PRAISE FOR JENNIFER LYNN BARNES

The Naturals Series

"*The Naturals* is *Criminal Minds* for the YA world, and I loved every page." —Ally Carter, *New York Times* bestselling author

★ "[A] tightly paced suspense novel that will keep readers up until the wee hours to finish." —*VOYA*, starred review

"It's a stay-up-late-to-finish kind of book, and it doesn't disappoint." —*Publishers Weekly*

"Even a psychic won't anticipate all the twists and turns." —*Booklist*

The Inheritance Games Series

"Barnes is a master of puzzles and plot twists. *The Inheritance Games* was the most fun I've had all year." —E. Lockhart, #1 *New York Times* bestselling author of *We Were Liars* and *Again Again*

"A thrilling blend of family secrets, illicit romance, and a high-stakes treasure hunt, set in the mysterious world of Texas billionaires. The nonstop twists kept me guessing until the very last page!" —Katharine McGee, *New York Times* bestselling author of *American Royals*

"Impossible to put down." —Buzzfeed

★ "Part *The Westing Game*, part *We Were Liars*, completely entertaining." —*Kirkus Reviews*, starred review

★ "This strong, *Knives Out*–esque series opener... provides ample enjoyment." —*Publishers Weekly*, starred review

"Not to be missed." —SLJ

Also by Jennifer Lynn Barnes

The Inheritance Games Saga

The Inheritance Games
The Inheritance Games
The Hawthorne Legacy
The Final Gambit
The Brothers Hawthorne

The Grandest Game
The Grandest Game
Coming next: *Glorious Rivals*

Games Untold

The Naturals
The Naturals
Killer Instinct
All In
Bad Blood
Twelve: A Novella

The Debutantes
Little White Lies
Deadly Little Scandals

The Lovely and the Lost

BAD BLOOD

A NATURALS NOVEL

#1 *New York Times* bestselling author
JENNIFER LYNN BARNES

LITTLE, BROWN AND COMPANY
New York   Boston

This book is a work of fiction. Names, characters, places, and incidents are the product of the author's imagination or are used fictitiously. Any resemblance to actual events, locales, or persons, living or dead, is coincidental.

Copyright © 2016 by Jennifer Lynn Barnes
Twelve copyright © 2017 by Jennifer Lynn Barnes
Excerpt from *The Inheritance Games* copyright © 2020 by Jennifer Lynn Barnes

Cover art copyright © 2023 by Katt Phatt. Cover design by Karina Granda.
Cover copyright © 2023 by Hachette Book Group, Inc.

Hachette Book Group supports the right to free expression and the value of copyright. The purpose of copyright is to encourage writers and artists to produce the creative works that enrich our culture.

The scanning, uploading, and distribution of this book without permission is a theft of the author's intellectual property. If you would like permission to use material from the book (other than for review purposes), please contact permissions@hbgusa.com. Thank you for your support of the author's rights.

Little, Brown and Company
Hachette Book Group
1290 Avenue of the Americas, New York, NY 10104
Visit us at LBYR.com

Originally published in hardcover and ebook by Hyperion, an imprint of Disney Book Group, in November 2016
Twelve originally published as an ebook by Hyperion, an imprint of Disney Book Group, in November 2017
Revised Trade Paperback Edition: May 2023

Little, Brown and Company is a division of Hachette Book Group, Inc. The Little, Brown name and logo are trademarks of Hachette Book Group, Inc.

The publisher is not responsible for websites (or their content) that are not owned by the publisher.

Little, Brown and Company books may be purchased in bulk for business, educational, or promotional use. For information, please contact your local bookseller or the Hachette Book Group Special Markets Department at special.markets@hbgusa.com.

Library of Congress Control Number: 2023932334

ISBNs: 978-0-316-54086-5 (pbk.), 978-1-4847-5854-0 (ebook)

Printed in New Jersey, USA

CCR, 04/25

For William, who helped Mommy copyedit this book when he was just five weeks old.

BAD BLOOD

YOU

Without order, there is chaos.

Without order, there is pain.

The wheel turns. Lives are forfeit. Seven masters. Seven ways of killing.

This time, it will be fire. Nine will burn.

So it has been decreed, and so it must be. The wheel is already turning. There is an order to things. And at the center of all of it—all of it—is you.

CHAPTER 1

The serial killer sitting across from me had his son's eyes. The same shape. The same color. But the glint in those eyes, the light of anticipation—*that's wholly your own.*

Experience—and my FBI mentors—had taught me that I could delve further into other people's minds by talking to them than by talking about them. Giving in to the urge to profile, I continued to appraise the man across from me. *You'll hurt me if you can.* I knew that, had known it even before coming to this maximum security prison and seeing the subtle smile that crossed Daniel Redding's lips the moment his gaze met mine. *Hurting me will hurt the boy.* I sank deeper and deeper into Redding's psychopathic perspective. *And the boy is yours to hurt.*

It didn't matter that Daniel Redding's hands were cuffed together and chained to the table. It didn't matter that there was an armed FBI agent at the door. The man in front of me was one of the world's most brutal serial killers, and if I let him past my defenses, he would burn his mark into my soul as surely as he'd branded the letter *R* onto the flesh of his victims.

Bind them. Brand them. Cut them. Hang them.

That was how Redding had killed his victims. But that wasn't what had brought me here today.

"You told me once that I would never find the man who killed my mother," I said, sounding calmer than I felt. I knew this particular psychopath well enough to know that he would try to get a rise out of me.

You'll try to burrow into my mind, to plant questions and doubts so that when I walk out of this room, a part of you goes with me.

That was what Redding had done months ago when he'd dropped that bombshell about my mother. And that was why I was here now.

"Did I say that?" Redding asked with a slow and subtle smile. "It *does* sound like something I might have mentioned, but . . ." He lifted his shoulders in an elaborate shrug.

I folded my hands on the table and waited. *You're the one who wanted me to come back here. You're the one who set the lure. This is me, taking the bait.*

Eventually, Redding broke the silence. "You must have something else to say to me." Redding had an organized killer's capacity for patience—but only on his own terms, not on mine. "After all," he continued, a low hum in his voice, "you and I have so very much in common."

I knew he was referencing my relationship with his son. And I knew that to get what I wanted, I'd have to acknowledge that. "You're talking about Dean."

The moment I said Dean's name, Redding's twisted smile deepened. My boyfriend—and fellow Natural—didn't know that I was here. He would have insisted on coming with me, and I couldn't do that to him. Daniel Redding was a master of manipulation, but nothing he said could possibly hurt me the way every word out of his mouth would have shredded Dean.

"Does my son fancy himself in love with you?" Redding leaned forward, his cuffed hands folding in imitation of my own. "Do you tiptoe into his room at night? Does he bury his hands in your hair?" Redding's expression softened. "When Dean cradles you in his arms," he murmured, his voice taking on a musical lilt, "do you ever wonder just how close he is to snapping your neck?"

"It must bother you," I said softly, "to know so incredibly little about your own son."

If Redding wanted to hurt me, he'd have to do better than trying to make me doubt Dean. If he wanted what he said to haunt me for days and weeks to come, he'd have to hit me where I was most vulnerable. Where I was *weak*.

"It must bother you," Redding parroted my own words back at me, "to know so incredibly little about what happened to your own mother."

The image of my mom's blood-soaked dressing room surged to the front of my mind, but I schooled my face into a neutral expression. I'd set Redding up to hit me where it hurt, and in doing so, I'd steered the conversation exactly where I wanted it to go.

"Isn't that why you're here?" Redding asked me, his voice velvety and low. "To find out what I know about your mother's murder?"

"I'm here," I said, staring him down, "because I know that when you swore to me that I would never find the man who killed my mother, you were telling the truth."

Each of the five teenagers in the FBI's Naturals program had a specialty. Mine was profiling. Lia Zhang's was deception detection. Months ago, she'd pegged Redding's taunting words about my mother as true. I could feel Lia on the other side of the two-way mirror now, ready to separate every sentence I got out of Dean's father into *truth* and *lies*.

Time to lay my cards on the table. "What I want to know," I told the killer in front of me, enunciating each word, "is exactly what kind of truth you were telling. When you guaranteed me that I would never find the man who murdered my mother, was that because you thought she'd been murdered by a *woman*?" I paused. "Or did you have reason to believe that my mother was still alive?"

Ten weeks. That was how long we'd been looking for a lead—any lead, no matter how small—on the cabal of serial killers who'd faked my mother's death nearly six years earlier. The group that had held her captive ever since.

"This isn't a casual visit, is it?" Redding leaned back in his chair, tilting his head to the side as his eyes—*Dean's eyes*—made a detached study of mine. "You haven't simply reached a tipping point, my words haven't been slowly eating away at you for months. You know something."

I knew that my mother was alive. I knew that those monsters had her. And I knew that I would do anything, make a deal with any devil, to bring them down.

To bring her home.

"What would you say," I asked Redding, "if I told you that there was a society of serial killers, one that operated in secret, killing nine victims every three years?" I could hear the intensity in my own voice. I didn't even sound like myself. "What would you say if I told you that this group is steeped in ritual, that they've been killing for more than a century, and that *I* am going to be the one to bring them down?"

Redding leaned forward. "I suppose I'd say that I wish I could be there to see what this group will do to you for coming after them. To watch them take you apart, piece by piece."

Keep going, you sick monster. Keep telling me what they'll do to me. Tell me everything you know.

Redding paused suddenly, then chuckled. "Clever girl, aren't you? Getting me talking like that. I can understand what my boy sees in you."

A muscle in my jaw ticked. I'd almost had him. I'd been *this* close. . . .

"Do you know your Shakespeare, girl?" Among his

plethora of charming qualities, the serial killer across from me had a fondness for the Bard.

" 'To thine own self be true'?" I suggested darkly, racking my brain for a way to reel him back in, to *make* him tell me what he knew.

Redding smiled, his lips parting to show his teeth. "I was thinking more of *The Tempest*. 'Hell is empty, and all the devils are here.' "

All the devils. The killer across from me. The twisted group that had taken my mother.

Seven Masters, a voice whispered in my memory. *The Pythia. And Nine.*

"From what I know of this collective," Redding said, "if they've had your mother for all these years?" Without warning, he surged forward, bringing his face as close to mine as his chains would allow. "She might be quite the devil herself."

CHAPTER 2

The FBI agent at the door drew his sidearm the moment Redding lunged toward me. I stared at the killer's face, inches from mine.

You want me to flinch. Violence was about power, about control—who had it and who didn't.

"I'm fine," I told my FBI escort. Agent Vance had worked with Agent Briggs off and on since I'd joined the Naturals program. He'd been tapped to stand guard because both Briggs and his partner, Agent Sterling, had decided to stay on the other side of the two-way mirror. They had a history with Daniel Redding, and right now, we wanted all of the psychopath's attention focused on me.

"He can't hurt me," I told Agent Vance, saying those words as much for my target's benefit as the agent's. "He's just being melodramatic."

Minimizing language, designed to keep Redding engaged in this game of verbal chess. I'd gotten him to admit that, at the very least, he knew of this group's existence. Now I needed to find out what he'd heard and who he'd heard it from.

I needed to stay focused.

"No reason to get testy." Redding settled back in his seat and made a show of holding his cuffed hands up in a mea culpa for Vance, who holstered his sidearm. "I am simply being candid." The edges of Redding's lips twisted as his attention returned to me. "There are things that can break a person. And once broken, a person—such as your mother—can be formed into something new." Redding tilted his head to the side, his eyes heavy lidded, as if he were caught in the midst of a particularly vivid daydream. "Something *magnificent*."

"Who are they?" I asked, refusing to take the bait. "Where did you hear about them?"

There was a long pause.

"Say that I did know something." Redding's face stilled. His voice was neither soft nor loud as he continued. "What would you give me in return?"

Redding was highly intelligent, calculating, sadistic. And he had only two obsessions. *What you did to your victims. And Dean.*

My fingers curved into fists on the table. I knew what I had to do, and I knew, without question, that I was going to do it. No matter how sick it made me. No matter how much I didn't want to say the words.

"Dean reaches for me more now than he used to." I looked

down at my hands. They were shaking. I forced myself to turn my left hand over and brought the fingers on my right hand to meet it. "His fingers entwine with mine, and his thumb . . ." I swallowed hard, my thumb making its way to my palm. "His thumb draws tiny circles on the palm of my hand. Sometimes he traces his fingers along the outside of mine. Sometimes . . ." My voice caught in my throat. "Sometimes I run my fingers along his scars."

"I gave him those scars." The look on Redding's face told me that he was savoring my words, would savor them for a very long time.

A ball of nausea rose in my throat. *Keep going, Cassie. You have to.*

"Dean dreams about you." The words felt like razor-edged sandpaper in my mouth, but I forced myself to continue. "There are times when he wakes up from a nightmare and can't see what's right there in front of him because the only thing that he can see is *you*."

Telling Dean's father these things wasn't just making a deal with the devil. This was selling my soul. It was dangerously close to selling Dean's.

"You won't tell my son what you had to do to get me to talk." Redding drummed his fingers along the tabletop, one after another. "But every time he reaches for your hand, every time you touch his scars, you'll remember this conversation. I'll be there. Even if the boy doesn't know it, *you* will."

"Tell me what you know," I said, the words ripping their way out of my throat.

"Very well." Satisfaction played along the edges of Redding's lips. "The group you're hunting looks for a specific type of killer. Someone who longs to be a part of something. A joiner."

This was the monster, giving me my due.

"I'm not much of a joiner myself," Redding continued. "But I am a listener. Over the years, I've heard rumors. Whispers. Urban legends. Masters and apprentices, ritual and rules." He tilted his head slightly to one side, watching my reaction, as if he could see the workings of my brain and found them enticing. "I know that each Master chooses his own replacement. I don't know how many of them there are. I don't know who they are or where they're located."

I leaned forward. "But you did know that they took my mother. You knew she wasn't dead."

"I'm a man who sees patterns." Redding enjoyed talking about what kind of man he was, demonstrating his superiority to me, to the FBI, to Briggs and Sterling, whom he must have suspected were hiding behind the glass. "Shortly after I was incarcerated, I became aware of another inmate. He'd been convicted of murdering his ex, but insisted she was still alive. There was never a body, you see. Just a copious amount of blood—too much, the prosecutors argued, for the victim to have lived."

Those words were familiar enough to send a chill down my spine. *My mother's dressing room. My hand fumbling for the light switch. My fingertips touching something sticky, something wet and warm and—*

"You suspected this group was involved?" I could barely hear myself ask the question over the deafening beating of my own heart.

One edge of Redding's mouth quirked upward. "Every empire needs its queen."

There was more to it than that. There had to be.

"Years later," Dean's father added, "I was moved to take on an apprentice of my own."

He'd taken on three, but I knew which one he was referencing. "Webber." The man had kidnapped me, loosed me in a forest, and hunted me. Like I was an animal. Like I was prey.

"Webber brought me information. About Dean. About Briggs. About you—and about Special Agent Lacey Locke."

Locke, my original FBI mentor, had started life as Lacey Hobbes, my mother's younger sister. She'd ended life a serial killer, re-creating my mother's murder over and over again.

Not a murder, I reminded myself. The whole time Locke had been killing women in my mom's image, my mother had been *alive.*

"You found out the details of my mother's case." I focused, as much as I could, on the here and now, on Redding. "You saw a connection."

"Whispers. Rumors. Urban legends." Redding fell back on what he'd said before. "Masters and apprentices, rituals and rules, and at the center of it all, a woman." His eyes gleamed. "A very specific kind of woman."

My lips and tongue and throat were dry—so dry, I almost couldn't force out the words. "What kind?"

"The kind of woman who could be formed into something magnificent." Redding closed his eyes, his voice humming with pleasure. "Something new."

YOU

You take the knife. Step by step, you make your way to the stone table, testing the balance of the blade in your hand.

The wheel is turning. The offering turns with it, chained to the stone, body and soul.

"All must be tested." You say the words as you drag the flat of the knife across the offering's neck. "All must be found worthy."

Power thrums through your veins. This is your decision. Your choice. One twist of your wrist and blood will flow. The wheel will stop.

But without order, there is chaos.

Without order, there is pain.

"What do you need?" You lean down as you whisper the ancient words. The knife in your hand angles into the base of the offering's neck. You could kill him, but it would cost you. Seven days and seven pains. The wheel never stops turning for long.

"What do I need?" The offering repeats the question, smiling as blood streams down his naked chest. "I need nine."

CHAPTER 3

"Well, that was cheerful." Lia jumped off the table she'd been sitting on.

Agent Vance had just delivered me to the observation area. Sterling and Briggs still had their twin gazes fixed on the room I'd vacated a few moments earlier. On the other side of the two-way mirror, guards pulled Daniel Redding to his feet. Briggs—competitive and ambitious and, in his own way, idealistic—would never view Redding as anything other than a monster, a threat. Sterling was more restrained, the type who kept her emotions on lockdown by following preset rules, including one that said that men like Daniel Redding didn't *get* to chip away at her control.

"I swear," Lia continued with a wave of her hand, "serial killers are so predictable. It's always all 'I want to watch you suffer' and 'let me quote Shakespeare while I imagine dancing on your corpse.'"

The fact that Lia was being so dismissive told me that the conversation she'd just witnessed had gotten to her almost as much as it had gotten to me.

"Was he lying?" I asked. No matter how hard I'd pressed, Redding had insisted he didn't know the name of the inmate whose ex's "death" had resembled my mother's, but I knew better than to take a master of manipulation at his word.

"Redding might know more than he's saying," Lia told me, "but he's not lying—or at least he's not lying about Ye Olde Consortium of Serial-Killing Psychopaths. He did stretch the truth a little about wanting to watch said psychopaths have their way with you."

"Of course Redding doesn't want to watch." I tried to match Lia's flippant tone in an attempt to make this—any of it—matter less. "He's *Daniel Redding*. He wants to kill me himself."

Lia arched one eyebrow. "You do seem to have that effect on people."

I snorted. Considering not one but *two* different serial killers had targeted me since I'd joined the Naturals program, I couldn't exactly argue the point.

"We'll track down the case Redding was talking about." Briggs finally turned to face Lia and me. "It might take some time, but if there's an inmate who matches Redding's description, we'll find him."

Agent Sterling laid a hand on my shoulder. "You did what you needed to do in there, Cassie. Dean would understand that."

Of course he would. That didn't make it better. It made it worse.

"As for what Redding said about your mother—"

"Are we done here?" Lia asked abruptly, cutting off Agent Sterling.

I knew better than to aim a grateful look in Lia's direction, but I appreciated the interference all the same. I didn't want to discuss the insinuations Redding had made about my mother. I didn't want to wonder if there was even a grain of truth to them, no matter how small.

My mentor got the message. As she led the way out, Agent Sterling didn't try to broach the subject again.

Lia wove one arm casually through mine. "For the record," she said, her voice uncharacteristically gentle, "if you ever"—*want to talk,* my brain filled in, *need to vent*—"ever," she repeated softly, her voice ringing with sincerity, "make me listen to you recount *The Erotic Hand-Holding Adventures of Cassie and Dean* again, I will exact vengeance, and that vengeance will be epic."

Next to deception detection, Lia's biggest specialty was providing distractions—some of which came with collateral damage.

"What kind of vengeance?" I asked, halfway grateful for the diversion, but also fairly certain that this was one time that she *wasn't* bluffing.

Lia smirked and let go of my arm. "Wouldn't you like to know?"

CHAPTER 4

We arrived home to find Sloane in the kitchen, cuddling a blowtorch. Luckily, Sterling and Briggs were still outside, exchanging words not meant for our ears.

Lia arched an eyebrow at me. "Do you want to ask? Or should I?"

Sloane tilted her head to the side. "There's a high probability that you're going to inquire about this blowtorch."

I obliged. "What are you doing with that blowtorch?"

"The earliest flamethrowers date back to the Byzantine empire in the first century AD," Sloane chirped. The words exited her mouth quickly enough to raise a red flag.

I amended my question. "What are you doing with that blowtorch, and who gave you caffeine?"

Michael chose that exact moment to saunter into the kitchen carrying a fire extinguisher. "You're alarmed," he said, taking in the expression on my face. "Also: mildly concerned I've lost my mind." He let his gaze travel to Lia. "And you're—"

"Not in the mood to have my emotions read?" Lia hopped up on the kitchen counter and allowed her legs to dangle, her dark eyes glittering as something passed unspoken between them.

Michael held her gaze for a moment longer. "That."

"I thought you were fundamentally opposed to giving Sloane caffeine," I said, shooting Michael a look.

"I am," he replied. "Most of the time. But you know what the song says: it's my three-day-long party, and I'll caffeinate my Sloane if I want to."

"Your party," I repeated. "As in your birthday?"

Michael gave me his most austere look. "Two days from now, I, Michael Alexander Thomas Townsend, will be a year older, a year wiser, and certainly old enough to supervise Sloane's use of the blowtorch. What's the harm in starting the festivities a little early?"

I heard what Michael wasn't saying. "You're turning eighteen."

I knew what that would mean for him—freedom. *From your family. From the man who turned you into a person who can spot even a hint of temper on a smiling face.*

As if on cue, Michael's phone rang. I couldn't read his face the way he could read mine, but I knew instinctively that Michael's father wasn't the kind of person who could just sit back and watch his last days of control tick by.

You won't answer, I thought, my focus still on Michael.

He can't make you—and two days from now, he won't ever be able to make you do anything again.

"Heaven forbid I be the responsible one." Lia slid off the counter and sauntered over to stand nose to nose with Michael. "But maybe Sloane shouldn't set stuff on fire."

"I *have* to," Sloane objected vehemently. "Michael's birthday is March thirty-first. That's in two days, and two days after that is—"

"April second," I finished for her. 4/2.

I could feel everything that Daniel Redding had said—about the Masters, about my mother—rushing back, the last ten weeks of dead ends on its heels. Nine victims killed every three years on dates determined by the Fibonacci sequence. That was the Masters' MO. It had been just over a week since the last Fibonacci date—March 21.

The next was April 2.

"We know the pattern," Sloane continued fiercely. "It starts this calendar year, and once it does, the new initiate will burn people alive. I've read everything I can find on arson investigation, but . . ." Sloane looked down at the blowtorch, her grip on it tightening. "It isn't enough."

Sloane's brother had been killed in Vegas by the UNSUB who'd turned us onto this group. She wasn't just vulnerable right now—she was bleeding. *You need to feel useful. Because if you couldn't save Aaron, what use are you—to anyone? What use could you ever be again?*

I understood now why Michael had given Sloane coffee

and gone for a fire extinguisher instead of confiscating the blowtorch. I slipped an arm around her. She leaned into me.

A voice spoke up behind us. "You're back."

All four of us turned. Dean didn't bat an eye at Sloane's blowtorch. One hundred percent of his attention was focused on Lia and me.

Our absence had definitely been noted.

Given where we had been and the fact that Dean shared my knack for profiling, that did not bode well.

"We're back," Lia declared, stepping between Dean and me. "Do you want to see what I let Cassie talk me into buying at the lingerie store?"

Dean and Lia had been the first two Naturals in the program. They'd been together for years before any of the rest of us had arrived on the scene. She was, in every way but blood, his sister.

Dean shuddered. "I will pay you fifty dollars never to say the word *lingerie* in my presence again."

Lia smirked. "No deal. Now"—she turned back to the rest of us—"I believe someone said something about recreational pyrotechnics?"

Before Dean could veto that suggestion, the front door opened. I heard footsteps—two pairs of them—coming toward the kitchen and assumed that they belonged to Sterling and Briggs. I was only half-right. Briggs wasn't accompanied by Agent Sterling. He was accompanied by Agent Sterling's father.

Director Sterling wasn't in the habit of making house calls.

"What's going on?" Dean beat me to the punch. His manner was non-confrontational, but it was no secret that when Director Sterling looked at Dean, he saw Dean's father. The FBI director was perfectly willing to use the son of a serial killer, but he didn't trust Dean—and never would.

"I received a call from Thatcher Townsend this morning." Director Sterling's words sucked the oxygen out of the room.

"I haven't been answering my phone this week," Michael commented, his voice deceptively pleasant, "so he called yours."

Before the director could respond, Agent Sterling arrived with Judd on her heels. Months ago, Judd Hawkins, who kept us fed and in one piece on a day-to-day basis, had also been given oversight of when and how the Naturals program was used. Director Sterling wasn't the type of person who appreciated oversight. He believed in acceptable costs and calculated risks—especially if the calculations were his.

"Townsend Senior turned me onto a case," Director Sterling said, addressing those words to Briggs and ignoring his daughter and Judd altogether. "I'd like you to take a look at it."

"Now?" Briggs asked. The subtext there was clear: *We have our first lead on the Masters in months, and you want us to do Michael's abusive father a favor* now?

"What Thatcher Townsend wants," Michael said tightly, "Thatcher Townsend gets."

Agent Sterling took a step toward him. "Michael—"

He brushed past her and out of the room, that same deceptively pleasant smile plastered to his face.

Briggs's jaw clenched as he turned back to the director. "What case?"

"There's a situation with Townsend's business partner's daughter," the director replied calmly. "And given his support of the Naturals program, he would like us to look into it."

"His support of the program?" Lia repeated incredulously. "Correct me if I'm wrong, but didn't the man more or less *sell* Michael to you in exchange for immunity from prosecution on a laundry list of white-collar crimes?"

Director Sterling ignored Lia. "It would behoove us," he told Briggs, each word issued with precision, "to consider taking this case."

"I believe that decision is mine." Judd's words were just as precise—and just as uncompromising—as the director's. A former marine sniper would have struck most people as an odd choice of housemother for a bunch of teenagers in an FBI training program, but Judd would have taken a bullet for any of us.

"Michael's father hits him," Sloane blurted out. She had no filter, no protective layer to keep her raw spots from the world.

Judd met Sloane's wide blue eyes for a moment, then held up a hand. "Everyone under the age of twenty-one, out."

None of us moved.

"I'm not going to ask you twice," Judd said, his voice low.

I could count on one hand the number of times I'd heard that tone in his voice.

We moved.

On my way out, Agent Briggs caught my arm. "Find Michael," he told me quietly. "And make sure he doesn't do anything . . ."

"Michael-ish?" I suggested.

Briggs eyed Director Sterling. "Ill-advised."

CHAPTER 5

We found Michael in the basement. When the FBI had purchased the house that served as our base of operations, they'd converted the bottom floor into a lab. Model crime scenes lined the walls. A quick scan of the room told me that Michael hadn't set anything on fire.

Yet.

Instead, Michael stood at the far end of the room, facing a wall that had been papered from ceiling to floor with photographs. *The Masters' victims.* I'd spent hundreds of hours down here, staring at that wall the way Michael was now. As I came to stand beside him, my gaze went automatically to two photos set apart from the rest.

One was a picture of a skeleton the authorities had found buried at a crossroads. The other was a photograph of my mother, taken shortly before she'd disappeared. When the police had uncovered the remains in the first picture, the working theory had been that they were my mom's.

Eventually, we'd discovered that my mother was alive—and that she was the one who'd killed our Jane Doe.

All are tested, a voice said from somewhere in my memory. *All must be found worthy.*

That was what one of the Masters, a serial killer known as Nightshade, had told me when we'd captured him. The Pythia was forced to prove her worth by fighting her predecessor—to the death.

Masters and apprentices, I could hear Daniel Redding saying lightly, *rituals and rules, and at the center of it all, a woman.*

Dean laid a hand on my shoulder. I forced myself to turn and meet his eyes, hoping he wouldn't see the naked vulnerability in mine.

Casting a glance at Dean and me, Lia walked up behind Michael and snaked an arm around his stomach, pulling him close. Dean narrowed his eyes at the two of them.

"We're on again," Lia informed us. "In a very big—and, might I add, overtly *physical*—way."

I knew better than to take Lia at her word, but Sloane played right into her hands. "Since when?"

Michael never tore his gaze from the wall. "Remember when Lia slammed me up against that wall in Vegas?"

It occurred to me then that Lia might *not* be lying. "You've been together since Vegas, and none of us knew?" I tried to wrap my mind around that. "You live in a house with three profilers and a marine sniper. How—"

"Stealth, deception, and an excellent sense of balance,"

Michael said, preempting the question. Then he glanced at Lia. "I thought you didn't want anyone to know."

"The weight of our treachery was weighing on my soul," Lia deadpanned. In other words: she wanted to distract Dean from thinking too hard about what was going on with me, and if she could also take Michael's mind off the chain of events that had brought him down here, all the better.

"I'm not really in the mood to be distracted," Michael commented. He knew Lia. Biblically. He knew exactly what she was doing, and right now, some part of him didn't want to be saved from the dark place. He turned back to the wall.

"I love you," Lia said softly. There was something intense in her tone, something vulnerable. No muss, no fuss, no misdirection. "Even when I don't want to, I do."

Despite himself, Michael whirled back around to face her.

Lia fluttered her eyelashes. "I love you like a drowning man loves air. I love you like the ocean loves the sand. I love you like peanut butter loves jelly, *and I want to have your babies.*"

Michael snorted. "Shut up."

Lia smirked. "I had you going there for a second."

Michael studied her expression, beyond the smirk, beyond the mask. "Maybe you did."

The thing about Lia that made her so difficult to read was that she would have said the exact same thing with the exact same smirk regardless of what she felt. She would have said it if she *was* falling in love with him. She would have said it if she was just jerking his chain.

"Question." Michael held up his index finger. "I know why Lia is looking particularly pleased with herself and why Cassie's wearing her profiling face, and I could make an educated guess about why Redding looks downright constipated every time Lia touches me, but why is Sloane wildly avoiding my gaze and shifting her weight to the balls of her feet like the effort of *not* saying something might actually cause her to explode?"

Sloane made her best attempt at looking inconspicuous. "There are over one hundred ninety-seven commonly used slang terms for a male's private parts!" she blurted out. And then, because she just couldn't help herself, she continued, "Also, Briggs, Sterling, and Judd are not up there debating the merits of taking your father's case!"

There was a beat of silence.

"As much as it pains me to say this, let's table the discussion of inappropriate slang for a moment." Michael's gaze went from Sloane to Lia, Dean, and me. "And someone can elaborate on this *case* of my father's."

"Director Sterling wasn't specific." Dean answered Michael's query, calm and ready to intervene if Michael tried to do something stupid. "All he said is that there's some kind of situation with your father's business partner's daughter."

Michael blinked. "Celine?" The name lingered on his lips for a second or two. "What kind of situation?" Michael must have been able to tell just from looking at us that we didn't know the answer to that question, because the next instant he made for the basement door, every muscle in his body taut.

Dean caught his arm as he passed. "Think, Townsend."

"I *am* thinking," Michael countered, stepping forward to get in Dean's face. "Specifically, I'm thinking that you have three seconds to remove your hand from my arm before I *make* you remove it."

"Michael." I tried and failed to get him to look at me.

"One," Michael told Dean.

"I do hope he says *two* next," Lia told Sloane wistfully. "Nothing says virility in a man like misplaced anger and counting to the number three."

That pierced Michael's bravado enough that he actually paused. "Celine Delacroix is the only person from my life before the program who ever gave a crap about me or bothered to see the kind of person that the great Thatcher Townsend *really* is," he told Dean. "If she's in some kind of trouble, I'm going. If I have to go through you to do it, I will."

"We're all going." Agent Briggs didn't mince words as he descended the basement stairs. He was the one who had recruited Michael to the program. He knew exactly what kind of man Thatcher Townsend was.

So why would he send Michael back there? Why would Judd agree? The fact that Agent Sterling wasn't with Briggs made me wonder if she'd fought them on this.

"You're telling me that we're just breaking camp and flying

to upstate New York?" Lia narrowed her eyes at Briggs. "Out of the goodness of our hearts?"

"Not out of the goodness of our hearts. And not because Director Sterling thinks Townsend Senior could prove useful down the road." Briggs looked to Michael. "Not even because a nineteen-year-old girl is missing, although we shouldn't stop caring about things like that, no matter how focused we are on taking the Masters down."

The word *missing* hit Michael like a physical blow. "Then why?" he asked.

Why would Director Sterling bring us this case? Why would Briggs and Judd willingly bring Michael back into his abusive father's sphere? Why would we drop everything to look for one girl?

I knew the answer in the pit of my stomach before Briggs said, "Because the police believe Celine was abducted eight days ago."

My heart thudded in my chest. *Eight days since the last Fibonacci date. Five days until the next one.*

"March twenty-first." Sloane's voice caught in her throat. "3/21."

"This girl disappeared on a Fibonacci date." Lia must have sensed Briggs was holding something back, because she tilted her head to the side. "And?"

There was a long pause.

"This girl disappeared on a Fibonacci date," Briggs repeated, "and the entire crime scene was soaked in kerosene."

YOU

The smell of burning flesh never really leaves you. Ash scatters. Skin scars. Pain subsides. But the smell is always there.

Pushing back against it, you concentrate. You know this slow and painful dance. You know the rules. But even as the wheel turns, the music changes. You can hear it. This time, you know something that the others don't.

You know her.

CHAPTER 6

Maybe Celine Delacroix was still alive. Maybe she hadn't been doused in kerosene. Maybe the person who had abducted her from her home hadn't burned her alive on March twenty-first.

But that wasn't a risk we could take. The entire team—plus Agents Starmans and Vance—were on the jet and flying to upstate New York in under an hour.

Near the front of the plane, Briggs checked his watch. Across the aisle from him, Agent Sterling thumbed through a copy of the case file, like she hadn't already memorized the entire thing. The lengths the two of them were going to in order to avoid eye contact might have triggered my interest if I hadn't been more focused on the fact that Celine Delacroix might be victim number one—*of nine*.

I felt the weight of that pressing down on me, suffocating me. Beside me, Dean's fingers brushed the tips of mine.

Every time he reaches for your hand, I heard Daniel

Redding whisper in my memory, *every time you touch his scars . . .*

I jerked my hand back.

"Cassie?"

"I'm fine," I said, falling back on a childhood habit and focusing on assessing the other occupants of the plane. Michael sat in a row by himself, Sloane and Lia side by side across the aisle. Near the front of the plane, behind Sterling and Briggs, Agent Vance—*short, compact, by the book, and pushing forty*—and Agent Starmans—*recently divorced, unlucky in love, and deeply uncomfortable with teenagers who saw more than they should*—awaited orders. They'd been a part of Briggs's team since before I'd joined the program, but hadn't started traveling with us until after Vegas.

Until every single one of us became a possible target.

That just left Judd. I could tell by the way he was sitting that he was armed. The plane hit cruising altitude before I could think too hard about why.

Agent Sterling stood and ditched the file in her hand for a digital version displayed on the flat screen at the front of the plane. "Celine Elodie Delacroix, nineteen-year-old daughter of Remy and Elise Delacroix." Agent Sterling began the briefing like this was any other day—and any other case. "Remy is a hedge fund manager. Elise runs the family's charitable foundation."

Agent Sterling didn't say a word about the Masters—or the Delacroix family's connection to Michael. I took my cue from her, setting aside conjecture in favor of focusing on the pictures on the screen. My first impression was that Celine Delacroix was the kind of girl who could make anything look elegant while giving off the general impression that *she* thought elegance was overrated. In the first picture, she wore her black hair wavy and chopped in artistic layers, the longest reaching past her chest and the shortest barely brushing the bottom of her chin. Her black cocktail dress was formfitting, and a gold medallion—most likely vintage—brought out the rich undertone of her brown skin. In the second picture, Celine's dark hair spiraled out around her head in seemingly endless curls. *Black pants. White blouse. Red heels.* My mind cataloged the details, even as I turned my attention to the final picture. Celine's tight curls were pulled into a loose bun on the top of her head, and her white T-shirt hung purposefully off both shoulders, revealing a white tank underneath.

You wear solid colors, not prints. You're always aware of the camera.

Agent Sterling continued, "Celine was reported missing by her college roommate when she didn't return to campus after spring break."

"Which campus?" Michael asked. I wondered why he was asking. I wondered why, if he and Celine had been at all close, he didn't already know.

"Yale." Agent Briggs was the one who answered Michael's question. "According to police interviews, Celine's friends were under the impression that she was joining them for a spring break trip to Saint Lucia, but she canceled at the last minute and went home instead."

Why? I wondered. *Did someone ask you to? Did something happen?*

"Our victim was reported missing by her college roommate." Sloane brought her feet up onto her seat and rested her chin on her knees. "It's statistically unlikely that such a report would be made immediately. The percentage of college students who return late from breaks increases in a curvilinear fashion as the school year proceeds to its close."

Agent Sterling recognized the question inherent in Sloane's statistic. "The report was made yesterday morning, after Celine's roommate had been unable to get ahold of her for three days straight and Mr. and Mrs. Delacroix confirmed that they hadn't heard from their daughter in several weeks."

A muscle ticked in Michael's jaw. "They didn't even know she went home, did they?"

"No," Agent Briggs replied evenly. "It appears Celine's parents were abroad at the time."

I integrated that into what I knew about our victim's last-minute trip home. *Did you know no one would be there? Did your parents even bother to tell you they would be gone?*

"If she wasn't reported missing until the twenty-eighth . . ." Sloane did the math and zeroed in on the money question. "How do we know she disappeared on the twenty-first?"

Agent Sterling clicked forward to the next slide in her

presentation. "Security footage," she clarified as a split-screen video began to play.

"Twelve cameras." Sloane cataloged them instantly. "Based on the coverage and the length of the hallways, I'd estimate the house is a minimum of nine thousand square feet."

Sterling enlarged footage of what appeared to be an in-home art studio. Celine Delacroix was visible, smack-dab in the middle of the frame. The date on the footage was March 21.

You were painting something. As I watched Celine, I tried to sink further and further into her perspective. *For you, painting is a whole-body endeavor. You move like you're dancing. You paint like it's a combat sport.* The footage on the screen was black-and-white, but the resolution was excellent. *You wipe the sweat from your brow with the back of your hand. There's paint on your arms, your face. You take a step back and—*

Without warning, the footage jumped. One second, Celine was on-screen, painting, and the next there was shattered glass everywhere. A broken easel lay on the floor. The entire studio had been ransacked.

And Celine was gone.

CHAPTER 7

Sterling and Briggs spent the remainder of the flight showing us crime scene photos and briefing us on the facts of the case. One thing was clear: our victim had fought.

She was stronger than you expected. I shifted my focus from Celine to the UNSUB. *You either lost control or you never had it. You weren't ready. Weren't worthy.*

That was guesswork as much as profiling. I needed to see the actual crime scene. I needed to stand where Celine had been standing. I needed to know her—to see her bedroom, examine her paintings, sort out exactly what kind of *fighter* she was.

"We'll set up our base of operations at a nearby safe house." As the plane began its descent, Agent Briggs laid out the plan. "Agent Starmans and Judd will accompany the Naturals to the safe house. Agent Vance, you're with us."

Us as in Briggs and Sterling. They'd scout out the scene

and major players before we were allowed anywhere near the case.

"Is this a bad time to point out that I'm on the verge of turning eighteen?" Michael asked. It was the first time he'd spoken since Agent Sterling had concluded her briefing. For Michael, that might have been a record. "Redding's eighteen. God knows when Lia's birthday *actually* is, but I think we can all agree that she doesn't need kid gloves."

"I cannot help noticing that you did not mention Cassie or me," Sloane told Michael, frowning. "I do not care for gloves of the kid or adult variety. Mittens conserve up to twenty-three percent more heat."

"None of you are coming with us." Agent Briggs was used to issuing orders. "The five of you are going to the safe house. We will deal you in on a need-to-know basis once the crime scene has been secured."

"So what I'm hearing," Michael replied as the plane touched down, "is that this is a *good* time to remind you that I am the only person here who knows Celine, the Delacroix family, or the local police department?"

"One guess as to how Townsend knows the local police department," Dean murmured beside me.

The debate continued as we de-planed, until Briggs snapped, "Michael, what are the chances that I'm going to change my mind?"

"Slim to none?" Michael guessed flippantly.

"*Infinitesimal* to none," Sloane corrected.

Michael shrugged as he descended the stairs to stand on the runway. "What are the chances that I'll do something stupid if you *don't* let me come, Agent Tightpants?"

Briggs didn't reply, which told me that Michael's threat had landed. Agent Sterling stepped in front of Michael before he could say anything else. "Briggs understands more than you think," she told him softly. She didn't provide any context for that statement, but I found myself wondering how Briggs had grown up, if he had firsthand experience with Thatcher Townsend's brand of parenting.

There was a long silence as Michael tried to ignore whatever emotions he saw on Sterling's face.

Agent Starmans, who'd been on our protection detail more than once in the last ten weeks, cleared his throat. "I'd really prefer you didn't make me spend my afternoon forcing you to stay put," he told Michael.

Michael offered him a dazzling smile. "And I'd prefer if you didn't peruse online dating profiles on your work phone." He winked at the mortified agent. "Dilated pupils, slight smile, followed by visible agonizing about how to compose just the right message? It's a dead giveaway every time."

Starmans clamped his mouth shut and strode to stand next to Agent Vance.

"Now that was just mean," Lia commented.

"Who?" Michael countered. "Me?"

I knew him well enough to know that if he decided to do something stupid, Starmans wouldn't be able to stop him. *When you're hurting, you hurt yourself.* I wanted to stop there but couldn't, because I knew exactly where Michael's love affair with self-destruction came from. *If you can't keep someone from hitting you, you* make *them hit you, because at least then you know it's coming. At least then you know what to expect.*

Turning away from Michael before he could read the expression on my face, I saw a row of gleaming black Mercedes SUVs parked at the edge of the private airstrip. Four of them. A closer inspection revealed that the keys were in the ignitions and that each of the four had been stocked with sparkling soda and fresh fruit.

"No warm nuts?" Lia commented, her voice dry. "And they call this hospitality."

Michael offered her his most careless smile. "I'm sure my father will remedy any disappointment. We Townsends pride ourselves on hospitality."

Your father arranged for transportation. Four SUVs, when two would do. I tried not to read too much into the way Michael had grouped himself in with his father, like Townsend men were Townsends first and anything else was a distant second—no matter how far they'd run.

"We're not visiting dignitaries," Briggs said flatly. "We're not clients Thatcher Townsend needs to woo. This is a federal investigation. The local field office is perfectly capable of supplying us with a car."

Sloane raised her hand. "Will that car have three rows of

42

air bags, a seven-speed automatic transmission, and a five hundred fifty horsepower engine?"

Lia raised her hand. "Will that car have warm nuts?"

"Enough," Sterling declared. She turned toward Michael. "I think I speak for everyone here when I say that I don't care about your father's *hospitality*, except insofar as it tells me that he's grandiose, prone to unnecessary gestures, and seems to have conveniently forgotten the fact that we've already seen behind the man behind the curtain. We know exactly what he is."

"Behind the curtain?" Michael said loftily, striding toward the farthest SUV. "What curtain? My father would be the first to tell you: with Townsends, what you see is what you get." He pulled the keys out of the ignition and tossed them in the air, catching them lazily in one hand. "Based on the set of Agent Sterling's mouth, not to mention those impressively deep brow ridges Agent Briggs is working, I have inferred that the FBI won't be accepting dear old Dad's gesture of goodwill." Michael gave the keys another toss. "But I will."

His tone dared Sterling and Briggs to argue with him.

"I call shotgun." Judd knew how to pick his battles. My gut said that, on some level, he knew that Michael saw accepting his father's gifts as akin to taking punches.

You take whatever he dishes out. You take and you take and you take—because you can. Because people would expect you to turn down his gifts out of spite. Because anything you could take from him, you would.

Michael caught my gaze. He always knew when I was profiling him. After a long moment, he spoke. "It appears we're going to the safe house. Judd's got shotgun. Lia?" He tossed her the keys. "You're driving."

CHAPTER 8

Riding with Lia was a bit like playing Russian roulette. She had a need for speed and a liar's disregard for limitations. We barely made it to the safe house in one piece.

Michael shuddered. "I think I speak for all of us when I say that I am in dire need of either an adult beverage or a live feed on Sterling and Briggs as they dig into this case."

Agent Starmans opened his mouth to reply, but Judd gave a quick shake of his head. We were here. We were under armed guard. We were safe. Judd knew as well as I did that, left to his own devices, Michael wouldn't be any of those things for long.

The last time you went home, you came back covered in bruises and spiraling out of control. I couldn't keep my mind from going there as Judd set up the video and audio feeds. *And now, a girl you know is missing. One of the so-called Masters might have burned her alive.*

Within minutes, the view from Briggs's lapel pin came into focus on Judd's tablet. We saw what Briggs saw, and all I could think, as Briggs and Sterling climbed out of their FBI-issued SUV, was that if this case was anything other than open-and-shut, none of us would be able to keep Michael from spiraling for long.

The Delacroix house was modern and vast. It was also, we soon learned, unoccupied. Celine's parents had apparently decided to meet with the FBI on more neutral ground.

"Home, sweet home." A sardonic edge crept into Michael's voice a few minutes later as the house next door to the Delacroix's came into view on the camera.

Large, I thought. *Traditional. Ornate.*

"Most people call it Townsend House," Michael said lightly, "but I prefer to think of it as Townsend Manor."

The more Michael joked, the more my heart thudded in my throat on his behalf. *You were supposed to be done with this place. You were supposed to be free.*

"Is that a turret?" Lia asked. "I love a man with a turret."

If Michael was going to crack jokes about his own personal hell, Lia would find a way to one-up him. They'd both had plenty of practice over the years at making the things that mattered most matter least.

On-screen, Briggs and Sterling made their way to the front porch. Briggs rang the bell. *One Mississippi. Two Mississippi.* The massive mahogany front door opened.

"Agent Briggs." The man who'd answered the door had thick charcoal-brown hair and a voice that commanded attention: rich and baritone and warm. He reached out and clapped a hand on Agent Briggs's shoulder. "I know you can't have appreciated the lengths I went to in order to get you here, but if I didn't do everything possible to help Remy and Elise at a time like this, I would never forgive myself." He turned from Briggs to Sterling. "Ma'am," he said, holding out a hand. "Thatcher Townsend. The pleasure is mine."

Sterling took the proffered hand, but I knew in my gut that she wouldn't offer the man even a hint of a smile.

"Please," Townsend said smoothly, stepping back from the threshold, "come in."

This was Michael's father. I tried to wrap my mind around that fact. He had Michael's air of confidence, Michael's presence, Michael's irrepressible charm. I waited for something to ping my inner profiler, for some hint, however small, that the man who'd answered that door was a monster.

"He hasn't lied yet," Lia told Michael.

Michael flashed her a sharp-edged smile. "It's not lying if you believe every word you say."

I'd expected Thatcher Townsend to be a man who threw his weight around, a man who needed to *own* and *possess* and *control*. I'd expected someone like Dean's father, or Sloane's. At the very least, I'd expected a man whose demons might be invisible to the average person, but not to me.

Nothing.

"What can you tell us about your father's business partner?" Dean asked Michael as the introductions got under way on camera.

"Remy Delacroix?" Michael shrugged. "He likes pretty things and pretty people. He likes being in control. And, God knows why, he likes my father. The two have been in business together since before I was born. Remy frowns when he's unhappy, snaps when he's angry, and hits on anything in a skirt."

What you see is what you get. Earlier, when Michael had said those words, he'd been parroting his father. And he'd been lying. Thatcher Townsend wasn't transparent. If Michael's father had been as easy to read as Remy Delacroix, Michael never would have become the type of person who could read a world of meaning in the blink of an eye.

"So you're saying we'll know fairly quickly if Delacroix had anything to do with his daughter's disappearance." I focused on that in an effort to help Michael do the same.

"I'm saying that Remy wouldn't touch a hair on Celine's head." Michael kept his gaze locked intently on the screen. "As I said, he likes pretty people, and CeCe's been beautiful since the day she was born."

Lia didn't stiffen, didn't bat an eye, didn't so much as lean away from Michael. But she would have heard the truth in those words. She would have heard the affection when Michael referred to Celine Delacroix as CeCe.

"Whatever resources you need, you'll have them." Remy Delacroix's words brought my attention back to the video feed. He looked like a shadow of Michael's father: slightly shorter, slightly blander features, more tightly wound. "I don't care what it costs. I don't care what laws you have to break. You get my little girl home."

Agent Sterling didn't tell the man that the FBI wasn't in the business of breaking laws. Instead, she eased him into questioning with a query that should have been easy to field. "Tell us about Celine."

"What is there to tell?" Delacroix replied, obviously agitated. "She's a nineteen-year-old girl. A damn Yale student. If you're trying to say that she might have done something to bring this on herself—"

Beside him, his wife laid a hand on his arm. I knew from reading the case file that Elise Delacroix was older than her husband, a former economics professor with an Ivy League education and the connections to match. As Remy's ranting subsided, Elise glanced at Michael's father, and after a moment, Thatcher went to pour his business partner a drink.

"What do you see?" I asked Michael.

"On Remy's face? Agitation. Part bluster, part fear, part righteous indignation. No guilt."

I wondered how many parents *wouldn't* feel guilty if they'd discovered their daughter had been missing for nearly a week before anyone had noticed.

"Celine is independent," Elise Delacroix told the agents once her husband had a drink in his hand. She was an elegant African American woman with her daughter's tall, lithe build and shoulders she kept squared at all times.

"Passionate, but unfocused. She has her father's temper and my drive, though she tries her best to hide the latter."

That the woman had mentioned her husband's temper to the FBI stuck out to me. *You have to know that the parents are always suspects in cases like these. Either you have nothing to hide or you simply don't care about throwing your husband under the bus.*

"Elise is always in control," Michael told me. "Of her husband, of her emotions, of the family image. The one thing she can't control is Celine."

"Does she miss her daughter?" Dean asked, his eyes still on the screen.

Michael was quiet for the longest time as he watched Elise Delacroix. The tone in her voice never changed. The control she exerted over her facial features never wavered.

Michael managed an answer to Dean's question. "She's broken. Terrified. Guilt-ridden. And disgusted—with her husband, with herself."

"With Celine?" I asked quietly.

Michael didn't answer.

On-screen, Agent Briggs had moved on to establishing a time line, and I tried to put myself in Celine's shoes, growing up with a father who, when asked about his daughter, said there was nothing to tell, and a mother whose first instinct had been to talk about her daughter's temper and drive.

Independent, I thought. *Passionate. Stubborn.* I could see shades of Elise in the Celine from the pictures. *Solid colors, not prints. You paint like you're dancing, paint like you're fighting—and you look at cameras like you know the secrets of the world.*

In the background of the feed, Thatcher Townsend made two more drinks: one for Elise and one for himself. It occurred to me for the first time to wonder where Michael's mother was. It also occurred to me to wonder why Remy and Elise had chosen to give this interview in the Townsends' house.

"What's your father feeling?" I asked Michael, hating myself for asking, but knowing we had to treat this like any other case.

Michael scanned his father's face as Thatcher held, but didn't drink, his bourbon on the rocks. Within seconds, Michael was texting Agent Briggs.

"You want to know what I see when I look at my father, Colorado?" he asked, his voice utterly devoid of emotion, like whatever he'd read on Thatcher Townsend's face had numbed something inside him, deadened it like a dentist would before removing a dying tooth. "Beneath that somber expression, he's furious. Affronted. Personally insulted."

Insulted by what? I wondered. By the fact that someone took Celine? By the FBI's presence in his home?

"And every time someone says CeCe's name, he feels exactly what he's always felt, every time he's looked at Celine Delacroix since she was fourteen years old." Michael's words set my gut to twisting, deep inside me. *"Hunger."*

YOU

You know the Seven, almost as well as they know you. Their strengths. Their weaknesses. The Masters thirst for power. They drape you in diamonds—one for each victim. Each sacrifice. Each choice.

Diamonds and scars, scars and diamonds. The men who've turned you into this pretty, deadly thing go out into the world. They live their lives. They prosper.

They kill.

For you.

CHAPTER 9

Hunger wasn't an emotion. It was a need. A deep-seated, biological, primitive need. I didn't want to even think about what might make a grown man look at a teenage girl that way, why Thatcher Townsend might be personally insulted that someone had dared to abduct the daughter of a family friend.

"Gloves." Agent Sterling held a pair out to each of us. She and Agent Briggs hadn't responded to Michael's text. Instead, Agent Starmans had eventually been the one to tell us that we'd been cleared to visit the crime scene.

You chose to come home over spring break. As I put on the gloves, I tried to slip back into Celine's perspective. *You had to at least suspect your parents wouldn't be here.* I stood at the threshold to Celine's studio. Crime-scene tape had it blocked off. From the looks of it, the studio had been a cabana or single-room guesthouse at some point. It was detached from the main house, overlooking the pool.

Even from the doorway, the smell of kerosene was overwhelming.

"Signs of forced entry." Sloane came to stand beside me, scanning the door. "Light scratches around the lock. There's a ninety-six percent probability that further analysis would reveal dents on the pins inside the lock."

"Translation?" Lia asked. Beside her, Michael closed his eyes, an elongated blink that made me wish that I were half as good at reading his emotions as he was at reading mine.

"The lock was engaged. Someone picked it." Sloane ducked under the crime-scene tape, her blue eyes taking everything in as she methodically scanned the room.

You locked the door. I stood in the doorway a moment longer, trying to picture Celine inside. *You came out here to paint, and you locked the door.* I wondered if that had been force of habit—or if she'd had a reason to turn the lock. Taking my time, I entered the studio, careful to avoid the evidence markers on the floor.

Shattered glass. A broken easel. My mind superimposed the images from the crime scene photos onto the markers on the floor. A second table was overturned near the far wall. A curtain had been pulled down, torn. There were drops of blood on the floor, a hand-shaped smear on the inside of the door frame.

You fought.

No, I thought, my heart thrumming in my chest. Using the word *you* kept me at a distance. That wasn't what I wanted. That wasn't what Celine needed.

I fought. I pictured myself standing in the middle of the studio, painting. Without meaning to, my body assumed the position we'd seen Celine in right before the security footage had cut out. My right arm was elevated, a pretend brush held in my hand. My torso twisted slightly to one side. My chin rose, my eyes on a phantom painting.

"The door was locked," I said. "Maybe I heard someone outside. Maybe I heard the light sound of scratching. Maybe the hairs on the back of my neck stood straight up."

Or maybe I was so consumed by painting that I didn't hear a thing. Maybe I didn't see the doorknob turn. Maybe I didn't hear it open.

"I was quiet." Dean stood at the door, staring at me. My first instinct had been to get inside Celine's head. His first instinct was always to profile the UNSUB. "There will be a time for noise, a time for screams. But first I have to get what I came for."

I saw the logic in what Dean was saying: the UNSUB had come here for Celine. She hadn't been a random target. A killer choosing his victims randomly wouldn't have chosen a girl protected by a state-of-the-art security system. Only someone who'd been watching her would have known she was here alone.

"You thought you could slip in and take me," I said, my eyes on Dean. "You thought that if you were quiet enough and quick enough, you could subdue me before I'd put up much of a fight."

You thought wrong.

Dean ducked under the tape and crossed the room. Standing behind me, he placed a hand over my mouth and pulled my body back against his. The motion was careful, slow, but I let myself feel it the way Celine would have. On instinct—and moving just as slowly as Dean had—I bent forward, thrusting my elbows back into his stomach. *The brush,* I thought, *in my hand.* I moved as if to stab him in the leg, and at the same time, I bit the hand that held me. Lightly. Gently.

Celine would have bit her captor hard.

Dean pulled back, and I escaped his grasp.

"I'm screaming by this point," I said. "As loud as I can. I rush for the door, but—"

Dean came up behind me again. As he mocked grabbing me, I went for the edge of the closest table. *If I hold on tight enough, you can't—*

"Not that way," Sloane said suddenly, breaking into my thoughts. "Based on the pattern of the debris we saw in the crime scene photos, the contents of the table would have been knocked off the table from *this* side." She came around to the far side of the table and mimicked the motion it would have taken, sweeping her arms over the table lengthwise.

I frowned. *That side of the table?*

"Maybe it wasn't me," I told Dean after a moment. "If I was terrified and fighting for my life, the first chance I got, I would go for the door."

Unless I was looking for a weapon. Unless I had reason to believe that I could fight and win.

Dean's hands clenched themselves slowly into fists. "I

could have done it." He swept his hands over the table, a vein in his neck jumping out against his suntanned skin. "To scare you. To *punish* you."

I pictured glass flying everywhere. *This studio is mine. My space. My haven.* What Dean was saying made sense only if the UNSUB knew that—and only if he'd known, on some level, that Celine would stay and fight.

That she wouldn't run.

I took in the rest of the room and integrated it with what I'd seen in the initial crime scene photos. *The overturned table. The curtain, torn down from the rod. The broken easel. The remains of Celine's painting, broken and dying on the floor.*

"What about the kerosene?" Lia had been remarkably quiet while we'd been profiling, but she'd reached the limit on biting her tongue.

Her question jarred me out of Celine's perspective and into the UNSUB's. *If you'd planned to abduct her, you wouldn't have brought the kerosene with you. And if you'd planned to burn her alive here, you would have torched the place.*

"Maybe I couldn't do it," Dean said softly. "Maybe, going in, I didn't realize what it would be like." He paused. "How much I would like it."

How much you would like the fight. How much you would like her fury, her terror. How much you would want to make this one last.

"The good news," I said, my voice horrible and bitter and low, "is that if this is the work of one of the Masters, she's definitely his first."

CHAPTER 10

Sloane was still analyzing the physical evidence, but I'd seen all I needed to see—all I could stand seeing. A small part of me couldn't help drawing parallels between this crime scene and the first one I'd ever seen—my mother's.

She fought. She bled. They took her.

The difference was that Celine had been taken on a Fibonacci date, and that meant that if this was the work of the Masters, we weren't looking for a missing girl, a potential Pythia.

We were looking for a corpse.

"I'd like to see the victim's bedroom," I said. I owed it to Celine Delacroix to get to know her, then to come back down here and walk through it all over again, until I found whatever it was that we'd been overlooking.

That was what profilers did. We submerged ourselves in the darkness again and again and again.

"I'll take you to Celine's room." Michael didn't wait for permission before he started walking toward the main house. I caught Agent Sterling's gaze. She nodded for me to follow Michael.

"I'll wait down here," Dean told me.

When we'd been profiling, I hadn't felt the crushing distance between us, but now, my mind went to the secrets I was keeping from him, his father's mocking words.

"I want to go over the scene again," Dean continued. "Something about this doesn't feel right."

Nothing feels right, I thought. And then, deep inside of me, something whispered, *Nothing ever will.* I would give everything I had to this case. I'd give and give, until the girl I'd been—the girl Dean had loved—was gone, worn away like a sand castle swept out with the tide.

Ignoring the dull ache that accompanied that thought, I turned and followed Michael into the house. Lia fell in beside me.

"You're coming with?" I asked.

Lia gave a graceful little shrug. "Why not?" The fact that she didn't even *try* to lie about her motivations gave me pause. "Keep up," Lia told me, breezing past. "I'd hate to have any alone time whatsoever with Michael in his exgirlfriend's room."

Michael had said that Celine was the one person who'd cared about him growing up. He'd said that she was beautiful. He'd called her by a nickname. And Lia and Michael's on-again off-again relationship had a tendency to end badly.

Every time.

We caught up with Michael just as he halted at the threshold of Celine's room. As I came to stand next to him, I saw the thing that had made him pause.

A self-portrait. I didn't question the instinct that said that Celine had painted this piece herself. It was big, larger than life. Unlike the photographs I'd seen of our victim, this painting showed a girl who wasn't elegant, didn't want to be. The paint was thick and textured on the canvas, nearly three-dimensional. The strokes were rough and visible. Celine had only painted herself from the shoulders up. Her skin was bare, dark brown and luminescent. And the expression on her face . . .

Naked and vulnerable and fierce.

Beside me, Michael stared at the painting. *You're reading her,* I thought. *You know exactly what the girl in that painting is feeling. You know what the girl who painted it was feeling. You know her like you know yourself.*

"She didn't use a brush." Lia let that comment register before she continued. "CeCe dearest painted that one with a knife."

My brain instantly integrated that tidbit into what I knew about Celine.

"How much do you want to bet our knife-wielding Picasso cleans her brushes with kerosene?" Lia asked. "Turpentine would be more common, but I'm guessing Celine Delacroix doesn't do common. Does she, Michael?"

"You a profiler now?" Michael asked Lia.

"Just an aficionado of fine art," Lia retorted. "I lived in a bathroom at the Metropolitan Museum of Art for six weeks, back when I was on the streets."

I raised an eyebrow at Lia, utterly unable to tell if that was true or a bald-faced lie. In response, Lia pushed past Michael and into Celine's room.

"If Celine cleans her brushes in kerosene," I murmured, thinking out loud, "she would have had some on hand. Not a ton, but . . ."

But enough that you might not have had to bring it with you. I paused. *And if you didn't bring it with you, you might never have intended to burn her alive.*

It could have been a coincidence. All of it—the date, the kerosene.

"You think the FBI doesn't realize that some people use kerosene as a paint thinner?" Michael asked me, reading my thoughts in my expression. "You really think Briggs and Sterling didn't go down that road before they took this case?"

Back at the crime scene, the smell of kerosene had been overwhelming. This wasn't a little spill we were talking about here—but for some reason, Lia had wanted me to entertain the possibility that it was.

Why?

Michael stepped over the threshold and into Celine's room. After one last glance at Lia, I followed.

"Two more paintings on the walls," I commented, breaking the silence. Celine had hung the paintings side by side, matched pieces of an eerie, abstract set. The canvas on the left appeared to be painted entirely black, but the longer I stared at it, the easier it was to see a face staring back from the darkness.

A *man's face.*

It was subtle, a trick of light and shadows in a painting that, at first glance, held neither. The second canvas was mostly blank, with a few bits of shading here and there. It looked like a completely abstract painting, until you realized that the white space held its own design.

Another face.

"She doesn't paint bodies." Michael came to stand in front of the paintings. "Even in elementary school, Celine refused to draw anything but faces. No landscapes. Not so much as a single still life. It used to drive the art teachers her parents hired mad."

That was the first opening Michael had given me to ask him about this girl, this piece of his past that none of us had even known existed. "You've known each other since you were kids?"

For a moment, I wasn't sure Michael would answer the question.

"Off and on," he said finally. "When I wasn't at boarding school. When *she* wasn't at boarding school. When my father wasn't pushing me to make friends with the sons of people more important than a partner he already had eating out of his hand."

I knew that Michael's father had a temper. I knew he was

abusive, nearly impossible to read, wealthy, and obsessed with the Townsend name. And now I knew something else about Thatcher Townsend. *No matter how much money you make, no matter how high up the social ladder you climb—it will never be enough. You will always be hungry. You will always want more.*

"Good news." Lia's voice broke into my thoughts. When Michael and I looked over at her, she was removing a false bottom from a chest at the foot of Celine's bed. "The police took our victim's laptop into evidence, but they didn't take her *secret* laptop."

"How did you—" I started to ask, but Lia cut me off with a wave of her hand.

"I did a stint as a high-end cat burglar after I got kicked out of the Met." Lia set the laptop up on Celine's desk.

"We'll need Sloane to hack the—" Michael cut off as Lia logged on.

It wasn't password-protected. *You hide your laptop, but don't password-protect it. Why?*

"Let's see what we have here," Lia said, opening files at random. "Class schedule." I had just enough time to commit Celine's class schedule to memory before Lia moved on. She opened a new file—a photograph of two children standing in front of a sailboat. I recognized the little girl immediately. *Celine.* It took me longer to realize that the little boy standing next to her was Michael. He couldn't have been older than eight or nine.

"Enough," Michael said sharply. He tried to close the photo, but Lia blocked him. On the laptop's screen, I noticed the photo begin to shift, to change.

Not a photo, I realized after a long moment. *A video. An animation.*

Slowly, the children in the photo morphed, until I was looking at a nearly identical photograph of two teenagers standing in front of a sailboat.

Celine Delacroix, age nineteen, and Michael Townsend, now.

CHAPTER 11

"You got something you want to share with the class, Townsend?" Lia's tone was light and mocking, but I knew with every fiber of my being that this wasn't a joke to her.

You came up here because you thought he was hiding something. From you. From all of us.

While Dean and I had been profiling the crime scene, Lia had been watching Michael. She must have seen some kind of tell. Even if he hadn't *lied*, she must have noticed something that made her suspect . . .

What? What do you suspect, Lia?

"That's not a photograph." Michael gave Lia a look. "It's a digital drawing. Celine took creative license with the old photo and updated it. Obviously. Unless you didn't happen to notice that her schedule included a class on digital art?"

As a matter of reflex, I ran through the rest of Celine's schedule in my head. *Visual Thinking. Death and Apocalypse* in Medieval Art. Theories, Practice, and Politics of Human Rights. Color.

"When was the last time you saw her?" Lia asked Michael. "When you went home over Christmas?"

Michael's jaw clenched slightly. "I haven't seen Celine in nearly three years. But I'm touched that you're jealous. Really."

"Who says I'm jealous?"

"The emotion reader in the room." Michael glanced at me. "Maybe the profiler in the room can tell the lie detector that it's borderline pathological to be jealous of one of our vics?"

Vics. As in *victims.* The Michael I knew wasn't capable of thinking of someone he cared about that way. Celine Delacroix wasn't a nameless, faceless *victim* to him. And I couldn't help wondering—if Celine hadn't seen Michael in three years, how had she captured the way he looked now so precisely?

"Tell me you're not hiding something." Lia gave Michael what seemed to be a perfectly pleasant smile. "Go ahead. I dare you."

"I'm not doing this with you," Michael said through clenched teeth. "This isn't *about* you, Lia. This is none of your damn business."

They were so caught up arguing with each other that they didn't see the picture on the screen change again. This time, there was only one face depicted in the drawing.

Thatcher Townsend's.

"Michael." I waited until he looked at me to continue. "Why would Celine have a picture of your father on her computer? Why would she have drawn him?"

Michael stared at the computer screen, his face unreadable.

"Townsend, tell me you think this case has something to do with the Masters." Lia went for the jugular. "Tell me that you haven't known, from the second you saw that crime scene, that it does not."

"In five seconds," Michael said instead, his gaze intent on Lia, "I'm going to tell you that I love you. And if you're still in the room when I say it, you're going to know."

Whether he loved her. Whether he didn't.

If she'd known for certain that the answer was the latter, Lia wouldn't have moved. If no part of her wanted him to love her, she wouldn't have cared. Instead, she looked at Michael with something like hatred in her eyes.

And then she ran.

It was several seconds before I found my voice. "Michael—"

"Don't," he told me. "Because I swear to God, Colorado, if you say a single word right now, I'm not going to be able to keep from telling you exactly what combination of emotions I saw flash across your face when you started to think that Celine might not have been taken by one of your precious Masters."

My mouth went dry. If Celine had been taken by the Masters on a Fibonacci date, she was already dead. But if this case was unrelated, she might still be alive. And I . . .

I wasn't happy. I wasn't hopeful. Part of me—a sick, twisted part of me that I barely even recognized—*wanted* her to be a victim of the cabal. Because if she was their victim, there was a chance they'd left evidence behind. We desperately needed a lead. *I* needed something to go on.

Even though I knew Celine mattered to Michael. Even though he mattered to me.

YOU

Some things you remember. Some things you don't. Some things you'll shudder at—and some things you won't.

CHAPTER 12

When had I become a person capable of being disappointed that a missing girl might still be alive?

This is the cost, I thought as I left Michael alone in Celine's room and made my way back toward the crime scene. *Of being willing to make a deal with any devil, to pay any price.*

Dean took one look at my face and his jaw tightened. "What did Townsend do?"

"What makes you think Michael did anything?"

Dean gave me a look. "One: he's Michael. Two: he's scheduled for a meltdown. Three: Lia has been Miss Rosy Sunshine since she got downstairs, and Lia doesn't do roses *or* sunshine unless she's screwing with someone or deeply upset. And four . . ." Dean shrugged. "I may not be an emotion reader, but I know you."

Right now, Dean, I don't even know myself.

"I went to see your father." I wasn't sure if saying those

words to Dean was confession or penance. "I told him about us so that he'd tell me about the Masters."

Dean was quiet for several seconds. "I know."

I stared at him. "How—"

"I know you," Dean repeated, "and I know Lia, and the only reason she would have told me that there was something going on between her and Michael was to distract me from something worse."

I told your father what it's like when you touch me. I told him that he haunts your dreams.

"I don't know what that monster said to you." Dean held my gaze. "But I do know that he has a very particular reaction to anything beautiful, anything real—anything that's *mine*." His fingers lightly traced the edge of my jaw, then moved to lay flat on the back of my neck. "He doesn't get to do that anymore, Cassie," Dean said fiercely. "And you don't get to let him."

My chest tightened, but I didn't pull back from his touch. I didn't step away.

"Celine Delacroix wasn't taken by one of the Masters." I let the heat from Dean's skin warm mine. I pushed down the echo of his father's voice. "I'm not sure how, but Michael knew. Lia suspected he was hiding something. And a very large part of me wishes . . ."

"You wish there were a lead," Dean cut in. His Southern accent was more audible in those words than any I'd heard him speak in a long time. "You wish we had a trail to follow. But you don't wish this girl had been burned alive, Cassie.

71

You don't wish she'd died screaming. You're not capable of it."

He sounded so certain of that, so certain of me, even after what I'd told him. I thought of my mother, fighting her predecessor to death. *We never really know what we're capable of.*

I changed the subject. "You weren't surprised when I said that Celine hadn't been taken by one of the Masters."

"I suspected." Dean had stayed behind to walk through the crime scene again because something didn't feel right. I wondered why he'd seen it and I hadn't. I was supposed to be a Natural. I was supposed to be better than this. I'd recognized that this was our UNSUB's first time. Why hadn't I taken that a step further and seen that the Masters would never have allowed someone that out of control, that *messy* into their ranks?

"You were in the girl's head," Dean said softly. "I was in her assailant's. From her perspective, it wouldn't have mattered if the intruder had chosen her as the first of nine kills or if she was the one and only target. It wouldn't have mattered if there was an element of ritual to his movements or only desire and anger. Either way, she still would have fought back."

I closed my eyes, picturing myself in Celine's shoes once more. *You fought back. You didn't run. You knew the UNSUB. You might have been terrified, but you were angry, too.*

"Celine has a secret laptop," I told Dean. "The police missed it. And whatever's going on here, I think it has something to do with Michael's father."

CHAPTER 13

"We knew this was a long shot." Briggs addressed those words to Sterling, even though Dean and I were the ones who'd come bearing the news. "But the dates matched, and the MO was in the ballpark. We had to check it out."

"So you said." Sterling clipped the words. "And so said the director."

I thought back to what I'd seen of that exchange. Director Sterling had spoken only to Briggs—not to his daughter, not to Judd.

"Don't make this about your father," Briggs told Sterling, his voice low.

"I didn't. You did." Sterling's tone reminded me that Briggs was her ex-husband as well as her partner. "This was never a long shot, Tanner. If you'd asked me—if you or my father had even bothered to remember that there was a profiler in the room—I could have told you that there was too much anger here to fit with what we know about the Masters, too little control."

The implications of that statement hit me like a semi-truck. "You knew this case wasn't related to the Masters?" My voice came out strained. *You knew, and you let me believe—*

"I knew that a girl was missing," Agent Sterling said softly.

"And you never thought to share any of this with me?" Briggs's voice hardened.

An unflinching Sterling met his gaze. "You never asked." After a moment's silence, she turned to me. There was a subtle shift in her tone, one that reminded me that once upon a time, she'd told me that when she looked at me, she saw herself. "You can never let yourself become so focused on one possibility—or one case—that you lose your objectivity, Cassie. The moment a case becomes about what *you* need—revenge, approval, redemption, control . . . you've already lost. There's a thin line between following your gut and seeing what you want to see, and that's not a lesson I could teach you." She glanced back at Briggs. "We all have to learn that one on our own."

You're thinking about the Nightshade case. My profiling instinct went into overdrive. Years ago, Briggs and Sterling hadn't known that the killer they were hunting was one of the Masters. They hadn't known that when they went after Nightshade, he'd go after one of their own—Scarlett Hawkins. Judd's daughter. Sterling's best friend.

"And what the hell kind of lesson were you trying to teach

me?" Agent Briggs bit out. "Not to make decisions without discussing them with you first? Not to take your father's side on anything? Not to ask Judd to trust me?"

"I went above the director's head on the Naturals program for a reason," Sterling replied, emotional armor firmly in place. "My father is very good at his job. He's got a mile-wide Machiavellian streak. And he can be very persuasive."

"I made a judgment call," Briggs shot back. "This has nothing to do with your father."

"He always wanted a son," Sterling said quietly. "A driven, ambitious, sculpted-in-his-own-image son."

Briggs's whole body went taut. "Is this about Scarlett? You still blame—"

"I blame myself." Sterling dropped those words like a bomb. "This isn't about you, or my father. This is about not letting any of us get so obsessed with one case, with *winning*, that we don't see or care about anything else. Scarlett died on the altar of *winning*, Tanner. Masters or no Masters, I'll be damned before we do the same thing to these kids."

"And what about what *this* case is doing to Michael?" Briggs shot back. "Sacrificing his psychological well-being on the altar of your self-righteousness, *that's* just fine?"

"I hate it when Mommy and Daddy fight." Lia sidled up beside me. "Do you think they're going to get a divorce?" Lia had never met a grease fire she didn't want to throw water onto.

Briggs pinched the bridge of his nose.

"Briggs and Sterling are already divorced," Sloane said

helpfully as she peeled off her latex gloves and joined the melee.

Dean intervened before the situation could escalate. "We still have a missing person."

That was why Agent Sterling hadn't fought Briggs's decision to come here. I thought of Celine, thought of the insidious emotion that had risen up inside of me when I'd realized what this case was—and what it wasn't.

You don't wish this girl had been burned alive, Cassie. Dean's words echoed in my mind. *You don't wish she'd died screaming. You're not capable of it.*

I wanted that to be true.

"We have to find out who took Celine." My throat tightening, I wove my fingers through Dean's, Daniel Redding and his mind games be damned. "If she's alive, we have to find her. And if she's dead, we're going to find out who killed her."

I'd spent the past two and a half months in the basement, staring at the Masters' handiwork. I'd sat down across from the devil and offered him a deal. But no matter what I did, no matter what *we* did, the reality of the situation was that I might never find my mother. Even if we caught one of the Masters—or two or three—the endless cycle of serial murder might never stop.

There was so much that wasn't in my control. But this was.

"Where's Michael?" Sloane asked suddenly. "Ninety-three percent of the time when there is an emotional or physical altercation, Michael is within a four-foot radius of the action."

There was a beat of silence, and then Agent Briggs reiterated Sloane's question. "Where *is* Michael?"

"I left him in Celine's room," I said. What I didn't say—what I should have realized much earlier—was that I was willing to bet a lot of money that he hadn't stayed in that room for long.

CHAPTER 14

It didn't take long to figure out where Michael had gone. If he suspected his father had something to do with Celine's disappearance, he'd almost certainly gone to confront the threat head-on.

"You take the kids back to the safe house," Briggs told Sterling. "I'll go after Michael."

"Because the one person Michael will listen to when he's spiraling out of control is an authority figure," Lia chirped. "There is no possible way this could go badly, especially if you start issuing orders. Heaven knows people who've spent their lives as punching bags do best when they have absolutely no control over a situation and someone else dominates them completely."

Lia's finely honed sense of sarcasm was all the more effective when she made the words sound completely sincere.

"And what do you suggest?" Briggs asked sharply.

"That the four of us go," Lia retorted. "Obviously. Unless you really think that Thatcher Townsend is going to lose it and physically attack us all?"

"He won't," Dean cut in. "He cares about appearances." He paused. "If I'm Thatcher Townsend, if I did have something to do with the disappearance of Celine Delacroix? I'd put on an even better show than usual."

"And if Michael does his best to push his father over the edge?" Agent Sterling shot back. "If he goes on the offensive and his father snaps?"

Something dark and dangerous flashed in Dean's eyes. "Then Thatcher Townsend will have to go through me."

"If either of you question him," I said to the FBI agents before they could respond to the threat inherent in Dean's words, "the chances that Michael's father will snap are very small." Lia gave me a look that said *You are not helping*, but I plowed on. "Thatcher is grandiose and capable of enormous levels of self-deception. If he *does* snap, so long as there aren't any other adults there, he might actually give us the information we need."

Sloane cleared her throat and then made an attempt at helping my argument. "I would estimate that Michael's father is seventy-one inches tall, one-hundred and sixty-one pounds." When it became clear that none of us saw the relevance of that number, Sloane expanded: "I think we can take him."

Lia turned and batted her eyelashes at Judd, who'd approached the discussion midway through.

"Fine," Judd said after a long moment's deliberation. "But this time, you'll be the ones wearing cameras."

I reached out to ring the Townsends' front door, but Lia tested the knob and, finding it unlocked, let herself in. Eventually, she'd make Michael pay for the stunt he'd pulled back in Celine's room, but she'd come riding to his rescue first.

"Drink?"

The moment I heard Michael's voice, I crossed the threshold after Lia. I heard a faint clinking—glass on glass—and quickly surmised that Michael was pouring himself a drink and offering one to someone else.

I followed Lia through the house. Sloane and Dean did the same. In the living room—the same one where Briggs and Sterling had interviewed Celine's parents—we found Michael with his father.

Thatcher Townsend accepted the drink Michael had made him, then raised the glass, a devil-handsome smile playing around the edges of his lips. "You should have answered when I called," he told Michael, saying the words like a toast, like an inside joke that he and Michael shared. Just looking at Thatcher, I knew that this man was everyone's best friend. He was the perfect salesman, one who specialized in selling himself.

Michael raised his glass and offered his father a charming smile of his own. "I've never really excelled at *should*."

Once upon a time, Michael had almost certainly feared

the moments when his father's charming mask slipped. Now he took power from his ability to *make* it slip.

But Thatcher Townsend proceeded as if he hadn't heard the mocking undertone in Michael's voice. "How are you, Michael?"

"Handsome, prone to bouts of melancholy and questionable decision-making. And you?"

"Always so glib," Thatcher said with a shake of his head, smiling softly, as if he and his son were reminiscing. He caught a glimpse of the rest of us out of the corner of his eye. "It appears we have company," he told Michael. The older Townsend turned his attention to us. "You must be Michael's friends. I'm Thatcher. Please, come in. Help yourself to a drink if and only if you can resist the urge to report me to the FBI for contributing to the delinquency of minors."

Michael's father was magnetic. Charming, friendly, larger-than-life.

You live to be adored, I thought, *and no matter how often you hurt Michael, you never stop turning on the charm.*

"Michael, darling . . ." Lia strolled over to join father and son, winding her hand through Michael's. "Introduce us."

In the span of a heartbeat, Lia had donned a persona I'd never seen before. It was present in the way she held her head, the way she glided across the floor, the musical lilt in her voice. Michael narrowed his eyes at her, but must have been able to tell from the look on her face that he was lucky she hadn't chosen to make a more memorable entrance.

"This is Sadie," he told his father, tucking a hand around

81

Lia's waist as he introduced her by her alias of choice. "And by the door, we have Esmerelda, Erma, and Barf."

For the first time, I saw a flicker of annoyance cross Townsend Senior's face. "Barf?" He eyed Dean.

"It's short for Bartholomew," Lia lied smoothly. "Our Barf had a speech impediment as a child."

Like me, Dean must have suspected that there was a method to Michael and Lia's madness, because he didn't say a word.

"Question," Sloane said, raising her hand. "Am I Erma or Esmerelda?"

Thatcher Townsend gave every sign of being amused. "I see my son has found a place where he fits right in. I'm sorry my wife couldn't be here to meet you all. I'm sure Michael has told you she has an adventurous streak. She runs a free clinic here in town, but travels with Doctors Without Borders whenever she gets the chance."

It was hard to picture Thatcher Townsend with anything but a society wife. My gut said that he'd mentioned his wife's adventurous streak for the sole purpose of punishing his son for refusing him our real names. *Fists aren't your only weapon. You are a man of intellect—unless the boy forces you to become something else.*

"We'd like to ask you a few questions about Celine Delacroix." Dean was the one who cut to the chase.

"Now, Barf," Michael chided, "let the man finish his drink."

Thatcher ignored his son and focused his performance

on Dean. "Feel free to ask any questions you would like. Despite my son's insistence on treating everything like a joke, I can assure you that both Celine's family and I are taking this very seriously."

"Why?" Sloane asked.

"I'm afraid I don't follow," Thatcher said.

"Why are you taking this so seriously?" Sloane tilted her head to the side, trying to make this whole situation compute. "Why were you the one to call in the FBI?"

"I've known Celine since the day she was born," Thatcher replied. "Her father is one of my closest friends. Why wouldn't I help?"

A flicker of movement caught my eye as Lia held her index finger against the side of her thigh, a subtle, downward-pointing number one.

That's the first lie he's told. Given that we knew that Thatcher and Remy had been in business together before either of their children were born, I doubted Thatcher was lying about how long he'd known Celine, and that meant that he was lying about his relationship with Celine's father. *Maybe you don't consider him your friend. Maybe he crossed you. Maybe you're the type to keep your enemies close.*

"I appreciate that you want to find Celine." Thatcher addressed those words directly to Michael. "I do too, but, son, you are looking in the wrong place for those answers."

"Wrong place, wrong time." Michael took a sip of his drink. "Kind of my specialty."

I braced for Thatcher to snap. Dean moved subtly toward

Michael. Thatcher, however, just smiled as he shifted his gaze from Michael to another target.

"Sloane, isn't it?" he said, a demonstration that he'd known our real names all along. "I know your father."

Some people had a sixth sense for vulnerability. In that instant, I had no doubt that Thatcher Townsend had made his fortune using exactly that skill. My gut twisted, knowing what even the mention of her father would do to Sloane.

"Grayson Shaw and I have some mutual investments," Thatcher continued, tossing off Sloane's deadbeat father's name like they were old chums. "He told me that you're quite brilliant, but he didn't mention what a beautiful young woman you're becoming."

I didn't need Lia to tell me that Sloane's father hadn't said anything nice about her.

"I was very sorry," Thatcher said, his eyes catching Sloane's and holding them, "to hear about your brother."

My hand went for Sloane's, but she didn't latch onto it. Her arms hung listlessly by her sides.

"No," Lia countered, taking a sudden step forward. "You weren't sorry. You didn't really care much either way. And incidentally, when you told Michael that he was looking in the wrong place for *those* answers, the only reason that was true was that one little word, *those*." Lia's voice went sultry and low. "Sometimes a liar's biggest tells happen when he's speaking the truth."

The gloves were officially off. Thatcher Townsend could have come after me or Lia or Dean and we would have rolled with it. But he'd gone after Sloane, and he'd used her dead brother to do it. From the moment we'd walked into this room, father and son had been engaged in a game, each trying to out-maneuver the other, each determined to have the upper hand, the power, the control. That Thatcher had used Sloane to that end made me want to tell him just how transparent he was.

"What answers *should* Michael be coming to you for?" I asked instead. Sometimes, the best way to trap someone was to give them exactly what they wanted. In this case, control. "You're a powerful man. You keep your ear to the ground. What questions should we be asking?"

Townsend knew I was flattering him, but didn't care. "Perhaps if you gave me a bit of direction, I could be of service."

"Speaking of services . . ." Michael set his drink down. "What services was Celine providing you?"

"Excuse me?" Thatcher managed to sound both incredulous and offended. "What exactly are you suggesting, Michael? Whatever differences you and I have had, you can't believe that I had anything to do with Celine's disappearance."

"You always did enjoy telling me what I could and could not believe," Michael said softly. "I couldn't possibly believe that you'd meant to throw me down the stairs or that you'd intended to break my arm or that you'd held me underwater in the bathtub on purpose. What kind of man did I take you for?"

Thatcher didn't react to even one of Michael's accusations. It was as if he hadn't even heard them. "Do you honestly think that I killed Celine? That I abducted her? That I would harm that girl in any way?"

I could feel myself *wanting* to believe him, even though I knew he was capable of violence. That was the kind of power Thatcher Townsend held over people. That was how convincing the emotions on his face and in his voice were.

"Do you, Michael?" Thatcher pressed. "Do you think I had anything to do with Celine's disappearance?"

"I think you were screwing her."

Thatcher opened his mouth to reply, but Michael pressed on.

"I think you got tired of screwing her. I think you paid a visit to her the day she disappeared. I think you threatened her. Tell me I'm wrong."

"You're wrong," Thatcher said, without so much as a second's hesitation. I looked at Lia, but she gave no indication that the man was lying.

Michael took another step forward. Even though I couldn't see a hint of anger on Thatcher Townsend's face, my gut said that Michael could, that he'd been watching his father's rage building—at the accusation, at the fact that it had come from his own son, at the way his son had aired dirty laundry in front of outsiders, sullying the Townsend name.

"Don't tell me you have too much integrity, too much *class*, to sleep with your partner's daughter." Michael had a very particular reaction to rage. He threw fuel on the fire. Thatcher Townsend saw himself as the founder of a dynasty, the social equal of any man. He *needed* to be seen that way. And Michael knew exactly what the cost would be of taking that away. "You can take the boy out of the slums," he told his father lightly, "but you can't take the slums out of the man."

There was no warning, no tell on Thatcher's face. His fists didn't clench. He didn't make a single sound. But one second, Michael was standing in front of his father, and the next, I heard a *crack* and Michael was lying on the ground.

Thatcher had backhanded him. *You hit him hard enough to put him down and keep him down. But in your own mind, you're rewriting the story already. You didn't lose your temper. You didn't lose control. You won.*

You always win.

Dean stepped between Michael and his father as Lia dropped to the ground to check on Michael.

Thatcher Townsend just went to pour himself another drink. "You're welcome in my home," he told us as he exited the room. "And do let me know if I can be of any help."

CHAPTER 15

There was a difference between knowing that Michael's father was abusive and *seeing* it.

"I don't know about the rest of you," Michael said, pulling himself to his feet and wiping blood from his lip with the back of his hand, "but I thought that went well."

The casual tone in Michael's voice nearly undid me. I knew that he wouldn't want my pity. He wouldn't want my rage. And whatever I felt, he would see it.

"*Well?*" Dean repeated. "You thought that went *well?*"

Michael shrugged. "In particular, the fact that I introduced you to my father as my good friend Barf is a memory that I will treasure forever."

It doesn't matter unless you let it matter. I ached for Michael, for the boy he'd been, growing up in this house.

"Are you okay?" Michael asked Sloane.

She was standing beside me, very still, her breathing shallow and her skin pale. *Thinking about Aaron. Thinking about what just happened to Michael. Thinking about your father. Thinking about his.*

Sloane took three tiny, hesitant steps, then threw herself at Michael, latching her arms around his neck so tightly that I wasn't sure she would ever let go.

My phone rang. Once I saw Michael's arms curve around Sloane, I answered it.

"That did *not* go well." Agent Sterling's greeting reminded me that we were wired with video and audio feeds. "I won't ask if Michael's okay, and I won't say I told you so. I will, however, let you know that Briggs is looking forward to seeing Thatcher Townsend booked for assault."

I set the phone to speaker. "You have the entire group," I told Sterling.

For a moment, I thought she might repeat her statement about Michael's father, but she must have decided that Michael wouldn't thank her for it. "What did we learn?" she asked instead.

"When Thatcher said Michael was wrong, he wasn't lying." Lia leaned back against a grand piano, crossing one leg in front of the other. "But whether he meant that Michael was wrong about part of it or all of it, I couldn't say."

I replayed Michael's accusation in my head: *I think you were screwing her. I think you paid a visit to her the day she disappeared. I think you threatened her.* I tried to sink into Thatcher's perspective, but instead, found myself adopting Michael's. *You accused him of sleeping with her. You accused him of threatening her. You didn't say that you thought he took* her. *You didn't accuse him of breaking into her studio or trashing it in a rage.*

"Anything else?" Agent Sterling's voice broke into my thoughts, but as Lia reported on the only other relevant lie she'd caught—Thatcher's reference to Remy as one of his closest friends—my brain cycled right back to profiling Michael.

You didn't come in swinging. You didn't lose your temper. You said that this went well. I followed those facts to their logical conclusion: Michael didn't believe his father had physically harmed Celine in any way. *If you had, you would have swung back.*

I studied Michael—the bruise forming on his face, the way he was standing, the way he kept his body angled away from Lia's.

When Lia pressed you for answers in Celine's room, you said something guaranteed to make her run. And when I opened my mouth to continue the conversation . . .

Michael had done his best to push us away. He'd wanted to be in Celine's room alone. And something he'd seen there had led him to come have a drink and a conversation with his father.

The wheels in my head turned slowly at first, then faster. *You don't believe your father took her. But here you are.* Back in Celine's room, Michael had cavalierly referred to the girl as one of our vics. He'd come here to have a chat with his father, but had focused more on finding out if his father had threatened Celine—if he'd slept with her—than on finding out where Celine might be now.

Because you already know.

Michael took one look at my face and stepped toward me. I thought back to the crime scene. Dean and I had assumed that the shattered glass, the easel, the turned-over tables, all of the debris, had been the result of Celine fighting back against her assailant.

But what if there was no assailant? The possibility took root in my mind. Sloane had told us that the debris was the result of someone sweeping their hands across the table, knocking its contents violently to the floor. We'd assumed that the UNSUB had done it—to hurt Celine, to scare her, to dominate her.

But Celine was a person who painted her own self-portrait with a knife. She threw her whole body into everything she did. She was strong-willed. She was determined. *You have a temper.*

"She did it herself." I tested the theory by watching Michael's response to my words. "That's why you thought your father went to see Celine the day she disappeared. Something set her off."

"I have no idea what you're talking about." Michael's voice was absolutely devoid of emotion.

"Yes," Lia countered. "You do."

You trashed your own studio. I slipped back into Celine's perspective. *You swept the glass off the table. You broke the* easel. *You turned the table over. You soaked the place in kerosene. Maybe you were going to burn it. Maybe you were going to send the whole thing up in flames, but then you stopped, and you looked around, and you realized what the destruction you'd wreaked looked like.*

It looked like there had been a fight. Like you'd been attacked.

I wondered if that was all it had taken. I wondered if Celine had turned her artist's eye on the destruction, thinking of ways to make it look even more realistic. *The bloody handprint on the door. The drops of blood on the carpet.* I wondered how she'd figured out how to delete the security footage, if she'd picked the lock on her own studio door.

"An artistic challenge." Dean picked up where I'd left off. "A game. To see if she could fool everyone. To see how long . . ."

How long it would take them to notice you were gone.

"Someone care to tell me what I'm missing here?" Agent Sterling's voice blared from the phone, reminding me that she was still on the line.

"Michael's a liar," Lia said flatly. "And Celine Delacroix is a poor, pathological little rich girl who kidnapped *herself.*"

"Don't talk about her that way." Michael's response was instantaneous and instinctual. "Whatever she did, she had a reason for it."

"Did you pine after her when you were growing up?" Lia asked the question like the answer didn't matter to her in the least. "Did you pursue her, the way you got all moon-eyed over Cassie when she first showed up?" Lia was aiming below the belt. That was the only way she knew how to hit. "Did you convince yourself you weren't good enough for her," she said, her voice low, "because a person like you could only ever be *good enough* for someone as horrible as me?"

"You're being ridiculous," Michael told her.

"Do you love her?" Lia asked, her voice dripping with syrupy sweetness.

I could see Michael's temper fraying. He ran his thumb over his bloodied lip and stared at Lia. "Longer and better than I've loved you."

CHAPTER 16

We found Celine Delacroix the next morning, sitting on the edge of a dock a two-hour drive from her house—the same dock where she and Michael had been photographed years before. Beside me, Dean watched, stone-faced, as Michael walked toward the end of the dock—toward Celine. I couldn't make out the expression on her face when she spotted him. I couldn't hear his greeting or the words she offered in return. But I saw the exact moment when the fighter in Celine gave way to something softer.

Something vulnerable.

"This is what happens when they're together," Dean said, and I knew that he wasn't talking about Michael and Celine. "Michael knows exactly what Lia's feeling. Lia knows every time he lies to her. They hurt each other, and they hurt themselves."

I thought about everything that had happened: Michael's

confrontation with his father, his fight with Lia, the realization that we'd been dragged away from hunting for my mother's captors by what amounted to an elaborate prank. We'd been on this case for less than twenty-four hours, but even that felt like too much.

One day until Michael's birthday. Three days until April second. As I watched Michael sit down next to Celine, the countdown to the next Fibonacci date resumed in my head.

"Relax, Dean," Lia said, coming up behind us. "I'm fine. We found the girl. We saved the day. If you think I'm going to get all emotional over Michael Townsend, clearly I've been doing this cold-hearted shrew thing all wrong."

Michael didn't tell us what Celine had said. He didn't tell us whether she'd explained why she'd done what she'd done or what she'd hoped to gain by it. By midmorning, we were back on the plane, a whole herd of emotional elephants in tow.

Briggs didn't say a word to Sterling about the fact that she'd known from the get-go that this case had nothing to do with the Masters.

Sterling didn't say a word to Briggs about the way he'd jumped the moment her father had indicated how high.

Michael and Lia didn't acknowledge the angry words that had passed between them.

I didn't tell Dean that the night before, I'd dreamed of his father, of my mother, of blood on the walls and blood on her hands—and on mine.

Once we were in the air, Judd pulled me to the back of the plane. He settled into one seat and nodded toward another. I sat. For several seconds, he said nothing, like the two of us were sitting side by side on the front porch of the Quantico house, enjoying our morning coffee and a bit of quiet.

"Do you know why I said yes to this case?" Judd asked finally.

I turned the question over in my head. *You want the Masters as badly as I do.* They'd killed his daughter. But though this case had appeared related, my gut said that Judd—unlike the director and Agent Briggs—had watched Agent Sterling very carefully through the whole exchange.

He hadn't been backing Briggs's decision. He'd been backing hers.

"A girl was missing." I repeated the words Agent Sterling had said the day before. "A girl that Michael knew."

"Michael was coming back here." Judd had never doubted that—not for a second. "And when one of my kids goes down an emotional rabbit hole like that one, he—or she—sure as hell doesn't do it alone."

Judd gave those words a moment to sink in, then reached into his bag and pulled out a folder.

"What's this?" I asked when he handed it to me.

"A file someone tried very hard to bury," he replied. "While you were off gallivanting after Miss Delacroix this morning, one of Ronnie's contacts managed to dig it up."

Ronnie was short for Veronica—as in Agent Veronica Sterling.

"Inmate named Robert Mills." Judd resorted to speaking in fragments as my fingers found their way to the edge of the folder. "Convicted of murdering his ex-wife. Killed in prison not long after he was convicted."

The man Redding talked to. My grip on the edge of the folder tightened. *The one whose ex-wife's body was never found. The one who was taken, just like my mother.*

As I opened the folder, Judd caught my chin, and his weathered hands turned my face gently toward his.

"Cassie-girl, don't go down this rabbit hole alone."

CHAPTER 17

The information in the file was bare-bones. Robert Mills had been convicted of murdering his ex-wife. Despite the fact that her body had never been found, there had been a preponderance of physical evidence. His DNA was found at the crime scene, which was soaked in his ex-wife's blood. He had a history of violence. Mallory Mills had been living under an assumed name at the time of her murder; Robert had recently discovered her location. The police had found three blood-soaked bullets at the scene, and each had tested positive for Mallory's DNA. Forensic analysis of a gun found in a nearby Dumpster had revealed that at least six shots had been fired, leaving police to conjecture that the other three bullets had remained embedded in the victim's body.

The gun was registered to her ex-husband.

You were left, shot and bleeding, on the floor for more than five minutes. There were pools of blood—upwards of 42 percent of the blood in your body.

Beside me, Dean studied the crime scene photos on his phone. Back at the house, Agent Sterling was probably tacking up her copies of these pictures, one more piece of the puzzle on the basement wall. I'd chosen a different location to process what I'd read on the plane.

The cemetery.

I stared at my mother's name, etched into the tombstone: LORELAI HOBBES. I'd known before we'd buried the body that the remains we'd laid to rest there weren't hers. Now I was trying to wrap my mind around the fact that they might belong to Mallory Mills. This wasn't the first time I'd thought about the life my mother had snuffed out to save her own. But now I wasn't just thinking about the body six feet beneath us; I was thinking about a living, breathing woman, holding her image in my mind as I walked back through the evidence that had been used to convict her ex-husband of murder.

Three missing bullets. I imagined lying on my back, bullets burning in my gut, my chest, my leg. *You would have lost consciousness. Without immediate medical intervention, you would have died.*

"But the Masters chose you," I said, my voice so soft that I could barely hear the words. "Just like they chose my mother."

If I was right, Mallory Mills hadn't died of those gunshot

99

wounds. The Masters had shot her, then saved her. They'd taken her, framed her husband, and, once she'd healed, forced her to fight *her* predecessor to the death. They'd held her captive, right up until they'd taken my mother.

"What do they have in common?" Dean asked quietly.

"Mallory was in her early twenties." I fell back on facts. "My mother was twenty-eight when she disappeared. Both of them were young, healthy. Mallory's hair was dark. My mom's was red." I tried not to remember my mother's infectious smile, the way she'd looked dancing in the snow. "Both of them had been abused."

My mother had left home at sixteen to escape a father more monstrous than Michael's. And Mallory Mills? There was a reason she'd been living under an alias, a reason that the district attorney was able to convict her ex without a body.

You choose women who have experienced violence firsthand. You choose fighters. You choose survivors. And then you make them do the unthinkable to survive.

I wanted to step toward Dean. I wanted to close my lips over his, to forget about Mallory Mills and my mother's name on this tombstone and every single thing I'd read in that file.

But I couldn't. "When I went to see your father, he quoted Shakespeare at me. *The Tempest.* 'Hell is empty, and all the devils are here.' "

Dean knew his father well enough to read between the lines. "He told you that your mom might not just be their captive. He told you she might be one of them."

"We don't know what those monsters have done to her, Dean. We don't know what she's had to become to survive." A chill settled over my body, even though I could still feel the heat from Dean's. "We do know that she's not just another victim. She's the Pythia. *Lady Justice*—that's what Nightshade called her. *Judge and jury*. Like she was one of them."

"Not by choice." Dean said the words I needed to hear. That didn't make them true.

"She *chose* to kill the woman we buried." Saying those words was like tearing off a bandage, followed by five or six layers of skin.

"Your mother chose to *live*."

That was what I'd been telling myself for the past ten weeks. I'd spent more nights than I could count staring up at my ceiling and wondering: Would I have done what she did if I'd been the one forced to fight for my survival? Could I have killed another woman—the previous Pythia, pitted against me in a battle to the death—to save myself?

As I had dozens of times before, I tried to put myself in my mother's shoes, to imagine what it must have been like for her after she'd been taken. "I wake up in near-darkness. I should be dead, but I'm not." My mom's next thought would have been of me, but I skipped over that and on to the realizations that must have been racing in her mind once she'd pieced together what had happened. "They cut me. They stabbed me. They took me to the brink of death. And then they brought me back."

How many women, other than my mother and Mallory Mills, shared this story? How many Pythias had there been?

You wait for them to heal, and then . . .

"They lock me in a room. I'm not the only one there. There's a woman coming toward me. She's got a knife in her hands. And there's a knife beside me." My breath was jagged. "I know now why they came so close to killing me, why they brought me back." To my ears, my voice even *sounded* like my mother's. "They wanted me to look Death in the eyes. They wanted me to know what it felt like so that I would know, beyond any shadow of a doubt, that I wasn't ready to die."

I pick up the knife. I fight back. And I win.

"The Masters stalk these women." Dean pulled me from the darkness. He didn't use any of our profiling pronouns—not *I* or *we* or *you*. "They watch them. They know what they've been through, know what they've survived."

I stepped forward, stopping just short of resting my face on his chest. "They watched my mother—for weeks or months or *years*, and I can't even remember the names of all the towns we lived in. I'm the closest thing we have to a witness, and I can't remember a single useful detail. I can't remember a single face."

I'd tried. I'd spent years trying, but we'd moved so often. And each time, my mother had told me the same thing.

Home isn't a place. Home is the people who love you. Forever and ever, no matter what.

Forever and ever, no matter what.

Forever and ever—

And that was when I remembered—I wasn't the only one my mother had promised to love. I wasn't the only witness. I didn't know what had been done to my mother or who she'd become. But there was someone who did. Someone who knew her. Someone who loved her.

Forever and ever, no matter what.

CHAPTER 18

My sister, Laurel, was small for her age. The pediatrician thought she was about four—healthy, except for a vitamin D deficiency. That, along with her pale skin and what little we'd been able to glean from Laurel herself, had led to the theory that she'd spent the majority of her life indoors—quite possibly underground.

I'd seen Laurel twice in the past ten weeks. It had taken almost twenty-four hours to arrange this meeting, and if Agents Briggs and Sterling had their way, it would be the last.

It's too dangerous, Cassie. For you. For Laurel. Agent Sterling's admonition rang in my ears as I watched the little sister I barely knew stand opposite an empty swing set, staring at it with an intensity at odds with her baby face.

It's like you can see something the rest of us can't, I thought. *A memory. A ghost.*

Laurel rarely talked. She didn't run. She didn't play. Part of me had hoped that she'd look like a kid this time. But she just stood there, ten feet and light-years away from me, as still and unnaturally quiet as the day I'd found her sitting in the middle of a blood-drenched room.

You're young, Laurel. You're resilient. You're in protective custody. I wanted to believe that with time, Laurel was going to be just fine, but my half sister had been born and bred to take a seat at the Masters' table. I had no idea if she was ever going to be okay.

In the weeks that Laurel had been in FBI custody, no one had been able to get any actionable information out of her. She didn't know where they'd been holding her. She couldn't—or wouldn't—describe the Masters.

"Based on the level of deterioration on that merry-go-round, I would estimate that this playground was built between 1983 and 1985." Sloane came to stand beside me. It had been Agent Sterling's suggestion to bring another Natural with us. I'd chosen Sloane because she was the most childlike herself—and the least likely to realize just how psychologically scarred Laurel really was.

Sloane squeezed my hand comfortingly. "In the Estonian sport of kiiking, players stand on a massive swing and attempt to rotate it three hundred and sixty degrees."

I had two choices: I could either stand here listening to every playground-related factoid Sloane could think of in her attempt to calm my nerves or I could talk to my sister.

As if she could hear my thoughts, Laurel pivoted, tearing her gaze away from the swing set and bringing it to me. I made my way toward her, and she turned her attention back to the swing. I knelt next to her, giving her a moment to acclimate to my presence. Sloane came and sat down one swing over.

"This is my friend Sloane," I told Laurel. "She wanted to meet you."

No response from Laurel.

"There are two hundred and eighty-five different species of squirrel," Sloane announced as a greeting. "And that's not counting any number of prehistoric squirrel-like species."

To my surprise, Laurel tilted her head to the side and smiled at Sloane. "Numbers," she said clearly. "I like numbers."

Sloane gave Laurel a companionable smile. "Numbers make sense, even when nothing else does."

I focused on Laurel as she took a tentative step toward Sloane. *Numbers are comforting,* I thought, trying to see the world through my little sister's eyes. *Familiar. To the men who brought you into this world, numbers are immutable. A higher order. A higher law.*

"Do you like swings?" Sloane asked Laurel. "They're my second favorite use of centripetal force."

Laurel frowned as Sloane began swinging gently back and forth. "Not like that," my sister told Sloane firmly.

Sloane slowed to a stop, and Laurel stepped forward. She reached out to trail her tiny fingers along the links of the swing's chains. "Like this," she told Sloane, pressing her wrist against the metal chain.

Sloane stood and mimicked Laurel's motion. "Like this?"

Laurel lifted the swing and wrapped the chain carefully

around Sloane's wrist. "Both hands," she told Sloane. As my four-year-old sister painstakingly wrapped the free chain around Sloane's other wrist, my brain finally processed what she was doing.

Chains on the wrists. Shackles.

I'd wondered what Laurel saw when she looked at the swing set, and now I knew.

"Bracelets," Laurel said, sounding as happy as I'd ever heard her. "Like Mommy's."

If I hadn't already been on the ground, those words might have brought me to my knees.

"Mommy wears bracelets?" I asked Laurel, trying to keep my voice even and calm.

"Sometimes," Laurel replied. "It's part of the game."

"What game?" My mouth was dry, but I couldn't afford to stop talking. This was the closest Laurel had ever come to telling me about the way she'd been forced to live, about our mother.

"*The* game," Laurel repeated, shaking her head like I'd just asked a very silly question. "Not the quiet game. Not the hiding game. *The* game."

There was a beat of silence. Sloane picked up the slack. "Games have rules," she commented.

Laurel nodded. "I know the rules," she whispered. "I know all of the rules."

"Can you tell Sloane the rules, Laurel?" I asked. "She wants to hear them."

My sister stared at Sloane's wrists, still wrapped in chains.

"Not Laurel," the little girl said fiercely. "Laurel doesn't play the game."

My name is Nine. That was one of the first things my sister had ever said to me. At the time, the words had sent chills down my spine because the group we were looking for had nine members. *Seven Masters. The Pythia. And the child of the Pythia and the Masters, the ninth member of their sadistic little circle.*

Nine.

"Laurel doesn't play the game," I repeated. "*Nine* does."

Laurel's tiny fingers tightened around the chain on the swing. "*Mommy knows,*" she said fiercely.

"Knows what?" I asked, my heart beating in my throat. "What does Mommy know?"

"Everything."

There was something off about the set of my half sister's features. Her face was strangely devoid of emotion. She didn't look like a child.

Not Laurel. Her words echoed in my head. *Laurel doesn't play the game.*

I couldn't do this to her. Whatever she was reliving, whatever she was *playing*, I couldn't send my sister to that place.

"When I was little," I said softly, "my mommy and I used to play a game. A guessing game." My chest tightened as a lifetime of memories threatened to overwhelm me. "We'd watch people, and we'd guess. What they were like, what made them happy, what they wanted."

Behavior. Personality. Environment. My mother had taught me well. Based on the other games my little sister had mentioned—*the quiet game, the hiding game*—I was betting my mom had taught Laurel some survival skills as well. What I *wasn't* sure of was whether the game that "Nine" played was another of my mom's creations, designed to mask the horrors of their situation—and the chains—from Laurel, or whether that one was a "game" of the Masters' design.

Laurel reached out a tiny hand to touch my cheek. "You're pretty," she said. "Like Mommy." She stared at and into me with unsettling intensity. "Is your blood pretty, too?"

The question trapped the air in my lungs.

"I want to see," Laurel said. Her little fingers dug into my cheek, harder and harder. "The blood belongs to the Pythia. The blood belongs to *Nine*."

"Look!" Sloane unwound her hands from the chains. She displayed her wrists for Laurel. "No more bracelets."

There was a pause.

"No more game," Laurel whispered. Her hand dropped to her side. She turned to me, her expression hopeful and childish and utterly unlike the one she'd worn a moment before. "Did I do good?" she asked.

You did so good, Cassie. I could hear my mom saying those words to me, a grin on her face when I'd correctly pegged the personalities of the family sitting next to us at a diner.

Sloane made an attempt at filling the silence. "There are

seven wonders of the world, seven dwarfs, seven deadly sins, and seven different kinds of twins."

"Seven!" Laurel tilted her head to the side. "I know *seven*." She hummed something under her breath: a series of notes, varying rhythm, varying pitch. "That's seven," she told Sloane.

Sloane hummed the tune back to her. "Seven notes," she confirmed. "Six of them unique."

"Did I do good?" Laurel asked me a second time.

My heart constricted, and I wrapped my arms around her. *You're mine. My sister. My responsibility. No matter what they did to you—you're mine.*

"You know the number seven," I murmured. "You did so good." My voice caught in my throat. "But Laurel? You don't have to play the game anymore. Not ever again. You don't have to be Nine. You can just be Laurel, forever and ever."

Laurel didn't reply. Her gaze fixed on something over my right shoulder. I turned to see a little boy spinning his sister on the merry-go-round.

"The wheel is always turning," Laurel murmured, her body going stiff. "Round and round . . ."

YOU

Soon.

Soon.

Soon.

Masters come, and Masters go, but the Pythia lives in the room.

CHAPTER 19

My conversation with Laurel had told me two things. First, whatever sway or position my mother held over the Masters, she was still a captive. Her "bracelets" were proof enough of that. And second . . .

"The blood belongs to the Pythia." I repeated my sister's words out loud. "The blood belongs to Nine."

"Knock, knock." Lia had a habit of saying the words in lieu of actually knocking. She also didn't bother to wait for a response before sauntering into the room I shared with Sloane. "A little birdie told me there was a seventy-two-point-three percent chance you needed a hug," Lia said. She raked her gaze over my face. "I don't do hugs."

"I'm fine," I said.

"Lie," Lia replied immediately. "Care to try again?"

It was on the tip of my tongue to say that, after the debacle at Michael's house, she probably wasn't *fine*, either, but

I had the good sense to know that pointing that out would not end well for me.

"You don't do hugs," I said instead. "What's your official position on ice cream?"

Lia and I ended up on the roof, a carton of white chocolate raspberry between us.

"Do you want me to tell you that your mother is still the woman you remember?" Lia asked, leaning back against the window frame behind us.

If I asked her to, Lia would make that statement sound utterly believable. But I didn't want her to lie to me. "Nightshade told us weeks ago that the Pythia leads the Masters in her child's stead." The words tasted bitter in my mouth. "But Laurel said they chain her wrists."

Part queen regent, part captive. Powerless and powerful. How long could a person withstand that kind of dichotomy before she did something—anything—to reclaim agency and control?

"My little sister calls shackles *bracelets*." I stared straight ahead, my grip on the spoon in my hands tightening. "She thinks it's a game. *The* game."

I fell silent.

"Well, I'm not bored yet." Lia waved her spoon at me, an imperious gesture that I should continue.

I did.

"It was like Laurel was two different people," I finished

several minutes later. "A little girl and . . . someone else."

*Some*thing *else.*

"She dug her fingers into the side of my cheek hard enough to hurt. She said she wanted to see my blood. And then, once Sloane took the swing chains off her wrists, it was like a switch had been flipped. Laurel was a little kid again. She asked me . . ." The words stuck in my throat. "She asked me if she did good, like—"

"Like she was *supposed* to be utterly creepy and borderline psychotic on cue?" Lia offered. "Maybe she was."

Lia had grown up in a cult. She'd told me once that someone used to give her presents for being a good girl. Beside me, she untied her ponytail, allowing her hair to flow free as she stretched her legs out toward the edge of the roof. *Change in appearance, change in posture.* I recognized Lia's method of shedding emotions she didn't want to feel.

"Once upon a time . . ." Lia's voice was light and airy, "There was a girl named Sadie. She had lines to learn. She had a role. And the better she played it . . ." Lia gave me a tight-lipped smile. "Well, that's a story for another time."

Lia didn't part with pieces of her past easily, and when she did, there was no way of telling if what she'd said was true. But I had gathered bits and pieces here and there— like the fact that her real name was Sadie.

Lines to learn, a role to play. I wondered what else Sadie and Nine had in common. I knew better than to profile Lia, but I did it anyway. "Whatever happened back then," I said softly, "it didn't happen to *you*."

Lia's eyes shone with a glint of emotion, like I was catching a glimpse of darkened water at the bottom of a mile-deep well. "That's what Sadie's mother used to tell her. *Just pretend it's not you.*" Lia's smile was sharp-edged and fleeting. "Sadie was good at pretending. She played the role. *I* was the one who learned how to play the game."

For Lia, shedding her old identity was a way of reclaiming power. Her "game"—whatever it had entailed—probably bore little resemblance to the specifics of what my mother was going through now, what Laurel had been raised to view as normal. But there were enough similarities between the two situations to make me wonder if my mom had encouraged my little sister to draw a line between "Laurel" and "Nine."

"And what about Sadie's mother?" I asked Lia. *Your mother*, I amended silently. "Did she take her own advice? Did she create a part of herself that nothing and no one could touch?"

Lia must have known, on some level, that I wasn't just asking about her mother. I was asking about mine. Was the woman who'd raised me the Pythia? Or was that a role she played? Had she segmented off a part of herself and buried it deep? If I found her, would there be anything left to save?

"You're the profiler," Lia said lightly "You tell—"

Lia cut off before finishing that sentence. I followed her

gaze to the walkway leading up to our house—and to the girl striding across it like it was a catwalk and she was the star of the show.

"Celine Delacroix." Lia's tone was only slightly less concerning than the twisted little smile that crossed her face as she stood. "This should be good."

CHAPTER 20

"Can't a girl come to visit her childhood best friend on his birthday?"

Lia and I made it downstairs in time to hear Celine explaining her presence to Michael. Sloane stood just behind him, a stubbornly protective expression on her face. I wondered if she was feeling protective of Michael—or of Lia.

"You followed us." Michael didn't sound entirely surprised.

"Followed," Celine repeated. "Bribed some people to keep tabs on you. Same difference." Without missing a beat, she turned to Sloane. "You must be one of Michael's friends. I'm Celine."

"You faked your own kidnapping." In Sloane's world, that passed for a greeting. "It is my understanding that is highly abnormal behavior."

Celine shrugged. "Did I fake a ransom note? Call in a phony tip to the police?"

"You're saying that you didn't do anything illegal." Dean entered the room and inserted himself into the conversation before Lia could.

"I'm saying that if someone wants to trash their own art studio and skip off to one of their vacation homes for a week, it's hardly *their* fault if someone assumes there's been foul play."

"And *I'm* saying," Sloane countered, "I'm saying . . ." She trailed off, uncertain of a proper comeback. "I'm saying that the average miniature donkey lives between twenty-five and thirty-five years!"

Celine grinned, the expression less practiced than any I'd seen cross her face. "I like her," she told Michael decisively. "She says what she's thinking. Our social circle could use more of that, don't you think?"

Your *social circle,* I corrected silently. *It's not Michael's. Not anymore.*

"In the interest of saying what we're thinking," Lia interjected, "if you're really here to celebrate Michael's birthday, perhaps we should get this party under way?"

Michael had the good sense to look alarmed.

"I'm thinking a game might be in order," Lia continued.

"A game?" Celine arched an eyebrow. "What kind of game?"

Lia looked at Michael, then smiled wickedly. "How about Never Have I Ever?"

I wasn't sure how Michael had intended to spend his birthday, but I suspected it wasn't sitting beside the pool in our backyard with Lia on one side and Celine on the other.

"The rules are simple," Lia said, dipping her toes into the pool. Even heated, it had to be chilly. "Everyone starts with ten fingers up. Each time someone names something you've done before, a finger comes down." She let that sink in, then started the game off with a bang. "Never have I ever been kidnapped, threatened, or shot by an UNSUB."

I saw the subtext there: whatever world Celine and Michael had shared, this was Lia's way of telling the other girl that she didn't know a thing about him now.

I lowered a finger. Dean and Michael followed suit.

Celine remained remarkably unruffled. "Never have I ever used the word *UNSUB* like that's a perfectly normal thing for a teenager to say."

Dean, Michael, Lia, and I all lowered fingers. Lia cleared her throat to get Sloane's attention.

"I don't say anything like it's perfectly normal," Sloane clarified. "Ninety-eight percent of the time I'm not normal at all." She paused. "Never have I ever not known the first hundred digits of pi."

Michael groaned. Every player but Sloane lowered a finger. I was down to seven, and we'd only been through three rounds.

"Your turn," Celine told me. "Make it a good one."

I glanced over at Lia. "Never have I ever lived in a bathroom at the Metropolitan Museum of Art."

Lia smirked, then slowly lowered the middle finger on her left hand.

"Seriously?" Celine asked.

Lia met the other girl's gaze, a dangerous glint in her eyes. "Seriously."

Dean must have sensed that the look in Lia's eyes didn't bode well—for Celine, for Michael, for Lia—because he chose that moment to enter the game. "Never have I ever," he said slowly, "made out with Michael Townsend."

"Someday, big guy," Michael told him with a wink. "If you're very, very good."

I stared at Dean, then lowered a finger. *Why would you say something like that?* I wondered, but as Lia lowered a finger, I realized exactly why Dean had chosen that statement.

Celine didn't move.

"Never have I ever," Michael said after a moment, "rashly assumed that my significant other was in love with a girl that I'd never met."

Lia lowered a finger and rearranged the fingers on her left hand so that only the middle finger was sticking up. "Never have I ever used the phrase *significant other*," she retorted.

"Technically," Sloane pointed out, "you just did."

Celine snorted. "Never have I ever had a thing for blondes," she said. And then, her eyes on Sloane, she shot our statistician a dazzling smile and lowered her own finger—meaning that she *did* have a thing for blondes.

You've never made out with Michael, I realized, *because Michael isn't your type.*

"Never have I ever not wanted a miniature donkey,"

Sloane offered, completely oblivious to the fact that Celine was flirting with her.

It was my turn again. "Never have I ever faked my own disappearance because of something Thatcher Townsend said to me."

Michael's father had denied that he'd slept with Celine, gone to see her the day she disappeared, and threatened her. But, as Lia had pointed out, his denial could ring true if he was telling the truth about any one of the three.

Maybe he didn't sleep with you, but went to see you anyway. Maybe he threatened you about something else.

Celine—brash and bold and fearless—lowered a finger.

"Never have I ever been threatened because of one of my father's business dealings." Dean took a shot next, but struck out.

Celine turned to Michael. "This is getting tedious," she told him. Clearly, whatever Thatcher Townsend had said to her, she wasn't in a sharing mood.

There was a moment of silence, and then Lia filled it. "Never have I ever *let* someone beat the crap out of me."

That brought Michael's attention from Celine to Lia. "You got me," he said, gesturing toward his swollen lip. "Very insightful."

Instead of replying, Lia dropped her left hand. It took me a moment to realize that, in doing so, she'd brought down her middle finger, too. With a start, I realized that was Lia's way of telling Michael that she'd been exactly where he was.

There was another long stretch of silence, and then: "Never have I ever been publicly acknowledged by my own father." Celine's voice was rough in her throat, like the exchange that had just passed between Michael and Lia had meant something to her, too.

Sloane stared at Celine. *Since my father had acknowledged me, I lowered a finger. So did Dean. So did Michael. So did Lia.*

But Sloane's fingers stayed up. "Are you illegitimate, too?" she asked Celine. There was no judgment in her voice, no awareness that the question wasn't the kind that people could politely ask.

Michael turned to look at Celine, searching her face for answers. "CeCe?"

If Celine was illegitimate, Michael clearly hadn't known. I thought about the emotions that he'd read on his father's face when Celine was missing. *Furious. Affronted. Personally insulted.*

Hungry.

A man like Thatcher Townsend hungered for things he couldn't have. Things that someone had denied him. *Things that are rightfully yours.*

Suddenly, I saw the whole situation from a different perspective—why Thatcher might have gone to see Celine, why Celine might have responded the way she had, why she'd followed Michael back here, why Thatcher Townsend had involved himself in the investigation from the get-go.

She has her father's temper, I thought, Elise Delacroix's

statement taking on new meaning in my mind. *Not Remy Delacroix's. Her father's.* Michael's *father's.*

Michael turned away from the secrets he saw laid bare on Celine's face. "As the birthday king, it is within my rights to demand a rumpus of *Where the Wild Things Are* proportions. And as it happens," he continued, masking his own emotions the way that only an emotion-reader could, "as the recipient of a recently released trust fund, I have a few ideas."

CHAPTER 21

Michael's idea of a party involved an amusement park rented out for the evening for our amusement and our amusement alone.

"Do I want to know how much this cost?" Dean asked.

"Doubtful," Michael replied. "Do I want to know why you have a phobia of integrating colors into your wardrobe? Almost certainly not!"

When I'd first met Michael, I'd found him difficult to profile. But now I understood. *Reading emotions was never your only survival mechanism.* He'd learned not to feel things, to turn everything into a joke, to shrug off revelations that shook his worldview to its core.

A quick glance at Celine told me that was a trait they shared. The edges of her lips quirked up in a slight smile. "Not bad," she told Michael, taking in the lights of the Ferris wheel in the distance.

"What can I say?" he replied. "Good taste runs in the family."

The subtext to those words was deafening.

Sloane frowned. "The number of taste buds one has is heritable, but that does not affect aesthetic or entertainment preferences, to the best of my knowledge."

Celine didn't miss a beat. "The brainy type," she declared loftily. "I approve."

Sloane was quiet for several seconds. "Most people don't."

My heart hurt at the matter-of-fact way Sloane said those words.

Her manner uncharacteristically gentle, Celine hooked an arm through Sloane's. "How would you feel about trying to win me a goldfish?"

Sloane clearly had no idea how to reply, so she went with the path of least resistance. "Goldfish don't have stomachs or eyelids. And their resting attention span is actually one-point-oh-nine times that of the average human."

As Celine led Sloane toward the carnival games, I started to follow, but Michael held me back. "She'll be fine," he told me. "Celine is . . ." He trailed off, then changed course. "I trust her."

"It's good to have someone you can trust." Lia's tone wasn't cutting, but that meant nothing. She was more than capable of coating razor blades in sugar.

"I never said you could trust me," Michael shot back. "I don't trust me."

125

"Maybe I'm saying that *you* can trust *me*." Lia played with the tips of her jet-black ponytail, making those words sound like nothing more than a lark. "Or maybe I'm saying that you absolutely *cannot* trust me not to wreak vengeance upon you in creative and increasingly absurd ways."

With that somewhat concerning statement, Lia hooked her arm through Dean's the way Celine had hooked hers through Sloane's. "I see a roller coaster with my name on it, Dean-o. You game?"

Lia rarely asked Dean for anything. He wasn't about to refuse now. As the two of them peeled off from the group, I pushed down the instinct to follow.

"And then," Michael murmured, "there were two."

We ended up in the house of mirrors.

"You're trying very hard not to profile me," Michael commented as we wove our way through the mazelike expanse.

"What gave me away?" I asked.

He tapped two fingers against my temple, then indicated the tilt of my chin. We passed a set of curvy mirrors that distorted our reflections, stretching them out, condensing them, the colors in my reflection blending into the colors in his. "I'll save you the effort, Colorado. I'm a person who wants what he can't have as a method of proving to himself that he doesn't deserve the things he wants. And for someone with my abilities, I have an uncanny knack for not seeing the obvious staring me in the face."

I read between the lines. "You had no idea. About Celine. About who her father really is."

"And yet the moment she said something, it made perfect sense." Michael paused, then tried out the words he'd been avoiding. "I have a sister."

I caught sight of myself in another mirror. The distortion made my face rounder, my body smaller. I thought of Laurel, staring at the swing set. *I have a sister, too.*

"Down-turned lips, tension in your neck, unfocused eyes seeing something other than the here and now." Michael paused. "You went to see *your* sister today, and no amount of Townsend Baby Daddy Drama can make you forget what you saw."

We hit the end of the house of mirrors and stepped back out onto the boardwalk. I bit back my response to Michael's statement when I saw Celine waiting for us. She was holding a fishbowl.

"Sloane won you a goldfish," Michael commented.

"Sloane won *all* of us goldfish," Celine corrected. "Girl is crazy good at carnival games. Something about 'doing the math.'"

I did some math of my own and decided that whether Michael wanted to or not, he *needed* to talk to Celine. And I needed to get away from the mirrors and the memories and the sudden reminder that the next Fibonacci date was less than thirty-six hours away.

I found Sloane sitting near the Ferris wheel, surrounded by goldfish in bowls. I sat down beside her. Whatever conversation Michael and Celine were having was drowned out by the music accompanying the Ferris wheel's turns.

The wheel is turning, I heard a tiny voice whisper in my memory, *round and round* . . .

Beside me, Sloane was humming. At first, I thought she was humming along to the music, but then I realized that she was humming the same seven notes, over and over.

Laurel's song.

Goose bumps rose on my arms. "Sloane . . ." I started to ask her to stop, but something about the expression on her face stopped me.

"Seven notes, six unique." Sloane stared at the Ferris wheel, watching it turn. "E-flat, E-flat, E, A-flat, F-sharp, A, B-flat." She paused. "What if it's not a song? What if it's a code?"

CHAPTER 22

Seven. I know seven. Laurel's words played on repeat in my head as we pulled into the driveway and I registered the fact that there were cars—*plural*—parked there. The lights were on, not just in the kitchen, but throughout the entire first floor.

Something's wrong.

I was out of the car before Michael had even pulled it to a stop. On my way to the front door, I passed a trio of agents. *Agent Vance. Agent Starmans.* It took me a moment to place the third—one of the two agents on Laurel's detail.

No.

I burst through the front door to find Briggs talking to another agent. From behind, I couldn't make out the other man's features, and I told myself that I was overreacting. I told myself that I didn't recognize him.

I told myself that Laurel was fine.

And then the man turned. *No. No, no, no—*

"Cassie." Agent Briggs caught sight of me and brushed past the man. *Agent Morris.* My brain supplied the name. *Agent Morris and Agent Sides.* Two agents assigned to protect my sister.

It's too dangerous, Cassie, Agent Sterling had told me when she'd explained why my most recent sisterly meeting had to be the last. *For you. For Laurel.*

"Where is she?" I asked, my entire body shaking with the intensity of that question. On some level, I was aware that Briggs had laid a hand on my shoulder. On some level, I was aware that he was steering me into another room. "Both of the agents on Laurel's detail are here," I said, my jaw clenched. "They're supposed to be in hiding. With *her.*"

My eyes darted to either side of Briggs, like Laurel might be there. Like if I just looked hard enough, I would find her.

"Cassie. *Cassandra.*" Briggs tightened his grip on my shoulder slightly. I barely felt it. I didn't even realize that I was fighting him, frantically pushing him away, until his arms encircled my body.

"What happened?" I asked. My voice sounded alien. It felt foreign in my own throat. "Where's Laurel?"

"She's gone, Cassie." Briggs was the one who'd recruited me to the program. Of all the adults in our lives, he was the most focused, the most driven, the most likely to pull rank.

"Gone as in missing?" I asked, going suddenly still. "Or gone as in dead?"

Briggs relaxed his hold on me, but didn't let go. "Missing. We got a call from her protection detail several hours ago.

We issued an AMBER Alert, blocked off all outgoing roads, but . . ."

But it didn't help. You didn't find her.

"They have her." I forced myself to say the words. "I promised her she would never have to go back there. I promised her that she was *safe*."

"This isn't on you, Cassie," Briggs told me, moving his hand to my chin, forcing my eyes to his. "This program is my responsibility. *You* are my responsibility. I made the call to bring Laurel in."

I knew, without asking, that Briggs was thinking of the fight he'd had with Agent Sterling back in New York, about Scarlett Hawkins and Nightshade and the sacrifices we'd all made on the altar of *winning*.

"Where's Sterling?" I asked.

"Looking for leaks at FBI headquarters," Briggs replied. "Trying to figure out how the hell this happened."

It happened, I thought, the words tightening around my heart like a vise, *because I went to see Laurel.*

It happened because of me.

YOU

The child lies unconscious on the altar, her tiny limbs forming an X against the stone. So small. So fragile.

All must be tested. All must be found worthy.

Your own throat is raw, ringed with bruises. Your hands are shaking.

But the Pythia cannot show weakness.

The Pythia cannot falter.

Your hands close around the child's neck. You tighten your grip. The girl is drugged. The girl is sleeping. The girl would feel no pain.

But the Pythia's job is not protecting the girl.

You release your grip on the little one's throat. "The child is worthy."

One of the Masters—the one you call Five—reaches out and lays a hand on the girl's forehead. One by one, the others follow suit.

"There is," Five says, once the ritual has been observed, "one other matter that requires your attention."

By the time the little girl wakes up on the altar, they've slammed your body against the wall. You don't struggle as they chain your ankles and wrists.

The Pythia is judge. The Pythia is jury. Without order, there is chaos. Without order, there is pain.

CHAPTER 23

I bolted for my room. With each step, my brain sank further and further into the Masters' perspective. *Laurel will never be safe. You'll always find her. You made her, and hers is a glorious purpose. She is Nine, and the only way she leaves your custody is if you test her and she fails.*

Nightshade had told me that the Masters didn't kill children. But that hadn't stopped them from leaving one of Laurel's predecessors to die of thirst and heat exposure when he was six years old—just two years older than Laurel was now.

All must be tested. Nightshade's prescriptive statement echoed in my memory. *All must be found worthy.*

If I had been a normal person, I might not have been able to imagine what kind of test these monsters might design for a child. But I could—I could imagine it in horrifying detail.

You won't just hurt her. You'll make her hurt someone else.

"Cassie?" Sloane stood in the doorway to our room, hovering outside it, like a force field kept her at bay.

"Did you figure it out?" I asked her. "The code?"

Sloane took a ragged breath. "I should have figured it out faster."

"Sloane—"

"*Seven* isn't just a number." She didn't let me tell her that this wasn't her fault. "It's a person."

My heart thudded in my chest as I thought about the fact that my mother had almost certainly been the one to teach Laurel that song.

"Seven is a person," I repeated. "One of the seven Masters." My mouth was suddenly dry; my palms were sweating. Laurel had been safe, right up until the meeting where she'd passed on this information. "You know who he is?"

"I know who he *was*," Sloane corrected. "E-flat, E-flat, E, A-flat, F-sharp, A, B-flat. Those aren't just notes. They're numbers." She pulled a piece of paper out of her pocket. On it, she'd drawn an octave's worth of piano keys. "If you sit down at the piano and you number the keys, starting with middle C . . ." She filled the numbers in.

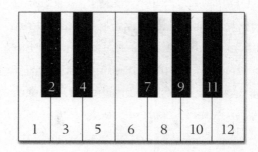

134

"E-flat, E-flat, E . . ." I said. "Four, four, five?"

"Exactly," Sloane said. "Seven notes translate into nine numbers—two digits each for A and B-flat. 445-97-1011."

It took me a moment to make the connection between what Sloane was saying and the fact that she knew one of the Masters' identities. "It's a Social Security number."

"That's the thing," Sloane replied. "It *isn't* a Social Security number—or at least, it's not anymore. I've been going in circles trying to figure out what else it could be, but then instead of cross-referencing it against *current* Social Security numbers, I decided to do a historical search."

"How much of this required illegal hacking?" a voice asked from the doorway. I looked up to see Lia and, behind her, Michael and Dean.

"Almost all of it," Sloane answered without skipping a beat. "When I went back a few decades, I found it. That Social Security number was given to a baby boy born in Gaither, Oklahoma, forty-three years ago. His name was Mason Kyle."

I could barely hear my own thoughts over the pounding of my heart. "Mason Kyle," I repeated.

"Why doesn't Mason show up in the database now?" Lia asked. "Is he dead?"

"That's the thing," Sloane replied, sitting down next to me on the bed. "Other than the Social Security number, there is virtually no record of Mason Kyle ever having existed. No birth certificate. No death certificate. No employment history. Whoever wiped his record wiped it clean. The only

135

reason I even found the Social Security number was that I hacked a decades-old archive."

This was what Laurel had given us. This was what I'd risked her safety for. This was why she was back in their hands.

To become a Master, you have to leave your old life behind. You have to erase all traces of your prior self. You used to be Mason Kyle, I thought, addressing the words to a phantom, *and now, you're a ghost.*

"That's it?" I asked Sloane, my stomach heavy, a slight roaring in my ears.

"When I heard Laurel was missing, I kept looking," Sloane said. "I looked and I looked and . . ." She bit her lip and then opened the tablet on her lap, angling it toward me. A picture of a young boy stared back at us. He was six, maybe seven years old. "This is Mason Kyle," Sloane said, "circa thirty-seven years ago. It's the one and only picture I was able to find."

The photograph was faded and fuzzy, like it had been scanned in by someone who didn't quite know how to work a scanner, but I could still make out most of the little boy's features. He had dimples. A smile missing one of its front teeth.

He could have been anyone.

I should have left Laurel alone. Instead, I led them right to her. The implication that the Masters were watching us— that they could be anyone, anywhere—made me think of Daniel Redding's chilling smile.

I wish I could be there to see what this group will do to you for coming after them.

"There's software that does age progressions," Sloane said softly. "If I can clean up the image and find the right parameters, we might be able to—"

I stood.

"Cassie?" Dean was the one who said my name. When he stepped toward me, I stepped back.

I didn't deserve comfort right now. I thought of Agent Sterling saying that Scarlett Hawkins had been sacrificed on the altar of ambition. I thought of the promise I'd made Laurel.

I lied.

CHAPTER 24

The backyard was pitch-black, except for the light from the pool. I'd come out here to be alone, but as I approached the water, it became apparent that I wasn't the only one looking for refuge.

Celine Delacroix was swimming laps.

As I went closer, I saw that she'd turned on the black light. Like the rest of the house, the pool had been designed to facilitate our training. The outline of a body glowed at the bottom of the pool. Spatter patterns—visible only under the black light—marred the pool's edge.

Months ago, Dean had shown me this. He'd tried to convince me to leave the Naturals program. He'd told me that murder and chaos wasn't a language that anyone should want to speak.

Realizing that she wasn't alone, Celine turned toward me, treading water. "No offense," she said, "but you all really suck at hiding the fact that you work for the FBI."

This girl was Michael's sister. She was safe here. But if she hung around, she might not be for long.

"You should leave," I told her. "Go back to school."

Celine swam to the edge and pulled herself out of the pool, the water clinging to her body. She had to have been freezing, but didn't shiver. "I've never excelled at *should*."

I'd heard Michael say the same thing—more than once.

"Are you okay?" Celine asked.

"No." I didn't bother elaborating and turned the question around on her. "Are you?"

She sat down next to the pool, allowing her legs to dangle in the water, tilting her head back toward the sky. "I'm trying this new thing," she told me. "Ultimate honesty. No more secrets. No more lies." This was the girl from the painting— the one who painted her self-portrait with a knife. "So, in answer to your question, Cassie, I'm not okay. I am incredibly and quite possibly *irreversibly* screwed-up. That's what happens when you figure out at the ripe old age of seven that your father isn't your father—and that his best friend is. That's what happens when, at the age of fourteen, your mother drunkenly admits to your biological father that you're his. And that's what happens when said biological father finally figures out that you know and corners you in your own studio to tell you that your dad—the man who raised you, his business partner and supposed friend—ruined you. That you would be so much more if he'd been the one in control. That, if he'd had the chance, he could have stamped the bad blood out of you when you were young, just like he did for his son."

139

Bad blood. I could imagine Thatcher Townsend saying the words, could imagine him beating out of Michael the weaknesses he saw in himself. And then I thought of Laurel—the way she was being raised, the things she was expected to do.

The blood belongs to the Pythia. The blood belongs to Nine.

"How did you find out?" I asked, my voice hoarse, trying to concentrate on the present and not what my actions had cost the one person in this world that I'd sworn to protect. "When you were seven, how did you find out that Thatcher Townsend was your father?"

"I looked at his face," Celine said simply. "And I looked at my own—not just the features, not my eyes or my lips or my nose, but the basic underlying facial structure. The bones."

I searched Celine's face for a resemblance to Michael's father, but I couldn't see it.

Celine must have sensed some skepticism. "I never forget a face. I can take one look at a person and know exactly what their facial bones look like underneath the skin. Creepy, I know, but what can I say?" She shrugged. "I'm a natural."

My breath caught in my throat. Celine didn't know the details of the program—why the FBI had brought us here, what we could do. She didn't know what it meant to be a Natural, capital N. But I thought of Michael saying that ever since they were kids, she'd only drawn faces, of the digital photo she'd created of her and Michael. She'd taken a photograph of them as kids, and she'd mentally fast-forwarded with stunning accuracy.

There's software that does age progressions. Sloane's statement echoed in my head, and I thought about the role that genes had played in making each of us Naturals what we were. Our environments had honed our gifts—but the seed had been there from the beginning.

And Celine was Michael's sister.

"I meant it when I said you should leave," I told Celine, my voice sandpaper-rough in my throat. "But before you do, I need a favor."

CHAPTER 25

The face that stared back at me from Celine's drawing was one I recognized.

Nightshade.

The likeness Michael's half sister had drawn was eerily accurate, down to the boyish expression on the murderer's face.

Seven, I thought, my heart pounding viciously in my chest. *Seven Masters, seven ways of killing.* The progression went in a predictable order, starting with the Master who drowned his victims and culminating in poison. *Nightshade is Seven.*

Nightshade is Mason Kyle.

The part of me that had felt numb and hollow from the moment I'd realized that the Masters had Laurel began to crack, like ice under the force of a pick. In the past ten weeks, the FBI hadn't been able to uncover anything about Nightshade's background. Now we had his real name. We knew where he'd been born. And—most importantly—we knew that he'd tried very hard to bury that information.

You're the one who brought Laurel to Vegas. You're the one who told me where she was.

I felt like my gut had been ripped open, like everything inside of me was leaking out. The man in this drawing had killed Judd's daughter. He'd stalked us, and when we'd caught him, he'd wrapped Laurel up for me in a tidy little bow. *Why?* Had he been instructed to do so? Had it all been part of some twisted game?

I found Agent Sterling in the kitchen sitting opposite Briggs. Her hands were folded on the table, inches from his. *You won't let yourself touch him. You won't let him touch you.*

She was the one who'd brought me to Laurel. She wouldn't blame Briggs for this. She wouldn't blame me. After Scarlett's death, Agent Sterling had left the FBI—because she blamed *herself.*

"Celine Delacroix is a Natural." I spoke up from the doorway. Right now, wallowing in guilt wasn't a privilege any of us could afford. "She did an age progression of a photo Sloane found. Nightshade's name is Mason Kyle. We can use that." My voice broke, but I forced myself to continue talking. "We can use him."

CHAPTER 26

It took sixteen hours to set up the interview. On one side of the glass, Briggs and Sterling sat opposite Nightshade. On the other side, Dean, Michael, Lia, and I watched.

We'd left Sloane at home with Celine and Judd. The only adult on our side of the glass was Agent Sterling's father.

This will work, I thought, my throat tightening. *It has to.*

"I understand that you feel you have nothing to say to us." Agent Sterling began the interrogation like it was a conversation, treating the serial killer's feelings and desires like they were completely valid. "But I thought this picture might change your mind."

She laid an image on the table—not Mason Kyle, not yet. For now, Agent Sterling needed an entry point, something to tax the killer's capacity for silence—in this case, a picture of Laurel.

"Did you call her Laurel?" Agent Briggs asked. "Or Nine?"

No answer.

"They have her, you know." Agent Sterling's voice was even and calm, but there was something intense about it, like each word that passed her lips was a living, breathing thing. "We hid her, but not well enough. They found her. Maybe they always knew where she was. Maybe they were just biding their time."

I should have protected her, I thought fiercely. *I should have been there.*

Beside me, Dean laid a hand on the back of my neck. I wanted to lean into his touch, but didn't. I didn't deserve to be touched. I didn't deserve to feel safe. I didn't deserve to do anything but sit here and watch the man who'd killed Judd's daughter reach for the picture of Laurel.

"You brought her to Las Vegas with you," Agent Sterling said. "Why?"

"If I didn't know better," Briggs commented, once it became clear that Nightshade wasn't going to say anything himself, "I'd think that you cared for the child. That you *wanted* to get her away from the life she was living."

All Nightshade offered up in response to those words was another stretch of deafening silence.

"He wasn't happy when he found out the Masters had her again," Michael informed the agents. We were miked. Briggs and Sterling could hear us; Nightshade could not. "But he's not surprised, and he's not upset. If he's feeling anything right now, it's longing."

145

What are you longing for? Not Laurel. Something else. Someone else . . .

"Ask him about my mother," I said.

When the FBI caught you, you cashed in your last chip—your only chip—to speak to me. You took Laurel away from the other Masters. You told me things that no one outside of your hallowed walls was ever supposed to know.

"Did Lorelai ask you to get her little girl out?" Agent Briggs asked. "Did she whisper a desperate plea in your ear?"

The Pythia doesn't whisper. The Pythia doesn't plead. I could feel those words—or something like them—simmering just below the surface of Nightshade's silence. *The FBI cannot begin to fathom who and what the Pythia is—to you, to your brethren. You won't tell them.*

Silence is power.

"Show him Mason Kyle," Dean suggested beside me.

Take away his power, I thought, *take away his silence.*

Agent Sterling didn't say a word as she pulled out the photograph Sloane had found of Mason Kyle.

Michael let out a long whistle. "His chin just jutted out ever so slightly. He can barely keep his lips from pressing together. Look at the way his hands are folded on the table—there's tension in his thumbs."

"He's angry," I inferred. "And he's scared." I thought about everything I knew about Nightshade. "He's angry that he's scared and scared that he's angry, because he's supposed to be above things like that. He's supposed to be above it all."

My understanding of emotion came from a different

place than Michael's. It had nothing to do with the muscles in Nightshade's jaw or the glint in his eyes—and everything to do with knowing what a man who lives to win felt when he realized he'd bet everything on the wrong hand.

When he realized that he'd *lost*.

"This is an age progression of that photograph." Agent Briggs pulled out the sketch that Celine had done for us.

As Nightshade stared at his own face, Agent Sterling went on the offensive. "Mason Kyle, born in Gaither, Oklahoma, Social Security number 445-97-1011."

That was the sum total of what we knew about Mason Kyle, but that was enough. *We were never supposed to know your name. You were supposed to be a phantom, a ghost. Even sitting in a cell, you were supposed to have the power.*

"I'm a dead man." The words were barely audible. Months of silence had not been kind to the killer's throat. "I am not worthy."

To the Masters, that's a death sentence, I thought. *A Pythia who is not worthy dies in battle against her successor. When a child is shown to be unworthy of the mantle of Nine, they're left to die in the desert. And a Master who fails in his duty . . .*

"It will be painful. It will be bloody." Nightshade—Mason Kyle—stared through the agents, like they weren't even there. "She cannot afford to let it be otherwise—not after choosing to let me live until now."

My mouth went cotton-dry. *She* as in *my mother.*

"The Pythia?" Agent Sterling said. "She's the one who decides if you live or die?"

No answer.

"Let me talk to him," I requested. Neither Briggs nor Sterling gave any sign that they'd heard me. "Let me talk to him," I repeated, my fingers curling themselves into fists and releasing, again and again. "I'm the only one he's ever really spoken to. He won't tell you about my mother, because you're not a part of this. But in his eyes, I am—or at least, I could be."

The last time I'd spoken with this man, Nightshade had told me that maybe someday, the Pythia's choice—to kill or be killed—might be mine.

With a slight nod, Agent Sterling removed her earpiece. She set it on the table and turned up the volume so that Nightshade could hear.

"It's me." I struggled to find the right words. "Lorelai's daughter. Your Pythia's daughter." I paused. "I think my mother is the reason you took Laurel when you left for Vegas. You weren't supposed to. And you certainly weren't supposed to tell me where she was. You all but gift-wrapped her for me, knowing I would hand her over to the FBI. My sister hadn't been tested. She hadn't been deemed worthy or unworthy. And you let her go." Still no reaction, but I could feel myself getting closer. "You treated Laurel like a child—not like your future leader, not like *Nine*." I lowered my voice. "She told me about the game she plays, when my mother is in chains."

If I'd been on the other side of the glass, I would have leaned forward, invading his space.

148

"You know what I think? I think my mother wanted Laurel out. She can be very convincing, can't she? She can make you feel special. She can make you feel like you don't need anyone or anything else, as long as you have her."

"You sound like her. Your voice sounds like hers." That was all I got in reply—nine words.

"You took Laurel away from that place *for her*. You knew they'd find a way to bring the child back. You knew the other Masters wouldn't be happy with you—but you did it anyway. And now you're saying that my mother is going to tell the others that you have to die? Why?" I let that question hang in the air. "Why would she do something like that after all you've done for her?"

"Haven't you learned yet?" The reply was low and fatally amused. "The Pythia does what she has to do to survive."

"And to survive, she'll have to tell them to kill you?"

"You mentioned *the game*. But do you know what that *game* involves?"

I know it involves my mother chained to the wall. I know it involves blood.

"In order to render judgment, the Pythia must first be purified," Nightshade said. "To admit someone to our ranks, she must go through the Rite of Seven. Seven days and seven pains."

I didn't want to imagine the meaning behind that phrase, but I did. *Seven Masters. Seven ways of killing people. Drowning, burning, impaling, strangling, knifing, beating, poisoning.*

"Seven pains," I said, the thudding of my heart drowning

out the sound of my words in my own ears. "You torture her for seven days."

"If she rules the acolyte unworthy, he is discarded. We find another, and the process is repeated. Again. And again. And again."

You're enjoying telling me this. You like that it hurts me. Just like you like hurting her.

"Why did you save Laurel?" I asked dully. "Why take her with you when you knew they would take her back?"

There was no answer. I waited, letting the silence build, and when he showed no sign of breaking, I turned and walked out the door. My steps never faltered as I entered the interrogation room myself.

The expression on Briggs's face told me that I'd pay for this later, but my attention was focused wholly on Nightshade. He raked his eyes over my face, my body. He drank in every detail of my appearance, and then he smiled.

"Why bother helping *Nine* break free of the Masters if you knew they would get her back?" I repeated.

I could see Nightshade's thoughts in his eyes, see him searching my features for a resemblance to my mother.

"Because it gave the Pythia hope," he said, a smile crossing his lips. "And nothing hurts the way hope does when you take it away."

A flicker of white-hot rage burned inside of me. I stepped toward him, every muscle in my body taut. "You're a monster."

"I am what I am. And she is what she is. To save herself, she has condemned others. She will condemn me."

"After they torture her for seven days?" I said, my voice low.

Agent Sterling stood to prevent me from going any closer. Nightshade angled his head downward. His body shook. It took me a moment to realize that he was laughing—silent, amused laughter that made me physically ill.

"For lesser matters, a single rite of purification will do. If the Masters are feeling generous, they might even give her a choice."

A choice of how she's tortured. My stomach revolted, but I clamped my jaw closed, refusing to give in to the bile rising in my throat. "And what if they don't like the answer she gives them?" I asked, once I had control. "What if she tells them to let you live?"

"She won't." Nightshade leaned back in his seat. "Because if her judgment appears compromised, they'll purify her again."

Torture her again.

"Where is she?" I asked sharply. "Tell us where they are, and we can stop this. We can keep you safe."

"No, Cassandra," Nightshade said with an almost loving smile, "you can't."

YOU

This time, it was the knife. Five's weapon—quicker than some, slower than others.

Chaos and order, order and chaos.

Now you're on the floor, and your memory is full of holes. You don't remember Laurel coming back. You don't remember how or when she got the bruises on her throat.

But you do remember your blood dripping off of Five's knife. You remember the music and the pain and telling the Masters that the traitor had to die.

You remember Laurel dipping her fingers in your blood. Smiling, the way you taught her.

"Did I do good, Mommy?" she asks, curling up in your lap.

The wheel turns. You tried to stop it. But some things will not be stopped.

CHAPTER 27

The FBI put Nightshade in isolation and installed agents to watch him round the clock. By two A.M., he was dead.

The Masters can get to anyone, anywhere.

"Today is April second." I forced myself to say the words out loud, standing in front of the evidence wall in the basement.

4/2. The first of four Fibonacci dates in April.

"April fourth is next," I continued. "April fifth. April twenty-third."

"Cassie." Dean came up behind me. I'd been down here since we'd returned home. I'd barely blinked when we'd gotten word that Mason Kyle was dead.

"You need to sleep," Dean murmured.

I didn't reply, staring at the victims on the wall. I thought about the fact that for each string of nine victims, a Pythia had given the go-ahead. She'd deemed an acolyte worthy to kill, because if she didn't, the pain would start all over again.

You choose abuse survivors. You choose fighters. And you make them sentence others to die.

"Cassie." Dean stepped in front of me, blocking my view of the wall. "You can't keep doing this to yourself."

I can, I thought, *and I will.*

"Look at me." Dean's voice was familiar—too familiar. I didn't want comfort. "You've barely slept since Laurel went missing. You don't eat." Dean wouldn't let up. "It ends now, Cassie."

I pretended that I could see through him. I knew this wall well enough that I could hold each and every photo in my mind's eye.

"When we discovered that my father had a copycat, I withdrew. I beat at a punching bag until my knuckles were bloody. And do you remember what you did?"

Tears threatened my eyes. *I knelt in front of you and wiped the blood from your knuckles. I pulled you back from the edge every time you went too far.*

Dean latched one arm around my torso and the other around my knees and lifted me into his arms, physically prying me away from the wall. I could feel his heart beat in his chest as he carried me toward the basement door.

Drop me, I thought, my body going stiff as a board. *Just drop me. Just let me go.*

Dean held me close as he carried me all the way to my

room. He sat down on the end of my bed. "Look at me." His voice was gentle—so gentle, it undid me.

"Don't," I choked out.

Don't be gentle. Don't hold me. Don't save me from myself.

"You think what happened to Laurel is your fault."

Stop, Dean. Please don't make me do this. Please don't make me say the words.

"And you've always believed, deep down, that if you hadn't left your mother's dressing room that day, if you'd just come back sooner, you could have saved her. Every time the police asked you a question you couldn't answer, what you heard was that you weren't enough. You weren't enough to save her. You weren't enough to help them catch the people who did it."

"And now they're hurting her." The truth burst out of me like shrapnel, exploding with deadly force. "They're torturing her until she gives them what they want."

"Permission," Dean said softly. "Absolution."

I rolled away from him, and he let me. Days' worth of exhaustion caught up to me in an instant, but I couldn't close my eyes. I let myself sink into my mother's perspective. "It's not that I don't have a choice," I said softly, not bothering to tell him that I wasn't speaking for myself anymore, that I was speaking for her. "I always have a choice: Do I suffer, or does someone else? Do I fight it? Do I fight them? Or do I play the role they've cast me in? Do I have more control, more power, if I *make* them break me or if I play the

Pythia so well that they stop thinking of me as a thing that can be broken?"

Dean was quiet for several seconds. "Against the seven of us," he said finally, "you will always be powerless." He bowed his head. "But against any one of us, you hold the cards."

I thought of Nightshade, dead in solitary confinement. "If I say you die, you die."

"But first, one in our number has to ask."

The Pythia passed judgment, but she didn't bring the cases. One of the Masters had to present an issue for her to rule on—and before making a decision, she was tortured. If enough of the Masters opposed her answer, she was tortured again.

"You chose me because I was a survivor," I whispered. "Because you saw in me the potential to become something more."

"We chose you," Dean countered, "because at least one among us believed that someday you might come to like it. The power. The blood. Some of us want you to embrace what you are. Some of us would rather you fight it—fight us."

This group followed very specific rules. After their ninth kill, they were done—permanently. "What you do to me is the closest any of you can come to reliving the glory. You drag a knife across my skin or watch it blister under a flame. You hold my head under water or make me watch as you push a metal rod through my flesh. You close your fingers around my neck. You beat me." I thought of Nightshade. "You force your most painful poison down my throat. And every time you hurt me, every time you *purify* me, I learn more about you. Seven different monsters, seven different motivations."

My mother had always excelled at manipulating people. She'd made her living as a "psychic," telling people what they wanted to hear.

"Some of us," Dean said after a moment's thought, "are easier to manipulate than others."

I thought again of Nightshade. My mother hadn't ordered his death when he'd been captured. The Masters had almost certainly presented the matter for her judgment, but she'd held out—and at least some subset of them had let her.

"Nightshade was a newly minted member of this group when they took my mother," I said slowly, trying to think of facts—any facts—that might shed light on their dynamic. "He completed his ninth kill two months before she was taken." I forced myself back into my mother's point of view. "He was competitive. He was daring. He wanted to break me. But I made him want something else more. I made him want me."

"What he wanted was immaterial." Dean closed his eyes, his lashes casting shadows on his face. "The Pythia will never belong to one man."

"But one of you must have identified me as a potential Pythia," I said. I thought again about how new to the fold Nightshade had been when my mother was taken. "One of you chose me, and it wasn't Nightshade."

I waited for another insight, but nothing came, and that

nothing ate away at me like a black hole sucking every other emotion in. I couldn't remember who might have been watching my mother. I couldn't remember anything that might have told us how—and by whom—she'd been chosen.

Dean lay down beside me, his head on my pillow. "I know, Cassie. *I know.*"

I thought of Daniel Redding, sitting across from me and gloating about the way he'd inserted himself between Dean and me—every time our hands brushed, every gentle touch.

I don't need gentle right now. I let myself turn toward Dean, let my breath catch raggedly in my throat. *I don't want it.*

I reached for Dean, pulling him roughly toward me. His hands buried themselves in my hair. *Not gentle. Not light.* My back arched as his grip on my ponytail tightened. One second I was beside him, and the next I was on top of him. My lips captured his—rough and hard and warm and *real*.

I couldn't sleep. I couldn't stop thinking. I couldn't save Laurel. I couldn't save my mother.

But I could live—even when I didn't want to, even when it hurt. I could *feel*.

CHAPTER 28

I dreamed, as I had so many times before, that I was walking down the hallway toward my mother's dressing room. I could see myself reaching for the door.

Don't go in. Don't turn on the light.

No matter how many times I had this dream, I was never able to stop myself. I was never able to do anything but what I'd done that night. *Grapple for the light switch. Feel the blood on my fingers.*

I flipped the switch and heard a faint rustling, like leaves in the wind. The room remained pitch-black. The sound got louder. *Closer.* And that was when I realized it wasn't rustling leaves. It was the sound of chains being dragged over a tile floor.

"That's not how you play the game."

The room was flooded with light, and I whirled to see Laurel standing behind me. She was holding a lollipop, the kind she'd been staring at the first time I'd seen her. "*This* is how you play the game."

Hands slammed me back into the wall. Shackles appeared on my wrists. Chains slithered across the floor like snakes.

I couldn't breathe, couldn't see—

"You can do better than that."

It took me a moment to realize that the chains were gone. Laurel was gone. The dressing room was gone. I was sitting in a car. My mother was sitting in the front seat.

"Mom." The word was strangled by my throat.

"Dance it off," my mom told me. That had been one of her go-to phrases. Every time we'd left a town, every time I'd skinned a knee. *Dance it off.*

"Mom," I said urgently, suddenly sure that if I could just get her to turn around and look at me, she would see that I wasn't a little girl anymore. She would see, and she would remember.

"I know," my mom called back over the music. "You liked the town and the house and our little front yard. But home isn't a place, Cassie."

Suddenly, we weren't in the car anymore. We were standing on the side of the road, and she was dancing.

"We all have choices," a voice whispered behind me. Nightshade emerged from the shadows, his gaze on my mother as she danced. "The Pythia chooses to live." He smiled. "Perhaps someday that choice will be yours."

I woke with a start to find Dean asleep beside me and Celine Delacroix standing in the doorway.

"I came to say good-bye," she said. "Michael performed an impressive encore of your *you don't belong here and you need to leave* number."

If there was one thing my last conversation with Celine had taught me, it was that she *did* belong here. But I couldn't blame Michael for wanting to send her away. The rest of us were in this. We were already in danger.

Celine didn't have to be.

"When this is over—" I started to say.

Celine held up one perfectly manicured hand. "Unless you feel like letting me in on what *this* is—don't." She paused. "Take care of Michael for me."

I will. I couldn't make that promise out loud.

"And if you get a chance," Celine continued, a subtle smile pulling at the edges of her lips, "put in a good word for me with Sloane."

She didn't wait for a reply before strolling out the door.

Beside me, Dean stirred. "What do you need?" he asked me quietly.

I needed to do something other than stand in front of the wall in the basement, waiting for a body to show up. I needed to get out of this house.

I needed to follow up on the one lead we had.

"I need to go to Gaither, Oklahoma."

YOU

You forget sometimes what it was like Before. Before the walls. Before the chains. Before the turning of the wheel and the bleeding and the pain.

Before the rage.

They bring photographs to show you what they did to Seven. They place another diamond around your neck.

Your fingertips gingerly touch the edge of a photograph—proof of death. There was blood. There was pain. You did this. Judge and jury, you held his life in your hands.

You did this. You killed him.

You smile.

CHAPTER 29

The town where Nightshade had been born wasn't the kind of place where the FBI turned up on a regular basis.

"Gaither, Oklahoma, population 8,425," Sloane rattled off as we stepped out of the rental car. "In the early days of Oklahoma's statehood, Gaither thrived, but its economy collapsed during the Great Depression, and it never recovered. The population has dwindled, and the average age of residents has risen steadily for the past sixty years."

In other words, Gaither had more than its share of senior citizens.

"Three museums," Sloane continued, "thirteen historical landmarks. While local tourism is a substantial source of income for the city proper, the surrounding rural communities rely primarily on farming."

The fact that there was tourism in Gaither meant that we could get the lay of the land without announcing our intentions—or the fact that Agent Sterling was carrying a badge. Agent Briggs had stayed behind in Quantico. I didn't fool myself as to why.

April second. Today was a Fibonacci date, and Laurel's disappearance was almost certainly a harbinger of things to come.

Judd had accompanied us to Gaither, as had Agent Starmans. My gut said that Briggs had sent the latter to protect Sterling as much as the rest of us.

Don't think about that, I told myself as we began the walk down historic Main Street. *Think about Mason Kyle.*

I tried to picture Nightshade growing up in this town. The storefronts had a Victorian charm to them. Stone signs detailed the town's history. As I laid a hand flat on one of them, an odd feeling came over me. Like something was missing.

Like *I* was missing something.

"You okay?" Agent Sterling asked me. In an attempt not to look like a cop, she'd chosen to wear jeans. She still looked like a cop.

"I'm fine," I told her, glancing back over my shoulder, then forcing my eyes to the front. As we turned a corner, a wrought-iron gate came into view. Beyond it was a stone path, landscaped on either side with all manner of plants.

For a split second, I couldn't breathe, and I had no idea why.

Dean walked ahead and stopped at the sign in front of the gates.

"Either Redding is constipated," Michael said as he took in a subtle shift in Dean's body posture, "or things are about to get interesting."

I walked toward Dean, overcome with the uncanny sense that I knew what the sign was going to say. *Poison garden.* Those were the words I expected to see.

"Apothecary garden," I read instead.

"Apothecary," Sloane said, coming to stand next to us. "From the Latin word meaning *repository* or *storehouse*. Historically, the term was used to refer to both the historic version of a pharmacy and to the historic version of a pharmacist."

Without waiting for a reply, Sloane bopped past the gates. Lia followed her.

Dean slid his gaze over to me. "What do you think the chances are that it's a coincidence that Nightshade grew up in a town with an apothecary garden and"—Dean jerked his head toward the building next door—"an apothecary museum?"

A chill spread slowly down my spine. Nightshade's weapon of choice had been poison. There was a thin line between knowing the medicinal properties of plants and knowing how to use them to kill.

"I can sense this is a romantic moment for the two of you," Michael said facetiously, patting us each on the shoulder. "Far be it from me to ruin it." He strolled past us into the garden, but the way he glanced back tipped me off to the fact that he recognized the unsettled feeling twisting in my gut.

"If you folks think that garden's something," a voice called out, "you should venture inside."

An older man—my guess put his age in the neighborhood of seventy—came to the door of the apothecary museum. He was small and compact, with round spectacles and a voice at odds with his appearance: deep and scratchy and utterly uninviting.

A much younger guy came to stand behind the old man. He looked to be nineteen or twenty and wore his white-blond hair combed back, accenting a widow's peak hairline.

"The garden is free for all to enjoy," Widow's Peak said tersely. "Visitors to the museum are asked to make a donation."

He may as well have stuck a giant NO TRESPASSING sign over the building's entrance.

Agent Sterling moved to stand beside me. "I think we're fine with the garden for now," she told Widow's Peak.

"Figures," the boy muttered, retreating into the building. There was something about him that gave me the same unsettled feeling that had coated my body the moment I'd seen the wrought-iron gates.

"You folks stay cool," the old man advised us, his gaze lingering on Sterling. "Even in spring, Gaither heat has a way of sneaking up on you." Without another word, he followed Widow's Peak back into the museum.

Agent Sterling preempted any comment from Dean or me. "Walk through the garden, pretend you're enjoying this lovely spring day, and think about what you've learned," she advised.

You want us to take this slow. To avoid tipping our hand.

I did as instructed. St. John's wort. Yarrow. The alder tree. Hawthorne. As I passed each labeled plant in the garden, I parsed my first impressions. My gut said that the older man had lived in Gaither all of his life. Widow's Peak was protective of him—and of the museum.

You don't like tourists, but you work in a museum. That spoke of either a contradictory personality or a lack of employment options.

I turned on the path, following the loop back to the iron gates. As I reached them, I got that same sense of déjà vu I'd had when I saw the garden for the first time.

I'm missing something.

As I scanned the surrounding street, I pegged a pair of tourists, then turned my attention to a local walking her dog. She turned around a corner and disappeared. I didn't mean to do more than follow her around the corner to see what was on the next block, but once I started walking, I couldn't stop.

I'm missing something.

I'm missing—

Dean caught up to me. The others weren't far behind. I caught sight of our protection detail out of the corner of my eyes.

"Where are we going?" Dean asked.

I wasn't following the dog walker anymore. She'd gone one way, I'd gone another. Gaither's historical charm had melted away blocks back. Now there were houses—most of them on the small side and in need of repairs.

"Cassie," Dean repeated, "where are we going?"

"I don't know," I said.

Lia fell in beside us. "Lie."

I hadn't realized that I was lying, but now that Lia had called me out, it was clear. *I do know where I'm going. I know exactly where I'm going.*

The niggling feeling of déjà vu, the deeply unsettling *something* that had fallen over me the moment we'd stepped foot in this town, solidified into something more concrete.

"I know this place," I said. I hadn't been sensing something off about Gaither. I'd been sensing something *familiar*.

I know, my mom whispered in my memory. *You liked the town and the house and our little front yard—*

There had been so many houses over the years, so many moves. But as I came to a stop in front of a quaint house with blue siding and a massive oak tree that cast shade over the entire lawn, I felt like someone had tossed ice-cold water directly into my face. I could see myself standing on the front porch, laughing as my mom attempted to throw a rope over a branch on the oak tree.

I made my way to the tree and fingered the tattered rope swing that hung there. "I've been here before," I said hoarsely, turning back to the others. "I *lived* here. With my mother."

CHAPTER 30

Nightshade had been born in Gaither. Decades later, my mother had lived here. That couldn't be a coincidence.

Hyperaware of the blood rushing through my veins, I forced myself into the Masters' perspective. *Each of you chooses your own apprentice. Who chooses the Pythia?* I took a step toward the house, my heartbeat drowning out all other sounds.

"Nightshade wasn't the one who selected your mother." Dean's voice broke through the cacophony inside my head. "If he had . . . if *I* had," Dean said, shifting from third person to first, "I wouldn't have waited until Lorelai's daughter joined the Naturals program to introduce myself."

Frozen halfway between a memory and a nightmare, I thought of Nightshade—of the way his shoulders had shaken with laughter when I'd interrogated him, of his still, gray corpse. *If you didn't choose my mother, there's a good chance that the same person chose you both.*

"This changes things." Agent Sterling whipped out her cell phone. She'd brought us here hoping to gain some information about Mason Kyle—who he had been before becoming Nightshade, how long ago he'd disappeared from this town. She hadn't expected to find a direct tie between Gaither and the Masters.

I forced air into and out of my lungs, forced my racing heart to slow. *This is the break we've been waiting for. This is our chance.* And based on the unearthly calm with which Agent Sterling had spoken, the way she'd gone from person to agent in two seconds flat—she knew it.

"There is a ninety-eight percent chance you're calling Agent Briggs." Sloane assessed Agent Sterling. "And a ninety-five-point-six percent chance that you're going to try to pull us out of Gaither."

You can't. My mouth was too dry to form the words. *I won't let you.*

"We came here looking for a needle in a haystack." Sterling's uncanny calm never faltered. "And we just found a sword. We'll have to reassess the risk involved in poking around Gaither. If Judd and I say you're out, you're out—no arguments, no second chances." Briggs's phone must have gone to voice mail, because Sterling didn't say anything else before she hung up.

"You're pushing down an adrenaline rush." Michael took his time reading Agent Sterling. "You're frustrated. You're scared. But more than anything, beneath the Agent Veronica Sterling mask, you look the way a thrill seeker does frozen at the top of the roller coaster, hovering on the verge of plunging down."

Agent Sterling didn't bat an eye at his commentary. "We'll have to reassess the risk," she said again. I knew that she was thinking about Laurel. About Scarlett Hawkins. About collateral damage and the true meaning of *risk*.

"I'm not going anywhere," I said, my voice as intense as Sterling's was calm. I'd spent years berating myself for the holes in my memory—for the fact that I couldn't remember half the places my mother and I had lived, for the fact that I hadn't been able to tell the police a single thing to help them identify the person or people who had taken her. I wasn't leaving Gaither, Oklahoma, without answers—about my mother, about Nightshade, about the connection between the two.

"I'll quit the program if I have to," I told Agent Sterling, my throat tightening. "But I'm staying."

"If Cassie's staying," Sloane said mutinously, "I'm staying."

Dean didn't have to say that he was staying, too.

"I do find Cassie borderline tolerable," Lia commented casually.

"It would be a shame to leave *borderline tolerable* behind." Michael smiled in a way that wasn't really a smile, his skin pulling tightly against the remnants of bruises.

"Judd." Agent Sterling turned for backup, her voice tightly controlled. I wondered if Michael could hear a full spectrum of emotion underneath that control. I wondered how close Veronica Sterling was to becoming the woman she'd been before Scarlett was murdered—someone who felt things deeply. Someone who acted before she thought.

Judd looked at me, then at each of the others in turn, before casting a sideways glance at Agent Sterling. "First rule of raising kids, Ronnie?" he said, in a way that reminded me that he'd had a hand in raising her. "Don't forbid them from doing something if you're certain they're going to do it anyway." Judd's discerning gaze landed back on me. "It's a waste of a good threat."

An hour later, Agent Briggs still hadn't returned Agent Sterling's call.

Today is a Fibonacci date, and Briggs isn't answering his phone. I wondered if he was knee-deep in a crime scene—if it had begun.

"We need some ground rules." Agent Sterling had checked us into Gaither's one hotel, assigning Agent Starmans to continue trying to get through to Briggs as she briefed the rest of us. With controlled and precise movements, she laid a collection of small metallic objects on the coffee table, one after another.

"Tracking beacons," she said. "They're small, but not undetectable. Keep them on your persons at all times." She waited until we'd each picked up a beacon—about the size and shape of a breath mint—before continuing. "You go nowhere alone. You're in pairs—or more—at all times, and don't even think about ditching whichever of us is on your protection detail. And finally . . ." Agent Sterling pulled two guns out of her suitcase and checked to make sure the safeties were on.

"You know how to handle a firearm?" Agent Sterling looked at Dean, who nodded, before she shifted her gaze to Lia. I wondered if the two of them had been trained to handle weapons before I'd joined the program, or if Agent Sterling had singled them out because of experiences in their pasts.

Lia held her hand out for one of the guns. "I do indeed."

Judd took first one gun, then the other from Agent Sterling. "I'm only going to say this once, Lia. You don't draw your weapon unless your lives are in imminent danger."

For once, Lia bit back her smart-mouthed reply. Judd gave her one of the guns, then turned to Dean.

"And," he continued, his voice low, "if your lives *are* in danger and you *do* draw your gun? You'd better be prepared to shoot."

You've already buried your daughter. I translated the meaning inherent in Judd's words. *Whatever the fallout, you won't lose us.*

Dean's hand closed around the gun, and Judd turned eagle eyes to Michael, Sloane, and me. "As for the rest of you hooligans, there are two types of people in a town this size: people who like talking and people who really, really don't. Stick to the former, or I will jerk the lot of you out of here so fast you get whiplash."

There was no questioning that order. I could hear the military man in Judd's cadence, his tone.

"This is an information-gathering mission," Sloane translated. "If we see a hostile . . ."

Do not engage.

CHAPTER 31

The best place to find people who wanted to talk was the local watering hole. In this case, we quickly zeroed in on a diner. It was just far enough away from the historic part of town to serve primarily locals, but not so far that they didn't get the occasional tourist—perfect.

MAMA REE'S NOT-A-DINER. The sign above the door told me pretty much everything I needed to know about the establishment's owner.

"But Cassie," Sloane whispered as we stepped into the restaurant. "It *is* a diner."

A woman in her early sixties looked up from behind the counter and gave us the once-over, as if she'd heard Sloane's whispered words. "Help yourself to any table you'd like," she called after she'd finished studying us.

I opted for a booth by the window in between a pair of senior citizens playing chess and a quartet of even older women gossiping over breakfast. Sloane wasn't kidding when she'd said the average age of Gaither's citizens was on an incline.

Lia and Sloane slid into the booth beside me. Dean and Michael took the other side, and Sterling and Judd helped themselves to stools at the counter.

"We don't do menus." The woman who'd told us to take a seat—Mama Ree, I was guessing—set five waters down on our table. "Right now, it's breakfast. In about ten minutes, it'll be lunch. For breakfast, we have breakfast food. For lunch, we have lunch food. If you can think of it, I can cook it, so long as you're not expecting anything fancy."

She said *fancy* like it was a dirty word.

"I could go for some biscuits and gravy." Dean's Southern accent got a smile out of the woman.

"Side of bacon," she declared. It wasn't a question.

Dean was nobody's fool. "Yes, ma'am."

"French toast for me," Lia requested. Ree harrumphed—my gut said *French* cut too close to *fancy*—but wrote down Lia's order nonetheless before turning her attention to me. "And for you, missy?"

Those words took me back. This wasn't my first time at the Not-A-Diner. I could see myself in a corner booth, crayons spread out on the table.

"I'll have a blueberry pancake," I found myself saying. "With strawberry sauce and an Oreo milkshake."

My order caused the unflappable woman to pause, as if that combination was familiar to her, the way the apothecary garden had been to me.

You're not the type to gossip with outsiders, I thought. *But you might share some interesting tidbits with one of Gaither's own.*

"You probably don't remember me," I said, "but I used to live in Gaither with my mother. Her name was—"

"Lorelai." Ree beat me to it. Then she smiled. "And that would make you Lorelai's Cassie, all grown up." She gave me another once-over. "You favor your mother."

I wasn't sure whether that was supposed to be a compliment—or a warning.

Get her talking, I thought. *About Mom. About the town. About Mason Kyle.*

"I don't remember much about living here. I know it was probably only for a couple of weeks, but—"

"A couple of weeks?" Ree raised both eyebrows so high that they nearly disappeared into her graying hairline. "Cassie, you and your mama lived here for almost a year."

A year? I felt like she'd punched me in the stomach. I could forgive myself for forgetting a couple of weeks out of a largely transient childhood, but a year? An entire year of my life that—if I'd even remembered the town's name—might have given the police a lead on my mother's case years ago?

"You were a bitty thing," Ree continued. "Six or so. Quiet. Well-behaved, not like my Melody. You remember Melody?"

The second I heard the name, I got a flash of a young girl with pigtails. "Your granddaughter. We were friends."

I never had friends. I never had a home. These were the truths of my childhood.

"How's your mama doing these days?" Ree asked.

I swallowed and looked down at the table in front of me. "She died when I was twelve."

Another truth of my childhood that had turned out to be a lie.

"Oh, honey." Ree reached out and squeezed my shoulder. Then, with the no-nonsense manner of a woman who'd raised multiple generations of children, she turned to Sloane and Michael and took their orders.

You know grief, I thought. *You know when to comfort and when to let things be.*

Once Ree made her way into the kitchen, Michael offered an observation.

"She was fond of your mother, but there's anger there, too."

If my mother and I had lived here for nearly a year, what had made us hit the road again? And what, exactly, had my mother left in her wake?

Our food arrived, and I spent the entire meal trying to decide how to get Ree talking. I needed details—about my mother's life in Gaither, about Mason Kyle's.

As it turned out, I didn't have to ask Ree to talk. Once we'd finished breakfast, she pulled up a chair. "What brings you back to Gaither?" she asked.

Murder. Kidnapping. Centuries of systematic torture.

"We brought Cassie's mom's ashes," Lia answered on my behalf. "Lorelai's body was discovered a few months ago. Cassie said this was the place she would have wanted to be lain to rest."

I'd already admitted to not remembering much about my time in Gaither, but Lia was Lia, and Ree believed every word out of her mouth.

"If there's anything I can do for you," Ree said plainly, "Cassie, honey, you just let me know."

"There is one thing." This was the opening I'd been waiting for. "If my mom and I were here for a year, that's the longest we ever lived anywhere. I can't remember much of it. I know my mother loved it here, but before I scatter her ashes . . ." I closed my eyes for a moment, allowing the real grief that lived inside me to make its way to the surface. "I'd like to try to remember why."

I wasn't anywhere near Lia's caliber as a liar, but I did know how to use the truth to my advantage. *The longest we ever lived anywhere. I can't remember much of it. I'd like to remember why.*

"I don't know how much I can tell you." Ree was nothing if not frank. "Lorelai was the type to keep to herself. She swept into town doing some kind of balderdash dog and pony show, claiming she was psychic—helping people 'connect to their dead loved ones,' reading fortunes." Ree snorted. "The city council wouldn't have let her stay for long, but Marcela Waite is a sucker for that kind of thing, and she's known for three things around these parts: loose lips, a rich, dead husband, and a tendency to badger city council members until they give her what she wants."

So far, this story was a familiar one.

"Your mama came in here two or three times those first

couple of weeks, with you in tow. She was young. Skittish, though she did a good job hiding it." Ree paused. "I offered her a job."

"Waitressing?" I asked. I'd worked as a waitress at a diner before Briggs had recruited me to the Naturals program. I wondered if some part of me had remembered my mother doing the same thing.

Ree pursed her lips. "I have a bad habit of hiring waitresses who've seen the ugly side of life. Most of them are running from something. I never knew what that something was for Lorelai—she didn't volunteer the information, and I didn't ask. She took the job. I gave her a good deal on rent."

"The blue house with the big oak tree," I said softly.

Ree nodded. "My daughter had recently vacated the premises. I had Melody and Shane with me, so it seemed a shame to let the house go to waste."

Vacated the premises. I translated those words based on the way that Ree had said them: *As in, took off and dumped her kids with you.*

It was easy to understand why Ree might have had a soft spot for a young single mother struggling to support her daughter.

Home isn't a place, Cassie. My mom's litany had stayed with me for years, but now I heard it differently, knowing that—however briefly—we'd had a home once.

"Was my mother close with anyone?" I asked Ree, memories swirling just out of reach. "Involved with anyone?"

"Your mama always did have an eye for good-looking

men." This was Ree, trying to be diplomatic. "Then again, she also had an eye for trouble."

Not that diplomatic.

Ree narrowed her eyes at Dean. "You trouble?" she asked.

"No, ma'am."

She turned to Michael. "You?"

He offered her his most charming smile. "One hundred percent."

Ree snorted. "That's what I thought."

The door to the restaurant opened then, and Widow's Peak from the apothecary museum walked in. Ree smiled when she saw him, the way she had when Dean had ordered biscuits and gravy.

"You remember Shane?" Ree asked me. "My grandson."

Shane. I could feel a memory hovering just out of reach. Ree started to stand.

"Did my mother know a man named Mason Kyle?" I asked before she could leave.

Ree stared at me. "Mason Kyle?" She shook her head, as if trying to clear it of memories. "I haven't heard that name in twenty-five years. He left Gaither when he was, what? Seventeen or so? Long before your mama came to town, Cassie."

As Ree made her way toward the counter—and her grandson—one of the older women at the table behind us clucked her tongue. "Shame what happened to the Kyle family," she said. "Downright tragic."

"What happened?" Sloane asked, twisting in her seat.

The old man playing chess on the other side of us turned to look at her. "Got killed," he grunted. "By one of *those people.*"

What people?

"Poor little Mason wasn't more than nine or so," the tongue-clucking woman said. "Most people hereabouts think he saw the whole thing."

I pictured the little boy from the photograph, then thought of the monstrous killer he'd become.

"Enough." It was clear from the tone in Ree's voice and the immediate reactions of those around us that her word was law. With a nod, she turned back to her grandson. "Shane, what can I get y—"

Before the question was out of her mouth, Shane saw something out the window. His whole body tensed, and he slammed out of the diner and charged into the street.

I looked out the window in time to see him striding toward a group of a dozen or so people. They walked in lines of four. *Various ages. Various ethnicities.* Every single one of them was dressed entirely in white.

Shane attempted to approach a girl standing behind the others, but a man with thick hair—ink-black and shot through with gray—stepped in front of him.

"Going to go out on a limb," Lia said, her eyes locked on the oncoming confrontation, "and guess that *those people* are emissaries from the friendly neighborhood cult."

CHAPTER 32

Those people. That was the phrase the man playing chess had used to describe the murder of Mason Kyle's family, thirty-some-odd years before.

Michael tossed three twenties on the table, and all five of us made our way out the door.

"Mel." Shane tried to sidestep the man with the graying hair. *"Melody."*

"It's all right, Echo," the man told the girl Shane had addressed as Melody. "Speak your truth."

A girl I almost recognized—the way I'd almost recognized Shane—stepped forward. Her eyes were on the ground. "I'm not Melody anymore," she said, her voice light and wispy, barely more than a whisper. "I don't want to be Melody. My second name—my true name—is Echo." She lifted her eyes to her brother's. "I'm happy now. Can't you be happy for me?"

"Happy for you?" Shane repeated, his voice catching in his throat. "Mel, you can't even talk to me without glancing at him to make sure what you're saying is okay. You gave up college—*college*, Melody—to join the soul-sucking *cult* that stole our mother away from us when we were kids." Shane's fingers curled into fists. "So, no, I can't be *happy* for you."

"Your mother was lost." The man in charge addressed those words to Shane, his manner almost gentle. "We attempted to provide solace, offer her a simpler way of life. I was as grieved as you were when she chose a different path."

"You're the *reason* she left town!" Shane exploded.

His opponent's demeanor never wavered. "Serenity Ranch is not for everyone. We cannot help everyone, but those we can help, we do." He glanced at Melody, so subtly that if I hadn't been looking for it, I wouldn't have noticed.

"I've found my Serenity," Melody recited, her voice expressionless, her eyes glassy. "In Serenity, I've found balance. In Serenity, I've found peace."

"Are you on something?" Shane demanded before whipping back around to the man he'd confronted. "What did you give her? What have you *been* giving her?"

The man stared at and into Shane for a moment or two and then bowed his head. "We must be going."

"We're about three seconds away from Draco Malfoy over there throwing a punch," Michael said, his voice low. "Three . . . two . . ."

Shane punched the man. As the cult leader wiped blood off his lip with the back of his hand, he looked at Shane and smiled.

It didn't take Agent Sterling long to dig up information on Serenity Ranch. The man in charge was named Holland Darby. He'd been investigated by local authorities dozens of times going back more than thirty years, but no proof of wrongdoing had ever been established.

The earliest complaints dated to the establishment of the Serenity Ranch commune on the outskirts of Gaither more than three decades earlier. According to the files Agent Sterling had acquired, Holland Darby was a collector of drifters and strays, but over the years, he'd wooed more than a few young, impressionable locals to his side, too. *Never anyone under the age of eighteen. Never any males.*

That told me what I needed to know about Holland Darby. *You dot your I's and cross your T's. If you harbored minors, you could run afoul of the law, and whatever you're doing out at Serenity Ranch, the last thing you want is cops on your property. Your followers include both men and women, but when it comes to locals, you prefer females—the younger, the better, so long as they're legal.*

"He brought Melody to town as a test." Lia's tone gave no clue to the fact that this was personal to her, that Holland Darby had raised memories she kept buried deep. "Darby wanted Shane to see his sister. He wanted Melody to make it clear that *they* are her family now."

The less contact Melody has with her family, the easier she is to manipulate, but the more times she looks them in the eyes and chooses you, the more certain she'll be that they won't forgive her. That they can't *forgive her, and that even if she wanted to leave Serenity Ranch, she could never go home.*

"Clearly," Lia said, standing up, "the Gaither Hotel is only passingly familiar with proper air-conditioning." She pulled her hair back and off her neck. "I'm going to change into something cooler."

Lia's expression dared us to argue that her need for a wardrobe change had nothing to do with the temperature. Beside me, Michael watched her walk away. No matter how good she was at hiding her emotions, he was better at reading them. *He knows what you're feeling. You know that he knows.*

After another moment, Michael followed her into the bedroom. I could see exactly how this was going to play out—the push and pull between them, Michael trying to bring her emotions to the surface, Lia throwing the fiasco with Celine in his face.

"I believe," Sloane said, filling the silence, "that there is approximately an eighty-seven percent chance that Michael and Lia will end up making out or otherwise engaged in acts of physical—"

"Let's turn our attention back to the case," Agent Sterling cut in. "Shall we?" She fell into lecture mode. "There were dozens of complaints filed about Serenity Ranch when Holland Darby first began buying up large chunks of property on the outskirts of town thirty-three years ago. If I had to guess, I'd say that most of the complaints were baseless or manufactured—no one wanted drifters, runaways, and former drug addicts taking up residence on what used to be family farms." Agent Sterling set those complaints aside and opened the thickest file. "Approximately nine months after the establishment of Serenity Ranch, the local sheriff's department opened up an investigation of the group's involvement in the murders of Anna and Todd Kyle."

"Nightshade's parents?" I asked. Sterling nodded. For the next hour, she, Dean, Sloane, and I pieced through every bit of evidence the investigation had managed to obtain.

It wasn't much.

At the time of the murders, Anna and Todd Kyle were a young married couple with a nine-year-old son. Anna's father, Malcolm Lowell, lived with them. Reading between the lines, I inferred that Malcolm was the one with money—the one who'd owned the house, the one who'd refused to sell his land to Holland Darby when the interloper was buying up all of their neighbors'. There had been some kind of altercation involving the two men. Words were exchanged. Threats were implied.

And that night, someone had broken into Malcolm Lowell's house, butchered his daughter and son-in-law, and viciously attacked Malcolm, stabbing him seventeen times and leaving him to bleed out on the floor. According to the police report, nine-year-old Mason had been home the whole time.

Did you hear them screaming? Did you hide? The old woman at the diner had said that most people in Gaither believed that Mason Kyle had seen his parents murdered, but the report gave no such indication.

Malcolm—Nightshade's grandfather—was the one who had called 911. By the time medical assistance had arrived, he had been holding on to his life by a thread. The old man survived. His daughter and son-in-law had not. In the aftermath of the attack, Malcolm Lowell had been unable to provide a physical description of his attacker, but suspicion had fallen almost immediately on the occupants of Serenity Ranch.

"I've been working on a time line." Sloane had made use of the hotel's complimentary notepad, ripping out page after page and laying them along the floor, scrawling a note on each. She pointed to the leftmost one. "Thirty-three years ago, Holland Darby establishes his commune on the outskirts of town. Less than a year after that, Anna and Todd Kyle are murdered. Twenty-seven years ago, the poison Master who would eventually go on to choose Nightshade as his apprentice killed nine people, completing his initiation into the Masters' ranks."

I followed the logic of Sloane's calculation: Nightshade had completed his initiation kills six years earlier. The cult operated on a twenty-one-year cycle. Ergo, the poison Master before Nightshade had been initiated two to three years *after* Anna and Todd Kyle had been murdered.

What's the connection?

"Scenario one," I said. "The Master who eventually trained Nightshade as his apprentice lived in Gaither during the time of the murders. We know the Masters favor Pythias who have violence and abuse in their past—it's possible a similar criteria is used in the selection of killers." I closed my eyes for a moment and let the logic take hold. "The previous Master knew what Mason had seen and survived, and marked him for recruitment."

Dean met my gaze. "Scenario two: I'm the Master who recruited Nightshade. I'm also the person who killed Anna and Todd Kyle. I was never caught, and the case got just enough local press to attract the attention of the Masters, who offered to channel my potential into *so much more*." He ran the tips of the fingers on his right hand over my left. "I accepted the offer and learned to kill without a trace, without mercy."

Beside me, Sloane shivered.

"Years later," Dean continued quietly, "when it was time for me to choose an apprentice of my own, I remembered Mason Kyle. Maybe I didn't realize he was in the house when I killed his family. Or maybe," he continued, his voice nothing like his own, "I chose to let him live. Either way, he's mine."

Silence fell over the room. If Nightshade's parents had been murdered by one of the Masters, solving the Kyle murders might lead us straight to the person who'd recruited Nightshade.

Find one Master, follow the trail.

"Scenario three." Agent Sterling, who had been remarkably quiet as Dean and I had sorted through our thoughts, added her voice to the mix. "The UNSUB in the Kyle murders killed Nightshade's parents *so that* little Mason Kyle would be more suited to becoming a killer himself someday." She stood up and began pacing the room. I'd never seen her so intent. "I know the Nightshade case inside and out. The killer we were looking for was brilliant, narcissistic, with a need to win and to one-up all competitors. And yet, during his last interrogation, Nightshade accepted that the Pythia was going to have him killed. He didn't fight it. He didn't turn on the other Masters to save himself."

"He was loyal," I translated.

"You think that loyalty might date back to childhood." Dean lifted his gaze to Sterling's. "You think our UNSUB started grooming Nightshade to join the Masters when he was just a boy."

Sloane frowned. "Nightshade's parents were killed one thousand, eight hundred, and eighty-seven days *before* Nightshade's Master completed his own initiation kills," she pointed out. "Barring anomalies in the space-time continuum, it seems unlikely that someone could have begun grooming an apprentice to take their place before that someone *had* a place."

Sloane's hands fluttered, a sure sign of anxiety. She calmed herself, turning to the remainder of the time line. "Nine years after Mason Kyle's parents were murdered, Mason left Gaither and never came back. That puts his exodus at roughly twenty-four years ago. About twelve years after that, Cassie and her mother moved to town." Sloane's blue eyes darted toward mine. I could see her trying to calculate the odds that continuing would hurt me.

I saved her the trouble. "Six years after my mom and I left Gaither, Nightshade killed nine people, taking his seat at the Masters' table. Less than two months after that, my mother was taken."

My mom and Nightshade had lived in this town more than a decade apart. But one or more of the Masters must have kept tabs on them thereafter. *You have a long memory. You have an eye for potential. And you can be very, very patient.*

"Assuming the attack on the Kyle family was perpetrated by someone aged sixteen or over," Sloane said, "we're looking for an UNSUB no younger than his late forties—and possibly substantially older."

I thought of the senior citizens back at the diner, the old man who'd invited us into the apothecary museum.

"We need to know what the police didn't put in the official file," Dean said. "Gossip. Theories."

"Luckily for you," Lia commented, strolling back into the room, "gossip is one of my specialties." She was wearing a long black skirt and a multilayered top that hung off her shoulders. She'd rimmed her eyes in thick, dark liner, and wore two-inch-wide copper bangles on her wrists. "On a scale of one to ten," she said, "how psychic do I look?"

"Six-point-four," Sloane replied without hesitation.

"Psychic?" I asked. I was fairly certain I did not want to know where this was going.

"Lia and I were talking about our little chat with Ree at the Not-A-Diner," Michael said, coming up behind Lia with a look on his face that made me think they'd been doing a lot more than talking. "And we both seemed to recall Ree saying something about a widow with a big mouth and a penchant for psychics."

Lia arched an eyebrow at me. I knew that eyebrow arch. It did not bode well.

"No way," I said. "I spent most of my childhood helping my mom con people into thinking she was psychic. I'm not going to help you do the same."

Sloane looked at me, looked at Lia, then looked at me again. "There is a very high probability," she whispered, "that Lia's about to tell you that you're lying."

CHAPTER 33

It could be worse, I told myself as I adjusted the camera pin on my lapel and Lia leaned forward to ring the town gossip's doorbell. *Lia could have chosen a more destructive outlet for her issues.*

"Can I help you?" The woman who answered the door was in her early fifties, with vivid red hair that wouldn't have looked natural even if she were two decades younger. Her sense of fashion tended toward skintight and shiny.

You wear bright pink lipstick, even in your own home. The house is classic, understated—everything you're not.

"If you're Marcela Waite, I believe that we can help you," Lia murmured.

Even a Natural liar's credibility could only take us so far. As much as I loathed doing it, I picked up the slack. "My name is Cassie Hobbes. You knew my mother, Lorelai. She helped you connect to loved ones on the other side."

Recognition sparked in Marcela's eyes.

"Forty-four percent of psychics believe in UFOs," Sloane blurted out. "But twice that believe in extraterrestrials."

"The spirit realm speaks to Sloane in numbers," Lia said solemnly.

"You have four dogs buried in your yard." Sloane rocked back on her heels. "And you replaced four hundred and seventy-nine shingles on your roof last year."

Marcela's hand flew to her chest. Clearly, it had not—and would not—occur to her that Sloane was simply good at math and extremely observant.

"Do you have a message for me?" Marcela asked, her eyes alight.

"My mother passed away several years ago," I said, sticking to the story we'd told Ree. "I came to Gaither to scatter her ashes, but before I do . . ."

"Yes?" Marcela said breathlessly.

"Her spirit asked me to come here and do a reading for you."

I was a horrible person.

As Marcela Waite served us tea and sat down across from me in her formal sitting room, I pushed down a stab of guilt and forced myself to focus on her BPE instead. *Behavior. Personality. Environment.*

This was your husband's house. He came from money. You didn't. He never pressured you to change, and you haven't—but you also haven't altered his décor. My gut said that she'd loved him.

"You're a very spiritual person," I said, feeling more like my mother than I had in a very long time. "I'm sensing that you have a touch of the Gift yourself."

Most people liked to consider themselves intuitive, and 90 percent of this job was telling the client what they wanted to hear.

"You've been having dreams," I continued. "Tell me about them."

As our hostess launched into a description of her dream from the night before, I wondered how my mother could have done this for so many years.

You did what you had to do, I thought. *You did it for me.* But deep down, I also had to admit, *You liked playing the game. You liked the power.*

It took me a moment to realize that Marcela had stopped talking.

"There are two sides to the dream you've described," I said automatically. "The different sides represent two paths, a decision you have to make."

The trick to my mother's trade had always been to stay vague until the client gave you cues about how to proceed.

"New versus old," I continued. "To forgive or not to forgive. To apologize or to bite your tongue." There was no reaction from Marcela, so I got a bit more personal. "You wonder what your husband would want you to do."

That opened the floodgates. "His sister has been so nasty to me! It's pretty rich, the way she looks down on me when *she's* on marriage number four!"

Your husband's sister never thought you were good enough for him—and she let you know it from day one.

Sloane cleared her throat. "There are fifty-six anagrams of the name Marcela, including *caramel, a calmer,* and *lace arm.*"

Marcela gasped. "Caramel was my Harold's favorite candy." Her brow furrowed. "Harold wants me to be calmer? More patient with his sister?"

Lia took that as her cue. "I smell caramel," she said, her eyes focusing on something in the distance. "Harold is here. He's with us." She latched on to my hand as she turned her weighty gaze to Marcela Waite. "He wants you to know that he knows how his sister can be."

"He didn't always see it when he was alive," I added, elaborating on Lia's statement to make it more consistent with my profile of Marcela. "But he sees everything now. He knows it's hard, but he's counting on you to be the bigger person. Because he knows you can be."

"He said that?" Marcela asked softly.

"He doesn't say much," I replied. "In spirit form, he doesn't have to."

Marcela closed her eyes and bowed her head. *You needed to hear that he supports you. You needed to remember that he loved you, too.*

I could almost believe that we were doing a good thing here, but then Lia arched her back, her body contorting itself into an unnatural position.

"*Help.*" Lia pitched her voice into a high, nails-on-chalkboard whisper. "*I can't find my son. There's blood. So much blood—*"

I gave Lia's hand a warning squeeze. This wasn't how I would have chosen to bring the conversation around to the Kyle murders, but Lia—in true Lia fashion—hadn't left me much of a choice.

I forced myself not to roll my eyes. "Tell me your name, spirit," I said.

"Anna," Lia hissed. "My name was Anna."

CHAPTER 34

Luckily for us, Marcela Waite—like most gossips and lovers of gold lamé leggings—had a finely tuned sense of melodrama. I was fairly certain she'd enjoyed Lia's performance even more than talking to her dead husband.

"It must have been Anna Kyle," Marcela told us, tapping red fingernails against the side of her teacup. "I was nineteen when she and her husband were murdered. That poor woman."

"What happened?" I asked. We'd put on our show. Now it was time for the town gossip to put on hers.

"Anna Kyle was stabbed to death in her own kitchen. The husband, too," Marcela said in a hushed voice. "And Anna's daddy barely made it out alive."

"And her son?" I asked. "She said she couldn't find her son."

"He was there," Marcela told us. "Saw the whole thing." That echoed the sentiment we'd heard at the diner, but contradicted the official report that Agent Sterling had dug up. "You ask me, there was something not quite right with that boy. He was a rowdy one, always running around with the children of *those people*."

I filed the reference to *those people* away for future consideration.

"How awful," Lia murmured. "It's a miracle the killer left the boy alive."

Marcela pursed her lips. Even without Michael present to read her, I recognized the look of a woman on the verge of saying something that she knew she shouldn't.

"I don't hold with gossip, mind you," Marcela hedged, "but some folks say that little Mason knew the killer. Some folks think he didn't just witness the murders." She lowered her voice to a whisper. "They think he watched."

Sloane frowned. "Why would anyone think that?"

Marcela didn't even try to resist answering. "I told you about Anna's daddy? He was stabbed over and over, had to have surgery, and when he woke up, he told the police he never saw the attacker."

"But?" Lia prompted.

"But after that, Malcolm Lowell refused to have anything to do with his grandson. He wouldn't take custody of his own flesh and blood, couldn't even *look* at him. Old Malcolm never spoke a word to the boy again."

I could see how this would play out in a small town, how it had played out for Nightshade. *At first, people felt sorry for you. But after your grandfather woke up, after he insisted to the police that he hadn't seen his attacker, people started asking questions. What if he was lying? What if he was protecting someone?*

What if that someone was you?

"What happened to Mason?" Sloane asked, her hands worrying at each other in her lap. "His parents died. His family didn't want him. Where did he go?"

The question struck close to home for Sloane.

"A local couple took the Kyle boy in," Marcela said, taking another sip of her tea. "Hannah and Walter Thanes."

"Do they still live in Gaither?" Lia asked casually.

Marcela set her teacup down on the tray. "Hannah passed away several years ago, but Walter is still local. He runs the apothecary museum down on Main Street."

YOU

You know better than to enjoy the quiet moments. You know better than to watch Laurel sleeping and think, even for a moment, that she's just a child.

"She looks peaceful, doesn't she?" Five's voice is like oil on your skin.

He's holding the knife.

"What are you doing here?" It pays sometimes to be haughty, to remind the sadists that you may be at their mercy, but they're at your mercy, too.

"I had some interesting news from an old friend."

You don't take the bait.

Five smiles at your silence. "It appears the FBI has made an appearance in Gaither." He drags one finger over the edge of his knife blade. Lightly. Carefully.

You give him a dead-eyed stare. "What the FBI is or is not doing is none of my concern."

"It is," Five replied, pressing the knife blade into the tip of his own finger and drawing blood, "when it involves your daughter."

CHAPTER 35

The others met us outside the apothecary museum.

"Sterling's conflicted about letting us on the front lines, Judd has that look on his face that he gets when he's thinking about Scarlett, and Agent Starmans desperately has to go to the bathroom," Michael murmured to Lia and me. "In case you were wondering."

I glanced over at Agent Starmans, who quickly excused himself to use the facilities inside. Judd reached into his back pocket, pulled out his worn leather wallet, and handed Sloane a rumpled twenty-dollar bill.

"Donation," he told her. "For the museum."

As Sloane closed her hand around the bill, I let my eyes meet Agent Sterling's. *You hate that I'm the one who has a plausible reason to be asking questions. You hate that people in Gaither will talk to me. But more than anything, you hate that you don't hate putting us in the line of fire nearly as much as you should.*

Dean reached for the door to the museum, then held it open for Sterling. "After you," he said, a gesture an onlooker would have taken for Southern chivalry, but that I recognized as an unspoken promise: we'd follow her lead.

Sterling entered first, the rest of us on her heels.

"Afternoon, folks." Walter Thanes stood behind the counter, looking as much a relic as anything housed in these walls.

Sloane held out the bill Judd had given her. Thanes nodded to a wooden box on the counter. As Sloane slipped the money into the box, I forced myself to turn away from the man who'd raised Nightshade, and perused the shelves.

Hundreds of bottles with faded labels lined one wall. Rusted tools sat on proud display in front of beakers made of cloudy glass. On the counter beneath them there was a thick leather-bound book, the pages yellowed and the ink faded with age. As I took in the handwritten title scrawled across the top, my heart stilled in my chest.

Poison Register—1897.

I thought of Nightshade, of the poison he'd used to kill Scarlett Hawkins—undetectable, incurable, painful. I pushed down a shudder as a presence beside me cast a shadow over the page.

"To buy medicines that could prove poisonous, patrons were required by the apothecary to sign for them." Walter Thanes ran the tip of his finger lightly over the entries on the register. "Laudanum. Arsenic. Belladonna."

I forced my attention from the open page to the old man.

Thanes smiled softly. "The line between medicine and poison was quite thin, you know."

That line appeals to you. Immediately, my brain went into overdrive. *You find poisons enthralling. You took Nightshade in when he was just a boy.*

"Was the museum an actual apothecary at some point?" Agent Sterling asked, pulling our suspect's attention away from me.

Thanes clasped his hands in front of his body as he crossed the room toward her. "Oh, yes. My grandfather ran Gaither's apothecary as a young man."

"A dying art," Sterling murmured, "even then."

Those words registered with Thanes. He liked her, liked talking to her. "Quite a brood you have here," he commented.

"My niece and her friends," Sterling replied smoothly. "Cassie and her mother lived here when Cassie was young. When I heard the whole group was planning a trip to Gaither, I thought they could do with some adult supervision."

Lia sidled up beside me, giving every appearance of being entranced by an old-fashioned scale the exact color and texture of a rusted penny. "Fun fact," the deception detector said under her breath. "The part about adult supervision was true."

Behind us, Thanes processed Agent Sterling's statement. "I suppose that would make you Lorelai's sister."

Hearing my mother's name on his lips had a visceral effect on me. I wanted to turn to face him, but my feet were cemented to the ground.

You knew my mother.

"Do you have any children?" Agent Sterling asked, the question completely natural—and completely benign—on her tongue. I made my way along the outside wall, turning so that I could sneak a look at the old man's reaction.

"Anger," Michael murmured, coming up behind me and speaking directly into my ear. "Bitterness. Longing." He was quiet for a moment. "And guilt."

The fact that Michael mentioned guilt last told me that it was the faintest of the three. *Because it's faded over the years?* I wondered. *Or because you're constitutionally incapable of feeling more than the slightest twinge?*

"I had a boy." The old man's answer to Sterling's question was clipped and gruff. "Mason. Took off when he was about seventeen. It just about broke my wife's heart."

A glance at Lia told me that she hadn't detected a single lie in those words.

"Mason," I repeated, doing my best impression of a curious teenager. I let myself hesitate, then said, "Some people were talking at Ree's this morning." I averted my gaze, tentative enough to suggest that I knew better than to say what I was about to say. "About the murders of Anna and Todd Kyle . . ."

"Cassie," my "aunt" said sharply, reinforcing the idea that I was a kid who'd just crossed a line.

"It was a horrible thing." Thanes closed his fingers around an old-fashioned bottle marked with a skull. "I never cared for Anna's father. He married a local girl, but never made much of an effort with folks here in town. His wife died when Anna was six or so, and he raised that little girl alone in his big house on the hill—too good for this town, from day one." He shook his head, as if trying to clear it of memories. "Malcolm flat-out ignored the rest of us, but he clashed with Holland Darby and his followers. That never turns out well for anyone in these parts."

I cast a glance at Agent Sterling, as if I were debating whether or not it was worth the risk to stop biting my tongue. "Anna and Todd Kyle were murdered. And their son . . . Mason . . ."

The old man stared at me for a moment. "My wife and I couldn't have children. It seemed like the Christian thing to do. And Mason . . ." Thanes closed his eyes. "Mason was a good boy."

Based on the way this conversation had unfolded, I could see two possible versions of Walter Thanes. One was an old man who'd tried to do his best by a damaged boy who'd thanked him by taking off as soon as he was old enough to shake the Gaither dust off his feet. The other was an incredible actor, one whose grief had less to do with the boy who'd left town and more to do with the man Mason Kyle had become.

Nightshade had failed the Masters.
Nightshade had gotten caught.
Nightshade had become a liability.

The sound of a bell tore me from my thoughts as the

front door to the museum opened. Instinctively, I turned away, busying myself with another shelf of relics.

"Walter." The voice that greeted Thanes was smooth and pleasantly pitched. *Non-confrontational.*

"Darby." Thanes offered little more than a clipped greeting in return. "Can I help you with something?"

Darby, I thought, suddenly glad that I'd turned away. *As in Holland Darby?*

"I understand Shane had a run-in with my father." Those calmly spoken words filled in the blanks. The speaker wasn't the older Darby. It was—apparently—his son. "I was hoping to have a word with the boy."

"I'm sure Shane would be grateful for your concern, doctor," Thanes said, in a tone that suggested the opposite. "But I gave him the afternoon off, told him to get his act together before he comes back here."

The response from Darby's son was measured. "I would hate to see Shane prosecuted for assault. And we both know that my father is capable of baiting him into a confrontation and then pressing charges."

There was another long silence, and then Walter Thanes abruptly changed the subject. "These folks were asking questions about Mason, about what happened to Anna and Todd Kyle. Maybe I'm not the one they should be asking."

I remembered what Marcela Waite had said about Mason Kyle running around with the children of "those people."

You were friends with Mason Kyle. My brain went full

speed as I turned to get a better look at the man. Agent Sterling stepped forward, drawing his attention before his gaze could land on me.

This Darby had his father's dark hair, but thicker and without any trace of gray. His eyes were a light, nearly see-through blue. I put him somewhere in the neighborhood of his early forties, none of which explained the way my fingernails dug into the palms of my hands the second I saw him.

A heavy weight settled in the pit of my stomach. My mouth went dry, and suddenly I wasn't standing in the museum. I was hanging on to a rope swing, watching as a younger version of the same man laughed and swung my mom up onto the porch railing.

She was laughing, too.

I came out of the memory in time to register the man's introduction. "Kane Darby," he said, holding out a hand to Agent Sterling. "I'm a local physician, and as you've probably gathered, my father is not beloved in these parts."

Kane. My brain latched on to the name. I heard my mom saying it. I saw her standing in the moonlight, her hand woven through his.

"You were asking about Mason Kyle?" Kane continued, so even and calm that I knew he had a natural bedside manner. "We were childhood playmates, though we had little contact after his parents' murder."

I should have looked at Lia for some indication of whether or not Kane Darby was telling the truth. I should have thrown myself into profiling the man.

But I didn't.

I couldn't.

Feeling like the walls were closing in, I pushed past Lia, past Michael, past Dean, the world blurring until I made it out the door.

CHAPTER 36

My mother had never been the type of woman to fall head over heels. She'd gotten involved with my father when she was a teenager, longing to escape her abusive father's household. But when she'd found out she was pregnant, she'd run, not just from her father, but also from mine.

All I could think, as Dean followed me outside—Lia, Michael, and Sloane on his heels—was that Kane Darby had held my mother's hand. He'd danced with her in the moonlight.

He'd made her smile.

Your mama always did have an eye for good-looking men. Ree's words echoed in my head. *Then again, she also had an eye for trouble.*

I tried to remember something, *anything* else about my mother's relationship with the cult leader's son, but came up empty. My time in Gaither was a black hole.

Viewing that memory loss with a profiler's eye, I asked the obvious question. *What is my subconscious trying so hard to forget?*

I crossed the street. Vaguely, I was aware that the others stuck close to me, that Agent Starmans had reappeared and was trailing a discreet distance behind us.

"I'm going to go out on a limb and guess that Kane Darby has daddy issues." Michael did me the favor of not commenting on *my* emotions. "The good doctor really was as calm as he seemed—right up until the point where he mentioned his father."

"What about Mason Kyle?" I asked. "What did Kane Darby feel when he heard Nightshade's name?"

"Sometimes one emotion can mask another." Michael paused. "What I got off the good doctor was a combination of anger, guilt, and dread. Whatever else might have been buried underneath, that particular cocktail of emotions is something Kane Darby has felt before. Those three emotions are intertwined for him, and when they arrive, they arrive all at once."

"Anger that someone else has all of the power and you have none." Lia strolled ahead of the rest of us, turning to walk backward, light on her toes. "Guilt, because you've been conditioned to believe that there is no greater sin than disloyal thoughts." She turned back around. "And dread," she finished softly, her face hidden from view, "because you know, deep down, that you will be punished."

You're not talking about Kane Darby.

"In other words," Michael translated, acting as if Lia hadn't just shown us a glimpse of her deepest scars, "the good doctor has daddy issues."

Like Lia, Kane Darby had been raised in a cult. Based on the fact that he'd spoken negatively about his father, I assumed that, like Lia, he'd gotten out.

But you didn't leave town. You didn't cut all ties. You didn't start anew.

"Kane Darby and my mother were involved," I admitted. Lia had been honest. The least I owed the group was the same. "I don't remember much, but from what I've been able to piece together . . ." I closed my eyes, picturing the look on my mother's face, my throat tightening around the words. "She might have loved him."

There was a beat of silence, and then Sloane picked up the conversational slack. "Counting the bellman at the front desk and various casual encounters, we've spoken with a dozen Gaither citizens in the past three hours. And of everyone we've spoken to or observed, there's only one person we've identified as having a close relationship of some sort with both Nightshade and Cassie's mother."

Kane Darby. I willed myself to remember something else about him, any interaction I'd had with him as a child, no matter how small.

"Darby the younger would have been all of ten years old when Nightshade's parents were murdered," Dean commented.

"And I was nine," Lia countered lightly, "when I killed a

man dead. Children are capable of horrible things, Dean. You know that."

Sometimes, I thought, seeing the world through Lia's eyes, *you have to become the monster to survive.*

I thought of Laurel, held captive alongside my mother; of Kane Darby, growing up under his father's thumb; of Nightshade, whose parents had been murdered in their own home. And then I thought about the holes in my own memory, how much of what I'd thought I knew about my own childhood had turned out to be a lie.

"We need more info on Kane Darby," I said, my stomach flipping as a plan solidified in my mind. "And I think I know how to get it."

YOU

You should have known that it would come to this, that Cassie would remember. The wheel turns. The die is cast.

It is only a matter of time before the Masters ask you to pass judgment.

You showed no weakness when Five told you of your daughter's arrival in Gaither, no hint that his words had hit their target. But in the hours since, you've felt the shift coming, felt yourself on the verge of becoming someone else.

Something else.

When the acolyte—no longer an apprentice, not yet a Master—comes to present his work for your approval, to add a diamond to the collection around your neck, you're ready.

This one is young. This one wants your admiration. This one you can use.

You listen. You nudge. You lay a hand lightly on the flesh of his chest, tracing a symbol—seven circles around a cross. You whisper in the acolyte's ear.

You are powerful, *you murmur*. You will be the best among them, if you choose your targets well.

You offer immortality if he is worthy. If he will do as you say.

Lorelai would shudder at your words—at your plan. But Lorelai isn't here anymore. Cassie doesn't need Lorelai.

She needs the Pythia.

She needs the monster.

She needs you.

CHAPTER 37

When Agent Sterling caught up to us, she sent everyone back to the hotel but Dean and me. I told her what I wanted to do. She made me lay out the pros and cons. She made me walk through it again and again. She listened to my arguments and, finally, she agreed. The three of us would go back to the quaint blue house where I'd spent a year of my childhood. Barring any unforeseen complications, I would see if the current occupant would let me poke around inside. With luck, we might knock loose a few memories.

Eventually, Agent Sterling might have to blow her cover and approach Kane Darby as an FBI agent. Eventually, we could directly interrogate him about Nightshade *and* my mother. But for now, we needed to know who we were dealing with, and that information was locked in my mind.

"I'd tell you that you don't have to do this," Dean murmured as the house came into view, "but I know that you do."

Less than a year ago, I'd gone with Dean to his childhood home. I'd knelt in the dirt with him, searching for his mother's initials on a weatherworn picket fence. At the time, it hadn't even occurred to me that someday, he might be returning the favor.

"Maybe we should have brought Townsend with us."

Dean's comment got an eyebrow arch out of me. "So he could make inappropriate comments and lighten the moment? Or so he could tell you exactly what I'm feeling?"

Dean considered his answer very carefully. "The one that's not going to get me a speech about how you can take care of yourself."

I snorted and walked toward the front porch. As I made my way up the steps, the second one creaked.

"Gotcha!" I jump from the step onto the porch and wrap my arms around Mommy before the creaking can give me away.

"On the contrary . . ." Mommy picks me up and dangles me upside down. "I've got you!"

"Cassie." Dean's voice broke through the memory. At first, I thought he was worried about me, but as I processed my surroundings, I realized that he was more concerned with the person who'd just opened the front door.

"Shane," I said, taking in Ree's grandson's appearance. Somehow, I hadn't expected the house to be occupied. "I don't know if you remember me, but I used to live here."

Shane stared at me with every bit as much disdain as we'd gotten from him at the museum. "So?"

"So I'd like to look around a little," I returned. "I don't know how much your grandmother told you—"

Before I could finish that thought, Shane headed back into the house. He let the door slam behind him, but didn't lock it. I took that as an invitation and reached for the doorknob.

When Shane realized I'd followed him into the house, he stared at me for a moment. "You didn't use to be this brave."

"You didn't use to be so antisocial," I countered.

Shane snorted. "You know what they say, Red: dance it off."

Hearing my mother's words come out of his mouth hit me like a jolt of electricity. This was real. My mom and I hadn't just lived here. We'd put down roots. We'd had people in our lives. We'd had something to miss when we hit the road.

"You want to look around?" Shane said, his surly tone softening ever so slightly. "Far be it from me to stop you. I just live here."

Wordlessly, I took Shane up on his invitation and began making my way through the house. *Entryway. Kitchen. Small spiral staircase.* I knew before I took the first step that at the top of the stairs, I'd find two bedrooms. When I came to stand in the doorway of the room that had been my mother's, another memory hit me with the force of a tidal wave.

Nightmare. It's dark. I want my mom. But Mommy isn't alone.

"I don't deserve you." Mommy has her back toward Kane. "I

told you about the kind of man my father is. I didn't tell you that I have a younger sister. I left her in that hellhole, and I never looked back."

I rub at the corners of my eyes. *Sister? Mommy doesn't have a sister. Just me.*

It's just Mommy and Kane and me.

I shift. The floor creaks beneath me. They turn—

The rest of the memory was less vivid. I didn't feel it, didn't live through it again, but I knew what had happened—knew that my mother and Kane had turned to see me, that Kane had been the one to bend down to my level, to pick me up. I knew that he'd told my mother that he was the one who didn't deserve her.

Didn't deserve *us*.

"You okay?"

I wasn't sure how long Dean had been standing behind me, but I let my body lean back into his. I let myself feel his warmth, the way my mother had felt Kane's.

"I knew that Kane and my mom were involved," I said, the words like sandpaper in my throat. "I didn't realize that he was part of my life, too."

Kane Darby and my mother hadn't just been involved. They'd been serious.

If you were serious about him, I thought, picturing my mom the way she'd looked in the memory, *if he was serious about us, why did we leave?* As I descended the spiral staircase, my stomach twisted. I felt the way I did every time I dreamed about my mother's dressing room.

Don't go in there. Don't open the door.

My gaze locked on the foot of the stairs. My heart raced, but a memory never came. I just stood there, until I heard a loud crash from the kitchen. I made a beeline for the noise, but Agent Sterling cut me off. She gave me a warning look and then led the way into the kitchen herself.

Shane was standing over the sink, blood dripping from his hand, a broken glass on the floor.

Blood.

Go back to sleep, baby, my mother's voice whispered from somewhere in my memory. *It's just a dream.*

"Have an accident?" Agent Sterling asked Shane.

Shane ignored Sterling and narrowed his eyes at me. "You shouldn't have come back here, little Red."

"Watch it." Dean's voice was low and full of warning.

Shane ignored him. "The last thing Gaither needs is outsiders buying into what Serenity Ranch is selling. You should tell your little friend that," he continued, his voice dripping with venom, "*if* you see her again."

For a moment, I felt like I was watching this interaction from outside my body.

"What little friend?" I asked.

Shane didn't answer. He grabbed a paper towel, pressed it onto his bleeding hand, then tried to storm past us. Agent Sterling stopped him. For the first time since we'd come to Gaither, she took out her badge.

"I'm with the FBI," she said. "And you need to back up and explain exactly what you meant just now."

Shane looked from Sterling's badge to me and then back again. "Holland Darby is on the FBI's radar?" It was clear from the tone of Shane's voice that he was trying very hard not to get his hopes up.

Agent Sterling let Shane's explanation stand.

"What about the girl who was with you?" Shane asked. "Is she FBI, too? Is that why I just got a call from a buddy of mine that she's out there, asking to join them?"

The girl who was with you. I'd had a plan to find out more about Kane Darby. But apparently, I wasn't the only one. All roads in Gaither led back to the friendly neighborhood cult, and it didn't take much profiling for me to figure out which of my fellow Naturals might have decided to follow up on that lead.

On her own.

CHAPTER 38

Serenity Ranch was less of a ranch than a compound, surrounded by a ten-foot-tall fence on all sides. Agent Sterling parked her car outside the main gate.

"Stay here," she told us.

Clearly, she wasn't thinking straight. Lia was the closest thing to family that Dean had. Before he could latch his hand around the door handle, I reached out to stop him.

"I know," I said. "Lia did something stupid, and you weren't there to stop her. And now she's in there playing a very dangerous game with very dangerous people. But you need to calm down, because you saw the way that Darby was with Shane. He wanted Shane to take a swing, and he'll want the same thing from you."

Power. Control. Manipulation. This was the language that Holland Darby spoke. It was a language that Dean and I knew all too well.

Dean's entire body was tense, but he forced himself to

breathe in and breathe out. "Lia was seven when her mother joined a religious commune," he said, his voice rough in his throat. "Lia's mom was in this country illegally, and after what she'd been through, the man in charge seemed like a savior." Dean closed his eyes. "To Lia, he was something else."

I thought of Lia, learning to recognize deception. Lia, learning to lie.

"Lia likes high places," Dean continued softly, "because her mother let a man like Holland Darby stick Lia in a hole in the ground for days at a time. Because six-year-old Lia didn't have a humble spirit. Because she wouldn't take forgiveness when it was offered. Because she didn't repent her sins."

Dean forced himself to stop, but my mind was reeling at the implications. As a child, Lia had gotten locked into a battle of wills with a man who dealt in power, manipulation, and control. The kind of man who benevolently offered forgiveness, so long as you accepted that your salvation was his to give. From the moment Lia had seen *those people* in town, from the moment she'd read about Serenity Ranch, she was a ticking time bomb.

Power. Control. Manipulation. Lia had known that approaching Holland Darby as tourists wouldn't work. Approaching him as the FBI would only cause him to close ranks. But approaching him as a lost soul in need of redemption?

You'll play his game better than he does. You'll find out

what he's hiding. And if it costs you—*whatever it costs you*—so be it.

"I'm not going to take a swing at anyone." Dean did his best to look like he *wasn't* on the verge of letting his darkest self come out to play. "But I'm also not staying in the car."

"Good," I replied as the cult leader approached the gate where Agent Sterling stood. "Because neither am I."

CHAPTER 39

"How may I help you?" Holland Darby's voice was pleasant and smooth, more powerful and magnetic than his son's.

Agent Sterling didn't so much as glance at Dean and me as we came to stand behind her. "I'm here for Lia," she said. Her tone wasn't argumentative. She was simply stating a fact.

"Of that, I have no doubt," Darby replied. "Lia is a very special young lady. May I ask what your relationship to her is?"

On either side of the gate, Holland Darby and Agent Sterling stood with their arms hanging loosely by their sides. Both of them were preternaturally calm.

"I'm her legal guardian." Agent Sterling went for the jugular. "And she's a minor."

If there was one thing that we knew about Holland Darby,

it was that he took pains to stay just this side of the law. The word *minor* was his kryptonite, and Agent Sterling knew it.

You would hate to part with such a prize, but if she's not eighteen . . .

"I haven't been a minor for three months." Lia came to stand behind the cult leader. She was dressed in a white peasant top and flowy white pants, barefoot, her hair loose and free.

"Lia." Dean didn't say more than her name, but there was a wealth of warning in that single word.

"I'm sorry," Lia told Dean softly. "I know this hurts you. I know that you want to make it all better, to make *everything* better, but there is no better, Dean. Not for someone like me."

A masterful liar wove truth into deception. Lia could say the words *someone like me* and mean them.

"I believe there is a *better*." Holland Darby took the opening that Lia had left him. "For everyone, Lia, even you."

Even you. Those two words belied the gentleness in his tone. He was already undermining her, already sowing the belief that she was less, that she was unworthy, but that *he* could believe in her despite her unforgivable flaws.

For a brief instant, Lia's eyes met mine. *You know exactly what you're doing,* I thought. *He's a doll-maker who likes broken toys, and you know how to play the shattered, broken doll.*

Agent Sterling almost certainly saw that as clearly as I did, but she had no interest whatsoever in allowing one of her charges to play this game. "Lia, you have two choices. The first is to get your ass out here in the next five seconds. And the second choice?" Agent Sterling took a single step forward. "It's one that you're really not going to like."

Lia—being Lia—heard the truth in that statement. I expected her to bait Agent Sterling further, but instead, she shrank back.

Vulnerable. Broken. Weak.

Holland Darby held up a hand. "I will have to ask you to moderate your tone." He stepped in front of Lia, blocking her bodily from Sterling's view. "This is a simple place, and we abide by simple rules. Respect. Serenity. Acceptance."

Agent Sterling stared the man down for a moment, and then she reached for her back pocket—*for her badge,* I realized. Dean's hand caught Sterling's before she could pull it out. He looked toward Lia, who stepped tentatively out from behind Darby, every motion, every gesture of vulnerability a lie.

"I hope you find what you're looking for," Dean told Lia. There was anger in those words, but also a message. He was telling her that he saw through her act—that he knew why she was here, and he knew that it had nothing to do with finding serenity and everything to do with finding out what Holland Darby was hiding.

Lia smiled sadly before retreating behind Darby's form. "I hope so, too."

CHAPTER 40

The second we walked past Agent Starmans, who was stationed in the hallway, and into the hotel room, Michael scanned our faces. "You spoke to Lia," he concluded. "Where is she?"

"She infiltrated Serenity Ranch." Sterling addressed those words to Judd, who didn't look any happier about Lia's absence than we were.

"Lia infiltrated a cult," Michael repeated. He shot an incredulous look at Dean. "And you didn't drag her home kicking and screaming?"

"Don't start with me, Townsend." A muscle in Dean's jaw ticked.

"Consider me warned."

Judd ignored the tension brewing between Michael and Dean and focused his attention on Agent Sterling. "Is Lia in any immediate danger?"

Agent Sterling's answer was as terse as Judd's question. "I don't think Darby has avoided formal charges for this long by overtly abusing newcomers before he's had a chance to fully indoctrinate them."

In other words, as long as Holland Darby bought the persona Lia was presenting to him—the lost lamb in need of guidance—she was probably safe.

For now.

"Will she be discreet?" Judd addressed that question to Dean.

"Discreet?" Michael repeated incredulously. "Are we talking about the same Lia Zhang here? The one who expresses her displeasure with relationship partners by threatening to duct-tape them naked to the ceiling?"

"Lia knows how this game is played," Dean told Judd. And then he turned back toward Michael, the muscles in his neck and shoulders as tense as his jaw. "So *now* you and Lia are in a relationship?"

"Excuse me?"

"You weren't 'in a relationship' in New York when we went to find Celine," Dean said. "The second things got tough, you pushed Lia away."

"I'm confused, Redding," Michael said, taking a lazy step toward Dean. "Is talking about our feelings something you and I do now?"

Leaving Lia at Serenity Ranch had taken everything Dean had. He'd done it because he trusted her, because trusting Lia and offering her honesty in exchange for every lie was the way he'd made it past her walls. But walking away had cost him. His temper was already frayed, and Michael's flippant tone wasn't helping.

"You're not good enough for her," Dean told Michael, his voice low. "If you were even the least bit capable of caring about anyone but yourself, Lia wouldn't have gone in alone. She did this *to* you as much as *for* the rest of us."

"Dean," I said sharply.

Michael held up a hand. "Let the man speak, Colorado. I do love it when he-who-has-literally-tortured-someone-in-this-room casts stones."

"Michael." As the person Dean had tortured, back when he was a child trying to help her escape his father's grasp, Agent Sterling didn't appreciate the reference.

"You should have known," Dean told Michael between gritted teeth. "If Lia was on the verge of taking off, if this case cut too close to home, if she was itching to get out of her own skin, if she *needed* to fight back—you should have known."

"You think I don't know that?" Michael got in Dean's face. "You think I wanted her to leave?"

For a moment, I thought Dean would de-escalate things. But then he leaned forward to speak directly into Michael's ear. "I think you don't know how to do anything but take a punch."

One second, they were standing there, and the next, they were on the floor. Michael swung at Dean, who grappled for better positioning and pinned Michael to the ground.

"Stop." The word exited Sloane's mouth in a whisper. *"Stop. Stop. Stop!"*

She'd been silent since we'd made it back, and as her volume escalated to a yell, the boys froze.

I'd never seen Dean pick a fight with Michael before. I'd never seen the two of them in an all-out brawl.

"It's not Michael's fault." Sloane's voice was barely audible. "It's mine." She moved backward until she hit the wall. "I saw Lia leaving. She asked me not to tell." Sloane sucked in a breath, her middle finger on her right hand tapping against her thumb. She was counting something—counting and counting and unable to pull it together. "We'd just gotten back, and she changed clothes. She was wearing white, and Lia only wears white thirteen percent of the time. I should have known."

"Sloane," Judd said gently. "Sweetheart . . ."

"I offered to go with her," Sloane continued, picking up the pace of both her words and her tapping. "She said no. She said . . ." Sloane looked down. "She said I'd just get in the way."

You knew how much that would hurt Sloane, Lia. You knew. Objectively, I could see that Lia had been trying to protect our most vulnerable member, but Sloane didn't know that. She wouldn't understand it even if I tried to explain what the combination of anger, fear, and dread that Michael had seen in Kane Darby had drudged up for Lia.

Years later, it can still hit you in a moment.

Dean was wrong. This wasn't about Michael, or what had

happened in New York, or any of us. This was about ghosts that Lia had never faced.

Agent Sterling's phone rang then, and as I told Sloane that none of this—*none* of it—was her fault, my brain was already processing the shift in my mentor's demeanor. The identity of the caller was clear in the way Sterling stood, her shoulders squared to ward off emotion, her free hand dangling loosely by her side.

"I take it you got my messages about Gaither." Sterling didn't say that Briggs should have called her back sooner. She didn't ask why he hadn't. "Lia's gone AWOL to infiltrate the local cult." Agent Sterling set the phone to speaker—one more layer of distance between herself and Briggs. "If the man in charge is hiding something, Lia will find it. But if he realizes she's looking—if anyone in his camp suspects she's with the FBI—this won't go well."

There was silence on the other end of the line for a moment. "Am I on speaker?" Briggs asked, his tone reminding me that he didn't have his ex-wife's impenetrable control.

"You are."

Briggs processed Agent Sterling's answer—and her tone—before proceeding. "What do we think the chances are that someone in the Gaither cult has ties to the Masters?"

I registered the logic behind that question. We'd come to Gaither looking for members of one cult; we'd found another. *Those people* had been implicated in at least one set of murders—those of Anna and Todd Kyle. What were the chances that there were more victims? Lia's situation was precarious enough, but if the Masters had a tie to Serenity Ranch, she could be in more danger than we knew.

"The killings started today," I said, reading into the fact that it had taken him this long to return Agent Sterling's call. "Didn't they?"

"April second." Sloane shivered. "4/2."

Briggs's silence answered that question. Finally, he elaborated. "Victim was a female," he said, clipping the words. "Early twenties, abducted from a college campus. She was found in an open field, strapped to a scarecrow's post."

Burned alive, I filled in. I swallowed hard.

"We can't leave Gaither," Dean told Briggs. "Not without Lia."

"I'm not asking you to." Agent Briggs was the type of person who developed and executed plans, the type who never backed down. "You keep working the case in Gaither," he continued. "Give Lia the chance to dig into Darby. And then, Ronnie?"

Agent Sterling didn't bat an eye at the nickname or the emotion that made its way into Briggs's voice as he said it.

"Get her out."

YOU

You aren't surprised when they come for you. You don't remember the hours following your conversation with Five, but you remember his words. You knew that it was only a matter of time before you were asked to pass judgment.

Of the nine seats at the table, four are filled at this midnight conference. Yours makes five.

"There is a threat." Five has laid his knife on the table for you to see. "I believe the situation to be worthy of the Pythia's counsel."

There is a promise in his tone. He will slice and dice and cut and bleed you, then ask you whether your daughter and her friends should live or die.

"There is no threat." You speak like one who knows the truth of things, like one who has seen that which mortal eyes may never see.

They pay you no heed.

Two is on the verge of losing his seat to the acolyte. This may be his last chance to hear you scream, to burn you, if Five and his knife prove less than convincing. Four believes himself a man of great discernment. You can already feel his fingers closing in around your neck.

It would be so easy to run and hide, deep inside your own head. To go away from this place—from the pain.

"The FBI is closing in." The fifth member of this quorum is the one who has never laid a hand on you. The one you loathe. The one you fear. "In my judgment, their very presence in Gaither makes this group a threat."

"They are not yours to judge." Your voice is dangerous, low. This is the lie that you must sell. You are what they have made you. You are judge and jury, and without a fifth vote, they cannot put you through the rites.

It will happen. Tomorrow, the next day at the latest, but for now . . .

The door opens. You recognize the person who stands there, and you see now what you should have seen before.

There are nine seats at the table. You sentenced Seven to die. You knew his seat would not remain empty. You knew that the Master who trained him would return to the fold.

But you didn't know . . . didn't know . . .

"Shall we begin again?" Five picks up his knife, his smile spreading.

Six seats filled. Five votes, excluding yours.

CHAPTER 41

The next morning, we still hadn't heard from Lia. If Ree noticed we were one short as we slid into our booth at the Not-A-Diner, she didn't comment on it. "What can I get you?"

"Just coffee." Dean's voice was barely audible. He hadn't slept and wouldn't until Lia was out of that place.

"Coffee," Ree repeated, "and a side of bacon. Cassie?"

"Coffee."

Ree didn't even ask Sloane and Michael what they wanted. She gave us a look. "I heard your friend has fallen under Holland Darby's spell."

I wondered if she'd also heard—from her grandson—that we were with the FBI. *You might not say anything if you had. You know how to keep a secret. You know when to keep your mouth closed.*

"Lia's coming back." Dean's voice was quiet, but his expression was hard.

Ree eyed Dean. "That's what I thought when my daughter joined Darby's flock. She split town, and I never heard from her again."

"You weren't surprised when your daughter left." Michael was entering dangerous territory, pressing Ree on this, but I let him do it.

"Her daddy hightailed it out of Gaither when I was pregnant. Sarah was always more like him than me—full of big dreams and restless in her own skin, always looking for the promise of something *more*."

"Holland Darby is big on promises," Dean commented, assessing Ree. "You're not."

Ree pursed her lips. "We, every one of us, reap what we sow. I hope your friend makes it out, but don't let her choices pull you down in the meantime. Life is full of drowning people, ready and willing to drown you, too."

The door to the diner opened. With a harrumph at the person who stood there, Ree disappeared back into the kitchen. Beside me, Dean laid one hand over mine.

The person who'd just walked in was Kane Darby.

I knew, from the moment that his gaze landed on our table, that he hadn't seen me the day before at the apothecary museum, but that he recognized me now.

"Gut-punched," Michael told me under his breath, his eyes methodically scanning Kane's face, his posture. "Like he can't decide whether to smile or throw up."

Staring at the man, I could suddenly remember riding on his shoulders when I was very small. If Michael had read my expression, he probably would have said that I looked gut-punched, too.

"If you need an icebreaker," Sloane told me, pitching her voice in a whisper, "you should tell him that eighty percent of Americans believe that a weevil is similar to a weasel, when in reality, it's a type of insect."

"Thanks, Sloane." I squeezed Dean's hand once, then stood, crossing the room until Kane Darby and I were standing face to face.

"You look like your mother." Kane's voice was muted, like he thought I was a dream and if he spoke too loudly, he might wake up.

I shook my head. "She was beautiful, and I'm . . ." I searched for the right words. "I can fade into the background. She never learned how."

I realized, as I said those words, that there was a part of me that had always believed that if my mother and I were more alike, if she'd been less of a performer, if she hadn't been the center of attention just walking through a room, she might still be here.

"Women shouldn't have to fade into the background to be safe." Kane's response told me that he could read me, nearly as well as I could read him.

"You heard what happened to my mom?" I asked, my voice hoarse.

"It's a small town."

I assessed him for a moment, then went straight for the jugular. "Why did my mother leave you? We were happy here. *She* was happy. And then we left, with no warning, in the middle of the night." Until I'd said the words, I hadn't realized that I had any memory of leaving Gaither, other than dancing with my mother on the side of the road.

Kane looked at me, really looked at *me* this time, instead of just seeing my mom in my features. "Lorelai had every right to leave, Cassie, and every right to take you with her."

"What happened?" I repeated the question, hoping for an answer.

"This town wasn't a good place for your mom, or for you. I kept things from her. I thought I could shield her from what it meant to be with me, here."

"Your father isn't well-liked in Gaither." I spoke out loud, instead of profiling him in my head. "You broke away from him, but you stayed local." I thought back to the memory of Kane sweeping me into his arms after a nightmare. "When my mom and I left, you didn't follow."

Did you resent her for leaving? Did you keep track of her? Did you find a way, years later, to make her yours?

I couldn't ask a single one of those questions out loud. So instead, I asked him about Lia.

Kane glanced around the diner. "Can we take a walk?"

In other words, he didn't want an audience for what he was about to say. Knowing I would catch hell for it, I followed him out the door.

"My father prizes certain things." Kane waited until we were a block away from the diner before he began speaking. "Loyalty. Honesty. Obedience. He won't hurt your friend.

Not physically. He'll just slowly become more and more important to her, until she's not sure what she'd be without him, until she'll do anything he asks. And any time she doubts herself or doubts him, there'll be someone there to whisper in her ear about how lucky she is, how special."

"Were you lucky?" I asked Kane. "Special?"

"I was the golden son." His voice was so even, so controlled, that I couldn't hear even a tinge of bitterness underneath.

"You left," I commented. When that didn't engender a response, I pressed on. "What happens if Lia wants to leave?"

"He won't stop her," Kane said. "Not at first."

Those three words sent a chill down my spine. *Not at first.*

"I wish I could do something, Cassie. I wish that I'd had any right to keep your mother here, or to go after her once she was gone. But I am my father's son. I made my choices long ago, and I accept what those choices have cost me."

I'd wondered why Kane Darby had stayed in Gaither. *What if staying isn't an act of loyalty? What if it's penance?* My mind traveled back to Mason Kyle, Kane Darby's childhood friend.

What choices did you make? What exactly are you repenting?

"I never stopped thinking about you." Kane stopped walking. "I know I wasn't your father. I know that, to you, I'm probably just some guy who briefly dated your mom. But, Cassie? You were never just some kid to me."

My chest tightened.

"So, please, listen to me when I say that you need to leave Gaither. It isn't safe for you to be here. It isn't safe for you to be asking questions. Your friend will be okay at Serenity, but you wouldn't be. Do you understand what I'm telling you?"

"You're telling me that your father is a dangerous man." I paused. "And that my mother left this town for a reason."

YOU

Five admires his handiwork as blood drips down your arms, your legs. It will be hours before the others return. Hours before they ask you if Cassie and her friends should die.

No. No. No.

That's Lorelai's answer. That will always be Lorelai's answer. But Lorelai isn't strong enough to bear this. Lorelai isn't here right now.

You are.

CHAPTER 42

There was a thin line between a warning and a threat. I wanted to believe that Kane Darby had been warning me, not threatening me, when he'd suggested I leave town, but if my time with the FBI had taught me anything, it was that violence didn't always simmer just below the surface. Sometimes, the serial killer across from you quoted Shakespeare. Sometimes, the most dangerous people were the ones you trusted most.

Kane Darby's non-confrontational manner wasn't any more *natural* than Michael's tendency to wave red flags at any and all passing bulls. That kind of steadiness could have come from one of two places: either he'd grown up in an environment where emotion was seen as unseemly—and outbursts were punished accordingly—or staying calm had been his way of seizing control in an environment where someone else's volatile emotions had served as land mines.

As I rolled that over in my mind, Dean fell in beside me. "I made a promise to the universe," he said, "that if Lia gets out of this unscathed, I'll go forty-eight hours without brooding. I will purchase a colored T-shirt. I'll sing karaoke and let Townsend pick out my song." He cast a sideways glance at me. "Did you learn anything from talking to Darby's son?"

The answer to Dean's question sat heavy and unspoken in my throat as we made our way down Main Street, past Victorian storefronts and historical markers, until the wrought-iron gate of the apothecary garden came into view.

"Kane said that he was the golden son," I said finally, finding my voice. "He blames himself for that. I think staying in Gaither was a form of penance for him—punishment for, and I quote, 'choices' he made 'long ago.'"

"You're talking about him," Dean observed. "Not to him."

"I'm talking to you."

"Or," Dean countered softly as we came to a stop outside the garden, "you're scared to go too deep."

In the entire time I'd known him, Dean had never pushed me further into another person's perspective than I wanted to go. At best, he curtailed his protective instincts, profiled with me, or got out of my way—but right now, I wasn't the one that Dean would have given anything to protect.

"You came very close to remembering something back at your old house. Something that a part of you is desperate to forget. I know you, Cassie. And I just keep thinking that if you forgot an entire year of your life, it wasn't because you were little, and it wasn't the result of some kind of trauma. You've been through two lifetimes of trauma, just since I've met you, and you haven't forgotten a thing."

"I was a child," I countered, feeling like he'd hit me. "My mother and I left in the middle of the night. We didn't tell anyone. We didn't say good-bye. Something happened, and we just *left*."

"And after you left"—Dean took my hand in his—"it was just you and your mother. She was all you had. You were her everything, and she wanted you to forget. She wanted you to dance it off."

"What are you saying?" I asked Dean.

"I'm saying that I think that you forgot the life you lived in Gaither for *her*. I'm saying that I don't think you're the one that your brain was protecting. I think it was protecting the only relationship you had left." Dean gave me a moment to process, then pushed on. "I'm saying that you couldn't afford to remember the life you had here, because then you would have had to be angry that she took it away." He paused. "You would have to be angry," he continued, switching to the present tense, "that she made sure you never had that again. She made you the center of her life and herself the center of yours, and knowing what we know now—about the Masters, about the Pythia—I think you're even more terrified than you were as a child about what might happen if you do remember Gaither."

"And that's why I'm using the third person when I talk to you about Kane Darby?" I asked sharply, stepping past the gates and walking the stone path of the apothecary garden, Dean two steps behind me. "Because getting close to him might mean getting close to my mother? Because I might remember something I don't want to know?"

Dean walked behind me in silence.

You're wrong. I'd done everything I could to see my mother through a profiler's eyes and not a child's. She'd been a con woman. She'd made sure that I had no one to depend on but her.

She'd loved me more than anything.

Forever and ever, no matter what.

"Maybe I did forget Gaither for her sake," I said quietly, allowing Dean to catch up with me. "I was good at reading people, even as a kid. I would have known that she didn't want to talk about it, that she needed to believe that none of it had mattered, that the two of us didn't need anyone or anything else."

My mom had let herself care about Kane Darby. She'd let him in—not just into her life, but into mine. Based on the rest of my childhood, she'd learned her lesson.

What happened? Why did you leave him? Why did you leave Gaither?

I came to a standstill in front of an oleander, its reddish pink blooms deceptively cheerful for a poisonous plant. "Kane said that Lia would be safe," I told Dean, cutting to the heart of the matter. "For now." I wanted to stop there, but I didn't. "He also said that I wouldn't be safe in her position."

"Darby doesn't know who and what Lia is." Dean captured my gaze, unwilling to let me look away. "If you wouldn't be safe there, she's not, either." This was Dean asking me to stop pulling back, asking me to *remember*. And all I could think was that he shouldn't have had to ask.

I swallowed, my mouth dry as I began profiling Kane—the right way this time. "My mother once told you that she didn't deserve you, but she didn't know your secrets, the choices you had made." Saying the words out loud made them real. I kept my gaze on Dean's, let his deep brown eyes steady me, even as I could feel my entire life—my entire worldview—begin to shift under my feet. "You said that you didn't deserve her, didn't deserve *us*. But you wanted it—you wanted a family, and you were good at being there for her and for me." Saying the words physically hurt, and I had no idea why. "There had to be some shred of that desire, some kernel of what it meant to be a family in your background. Setting aside *loyalty*, *honesty*, *obedience*, and any other buzzword that dominated your childhood, you cared about people. And because you cared, you did horrible things."

Kane Darby was a man who'd been punishing himself for decades. Maybe he'd let himself believe, when he'd met my mother, that it was finally enough. That he could have her. That he could have a family.

But yours will never let you go.

I thought about Kane trying to intervene with Shane, trying to mitigate his own father's harm. And then I thought about Dean, standing beside me in this garden, his blond hair falling into his face. What Kane had been to my mother, Dean was to me. Like Kane, Dean had spent years keeping a tight rein on his emotions. He'd spent years convinced that there was something dark and twisted inside of him, and that if he wasn't careful, he would someday become his father.

All of us had a way of regaining the control that life had taken from us. For Sloane, it was numbers. For Lia, it was keeping her true self buried beneath layers of lies. Michael intentionally provoked anger instead of waiting for someone else's fuse to blow. Dean did everything he could to keep his emotions in check.

And I use knowing things about people as an excuse to keep them from knowing me.

Becoming a part of the Naturals program had meant letting a piece of that control go. *For years, you were my everything.* I wasn't talking to Kane now. I was talking to my mother. *You kept me from my father's family. You made me the center of your world and yourself the center of mine.*

I wrapped my arms around Dean's neck. I felt his pulse, steady against mine. His fingertips traced the edge of my jaw. I pressed my lips to his, let them part. I tasted and wanted and *felt* him, and I remembered:

Mommy kissing Kane—

The first day of school—

Coloring at Ree's—

Melody, in the garden. "What's the matter, scaredy-cat?" Melody is pigtails and skinned knees and bossy hands on bossy hips. "It's just the poison garden!" She squats down next to a plant. "If you don't come in, I'm going to eat this leaf. I'll eat it right up and die!"

"No, you won't," I say, taking a step toward her. She plucks a leaf off the plant and opens her mouth.

"You kids stop horsing around in there!"

I turn around. There's an old man standing behind us. He looks mad and mean, and he's wearing long sleeves, even though it's summer. Rough white lines and ugly puckered pink ones snake out from underneath his shirt.

Scars.

"How old are you?" the man demands. I know with all of my being that he's wearing long sleeves because those aren't his only scars.

"I'm seven," Melody answers, coming to stand beside me. "But Cassie's only six."

The memory jumps, and suddenly I'm running home. I'm running—

Nighttime now. I'm in bed. There's a thump. Muted voices.

Something's wrong. I know that, and I think about the old man in the garden. He got mad at Melody and me. Maybe he's here. Maybe he's angry. Maybe he's going to eat me right up.

Another thump. A scream.

Mommy?

I'm at the top of the stairs now. There's something at the bottom.

Something big.

Something lumpy.

And suddenly, my mother is on the stairs, kneeling in front of me. "Go back to sleep, baby."

There's blood on her hands.

"Did the old man come?" I ask. "Did he hurt you?"

My mother presses her lips to my head. "It's just a dream."

I came out of the memory with my body still pressed against Dean's, my head buried in his shoulder, his hands combing gently through my hair.

"There was blood on my mother's hands," I whispered. "The night my mom and I left Gaither, I heard something. A fight, maybe? I went to the top of the stairs, and there was something at the bottom." I swallowed, my mouth so dry the words wouldn't come. "There was blood on her hands, Dean." I forced them out anyway and didn't let myself stop. "And then we left."

I thought about the rest of the memory.

"There's something else?" Dean asked.

I nodded. "The day we left," I said, pushing back from his chest, "I'm fairly certain I met Malcolm Lowell."

CHAPTER 43

Nightshade's grandfather still lived in a house on a hill overlooking the Serenity Ranch compound. Malcolm Lowell was pushing ninety, confined to a wheelchair, and—as his home health aide informed Agents Sterling and Starmans—not up for visitors.

Agent Sterling didn't take no for an answer.

Back at the hotel, I sat between Dean and Sloane as we watched the live feed from Sterling's lapel camera, all too aware of the risk Agent Sterling was taking by flashing her badge. If word got around that Sterling was FBI, Holland Darby might start to consider Lia a liability.

As the nurse reluctantly allowed Sterling and Starmans into the massive house, my mind went to what I'd remembered. *The stairs. Something at the bottom.*

In my six-year-old mind, the scary old man who'd yelled at Melody and me and the events that had transpired that night were integrally related, but from a more mature perspective, I could see that they might well be two independent, traumatic events, linked in my mind only by their proximity to each other in time.

An intimidating old man had scared me. And that night, something had happened—something that had ended with blood.

"Mr. Lowell." Agent Sterling took a seat across from a man who appeared no older than he had a decade earlier. He was wearing a long-sleeved shirt, just as he had then.

The scars were still visible.

As a child, they'd scared me. Now, they told me that Malcolm Lowell had woken up every day for the past thirty-three years with a very visible reminder of the attack that had left his daughter and son-in-law dead.

"I'm Special Agent Sterling with the FBI." Agent Sterling let her posture mimic his—straight and uncompromising, despite his age. "This is Agent Starmans. We need to ask you some questions."

Malcolm Lowell was silent for several seconds, and then he spoke. "No," he said, "I don't believe you do."

She wants *to ask you some questions*, I thought. *There's a difference.*

"We have reason to believe that your family's tragedy may be related to a current serial murder investigation." Agent Sterling danced the line between offering specifics and offering truth. "I need to know what you know about the original murders."

Lowell's right hand crept up his left sleeve, running his

fingertips over a scar. "I told the police what I knew," he grunted. "Nothing else to tell."

"Your grandson is dead." Agent Sterling made no attempt to soften those words. "He was murdered. And we would like, very much, to find his killer."

I glanced to Michael.

"Grief," Michael said. "And nothing but."

Malcolm Lowell had disowned his grandson when the boy was nine years old, but more than thirty years later, he mourned his passing.

"If you know something," Agent Sterling said, "anything that might help us find the person who attacked you—"

"I was stabbed repeatedly, Agent." Lowell met Agent Sterling's gaze, his own uncompromising. "In my arms, my legs, my stomach, and my chest."

"Did your grandson witness the attack?" Agent Sterling asked.

No response.

"Did he participate in the attack?"

No response.

"He's shutting down," Michael told Agent Sterling over the audio feed. "Whatever emotions your questions might have provoked a couple of decades ago, he won't let himself feel anything now."

"Sound familiar?" Dean asked me.

I thought of Nightshade, stonewalling the FBI the exact same way his grandfather was now. He'd learned the power of silence firsthand.

"Ask him about my mother," I said.

Agent Sterling did me one better. She withdrew a picture—one I hadn't even been aware that the FBI had. In the picture, my mother was standing onstage, her eyes rimmed in thick black liner, her face alive with expression.

"Do you recognize this woman?"

"Eyesight isn't what it used to be." Malcolm Lowell barely even glanced at the picture.

"Her name was Lorelai Hobbes." Agent Sterling let those words hang in the air, using silence as her own weapon.

"I remember her," Lowell said finally. "Used to let her little girl run wild with Ree Simon's hellions. Trouble, the lot of them."

"Like your grandson was trouble?" Agent Sterling asked softly. "Like your daughter before him?"

That got a reaction. Lowell's hands balled themselves into fists, loosened, and balled up again.

"He's getting agitated," Michael told Sterling. "Anger, disgust."

"Mr. Lowell?" Agent Sterling prompted.

"I tried to teach my Anna. Tried to keep her home. *Safe*. And how did she end up? Pregnant at sixteen, sneaking out." His voice trembled. "And that boy. *Her* son. He cut a hole in the fence, found his way down to that godforsaken compound." Lowell closed his eyes. He lowered his head, until I couldn't make out a single one of his features onscreen. "That's when the animals started showing up."

"The animals?" Sloane said, cocking her head to the side.

Clearly, she hadn't foreseen that admission. Neither had I. The difference was that I knew immediately that when Malcolm Lowell said *animals*, he meant *dead animals*.

"They weren't clean kills." Lowell looked back up at the camera, a hard glint in his eyes. "Those animals died slowly, and they died in pain."

"You thought Mason was responsible?" Agent Starmans asked, speaking for the first time.

There was a long pause. "I thought he watched."

YOU

You've been chained to the wall for hours, bleeding for hours.

But really, you've been chained and bleeding for years. Before this place. Before chaos or order. Before knives and poison and flame.

You are the one who lay in Lorelai's bed as a child.

You took what she couldn't.

You did what she couldn't.

As the seconds and minutes and hours tick by, you can feel her, ready to stop hiding. Ready to come out.

Not this time. This time, you're not going anywhere. This time, you're here to stay.

Night falls. The Masters return. They have no idea who you are. What you are.

They're used to Lorelai's dramatics.

Let them see yours.

CHAPTER 44

I was aware, as the clock ticked past midnight, that another day had passed without answers. *April fourth.* Somewhere, Agent Briggs was waiting for the Masters' next victim to turn up, strapped to a scarecrow post and burned alive.

Unable to sleep, I sat on the counter of our kitchenette, staring out into the night and thinking about Mason Kyle and Kane Darby, dead animals, and the large, lumpy shape at the bottom of those stairs.

It was a body. I hadn't seen that at the age of six, but even with a fragmented memory, I knew it now. I'd been trying not to know it, trying not to *remember* since I'd gotten back in town.

"No offense, but you have the survival instincts of a lemming."

I jumped at the sound of those words and scrambled off the counter. Lia stepped out of the shadows.

"Relax," she said. "I come in peace." She smirked. "Mostly."

Lia was wearing the uniform I'd seen on the rest of Holland Darby's people, not the white peasant top she'd been wearing when I saw her last. In all the time I'd known her, she'd never ceded control of her wardrobe to another person.

In all the time I'd known her, she'd never looked so *blank*.

"How did you get past Agent Starmans?" I asked her.

"The same way I got out of Serenity Ranch. Sneaking around is just another form of lying, and God knows my body is even more talented at deception than my mouth."

Something in Lia's words triggered an alarm in my head. "What happened?"

"I got in, and I got out." Lia shrugged. "Holland Darby likes making claims. That he would never hurt me. That he understands me. That Serenity Ranch has nothing to hide. All lies. Of course, the most interesting piece of deception I picked up on wasn't from Darby. It was from his wife."

I tried to remember what the police files had said about Mrs. Darby, but she'd been little more than a footnote, a fixture in the background of the Holland Darby Show.

"She told me they had nothing to do with what happened to 'that poor family' all those years ago." Lia gave me a moment to process the fact that she'd seen deception in that claim. "And she said that she loved her son."

"She doesn't?" I thought of the Kane my mother had known. And then I thought about the body at the foot of the stairs, the blood on my mother's hands.

There was a thump. Had Kane been there? Had he done something? Had my mother?

It isn't safe for you to be asking questions. Kane's warning echoed in my mind. *Your friend will be okay at Serenity, but you wouldn't be.*

"Agent Sterling talked to Malcolm Lowell." As I sorted through the bevy of thoughts in my head, I caught Lia up on what I knew. "Back before Nightshade's parents were murdered, someone at Serenity Ranch had developed a fondness for killing animals."

"Cheery," Lia opined. She reached past me and helped herself to a four-dollar Dr Pepper from the mini fridge. As she did, I caught sight of her wrist. Angry red lines crisscrossed the exposed skin.

"You cut yourself?" My mouth went dry.

"Of course not." Lia turned her wrist over to examine the damage as she lied to my face. "Those lines just magically appeared and were not in any way a method by which to make sure Darby bought my story about how *empty* I feel inside."

"Hurting yourself isn't the same as donning a costume, Lia."

I expected her to shrug the words off, but instead she met my eyes. "This didn't hurt," she told me quietly. "Not really. Not in any way that mattered."

"You're not okay." My voice was every bit as quiet as hers. "You weren't okay before you went there, and you sure as hell aren't okay now."

"I forgot what it was like," Lia said, her voice absolutely devoid of expression, "to be special one moment and nothing the next."

I thought about what Dean had told me about Lia's childhood. *When you pleased him, you were rewarded. And when you displeased him, he put you in a hole.*

"Lia—"

"The man I grew up with? The one who controlled everything and everyone I knew? He never laid a hand on us." Lia took a sip of her soda. "But some days, you'd wake up and everyone would know that you were unworthy. Unclean. No one would speak to you. No one would look at you. It was like you just didn't exist."

I heard the implication buried in those words. *Your own mother would look right through you.*

"If you wanted anything—food, water, a place to sleep—you had to go to *him*. And when you were ready to be forgiven, you had to do it yourself."

My heart jumped into my throat. "Do what?"

Lia looked down at her angry red wrists. "Penance."

"Cassie?"

I turned to see Sloane standing a few feet away.

"Lia. You're home." Sloane swallowed. Even in dim lighting, I could see her fingers beginning to tap against her thumbs. "You two probably want to talk. Without me." She turned.

"Hold up," Lia said.

Sloane stayed where she was, but didn't turn back to face us. "That's what you were doing. Talking to Cassie. Because

Cassie's easy to talk to. She understands, and I don't." A breath caught in Sloane's throat. "I just blurt out stupid statistics. I get in the way."

"That's not true." Lia stalked toward Sloane. "I know I said it, Sloane, but I was lying."

"No. You weren't. If Cassie or Dean or Michael had been the one to catch you leaving, you wouldn't have said it. You wouldn't have meant it, because Cassie and Dean and Michael could go with you and lie and keep secrets and not say exactly the wrong things at exactly the wrong times." Sloane turned to face us. "But I can't. I *would* have been in the way."

Sloane was different from the rest of us. That was easy for me to forget—and impossible for Sloane to.

"So?" Lia retorted.

Sloane blinked several times.

"You can't lie worth a damn, Sloane. That doesn't mean you matter any less." Lia stared at Sloane for a few seconds, then seemed to come to a decision. "I'm going to tell you something," she said. "*You*, Sloane. Not Cassie. Not Michael. Not Dean. You know the Salem witch trials?"

"Twenty people were executed between 1692 and 1693," Sloane said. "An additional seven died in prison, including at least one child."

"The girls who started the whole thing off with their accusations?" Lia took another step toward Sloane. "That was me. The cult I grew up in? The leader claimed to have visions. Eventually, I started playing his game. I started having 'visions,' too. And I told everyone that my visions showed me that he was right, that he was just, that God wanted us to obey him. I built myself up by building him up. He believed me. And when he came into my room one night . . ." Lia's voice was shaking. "He told me that I was *special*. He sat on the end of my bed, and as he leaned over me, I started screaming and thrashing. I couldn't let him touch me, so I lied. I said that I'd had a vision, that there was a betrayer in our midst." She closed her eyes. "I said the betrayer had to die."

I killed a man when I was nine years old, Lia had told us months ago.

"If I had to choose between being like you and being like me," Lia continued, holding Sloane's gaze, "I'd want to be like you." Lia tossed her hair over her shoulder. "Besides," she said, shedding the intensity she'd borne a moment ago like a snake wriggling out of its skin, "if you were like Cassie and Michael and Dean and me, you wouldn't be able to do anything with this."

Lia reached into her back pocket and pulled out several folded pieces of paper. I wanted to see what was on them, but was still paralyzed by the words Lia had spoken.

"A map?" Sloane said, thumbing through the pages.

"A layout," Lia corrected. "Of the entire compound—the house, the barns, the acreage, drawn to scale."

Sloane wrapped her arms around Lia in what appeared to be the world's tightest hug.

" 'Drawn to scale,' " Sloane whispered, just loud enough that I could hear her, "are three of my favorite words."

CHAPTER 45

By the time the others woke up the next morning, Sloane had developed a complete blueprint of the Serenity Ranch compound.

Agent Sterling helped herself to a cup of coffee, then turned to Lia. "Pull a stunt like that again and you're out. Out of the program. Out of the house."

Not a threat. Not a warning. A promise.

Lia didn't bat an eye, but when Judd cleared his throat and she turned to face him, she actually winced.

"I can keep the FBI from treating you like you're disposable," Judd told Lia, his voice even and low. "But I can't make you value yourself." Next to Dean, Judd had been the one constant in Lia's life since she was thirteen years old. "I can't force you not to take chances with your own life. But you didn't see me after my daughter died, Lia. If something happens to you? If I go to that place again? I can't promise I'm coming back."

Lia found it easier to be the recipient of anger than affection. Judd knew that, just like he knew she'd read the truth in every word.

"Okay," Lia said, holding up her hands and stepping back. "I'm a bad, bad girl. Point taken. Can we focus on what Sloane has to say?"

Dean appeared in the doorway and registered Lia's presence. "You're okay."

"More or less." Lia's reply was flippant, but she took a step toward him. "Dean—"

"No," Dean said.

No, you don't want to hear it? No, she doesn't get to do this to you?

Dean didn't elaborate.

"Thank goodness you're home, Lia." Michael strolled into the room. "Dean is awfully prone to talking about *feelings* when you're MIA."

"Would this be an inappropriate time to say 'aha'?" Sloane interjected from the floor. "Because *aha!*"

If Sloane had been even the least bit capable of guile, I would have thought she'd come to Lia's rescue on purpose.

"What did you find?" I asked, earning a look from Dean that said he knew quite well that I *was* capable of throwing Lia a lifeline.

"I started with Lia's drawings and compared them to satellite photographs of the Serenity Ranch compound." Sloane stood, bouncing to the tips of her toes and walking the perimeter of the diagram she'd laid out on the floor.

"Everything lined up, except . . ." Sloane knelt to point a finger at one of the smaller buildings on her diagram. "This structure is roughly seven-point-six percent smaller on the inside than it should be."

"That's the chapel." Lia tossed her ponytail over her shoulder. "No specific religious ties, but you wouldn't know that from looking at it."

I could hear Melody's monotone in my memory. *In Serenity, I've found balance. In Serenity, I've found peace.*

I turned my attention back to Sloane. "What does it mean that the building is smaller on the inside than it should be?"

"It means that either the walls are abnormally thick . . ." Sloane caught her bottom lip in her teeth, then let it go. "Or there's a hidden room."

I didn't have to sink very far into Holland Darby's psyche to conclude that he was the kind of man who hid his secrets well. *That's your serenity. That's your peace.*

"Unfortunately," Agent Sterling said, "none of that gives me probable cause to search the property."

"No," Lia said, reaching into her pocket. "But this does."

She pulled a small glass vial out of her pocket. The liquid inside was milky white. "Not sure what it is," she said, "but Darby keeps his flock well-dosed."

"He's drugging them." Dean's stony face showed no signs of softening—toward her or toward the situation.

Agent Sterling took the vial from Lia. "I'll get this to the lab. If it's a controlled substance, I can get a warrant to search the compound."

Beside me, Sloane stared at the vial. "I'd give it even odds that it's some kind of opiate."

Your mother died of an overdose. I profiled Sloane as a matter of instinct, but another part of me couldn't help profiling someone else—some*thing* else. Nightshade and whoever in this town had recruited him.

There's a thin line between medicine and poison.

CHAPTER 46

It took twenty-four hours for Agent Sterling to get her warrant and another hour after that for the FBI to secure the compound—and, more to the point, the compound's owner. By the time Holland Darby and his followers had been sequestered and the five of us were allowed on the premises, I could feel the ticking of the clock.

Today is April fifth. The reminder thrummed through my veins as we approached the chapel. *Another Fibonacci date. Another body.*

Briggs hadn't called us. He hadn't asked for help. I shoved that thought out of my mind as I pushed open the chapel door.

"No religious iconography," Dean commented.

He was right. There were no crosses, no statues, nothing to indicate a tie with any established religion—and yet the room was clearly designed to call to mind a religious space. There were pews and altars. Tile mosaics on the floor.

Stained glass windows casting colored light into the room.

"We're looking for a false wall," Sloane said, pacing the perimeter of the room. She stopped in front of a wooden altar near the back. Her fingers deftly searched for a trigger, some kind of release.

"Got it!" Sloane's triumph was punctuated by the sound of creaking wood, followed by the whine of rusted hinges. The altar gave way to reveal a hidden room. I took a step forward, but Agent Sterling strode past me. Her right hand on her weapon, she held her left out to Sloane.

"Stay here," she said, stepping into the room herself.

"It's narrow," Sloane reported, peering into the darkness. "Based on my earlier calculations, it almost certainly runs the entire length of the chapel."

I waited, the steady fall of Agent Sterling's footsteps the only sound in the room. Dean came to stand on one side of me, Michael and Lia on the other. When Agent Sterling reappeared, she holstered her weapon and called for backup.

"What did you find?" Dean asked her.

If any of the rest of us had asked the question, Agent Sterling might not have responded, but given their history, she was incapable of ignoring Dean.

"A staircase."

The staircase led to a basement. *Not a basement,* I corrected myself when it had been deemed safe enough for us to enter. *A cell.*

The walls were thick. Soundproof. There were shackles

on the wall. There was a decomposed body in the shackles.

A second body lay on the floor.

The room smelled of decay and death—but it didn't smell *recent*.

"Based on the level of decomposition and taking into account the temperature and humidity levels in this room . . ." Sloane paused as she ran the numbers in her head. "I'd guess our victims have been dead between nine and eleven years."

Ten years ago, my mother and I had left Gaither.

Ten years ago, I'd seen a body at the bottom of the stairs.

"Who are they?" I asked the question that everyone was thinking. Who had Holland Darby chained up under his chapel? Whose bodies had been left here to rot and fade away?

"Victim number one is male." Sloane stepped closer to the body still shackled to the wall. The flesh was nearly nonexistent.

Bones and decay and rot. My stomach threatened to empty itself. Dean laid a hand on the back of my neck. I leaned in to his touch and forced my attention back to Sloane.

"The depth and thickness of the pelvic bone," Sloane murmured. "The narrow pelvic cavity . . . definitely male. Facial bones suggest Caucasian. I'd put height at around five foot eleven. Not a juvenile, and no signs of advanced age." Sloane studied the body for another thirty or forty seconds in silence. "He was shackled postmortem," she added. "Not before."

You built this room for something. For someone. I took in the size of the room. *You chained this man's body, even after death.*

"What about the other victim?" Agent Sterling asked. I knew her well enough to know that she'd already developed her own theories and interpretation of the scene before us, but she wouldn't contaminate a second opinion by letting us see even a hint of what that interpretation was.

"Female," Sloane answered. "I'd put her age somewhere between eighteen and thirty-five. No visible sign of cause of death."

"And the male?" Agent Starmans asked. "How did he die?"

"Blunt force trauma." Sloane turned to Agent Sterling. "I need to go upstairs now," she said. "I need to be not here."

Sloane had seen plenty of bodies, plenty of crime scenes, but since Aaron's death, victims hadn't just been *numbers* to her. Slipping an arm around her, I led her up the stairs. On the way, we passed Lia, who stood with her back up against Michael's body.

As Sloane and I made it up into the fresh air, I heard Lia's ragged whisper. "He put them in a hole."

YOU

Without order, there is chaos. Without order, there is pain.

That's Lorelai's chorus, not yours. You are chaos. You are order.

Five stands before you, sharpening his blade. It's just you and him. Two had his turn yesterday, a dozen burns on your chest and thighs. And still, you wouldn't tell them what they wanted to hear. You wouldn't tell them to eliminate the problem, to take whatever steps necessary to rid Gaither of the FBI.

Not yet.

Five steps forward, blade and eyes gleaming. Closer. Closer. The flat of the blade presses against the side of your face.

Without order, there is chaos. Without order, there is pain.

You smile.

They left you all day in this room, thinking that you were Lorelai. They left you, roaming free in a room with your own shackles, under the belief that the threat of retribution—to you, to Laurel—would keep you in line.

They were wrong.

You surge forward as the broken shackles fall away. You grab the knife and plunge it into your tormenter's chest. "I am chaos," you whisper. "I am order." You press your lips against his and twist the blade. "I am pain."

CHAPTER 47

Holland Darby and his wife were brought in for questioning. Neither one of them said a word. At my suggestion, Agent Sterling brought in their son. The teenagers among us were relegated to observing—in this case, from behind a two-way mirror.

"Devastation, resignation, fury, guilt." Michael rattled off the emotions on Kane Darby's face one by one.

I looked for some hint of what Michael saw, but I couldn't sense even a trace of emotion churning in Kane Darby. He seemed somber, but not on guard.

"Two bodies were found in a hidden room beneath your family's chapel." Agent Sterling mimicked Kane's manner: no muss, no fuss, no frills. No beating around the bush. "Do you have any idea how they came to be there?"

Kane looked Agent Sterling straight in the eye. "No."

"Lie," Lia said beside me.

"We're looking at one male victim and one female victim,

killed approximately ten years ago. Can you shed any light on their identities?"

"No."

"Lie."

I stared at Kane's familiar face, pushing back against any warmth the six-year-old inside of me still felt for the man. *You know who they are. You know what happened to them. You know what happened in that room. Why your father built it. Why he built the chapel.*

Why there were shackles on the walls.

Kane had told me that Lia would be safe at Serenity Ranch, but that I wouldn't be. I wondered now if I would have ended up down below.

I am my father's son. Kane's voice rang in my memory. *I made my choices long ago.*

I'd seen parallels between Kane's emotional control and Dean's. Dean had known what his father was doing to those women. At the age of twelve, he'd found a way to stop him.

You got out, Kane. But you didn't stop your father. Didn't stop it—whatever it was. You didn't leave town. You couldn't.

"He might talk to me," I told Agent Sterling over the audio feed. After a few more questions to Kane, she excused herself from the room.

"He won't talk to anyone," she told us, observing my mother's ex from behind the two-way mirror. "Not until we identify the bodies. Not until we know who they are. Not until this—all of it—is *real* and he reaches the point of no return."

Kane Darby had been keeping his father's secrets all his life. *Devastation. Resignation. Fury. Guilt.* The last two were the emotions we needed.

"What are the chances the FBI lab can ID the bodies?" I asked.

"With little more than skeletal evidence and no DNA to compare it to?" Agent Sterling returned evenly. "Even if they come up with something, it will take time."

I thought of today's date—and yesterday's. I thought about the fact that it was still unclear how this—any of it—was related to the Masters. I thought about my mother, shackled. The way that corpse had been shackled.

And then I thought about the corpse, the bones peeking out from beneath its fraying flesh. The face that didn't even look like a face.

I paused. *The face.* I could see Celine Delacroix in my mind's eye, her posture regal, her expression wry. *I can take one look at a person and know exactly what their facial bones look like underneath the skin.*

My mind reeled. What were the chances that Celine could do the reverse? That, given a picture of a person's facial bones, she could draw the face?

"Cassie?" Agent Sterling's tone told me this wasn't the first time she'd said my name.

I turned to catch Michael's eye. "I have an idea, and you're really not going to like it."

CHAPTER 48

We sent Celine photographs of our victims. And then we waited. Waiting was not one of the Naturals program's collective strong suits. Within an hour, Agent Sterling was out working the case again, but the rest of us were stuck twiddling our thumbs at the hotel. Waiting for Celine to put her skills to the test. Waiting for the truth. Waiting to find out if our efforts would lead us any closer to my mother.

"Dean." Of all of us, Lia was either the best at waiting or the worst. "Truth or dare?"

"Seriously?" I asked Lia.

Her lips tilted upward ever so slightly. "There's a certain tradition to it, don't you think?" She sat down on the arm of the couch. "Truth or dare, Dean?"

For a moment, I thought he would refuse to answer.

"Truth."

Lia looked down at her hands, examining her fingernails. "How long are you going to be mad at me?"

You don't sound vulnerable. You don't sound like the answer could break you.

"I'm not mad at you," Dean said, his voice cracking.

"He's mad at himself," Michael clarified loftily. "Also: me. Definitely me."

Dean glared at him. "Truth or dare, Townsend." Those words weren't issued like a question. They were a challenge.

Michael offered Dean a charming, glittering smile. "Dare."

For almost a minute, the two of them were caught in a staring competition. Then Dean broke the silence. "Agent Starmans is downstairs patrolling the perimeter of the hotel. I dare you to moon him."

"*What?*" Clearly, Michael had not been expecting those words to exit Dean's mouth.

"The term *mooning* arises from the vaguely moon-shaped form of the human buttocks," Sloane volunteered helpfully. "Although the practice dates back to the Middle Ages, the terminology was not common until the mid-1960s."

"Really?" I asked Dean. I was a natural profiler. He was my boyfriend, and I had in no way seen this coming. Then again, he *had* promised the universe a significant reduction in brooding if it returned Lia to us intact.

"You heard the man," I told Michael.

Michael stood up and dusted off his lapels. "Mooning Agent Starmans," he said solemnly, "would be my pleasure."

He stalked to the balcony, let himself out, waited for Agent Starmans to pass by, and then called down to the man. When Starmans looked up, Michael saluted him. With military precision, he turned and bared his backside.

I was laughing so hard, I almost didn't hear Michael as he came back in and turned to Dean. "Truth or dare, Redding?"

"Truth."

Michael crossed his arms over his waist in a way that made me think Dean was going to regret that choice. "Admit it: I've grown on you."

Sloane frowned. "That wasn't a question."

"Fine," Michael said, grinning, before returning to torture Dean. "Do you like me? Am I one of your closest bosom buddies? Would you cry your little heart out if I was gone?"

Michael and Dean had been at each other's throats for as long as I'd known them.

"Do. You. Like. Me." Michael repeated the question, this time with gestures.

Dean glanced at Lia, whose presence was a reminder that he couldn't get away with lying.

"You have your moments," Dean mumbled.

"What was that?" Michael cupped his ear.

"I don't *have* to like you," Dean snapped back. "We're family."

"Bosom buddies," Michael corrected loftily. Dean gave him a dirty look.

I grinned.

"Your turn again," Lia reminded Dean, nudging him with the tip of her foot.

Dean resisted the urge to target Michael. "Truth or dare, Cassie?"

There were very few things I kept from Dean—very few things he couldn't ask me, if he wanted to know.

"Dare," I said.

Sloane cleared her throat. "I would just like to point out," she said, "that this is one of only two-point-three percent of hotel rooms that come with a blender."

Hours ticked by. The blender and the minibar proved to be a dangerous combination.

"Truth or dare, Lia?" It was my turn, and I could feel reality creeping back up on us. Every round that went by was that much longer without hearing from Celine. It was that much closer until the point in time when Agent Sterling would either have to charge the Darby family or let them go.

"Truth," Lia replied. It was her first in a very long game.

"Why did you go after Darby alone?" I asked her.

Lia stood up and stretched, arching her back and twisting from one side to the other. She had the advantage in Truth or Dare.

No one else in this room could lie and get away with it.

"I got out," Lia said finally. "My mother didn't." She stopped stretching and stood very still. "I ran away when I hit puberty. By the time Briggs found me in New York . . ." She shook her head. "There was nothing left for us to save."

Nothing left of the cult. Nothing left of your mother.

"Some of Darby's followers will just find someone else to latch on to," Lia continued. "But there's at least a chance that with him in prison, some of them will go home."

I thought of Melody and Shane. And then I thought of Lia—younger and more vulnerable than the girl I knew now.

"Besides," Lia added flippantly, "I wanted to stick it to Michael for that stunt he pulled in New York." She turned on the tips of her toes. "Truth or dare, Sloane?"

"Would choosing truth involve a question about beagle and/or flamingo statistics?" Sloane asked hopefully.

"Doubtful," Michael opined.

"Dare," Sloane told Lia.

A slow, wicked grin spread over Lia's face. "I dare you," she said, "to hack into Agent Sterling's computer and change her wallpaper to the picture I took of Michael mooning our Agent Starmans."

CHAPTER 49

It took Sloane nearly half an hour to hack into Agent Sterling's laptop. Considering that this was Sloane we were talking about, that made Agent Sterling's computer security measures downright impressive. Our resident hacker was midway through uploading the picture Lia had taken when the computer beeped.

"Incoming e-mail," Lia said, reaching over Sloane to click the e-mail icon.

One second, we were in giddy Truth or Dare mode, and the next, it was like all traces of oxygen had been sucked from the room. The e-mail was from Agent Briggs. There were files attached. *Reports. Pictures.*

Within a minute, they filled the screen. The image of a human body, burned past all recognition, sent me to the ground. I sat down hard, unable to keep my arms from wrapping around my legs, unable to tear my eyes away from the screen.

I'd known, logically, that the killing had started again. I knew that there was an UNSUB out there making the transition from apprentice to Master. I'd even known the killer's MO.

Strung up like a scarecrow. Burned alive.

But there was a difference between knowing something and seeing it with your own eyes. I forced myself to look at a photograph of the victim—the person she'd been before her body was devoured by flames, before she was nothing but pain and scorched flesh and ash.

Her hair was long and blond, her pale skin offset by a pair of dark-rimmed hipster glasses. And the longer I looked at her, the harder it was to look away, because she didn't just look young and carefree and alive.

"She looks familiar." I hadn't meant to say those words out loud, but they exited my mouth like a crack of thunder.

Beside me, Sloane shook her head. "I don't recognize her."

Michael squeezed in beside us at the computer. "I do." He turned to look at me. "Back when we were investigating the Redding case, when you and Lia and I went to that frat party—you went off with the professor's teaching assistant, and I followed. With her."

I tried to recreate the scene in my memory. A college girl had been killed, the MO an exact match to Daniel Redding's. Michael, Lia, and I had snuck out of the house to do some recon on potential suspects. And one of the people we'd talked to was this girl.

"Bryce." Sloane read her name from the file. "Bryce Anderson."

I struggled to remember more about her, but other than the fact that she'd been in class with the first victim—and the fact that the class in question had been studying the Daniel Redding case—I came up blank.

"When you talked to my father . . ." Dean's voice was steady, but I knew exactly how hard he had to fight for that kind of detachment. "He indicated that he was aware of the Masters' existence. What are the chances that *they* have been keeping tabs on *him*?"

I saw the logic in Dean's question. If our victim had a connection to the Daniel Redding case, there was at least a chance that the UNSUB did as well.

The door to the hotel room opened before I could put any of that into words.

"This," Agent Sterling said sternly, coming into the room, "is the face of someone who is not going to say a word—*not a single word*—about the dubious decision-making that leads one to moon a federal agent." The edges of her lips turned up slightly. "Once we finish in Gaither, Agent Starmans has requested some time off." She took in the mood of the room and the expressions on our faces. "Have we heard anything back from Celine?"

In response, Sloane turned the laptop around, giving Agent Sterling a look at the screen. The poker face our mentor adopted in that moment told me, beyond any shadow of a doubt, that the files attached to this e-mail weren't news to her. She'd known the identity of the first victim—and somehow, she'd made the connection.

"You hacked my laptop." That was neither a question nor an accusation. Judd, who'd been giving us space for hours, chose that moment to join us, and Sterling met his gaze. "Is this the part where you tell me that reading them the riot act would be a waste of breath?"

Dean stepped toward her. "This is the part where you tell us about victim number two."

Bryce had been killed on April second. The next two Fibonacci dates were the 4/4 and 4/5—and today was the fifth. At a minimum, we had two victims. By midnight, we'd have three.

"Are we looking at the same geographical area?" I asked Sterling, hoping to prompt some kind of response. "Same victimology?"

"Does victim number two have a connection to my father?" Dean pressed. "Or that class on serial killers?"

"No."

That response didn't come from Agent Sterling. It came from Sloane.

"No. No. No." Sloane had turned the laptop back around. Her hands sat limp on the keys, and I realized that she'd opened the rest of the files attached to Briggs's e-mail.

My eyes stung as I took in the second crime scene. *Strung up like a scarecrow. Burned alive.* But it was the name typed onto the accompanying forms that explained the way

Sloane pressed her hands to her mouth and the garbled, high-pitched sound that made its way through her fingers.

Tory Howard.

Tory had been a person of interest in our Vegas case. She was a stage magician in her early twenties who'd grown up alongside our Vegas killer. And that meant that the common thread between our two victims wasn't the Redding case. It wasn't geographical. It was *us*. Cases we'd worked. People we'd talked to.

In Tory's case, people we'd saved.

"*She loved him, too.*" Sloane's hands weren't on her mouth anymore, but her voice was still garbled. Tory had been involved with Sloane's brother, Aaron. She'd grieved for him, like Sloane had. She'd recognized Sloane's grief. "Call Briggs." Sloane's voice was still quiet, her eyes pressed closed.

"Sloane—" Judd started to say, but she cut him off.

"Tanner Elias Briggs, Social Security number 449-872-1656, Scorpio on the cusp of Sagittarius, seventy-three-point-two-five inches tall." Sloane forced her blue eyes open, her mouth set in a mutinous line. "*Call him.*"

This time, when Agent Sterling dialed the number, Briggs picked up.

"Ronnie?" Briggs's voice cut through the air. In all the time I'd known him, he'd almost always answered the phone with his own name. I wondered what to read into the fact that this time, he'd answered with hers.

"You've got the entire group," Agent Sterling said, setting

the phone to speaker. "The kids hacked my computer. They saw the files."

"You should have told me," Sloane said fiercely. "When you found out the second victim was Tory." Her voice shook slightly. "I should have known."

"You had your plate full." Judd was the one who responded, not Briggs. "You all did." The former marine's characteristically gruff manner softened slightly as he moved toward Sloane. "You remind me of my Scarlett." Judd rarely spoke his daughter's name. It carried an unearthly weight when he did. "Too much sometimes, Sloane. Every once in a while, I fool myself into thinking that maybe I can protect *you*."

I could see Sloane struggling to understand—what Judd was saying, the fact that he'd been the one to make the call about keeping us in the dark.

"Today is April fifth." Lia's tone had sharp edges, but I couldn't hear even the slightest tinge of anger. "4/5. Where are we on victim number three?"

She'd asked the question because Sloane couldn't, and she'd asked it to remind Briggs, Sterling, and Judd that they couldn't lie to *her*.

Briggs kept his reply brief. "No crime scene. No victim. Not yet."

Yet. That word served as a reminder of every person we'd failed. While we'd been here in Gaither, searching for clues, two more people had died. Another would join them soon, join the *hundreds* of victims the Masters had murdered through the years.

"We need to go through our past cases," I said tersely, fighting back against the crushing reality that when we made mistakes—when we weren't good enough, when we were too slow—people died. "Identify persons of interest."

"Female persons of interest under the age of twenty-five," Dean said quietly. "Even if the other Masters have been suggesting victims that will make a point to the FBI, this is *my* test, and that's my type."

Dean's words sent a chill down my spine, because they gave life to a suspicion lurking just below the surface of my mind. Each Master chose nine victims. Victimology was one of the things that separated each Master from the next.

But this time, our killer wasn't the only one with a say in the kills.

This isn't just ritual. It's personal. No matter how many times I tried to slip into this UNSUB's head, I kept coming to the same conclusions. *Someone made it personal, because we're getting close. Because we're in Gaither.*

"The Masters had the apprentice kill Bryce and Tory because of us." I swallowed, but I couldn't stop the words from pouring out of my mouth. "I'm not sure if it's revenge or an attempt to lure us away from Gaither, but if we weren't here . . ."

On the other side of the room, Michael had his cell phone pressed to his ear. He said nothing, ending the call and trying a second time.

"Michael—" Lia started to say.

He slammed his fist into the wall. "Female," he said, like

it was a curse word. "Under twenty-five. With a connection to one of our previous cases."

For the first time since I'd known him, Michael's expression was transparent. *Terrified. Nauseated.*

And that was when I realized . . .

"Celine," I said. *Female. College-aged.* Bile rose in my throat. "She was the 'victim' in our most recent case. If they've been watching us . . ." A heavy feeling settled over my limbs. "She helped us identify Nightshade. And we just pulled her back into the case."

Not we, I thought, horrified. *Me. I was the one who suggested we call Celine—just like I went to see Laurel.*

"If she was there, she'd answer." Michael slammed his fist into the wall again and again, until Dean forcibly hauled him back. "With everything that's going on, she'd answer." Michael struggled violently against Dean's hold before stilling abruptly. "My call went to voice mail. Twice."

CHAPTER 50

No matter how many times we called Celine, her phone went straight to voice mail. Briggs sent a local field agent to her dorm to check on her, but she wasn't there.

No one had seen or talked to Celine Delacroix since we'd sent her the photos hours earlier.

"First they went after your sister, Colorado," Michael said dully, his eyes empty of emotion. "And now they've taken mine."

Lia crossed the room to stand in front of him. For no apparent reason, her hand snaked out to slap him across the face, and a moment later, she pressed her lips to his, kissing him hard. As far as distractions went, that was a one-two punch.

"Celine is fine," Lia said when she pulled back. "*She's going to be fine, Michael.*" Lia could make anything sound true. Her breath was ragged as she continued. "I promise."

Lia didn't make promises.

"She's only been missing a few hours," Sloane added. "And given that she has a history of kidnapping *herself*, statistically speaking . . ." Our numbers expert paused, her blond hair falling into her face. "She's going to be okay." Sloane didn't offer up a single number or percentage. Whatever numbers were flying through her head, she fought back against them for Michael and echoed Lia's words. "I promise."

Dean clapped a hand onto Michael's shoulder. Michael's eyes found their way to mine.

"She's going to be okay," I said softly. After everything we'd been through, everything we'd lost, I had to believe that. But I didn't promise. I couldn't.

Michael, taking one look at my face, would have known why.

A knock at the hotel room door broke the silence that had fallen over us. Judd stepped forward to prevent me from answering it. Looking through the peephole, he let his hand drop from the gun at his side and opened the door.

"You have a bad habit of disappearing, young lady."

I processed Judd's words before I registered the identity of the girl on the other side of the door.

"Celine?"

Celine Delacroix stood, designer suitcase in hand, her hair swept gently back from her face. "Two-dimensional skull photos blow," she declared in lieu of a greeting. "Take me to the bodies."

CHAPTER 51

It hadn't occurred to Celine to tell anyone she was going on an impromptu trip to Oklahoma. She'd turned her phone off on the plane.

"I told you." Lia smirked at Michael. "Say that I was right."

"You were right." Michael rolled his eyes. His voice softened slightly. "You promised."

"In the interest of ultimate honesty," Celine cut in, "I'm pretty sure that everyone present would appreciate it if you two got a room."

"I wouldn't," Dean grumbled.

"I am unbothered by displays of physical and emotional intimacy," Sloane volunteered. "The nuances and statistics underlying courtship behavior are quite fascinating."

The edges of Celine's lips quirked upward as she met Sloane's gaze. "You don't say."

Sloane frowned. "I just did."

"I could use some mathematical expertise for these facial

reconstructions." Celine cocked her head to the side. "You in, Blondie?"

Remembering Sloane's reaction to the bodies in the basement, I expected her to decline, but instead, she took a step toward Celine. "I'm in."

Agent Sterling, Celine, and Sloane left before the sun came up the next morning. I ended up along for the ride. In all my time in the Naturals program, this was my first visit to one of the FBI labs—in this case, a secure facility a two-hour drive from Gaither. After the medical examiner had finished her analysis of both bodies and a forensics team had gathered trace evidence from the clothing and skin, what little had remained of our victims' flesh had been stripped from the bones. The two skeletons lay side by side.

Agent Sterling cleared the room before allowing us in.

Celine stood in the doorway, taking in the long view before advancing on the skeletons, circling them slowly. I knew, just from her posture, that her eyes missed nothing. Her gaze latched on to the smaller skeleton—our female victim.

You see more than bones. You see contours. A cheek, a jaw, eyes . . .

"Can I touch her?" Celine asked, turning to Agent Sterling.

Sterling inclined her head slightly, and Sloane handed Celine a pair of gloves. Celine slipped them on and ran her fingertips gently over the woman's skull, feeling the way the bones curved and met up with each other. For Celine, painting was a whole-body endeavor, but this—this was sacred.

"Two-point-three-nine inches between her orbital cavities," Sloane said softly. "An estimated two and a half inches between her pupils and mouth."

Celine continued her exploration of the skull, nodding slightly. As Sloane rattled off more measurements, Celine reached for the sketch pad she'd laid on a nearby exam table. Within seconds, she had a pencil in hand and it was flying across the page.

As Celine drew, she stepped back from the rest of us. *You'll show it to us when it's ready. When it's done.*

It was several minutes before the sound of Celine ripping the paper out of her pad cut through the air. Without a word, she handed the picture to Sloane, set down her notepad, and turned her attention to the second skeleton.

Sloane brought the picture to me. I brought it to Agent Sterling. The woman staring back at us from the page was in her late twenties, pretty in an ordinary kind of way. A creeping feeling of familiarity tugged at me.

"Recognize her?" Agent Sterling asked me quietly, as Celine continued to work on the other side of the room.

I shook my head, but inside, I felt like nodding. "She looks . . ." The words hovered, just out of grasp. "She looks like Melody," I said finally. "Ree's granddaughter."

The instant that statement was out of my mouth, I knew.

I knew who this woman was. I knew that Ree's daughter—Melody and Shane's mother—hadn't skipped town after a brief stop at Serenity Ranch.

She'd never left.

I tried to remember anything else I could about the woman—anything I'd heard, anything I'd seen. Instead, I remembered what my mother had tried to keep me from seeing at the bottom of the stairs.

Something big.

Something lumpy.

Blood on my mother's hands . . .

I couldn't make out the face on the body. I couldn't tell if it was male or female.

Kane. Kane was there. The knowledge swept over me. *Wasn't he?*

Feeling like the world was falling out beneath me, I walked toward Celine, who'd picked up her sketch pad again. This time, I couldn't stop myself from watching as she drew.

She let me.

She let me watch over her shoulder, and slowly, a man's face emerged. *Jawline first. Hairline. Eyes. Cheeks, mouth . . .*

I took a step back. Because this time, there was no creeping feeling of familiarity, no searching the banks of my memory for some clue of who this body had belonged to.

I recognized that face. And suddenly, I was standing at the top of the steps again, and there was a body at the bottom.

I see it. I see the face. I see blood—

The man in the picture—the man in my memory, crumpled at the bottom of the stairs, the skeleton on the exam table, a decade dead—was Kane Darby.

YOU

The Masters find you sitting on the floor, the knife balanced on your knee. Five is in pieces beside you.

You look up, feeling more alive—more like yourself—than you ever have. "He was not worthy," you offer.

You are not weak. You are not Lorelai. You decide who lives, who dies. You are judge and jury. You are executioner. You are the Pythia.

And they will play your game.

CHAPTER 52

Impossible. That was the word for what Celine had drawn. Hours later, as I sat down across from Kane Darby at the nearest FBI field office, Agent Sterling on one side and Dean on the other, I found myself staring at his face—at those familiar features—my throat dry and my mind reeling.

You're alive. You're here. But it was your face in that sketch.

It was *his* face in my memory, *his* body crumpled at the bottom of the stairs, *his* blood on my mother's hands. There was an explanation, and I knew in my gut that I could make Kane give it to me, but just looking at him, I was frozen, like a diver standing at the edge of a cliff staring down at rough waves breaking against the rocks below.

"Did my mother ever mention the BPEs to you?" I asked Kane, somehow managing to form the words. "Behavior. Personality. Environment."

"Lorelai was teaching you the tricks of her trade," Kane

said. A decade on, I could still hear an echo of emotion when he said her name.

"She taught me well." I let that sink in, sounding calmer than I felt. "Well enough that the FBI finds my skills useful on occasion."

"You're a child." Kane's objection was predictable enough to steady me, grounding me in the here and now.

"I'm the person asking the questions," I corrected evenly. I knew instinctively that Agent Sterling had been right—if we'd tried this tactic without having identified our victims, I wouldn't have been able to get anything out of Kane.

But Celine's facial reconstructions had changed the game.

You'll know, in a moment, that this is real. That your family's secrets are coming out. That there's no use in fighting it.

That the power of penance pales next to confession.

"We've identified the bodies found at Serenity Ranch." I gave Kane enough time to wonder if I was bluffing, and then I glanced at Agent Sterling, who handed me a folder. I laid the first picture on the table, facing Kane.

"Sarah Simon," I said. "She joined your father's cult and then—by all accounts—skipped town when it wasn't what she'd hoped."

"Except she didn't." Dean took over where I stopped. "Sarah never left the property, because someone killed her first. Based on the autopsy, we're looking at asphyxiation. Someone—most likely a male—slipped his hands around her neck and choked the life out of her."

"Strangulation is about dominance." I was all too aware of how strange it must have been for Kane, who'd known me as a child, to hear me say those words. "It's personal. It's intimate. And afterward, there's a sense of . . . completion."

For the first time, Kane's expression faltered and something else peeked out from behind his light blue eyes. I didn't need Michael to tell me that it wasn't fear or disgust.

It was *anger*.

I laid the second picture down on the table, the one depicting a man with Kane's face.

"Is this a joke?" Kane asked.

"This is the face of the second victim," I said. *Impossible—but not.* "It's funny—no one in Gaither ever mentioned that you had a twin."

That was the only explanation that made sense—*not Kane crumpled at the bottom of the stairs. Not Kane covered in blood.*

"Maybe," I said, slanting my gaze to catch his, "no one in Gaither knew. You told me the other day that growing up, you were the golden son." I looked down at the photo. "Your brother was something else."

Sometimes, a profiler didn't have to know the answers. Sometimes, you just had to know enough to push someone else into filling in the blanks.

"My brother's name," Kane said, staring at the picture, "was Darren." The anger I'd seen in his eyes was replaced with another emotion, something dark, full of loathing and longing. "He used to joke that they'd gotten us mixed up at the hospital—that he was meant to be Kane. In his version, I was Abel."

"Your brother liked to hurt things." Dean read between the lines. "He liked to hurt you."

"He never laid a hand on me," Kane replied, his voice hollow.

"He made you watch," Dean said. He knew what that was like—viscerally, in a way he could never forget.

Kane dragged his eyes away from Celine's drawing. "He hurt a little girl back in California. He was the reason we moved to Gaither."

When Kane had moved to Gaither, he and his twin were all of nine years old.

"Darren was the reason your father started Serenity." I could see, now, shades in that action that went beyond the older Darby's thirst for power and adoration.

In Serenity, I've found balance.

In Serenity, I've found peace.

"Darren wasn't allowed to leave the property," Kane said. "We kept a close eye on him."

I'd theorized before that Kane had developed his unnatural calmness as a result of growing up around someone who was unstable, volatile, unpredictable.

"Your father's followers kept Darren a secret."

Kane closed his eyes. "We all did."

I thought of Malcolm Lowell, saying that his grandson

had found his way into the compound. I thought about the animals—

They weren't clean kills. Those animals died slowly, and they died in pain.

"Your brother and Mason Kyle were friends."

I thought of Nightshade and the monster he'd become. Had he been that way even as a child? A sadist?

"My parents thought Mason was good for Darren. Good for us. It was almost like . . ."

"Almost like you were normal kids," Agent Sterling filled in. "Almost like your brother didn't have a fondness for hurting animals—and people, when he could."

Kane's head bent so low that his chin nearly gouged his chest. "I let my guard down. I let myself believe that my parents were wrong about Darren. He wasn't broken. He'd just made a mistake. Just one mistake, that was all. . . ."

"And then came the Kyle murders." Dean knew, better than anyone, what it felt like to carry the blood of someone else's victims on your hands.

"Darren went missing that day." Kane closed his eyes, reliving what he'd seen as a child. "I knew he'd gone to Mason's. I followed, but by the time I got there . . ."

Anna Kyle, dead. Her husband, dead. Her father, dying . . .

"Mason was standing there," Kane said. "He was just . . . standing there. And then he turned, and he looked at me, and he said, 'Tell Darren—I won't tell.' "

I could hear Malcolm Lowell stating that he didn't think

his grandson had been the one to torture and kill the animals he'd found.

I think he watched.

"That was when your father built the chapel?" Agent Sterling asked. I translated the question—*the cell underneath the chapel. The shackles on the walls. Not for sheep in his flock who'd gone astray—for his own monstrous son.*

I tried to imagine being Kane, knowing that my father had locked my own twin away. Had Kane visited Darren? Had he seen the toll captivity was taking on him? Had he just left his own brother down there, day after day and year after year?

As if he could hear those silent questions, Kane closed his eyes, pain etched into his features. "You could catch Darren standing over a dying puppy and he'd tell you to your face that he didn't do it. He swore, up and down, that he'd had nothing to do with the attack on the Kyles." Kane swallowed. "My father didn't believe him."

You didn't believe him, either. You let your father lock him up. For years.

I understood now why Kane had never been able to leave town. No matter how disgusted he'd become with his father's manipulations, no matter how broken his family was, he couldn't leave his brother.

"He was my twin. If he was a monster, I was, too."

"Years later, you met my mother," I commented, my mind racing. "And things were going so well. . . ." My voice caught in my throat as I remembered Kane dancing with my mother on the front porch, Kane lifting me onto his shoulders.

"How does Sarah Simon tie in to all of this?" Agent Sterling redirected the conversation. "By all accounts, she joined Serenity more than two decades after the death of the Kyle family."

"I'd left Serenity by that point," Kane said, his voice hoarse enough to tell me that I wasn't the only one who'd been caught up in memories of my mother. "But from what I understand, Sarah spent a lot of time in the chapel."

I could hear the horror in the way Kane said *chapel*.

"Sarah found out about Darren," I said, my mind on the cell where Holland Darby had kept his son.

"She discovered the room. She snuck down to see him, probably more than once, and when he tired of playing with her, he killed her." Kane's voice was like a dull-edged knife. "He wrapped his hands around her neck, just like you said. Power. Domination. Personal. And then, he got out and came after me."

Not you, I corrected silently. *Power. Domination. Personal.*

"He went after the person you loved." I wondered how Darren had known about my mother, if he'd followed Kane to our house, but those questions died under the force of a memory that hit me with a tsunami's force.

Nighttime. There's a thump downstairs.

I put myself in my mother's position. *Did you think he was Kane at first? Did he try to hurt you? Did he wrap his fingers around your throat?*

You fought back.

I thought of my mother smiling, hours later, dancing with me on the side of the road. *You killed him.*

Kane's eyes were closed now, like he couldn't bear looking at me, couldn't bear remembering, but couldn't stop. "By the time I got to Lorelai's house, she was gone. You were gone, Cassie. And Darren's body was at the bottom of the stairs."

I saw the entire scene through his eyes: the brother he'd hated and feared and loved, dead. The woman he'd fallen for, responsible. *It was your fault he came after her. Your fault he hurt her.*

Your fault he was dead.

"Lorelai killed Darren in self-defense," Agent Sterling surmised. "Unless you'd told her about him, she probably thought that she'd killed you."

I tried to reconcile that with the mother I remembered, the mother I knew.

"You cleaned up the crime scene," Agent Sterling continued, offering Kane no respite. "You brought your twin's body home."

"I never told." Kane sounded like a boy, like the child who'd been forced to keep his family's secret, to carry his brother's burden.

"Your family locked Darren away, under the chapel," Sterling said softly. "He was dead, and they still put him in shackles. And Sarah Simon—you left her body down there. You let her family think she'd left town."

Kane had no response. Something had snapped inside of him. Something had broken. And when he finally did speak again, it wasn't to confirm Agent Sterling's statements.

"In Serenity, I've found balance," he said, a shadow of his former self. "In Serenity, I've found peace."

YOU

You've always protected Lorelai. Borne what she could not. Done what she could not.

But this time? You didn't kill for her.

You killed Five for yourself. Because you liked it. Because you could.

Lorelai is weak. But as the Masters take their seats at the table, you are not. Some want to punish you. Some want to take the knife forever from your hand. But others remember—what a Pythia is.

What a Pythia can be.

The Master who preceded Five—the man who chose and trained him and has reclaimed the empty seat, a man you recognize—puts an end to conversation when he hands you a diamond, bloodred, in honor of your kill.

This is a man used to leading. A man used to being in charge.

"There is a threat," the newcomer says. "I can take care of it."

He's talking about Gaither. About Lorelai's daughter and her little friends and how very close they are to discovering the truth.

You allow your gaze to capture his. "It's already taken care of."

The acolyte's third kill is already under way. The body should be showing up soon, and if victim two didn't send your message, this one will.

"And if the problem persists? If their investigation leads them to our door?"

"Well, then . . ." You turn the bloodred diamond in your hand. "In that case, I suppose you can ask for judgment once more."

CHAPTER 53

Kane's twin killed Ree's daughter. Darren tried to kill my mother, and she killed him in self-defense. I should have been overwhelmed. I should have had to fight to view the situation with detached eyes. But instead, I felt nothing.

I felt like this—all of it—had happened to someone else.

Lia, who'd been watching with Sloane and Michael from behind the scenes, confirmed that Kane Darby had believed every word he'd said, and I found myself turning toward Agent Sterling. "What's going to happen to him?"

"Kane will testify against his father," Sterling replied. "About the drugs, what his father did to Darren, the role he played in covering up the death of Sarah Simon. Given the extenuating circumstances, I think I can convince the district attorney to cut Kane a deal."

That wasn't what I'd been asking—not really. I was

asking where a person like Kane could go after something like this, how he could possibly move on.

Celine, who'd observed the debrief, cocked her head to the side and raised one manicured hand. "Just to clarify: we're actually buying the idea that a little kid killed two people and tried to kill a third, causing his parents to chain him up in a basement for twenty-three years, at which point in time he killed someone else, broke out, and got himself axed?"

There was a long pause. After a moment, Sloane answered her. "That seems to be an accurate depiction of the working theory."

"Just checking," Celine replied lightly. "On a related note, this is the most effed-up thing I've ever heard."

"Stick around," Lia told her. "The puppies and rainbows come *after* the murder and mayhem."

Agent Sterling snorted. But the moment of levity didn't last. I could see the FBI agent debating whether to open her mouth again. "I don't know if I buy Darren's involvement in the Kyle murders or not. Kane *believes* his brother killed them—that doesn't mean he's correct."

You showed up, Kane. The Kyles were dead. Mason, who had a history of watching as your brother slaughtered animals, asked you to tell Darren that he wouldn't tell. That single sentence had been enough to convict Darren in Kane's eyes, in his family's eyes. But that sentence had been spoken by a boy who grew up to become a vicious killer himself.

A boy *someone* had groomed for great things.

"We have the files from the Kyle murders." The fact that Dean hadn't spiraled into his own darkest memories—of being groomed, of *watching*—told me that even when normal wasn't an option, going on was. "There must be some way of seeing if the story lines up."

"The average ten-year-old male is fifty-four-point-five inches tall." Sloane popped to her feet and began pacing the claustrophobic quarters of the observation room. "As an adult, Darren Darby was only slightly above average height. Allowing for variable growth patterns, I would estimate his height at the time of the Kyle murders to be between fifty-four and fifty-six inches tall."

"I'm assuming that if we wait, we'll see where Blondie is going with this?" Celine asked the room at large.

"Anna and Todd Kyle were stabbed to death," Sloane told Celine, her eyes alight. "They were knocked to the floor prior to the attacks, making it difficult to gauge the height of their attacker. However, Malcolm Lowell put up more of a fight."

Without another word, Sloane pulled a thick file out of her bag. *The Kyle murders.* She flipped through the contents at hyperspeed, pulling photos and crime scene descriptions.

"I take it that's Malcolm Lowell?" Celine asked, staring down at a series of photos, each a close-up of one of Malcolm's knife wounds. I thought of the scars winding their way in and out of his shirt.

People assumed you stayed quiet for your grandson's sake—and maybe that's true. Maybe Mason helped Darren. Maybe he watched and smiled. But everything I knew about Malcolm Lowell told me that he was a proud man. *You isolated your family. You tried to control them.*

"This doesn't make sense," Sloane said, staring at the pictures. "The angle of entry, especially on the torso wounds . . . it doesn't make sense."

"So Malcolm Lowell *wasn't* stabbed by a child?" Michael asked, attempting to translate.

"This wound," Sloane said, zeroing in on one of the pictures. "The knife was wielded from Lowell's right side, suggesting a left-handed attacker. But the wound is too neat, too clean, and the shape suggests that the knife was held with the blade facing toward the ceiling. It entered the body at an angle of roughly one hundred and seven degrees."

"So Malcolm *was* stabbed by a child?" Michael tried again.

"No," Sloane said. She closed her eyes, every muscle in her body taut.

"Sloane," I said. "What is it?"

"I should have seen it." Sloane's words were barely audible. "I should have seen it before, but I wasn't looking."

"You weren't looking for what?" Agent Sterling asked her gently.

"He wasn't stabbed by a child," Sloane said. "And he wasn't stabbed by a left-handed adult." She opened her eyes. "It's there, if you're looking. If you run all possible scenarios."

"What's there?" I asked her quietly.

Sloane sat down hard. "I'm ninety-eight percent sure that the old man stabbed himself."

CHAPTER 54

What kind of determination would it take to stab a blade into your flesh over and over again? What kind of person could kill his own flesh and blood and then calmly turn the knife on himself?

I pictured myself holding a bloodied knife, pictured myself turning it inward, pictured the light glistening off the blade.

"I'm afraid Mr. Lowell is unavailable." The home health aide who answered Lowell's front door couldn't tell us much more than that. The old man had taken his leave shortly after Agent Sterling had interviewed him—and hadn't told a soul where he was going.

As I paced Lowell's house, looking for some shred of evidence, something to confirm Sloane's theory that he'd killed his daughter and son-in-law, then turned the knife on himself to bar suspicion, I couldn't help remembering the statement he'd given to Agent Sterling about the murdered animals.

You said that you believed that Mason had watched. I pictured the knife again, picture myself holding it. *It must have pleased you to be able to say those words, knowing Agent Sterling wouldn't see the truth behind them. You weren't talking about the way Mason watched Darren Darby kill those animals. You were talking about what your grandson watched you* do.

"What are you thinking?" Dean asked, slipping in beside me.

"I'm thinking that maybe Nightshade *did* see his parents murdered. Maybe he *did* watch." I paused, knowing that my next words would hit home for Dean. "Maybe it was a lesson. Maybe when Kane arrived later, Nightshade threw suspicion on Darren *because* little Mason Kyle had learned that a boy who tortured animals wasn't worthy of following."

Dean was quiet then, the kind of quiet that told me he'd gone to a dark and cavernous place in his own memory the moment I'd said the word *lesson*. Eventually, he clawed himself out.

"My daughter was a disappointment." When Dean spoke, it took me a moment to realize that he was speaking from Lowell's perspective. "I tried to raise her right. I tried to raise her to be worthy of my name, but she ended up being just another whore—pregnant at sixteen, defiant. They lived with me, Anna and her pathetic husband and the boy."

The boy. The one who would grow up to be Nightshade.

"You thought Mason was cut from your daughter's cloth," I said, picking up where Dean had left off. "And then he started sneaking out." By Malcolm Lowell's own admission, he had tried to cage his family. He'd tried to control them. I'd assumed that the proud old man would have considered Mason's behavior an affront.

But what if you didn't? Air entered and exited my lungs. I took a step forward, even though I didn't know what I was walking toward. *What if you considered Mason's little pastime a sign?*

"When the animals started turning up," Dean mused, his voice sounding uncannily like his father's, "I thought it might be the boy. Perhaps he had potential after all."

"But it wasn't Mason." I pressed my lips together as I thought about Kane, broken and hollow. "It was Darren Darby."

"A disappointment," Dean said harshly. "A sign of weakness. One that required an object lesson for my grandson about who he was and where he came from. *We are not followers. We do not watch.*"

Dean's words coated me like oil, bringing me back to my own encounter with Malcolm Lowell as a child.

You knew what it was like to feel the life go out of your victims. You knew the power. You wanted Mason to see you for what you really were, to know exactly whose blood ran in his veins.

Out loud, I let myself take that thought to its logical conclusion. "To kill his own family, to plan it out so coldly, to go as far as to calmly and brutally attack *himself* . . . By the time of the Kyle murders, Malcolm Lowell was already a killer."

Dean waited a beat and then took my statement a step further. "Already a Master."

A chill spread slowly down my spine, like the cracking of ice. *You were tested. You were found worthy. You'd already killed your nine.*

"The timing doesn't add up," I said, pushing down the urge to look over my shoulder, like the old man might be there, watching me the way he had when I was a child. "The poison Master who trained Nightshade—the one who chose him as an apprentice—didn't become a Master himself until years *after* the Kyle murders."

And that meant that if my instincts—and Dean's—were correct, Malcolm Lowell was not the poison Master.

You were something more.

"You groomed your grandson for greatness," I said, my heart thumping in my chest. "You saw the potential, and you made Mason a monster. You made him your heir." I paused. "You sent him to live with a man who knew—intimately knew—the thin line between medicine and poison."

Mason Kyle had left Gaither when he was seventeen years old. He'd attempted to bury all traces of his identity. He'd lived as a ghost for two decades *before* he'd become an apprentice and then a Master.

He knew it was coming. He always knew what he was meant to be. Even thinking about Nightshade, I never left the old man's perspective. *You made him in your own image. You made him worthy.*

A flicker of shadow was the only warning I had that Dean and I were no longer alone.

"Basements are actually relatively rare in Oklahoma," Sloane commented, popping up beside us. "But this house has one."

My heart had leapt into my throat before I'd realized that Sloane was the one who'd joined us. It stayed there as I turned the word *basement* over and over in my mind, thinking about the fact that Laurel had grown up inside and underground.

Thinking that Holland Darby might not be the only one in Gaither with shackles built into his walls.

I knew, logically, that it couldn't be that simple. I knew that my mother had probably never been here, knew that wherever the Masters kept her, wherever they conducted their business, it probably wasn't in one of their basements. But as I wound my way toward the basement, Dean and Sloane on my heels and Lia and Michael falling in beside us, I couldn't push down the roar building in my mind, the incessant thumping of my heart as I thought, *You built this house. For your wife. For your family. For what was to come.*

The basement floor was made of concrete. The beams overhead were covered in cobwebs. A surplus of cardboard boxes made the room's function clear.

Just storage. Just a room.

With no idea what I was looking for, I began to open boxes and go through the contents. They told a story—of a man who'd gotten started on his family later in life. Of the local girl he'd married. Of the daughter who'd lost her mother when she was six years old.

Six years old.

Suddenly, I was taken back to the day Malcolm Lowell had caught Melody and me in the apothecary garden.

"How old are you?" the man demands.

"I'm seven," Melody answers. "But Cassie's only six."

I was six years old when I met Malcolm Lowell. His daughter was six years old when her mother died. Mason Kyle was nine when he watched his grandfather murder his parents.

"Six," I said out loud, sitting down hard between the boxes, the concrete digging into the skin under my legs. "Six, six, and nine."

"Three plus three," Sloane rattled off, unable to stop herself. "Three times three."

The Masters kill nine victims every three years. There are twenty-seven—three times three times three—Fibonacci dates total. My hand brushed up against something etched into the concrete. I shoved a box to the side to get a better look.

Seven circles around a cross. It was the Masters' symbol, one I'd first seen etched into a wooden casket and later seen carved into a killer's flesh. Like Laurel, Beau Donovan had been raised by the Masters. Like Laurel, his mother was the Pythia.

"Beau was six years old when he was tested by the Masters," I said, looking up from the floor. "Six years old when they cast him out to die."

Beau—and Laurel—had been born for one purpose and one purpose alone.

Nine is the greatest of us, Nightshade had told me months ago. *The constant. The bridge from generation to generation.*

I traced my fingers around the outside of the symbol. "Seven Masters," I said. "The Pythia. And Nine."

If Laurel passed their tests, if she was *worthy,* someday she would take the ninth seat at the Masters' table. *But whose seat is it now?*

The greatest of us. The bridge from generation to generation. There had been awe in Nightshade's voice when he'd spoken those words. There had been *warmth.*

"I know that face, Colorado," Michael said, narrowing his eyes at me. "That's your holy *bleep* face. That's—"

I didn't wait for him to finish. "We were never looking for the poison Master who preceded Nightshade," I said, moving my finger from the outer circle to the inner cross. "We were looking for someone who'd been a part of the Masters for longer than twenty-seven years. Someone who held sway over the others. The whole time—we were looking for *Nine.*"

CHAPTER 55

Everything I knew about Malcolm Lowell fell into place. How many years had he spent being molded in the Masters' image, hidden away from the world? How old had he been when he'd finally been allowed a life outside those walls?

How many times had the Masters attempted to raise a new child to take his place?

There had been at least three Pythias in the past twenty years. *My mother. Mallory Mills. The Pythia who'd given birth to Beau.* In all likelihood, there had been more.

Had each woman had a child? Had all of the would-be Nines been tested and found unworthy? Turned out to die?

You don't care to be replaced.

Without meaning to, I began walking toward the stairs. I climbed them two at a time and headed for Agent Sterling, but when I reached the top, a familiar voice froze me in my tracks.

"I'm not going anywhere." That was Sterling—and her tone was steel.

"You are." When Director Sterling gave Briggs an order, Briggs took it—but the director's daughter was another matter.

"You're not authorized—" Agent Sterling started to say, but her father cut her off.

"I'm not authorized to tell the Naturals what cases they can and cannot work. You saw to that, Veronica. I am, however, authorized as your superior in this organization to pull *my* agents off of a case—and that includes you."

"We're *this close*. You can't—"

"I can and I am, Agent. I let you chase this lead, and you ran it into the ground. You've identified one individual connected with this group. Now Lowell is gone, and he's not coming back." The director's verbal onslaught stopped, but only for a moment. "Briggs has three bodies, Veronica. Three crime scenes, three victims, three sets of persons of interest. *That* is where your attention should be focused—and starting tonight, it will be."

There was a long pause—Agent Sterling donning her inner armor. "The last time you pulled me off a case, Scarlett had just been murdered." Sterling could be just as merciless as her father. "If you hadn't interfered then, we might not be in this position now."

"Have you even told the Hobbes girl about the third body?" Director Sterling shot back. His voice was soft, but his words hit me like a hammer to the chest.

He'd asked if she'd told me. Not Dean, not Lia, not Michael, not Sloane. *Me.* My throat tightened as I pictured the first two victims in my mind.

I pushed the door to the basement open and stepped out. "What about the third body?"

Michael came to stand beside me, his gaze locked on Agent Sterling's face. I had no idea what he saw there, but whatever it was had him stepping in front of me, like he could protect me from the answer to the question I'd just asked.

"The third victim," I reiterated, my voice dry and hoarse, focusing on Agent Sterling and ignoring her father. "You and Briggs never said anything about the third victim."

Michael glanced wordlessly at Dean, who moved to my other side, his body close enough to mine that I should have been able to feel the heat off of it.

I couldn't feel anything.

"Cassie . . ." Agent Sterling took a step forward. I took a step back.

"The first two victims were persons of interest in our prior cases," I said. "Following the same pattern . . ."

I trailed off, because even without Michael's ability, I could see in Agent Sterling's eyes that the third victim wasn't just a person of interest in one of our cases.

I'd thought that our killer's choice of victims was either meant as punishment for coming to Gaither or a distraction to lure us away.

Not us, I realized. *It was never about us.*

I went for my cell phone. It was dead. How long had it been since I charged it? How many phone calls had I missed?

"Cassie," Agent Sterling said again. "The third victim—you know her."

YOU

Too little, too late. If they'd discovered anyone's identity but Nine's, you could order the leak eliminated at the source— and, oh, how you'd like to see the old bastard bleed.

To make him *bleed.*

But he commands the others' respect—their reverence— and you're the one who's bleeding. You're the one they chain, the one they purify with flame and blade and fingers wrapped around your throat.

They want you to pass judgment. They want you to say yes.

Lorelai would die to protect Cassie. Lorelai would never give them what they want. But you aren't Lorelai.

When you say the words, they release you from the chains. Your body slumps to the floor. They leave you with nothing but a torch to light the tomb.

"Mommy?" The little voice echoes through this cavernous space as Laurel emerges from the shadows. You can see Lorelai in the child, see Cassie.

Lorelai tries to fight her way to the surface as Laurel comes closer, but you're stronger than she is.

"Mommy?"

Your gaze locks onto hers. Laurel is silent and still, and then, looking more like a ghost than a child, her eyes harden.

"You're not my mommy."

You hum under your breath. "Mommy had to go away," you tell her, stepping forward to caress her hair, a smile playing at the edges of your lips. "And Laurel? Mommy isn't coming back."

CHAPTER 56

When my phone was charged, I saw that I had a half-dozen missed calls—all of them from my grandmother. Nonna had raised seven children. She had nearly two dozen grandchildren.

One less now. I'd spent five years living with my father's family. Kate was the cousin closest to my own age, just three years my senior. And now, she was dead—strung up like a scarecrow and burned alive. Because of me.

You did this, I thought. I forced myself to repeat the words a second time, aiming them not at myself and not at the UNSUB.

Every instinct I had said that the person who'd marked my cousin for death was the one person I'd loved more than anything—forever and ever, no matter what.

You wanted me out of Gaither, didn't you, Mom? You wanted me safe. You wouldn't bat an eye at trading Kate's life for mine. You've done it before.

324

My mother had left her little sister—the sister she'd protected for *years*—with an abusive father as soon as she'd found out she was pregnant with me. She'd traded Lacey's future, her safety, for mine.

You knew that if the ties to our previous cases didn't work, if those didn't get me out of Gaither—this would.

"What are you going to do?" Sloane asked me quietly. We were back at the hotel.

"Malcolm Lowell is in the wind. We solved the Kyle murders." I paused, looking out the window at historic Main Street. "My mother knew exactly what I would do." I swallowed hard. "I'm going to go home."

I had one stop to make before leaving Gaither. I'd spent years not knowing if my mother was dead or alive. I'd lived that limbo, unable to mourn, unable to move on.

Ree Simon deserved to know what had happened to her daughter.

When we got to the diner, the others split off, giving me the space to do what needed to be done. As Michael, Dean, Lia, and Sloane slid into a booth, Agent Sterling came up beside me. "Are you sure you want to do this alone?"

I thought of my cousin Kate. We'd never been close. I'd never *let* her get close. Because I'd been raised to keep people at a distance. Because I was my mother's daughter.

"I'm sure," I said.

Sterling and Judd took seats of their own. Agent Starmans joined them several minutes later. It occurred to me, on some level, to wonder where Celine had gone, but when Ree saw me standing in front of the counter, I did what I could to keep myself in the moment.

To feel for her what I couldn't feel for myself.

After filling cups with coffee for both Sterling and Judd, Ree turned to me. She wiped her hands on her apron and gave me an assessing once-over. "What can I do for you, Cassie?"

"I have something to tell you," I said, my voice surprisingly solid, surprisingly even. "It's about your daughter."

"Sarah?" Ree arched her brows, her chin thrusting slightly outward. "What about her?"

"Can we sit down?" I asked Ree.

Once we were ensconced in a booth, I laid a folder on the table between us and removed the picture that Celine had drawn. "Is this Sarah?"

"Sure is," Ree replied steadily. "She looks a bit like Melody there."

I nodded. My mouth wasn't dry. My eyes weren't wet. But I felt those words, all the way to my core.

"Sarah didn't leave Gaither," I told Ree, taking her hand. "She didn't leave her kids. She didn't leave you."

"Yes," Ree replied tersely, "she did."

I amended my previous statement. "She never left Serenity Ranch." Knowing in my gut that Ree wouldn't believe me without proof, I withdrew a photograph from the file—Sarah's body.

Ree was smart. She connected the dots—and abruptly rejected the conclusion. "That could be anyone."

"Facial reconstruction says it's Sarah. We'll do a DNA test as well, but a witness has verified that Sarah was killed ten years ago by a man named Darren Darby."

"Darby." That was all Ree said.

You never looked for her. You never knew.

"Melody is home now." Ree stood abruptly. "I suppose I have you to thank for that." She said nothing, not a single word, about her daughter. "I'll get you some coffee."

Watching as Ree busied herself with the task, I pulled a picture up on my phone, one I'd taken months before of a locket that Laurel had worn around her neck—and the photo inside. In it, my half sister sat on my mother's lap.

How many times had I looked at this picture?

How many times had I wondered who—and what—my mother was now?

"Mind if I join you?" Celine slid into the booth across from me.

"Where have you been?" I asked, my gaze still on my mother's picture.

"Here and there," Celine replied. "Bodies don't creep me out. Murders do. I decided pretty quickly that Creepy Serial Killer House probably fell closer to your expertise than mine."

Ree returned with two cups of coffee, one for me and one for Celine. "Here you go."

Ree didn't want to talk. She didn't want this—any of it—to be real. I could relate.

"Who's that?" Celine asked, craning her head to get a better look at the photo on my phone.

"My mother," I replied, feeling like that answer was only half true. "And my half sister."

"I see the resemblance," Celine replied. Then she paused. "Mind if I take a closer look?"

She took the phone without waiting for a reply. I closed my eyes and took a long drink of my coffee. Instead of thinking about my mother, about Kate, strung up like a scarecrow and burned alive, about Nonna and what this would do to her, I fell back on an old game, profiling everyone around me.

Behavior. Personality. Environment. Without looking, I knew that Dean was facing away from me. *You want to come to me, but you won't—not until you know that I want you to.*

I switched from second person to third, playing this game the way I would have when I was young. *Michael is reading me. Lia is next to Dean, pretending that she's not worried. Sloane is counting—the tiles on the floor, the cracks in the wall, the number of patrons in the room all around her.*

I opened my eyes, and the room swam around me. I thought, at first, that there were tears in my eyes, that thinking of the family I'd found in the program had broken the dam inside of me and let in the grief for my family of blood.

But the room didn't stop spinning. It stayed blurred. I opened my mouth to say something, but words wouldn't come. My tongue felt thick. I was dizzy, nauseous.

My right hand found its way to the cup of coffee.

The coffee, I thought, unable to form the words out loud. Even my thoughts were scrambled. I tried to stand up, but fell. I grabbed for the booth, and my hand hit Celine's thigh instead.

She didn't move.

She's slumped over. Unconscious. I fought my way to my feet. The world kept spinning, but as I stumbled forward, I realized—the room was silent. No one was talking. No one was coming to help me.

Dean and Lia, Michael and Sloane—they were slumped in their booths, too.

Unconscious, I thought. *Or . . . or . . .*

Someone caught me under my armpits. "Easy there." Ree's voice came to me from a great distance. I tried to tell her, tried to make my mouth say the word, but I couldn't.

Poison.

"It's not that I don't appreciate what you did for Melody— or for Sarah." As the world went black, Ree leaned down. "But all must be tested," she whispered. "All must be found worthy."

CHAPTER 57

I woke up in darkness. The floor beneath me was cold and made of stone. My head hurt. My body hurt—and that was when I remembered.

Ree. The coffee. All of the others, slumped over . . .

I tried to push myself to my feet, but couldn't stand. My body felt heavy and numb, like my limbs belonged to someone else.

"It will wear off."

My head snapped up as my eyes searched through the darkness for the source of that voice. I heard the strike of a lighter, and a second later, a torch flamed to life on the wall.

Ree stood before me, looking every bit the woman I remembered. *No-nonsense. Warm.*

"You're one of them?" I meant it as a statement, but the words came out a question.

"I *was* retired." Ree obliged me with an answer. "Until my

former apprentice got himself killed." She gave me a look. "I understand I have you to thank for that."

"You recruited Nightshade."

She snorted. "*Nightshade.* Boy always did have notions—but I owed his grandfather, and the old man was insistent that I choose him as my heir."

"You owed Malcolm Lowell." My brain whirred. "Because he was the one who brought you to the Masters' attention."

Ree smiled fondly. "I was younger then. My no-good husband had left me. My no-good daughter was already showing signs of being her father's daughter. Malcolm started coming by the diner. Never was a man as good at seeing secrets as that one."

Secrets. Like the fact that you had a homicidal streak.

"Malcolm saw something in me," Ree continued softly. "He asked me what I would do if I ever saw Sarah's father again."

The man who left you, pregnant and alone.

"You would have killed him." The feeling was starting to come back into my body. I became hyperaware of the world around me—the rough stone floor, the crackling of the fire, the shackles on the wall. "He left you, and people who leave deserve what they get."

Ree shook her head fondly. "You always did favor your mama—good at reading people."

You tried to help my mom, and she left. She didn't even say good-bye. I thought back to Michael's read on Ree the first time we'd met her. He'd said that Ree had been fond of my mother, but that there was anger there, too.

"Were you the one who suggested my mother as Pythia?" I asked. "You knew that she was alone in the world, except for me. You had to have at least suspected that there was abuse in her past."

Ree didn't reply.

"You told me once that we, every one of us, reap what we sow. To become one of the Masters, you had to kill nine people." I paused, thinking of the victims on the wall back at Quantico. "You chose people who deserved it. People like your husband. People who *left*." When I didn't get a reaction, I continued. "Life is full of drowning people," I said, continuing to parrot her own words back at her, "ready and willing to drown you, too—unless you drown them first."

For a moment, I thought Ree might snap. I thought she might reach for me. But instead, she closed her eyes. "You have no idea how different the world looks once you know what it's like to watch some son of a bitch who abandoned his four kids crumple to the ground. His eyes roll back in his head. His body seizes. Then the pain comes. He scratches at himself, at the walls, at the floor—until his nails are bloody. Until there's nothing left but pain."

The picture Ree was painting was familiar. Beau Donovan had died from Nightshade's poison. He'd scratched at himself, at the floor . . .

You chose Nightshade. You trained him. You have a gift for poisons. It made sense. Statistically, poison was a woman's weapon. And when the patrons of the Not-A-Diner had started answering our questions about Mason Kyle's family, Ree had shut the conversation down with a single word. *Enough.*

I pushed myself unsteadily to my feet. I was still weak—too weak to be a threat.

"The people you killed deserved to die," I said, playing into her pathology. "But what about me? Is this what I deserve?"

I willed her to see me as the child I'd once been—one that she'd been fond of.

"I don't leave people," I continued. "I'm the one who gets left." My voice shook slightly. "What about my friends, back at the diner? Did they deserve to die?"

Until now, I hadn't let myself even think those words. I hadn't let myself remember Celine slumped in the booth across from me. *Michael and Lia and Sloane and Dean. Agent Sterling. Judd.*

I stared at the psychopath across from me. *Tell me they were unconscious. Tell me you just drugged them. Tell me they're alive.*

"You came to Gaither asking questions," Ree said sternly. "Running around with your FBI friends, making us wonder if there was some memory buried in your head—some clue—that would lead you straight to our door. You found Malcolm. It was only a matter of time before you found the rest of us, too."

"Are we still in Gaither?" I asked. "Are we nearby?"

Ree didn't answer the question. "There were some who wanted you dead—*all* of you," she said instead. "Others made a case for an alternative solution."

I thought about what Nightshade had told me about the Pythia. She was judge and jury. She was the one they tortured, purifying her so that she could pass judgment.

Again. And again. And again.

My mother had tried to get me out of Gaither. Had they broken her? Had she told them to bring me here?

The sound of a door creaking open ripped me from those thoughts. A figure in a hooded robe stood in the door. The hood fell down over his face, obscuring his features.

"I'd like a word with our guest."

Ree snorted. Clearly, she didn't think too much of the guy in the hood. The exchange told me something about the power dynamics at play here. *You're a veteran. He's a blowhard on the front lines for the first time.*

I turned my attention from Ree to the man in the hood. *You're young, and you're new. She's a Master, and you're not— not yet.*

I was looking at the man who'd killed my cousin. The one who'd killed Tory and Bryce. And there was something familiar about him, something familiar about his voice. . . .

"I told you once," the hooded figure intoned, "that if you gaze long enough into the abyss, the abyss will gaze back into you."

"Friedrich Nietzsche." I recognized the quote—and the haughty, overblown delivery. *"TA Geoff?"*

I'd met him on the Redding case, when he'd attempted to pick me up in the wake of a girl's death by sharing his "vast" knowledge of serial killers. I'd spent an evening in an abandoned lecture hall with this guy, Michael, and Bryce.

"It's Geoffrey," he corrected tersely, lowering his hood. "And *your* name isn't Veronica."

The last time we'd met, I'd given him a fake name. "Really?" I said. "That's the issue you really think is worth discussing here?"

When last we'd met, I'd pegged Geoffrey as being low on empathy and high on himself—but he hadn't struck me as a killer. *You weren't then. You weren't even an apprentice. Death was a game to you. It was abstract.*

How had the Masters found him?

"You're asking yourself how you could have been so wrong about me," Geoffrey said smugly. "I know all about you, Cassandra Hobbes. I know that you were investigating the Daniel Redding case. I know that you helped catch *his* apprentices." He offered me a twisted smile. "But you didn't catch me."

You killed Bryce—she always did get under your skin. Then the Pythia whispered in your ear. Did she play to your ego? Tell you who to kill? Was she the abyss, looking at and into you?

I took a step forward on legs that weren't as unsteady as they'd been a moment before. "You burned those girls." I let myself sound mesmerized, playing to his ego the way my mother had. "You strung them up, and you burned them, and you left no evidence behind." I stared at and into him. "You need nine, but the nine *you* will choose?" My voice was low, seductive as I advanced on him. "They'll make you legendary."

"Enough," Ree snapped. She stepped between Geoffrey and me. "She's playing you," she informed him. "And I don't have the time or stomach to stand here and watch."

Geoffrey's eyes narrowed. His hands hung loosely by his sides. One minute, he was just standing there, and the next, his left hand had reached for the torch. "Let me test her," he said. "Let me purify her, bit by bit."

The flame flickered. *You want to burn me. You want to watch me scream.*

"No," Ree said. "Your time will come—after your ninth kill and not a second before." She removed something from her pocket—a small, round tub, no larger than a container of lip gloss. "Over time," she told me, unscrewing the lid, "one builds up immunity to poisons."

She dipped her finger into a colorless paste.

I thought of Beau, who'd died screaming, and of everything Judd had told me about Nightshade's poison of choice. *Incurable. Painful. Fatal.*

Ree's left hand closed around my chin. She jerked my face to the side, her grip like steel.

Too late, I tried to fight. Too late, my hands tried to block hers.

She smeared the paste down my neck.

Some poisons don't have to be ingested. My heart thudded in my chest. *Some poisons can be absorbed through the skin.*

Ree let go of me and stepped back. At first, I felt nothing. And then, the world exploded into pain.

CHAPTER 58

My body was on fire. Every nerve, every inch of skin—even the blood in my veins was boiling.

On the ground. Seizing. God, help me—

Someone, help me—

My fingers scraped against my throat. On some level, I was aware that I was tearing at my own flesh. On some level, I was aware that I was bleeding.

On some level, I heard the screams.

My throat closed around them. I couldn't breathe. I was suffocating, and I didn't care, because all there was—all *I* was—was pain.

On some level, I was aware of the sound of footsteps rushing into the room.

On some level, I was aware of someone saying my name.

On some level, I was aware of arms hoisting me upward.

But all there was . . . all I was . . .

Pain.

I dreamt of dancing in the snow. My mother was beside me, her head tilted back, her tongue darting between her lips to catch a snowflake.

The scene jumped. I stood in the wings of the stage as my mother performed. My gaze fell on an old man in the audience.

Malcolm Lowell.

Without warning, my mother and I were back in the snow, dancing.

Dancing.

Dancing.

Forever and ever. No matter what.

I woke to the sound of beeping. I was lying on something soft. Forcing my eyes open, I remembered—

The poison.

The pain.

The sound of footsteps.

"Easy."

I turned my head toward the voice, unable to sit up. I was in a hospital room. The beeping machine beside me tracked the beating of my heart.

"You've been unconscious for two days." Director Sterling sat next to my bed. "We weren't sure you were going to make it."

We. I remembered the sound of footsteps. I remembered someone saying my name.

"Agent Sterling?" I asked. "Judd. Dean and the others—"

"They're fine," Director Sterling assured me. "As are you."

I remembered the poison. I remembered gasping for breath. I remembered the pain.

"How?" I said. Beneath the covers, my body shook.

"There's an antidote." Director Sterling kept his answer direct and to the point. "The window during which to administer it is small, but you should be back to your full strength soon."

I wanted to ask where they'd gotten the antidote. I wanted to ask how they'd found me. But more than anything, I wanted the others. I wanted Dean and Lia and Michael and Sloane.

Beside me, Director Sterling held up a small object for my inspection. I recognized it instantly—the tracking device Agent Sterling had given me. "This time my daughter had the foresight to activate the device." He paused.

For reasons I couldn't quite pinpoint, my breath caught in my throat.

"It's a shame," the director continued slowly, turning the device over in his hand, "that the tracking software that would have led the FBI here had been tampered with."

A chill slid down my spine.

"Dean," I said suddenly. "If he knew where I was, if they'd found me . . ."

"He'd be here?" Director Sterling suggested. "Given what I know of Redding's whelp, I tend to agree."

I surged upward and winced as something bit into my wrists. I looked down.

Handcuffs.

Someone had tampered with the tracking software. Someone had cuffed me to this bed. I looked back up at the director.

"This isn't a hospital," I said, my heart beating in my throat.

"No," he replied. "It's not."

"There's an antidote to the Masters' poison," I repeated what Director Sterling had told me earlier, my chest tightening. "But the FBI doesn't have it."

"No. They don't."

The poison the Masters used to kill was one of a kind. It was, I'd been told over and over again, incurable.

Because the only people who have the cure are the Masters.

I flashed back to the room with the shackles, to the poison, to the pain. I'd heard footsteps. I'd heard someone saying my name.

"For some of us," the director said, his voice low and smooth, "this has never been about murder. For some of us, it was always *power*."

There are seven Masters. And one of them is the director of the FBI.

Agent Sterling's father stood and stared down at me. "Imagine a group more powerful, more connected than any you could possibly conceive of. Imagine the most *extraordinary* men on earth, sworn to one another and a common cause. Imagine the kind of loyalty that comes from knowing that if one of you falls, you all fall. Imagine knowing that if you could prove yourself worthy, the world would be yours for the taking."

"How long?" I asked the director. *How long have you been one of them?*

"I was young," the director said. "Ambitious. And look how far I've come." He spread his arms out, as if he could gesture to all of the FBI, all of the power he held as its head.

"Masters only have a seat at the table for twenty-one years," I said. My voice was hoarse—from screaming, from hoping, from knowing that this was about to get worse.

"My time as an active member had come to an end," Director Sterling admitted. "But the Pythia rather obligingly slit my successor's throat." He withdrew a knife from his jacket pocket. "I can't say I mind. Certain privileges are only afforded to those with a seat at the table." He lifted the knife to the side of my face. I waited for the pain, but it didn't come. Instead, he lifted his free hand to the other cheek, trailing it gently over my skin. "Other privileges aren't impossible to obtain as an emeritus member."

I shuddered beneath his touch.

"Scarlett Hawkins." I fought the only way I could, cuffed and held at knifepoint. "You knew that she'd been killed by one of your brethren."

The director's knuckles tightened around the hilt of the knife. "Scarlett was never supposed to be a target."

"Nightshade killed her," I shot back. "He didn't care that she was one of yours."

Director Sterling angled the blade at the underside of my chin and pressed just hard enough to draw blood. "I made my displeasure known—at the time, and again . . . later."

He lowered the knife. I could feel the blood dripping down my neck.

"You killed Nightshade," I said, the truth coming into focus. "Somehow, you got past the guards—"

"I *chose* the guards," the director corrected, a light in his eyes. "I arranged the shift changes. I oversaw the prisoner's transfer myself."

I saw what I should have seen before—the kind of access he'd had, the fact that as soon as we'd had a break in this case, he'd sent us on a wild goose chase after Celine.

"You knew where Laurel was being held," I said, my voice cracking.

"The child is back in the proper hands."

I thought of Laurel staring at the chains on the playground. I thought of the way she'd said the word *blood*.

"You *monster*." The word ripped its way out of my mouth. "All this time, you treated Dean like he was less than human because of what his father had done, and the whole time, you were worse."

"The whole time, I was *better*." Director Sterling surged forward, his face inches from my own. "Daniel Redding was an amateur who thought himself an artist. And his son dared to lay a hand on *my* daughter?"

Show your hand, Director. Show me your weaknesses.

I saw the exact moment he recognized my strategy for what it was. His eyes were cold and assessing as he leaned back. "I watched the tape of your interview with Redding, you know." He let those words sink in. "And he was right. Your mother *is* the type of person who can be forged in the fire." He stood and began walking toward the door. "She's everything we could have hoped for—and more."

YOU

Cassie is here. They have her. That's hardly a surprise. You're the one who gave the word, the one who told the poison Master to take Cassie and let the FBI director use his resources to lay a false path for her team to follow—far, far away from all of you.

"It's not that I want to kill her," you murmur as Lorelai fights weakly for control. "But if it's her or us . . ."

The door opens. Nine enters. Malcolm. He stares at you, then glances over at Laurel, who's asleep in the corner. The child was born to replace him. He'll see her dead first.

"The first test will come when she's six," the old man comments, his voice eerily calm. "It'll be a kitten, perhaps, or a puppy. She'll need to take it slow. When she's nine, it will be a prostitute, bound and strapped to the table of stone. And when she's twelve . . ." His gaze flickers from Laurel back to you. "We'll strap you to the table."

You read between the lines. "You killed your own mother."

"And embalmed her corpse so that she could continue to sit at the table, perfectly preserved, for decades." He shook his head. "Eventually, she was replaced. Woman after woman, child after child, and none were worthy."

You can feel the blood thrumming in your veins as you remember the feel of the knife in Five's flesh.

You are worthy.

"It's been too long since you've been tested," Nine continues.

"There's something poetic, don't you think, about the nature of this one?"

He thinks you're Lorelai.

He thinks Cassie is *your daughter.*

He thinks there are some things you wouldn't do to survive.

CHAPTER 59

Rough hands grasped me as a bag was thrown over my head. I wasn't sure how long it had been since the director had left the room or who the men were who'd just entered it. I heard the handcuffs click open, and an instant later I was jerked to my feet.

This is it, I thought, unsure of where they were leading me or what might be waiting there.

I heard the creaking of metal. *A door?*

A hand in the middle of my back shoved me forward, hard enough to send me to the ground. My knees hit first, my hands catching the rest of my body moments before my face would have slammed into the ground. My palms registered the texture beneath them—*sand*—just before the hood was torn from my head.

I blinked against the blinding light, my eyes adjusting slowly enough that by the time I could make out the world around me, the men who'd brought me to this place were gone. I turned in time to see a metal gate slamming into the ground behind me.

I was locked in.

In where? I forced myself to concentrate. I was still indoors, but the ground was covered in sand, almost too hot to bear, like the desert sun had been shining down on it for days. The ceiling overhead was high and domed, made of stone and carved with a symbol I recognized.

Seven circles ringing a cross.

The room was circular, and recessed into the walls were stone seats, looking down on the sandpit below.

Not a pit, I thought. *An arena.*

And that was when I knew. *You poisoned me. You healed me.* Buried deep in my memory, I could hear the words Nightshade had spoken to me all those weeks ago. He'd told me that we all had our choices. He'd told me that the Pythia chooses to live.

Perhaps someday that choice will be yours, Cassandra.

The Masters had a history of taking women—women who had traumatic histories, women who were capable of being forged into something new. They brought their captives to the brink of death, close enough to taste it, and then . . .

A figure stepped forward from the shadows. My gaze flicked to either side, and I noticed seven weapons laid out along the wall behind me.

Seven Masters. Seven ways of killing.

The figure on the other side of the arena took another step forward, then another. I was aware of hooded figures filing into the seats above us, but all I could think was that if they'd brought me here to fight the Pythia, that meant that the woman walking toward me was someone I knew very well.

Her face was hidden by a hood, but as I made my way to my feet and stepped toward her, drawn like a moth to the flame, she lowered it.

Her face had changed in the past six years. She hadn't aged, but she was thinner and pale and her features looked like they'd been carved from stone. Her skin was porcelain, her eyes impossibly large.

She was still the most beautiful woman I'd ever seen.

"Mom." The word escaped my throat. One second, I was stepping hesitantly toward her, and the next, the space between us had disappeared.

"Cassie." Her voice was deeper than I remembered, hoarse, and when her arms wrapped around me, I realized that the skin on her face looked smooth in part because of contrast.

The rest of her body was covered in twisting, puckered scars.

Seven days and seven pains. I made a choking sound. My mother pulled me up against her, laying my head on her shoulder. She pressed her lips to my temple.

"You shouldn't be here," she said.

"I had to find you. Once I realized you were alive, once I realized they had you—I couldn't stop looking. I would *never* stop looking."

"I know."

There was something in my mother's tone that reminded me that we were being watched. Over her shoulder, I could see the Masters—six men and one woman, sitting in a line. *Director Sterling. Ree.* I tried to memorize the others' faces, but my gaze was drawn upward.

Malcolm Lowell sat above the others, his eyes locked on mine.

Nine is the greatest among us, the bridge from generation to generation. . . .

"We have to get out of here." I kept my voice low. "We have to—"

"We can't," my mother said. "There is no *out*, Cassie. Not for us."

I tried to pull back so that I could see her face, but her arms tightened around me, holding me close.

Tight.

In the stands, Ree caught my gaze and then shifted hers to the far wall. Like the one behind me, it was lined with weapons.

Six of them. *Not seven. Six.*

"Where's the knife?" I choked on the words. "Mom—"

The hand that had been stroking my hair a moment before grasped it tightly now. She jerked my head to the side.

"Mom—"

She raised the knife to the side of my throat. "It isn't personal. It's you, or it's me."

I'd been warned, over and over again, that my mother might not be the woman I remembered.

"You don't want to do this," I said, my voice shaking.

"But that's the thing," she whispered, her eyes lighting on mine. "I *do*."

CHAPTER 60

My mother would never have hurt me. My mother had left home for *me*. She'd left her own sister for *me*. She'd been my everything, and I'd been hers.

Whatever you are, you aren't my mother. That thought took root, deep in my brain, as I thought of Lia telling me that she'd been instructed as a child to pretend that the bad things hadn't happened to *her*. That the things she'd done hadn't been the work of *her* hands. I thought of Laurel telling me that *she* didn't play the game.

Nine did.

In Laurel's case, her inner Nine wasn't a full-fledged person. *But you are.*

"Seven days and seven pains," I said softly. "They tortured her. Over and over and over again. They forced themselves on her, one by one, until she was pregnant with Laurel."

I saw the exact moment that my captor realized I wasn't talking to myself.

"I wondered how a person could survive something like that, but that's the thing. *She* didn't survive it." The blade still against my neck, I pushed down the urge to swallow. "*You* did."

She loosened her grip on my hair.

People look at you, and they see her. They love her. But you're the strong one. You're the one who matters. You're the one who deserves to be seen.

"Were you born here?" I asked, watching her face for any clue that my words had hit their target. "Or have you been around for much, much longer?"

A bit more slack. It wasn't enough. She had the knife. I didn't.

"Do you have a name?" I asked.

No one has ever asked. No one has ever looked at you and seen.

The woman with my mother's face smiled. She closed her eyes. And then, she let me go. "My name," she said, her voice echoing loudly enough for the Masters to hear, "is Cassandra."

I scrambled backward, a chill spreading over my arms.

"Lorelai didn't even know I existed," the woman—Cassandra—said. "She didn't know that all of those times, when her father came into our room and she blacked out, it wasn't a mercy. It wasn't luck. It was *me*." Cassandra circled me, her stride predatory. "When you came along, when she named you, I liked to think that it was a thank-you, even if she didn't realize what she'd done." Cassandra's grip on the knife tightened. "And then you were there, and suddenly, Lorelai didn't need me so much anymore. She was stronger, for *you*. And I was locked away."

Step by careful step, I made my way toward the back wall, toward the weapons, profiling her with every step. *You're in control. You're strong. You do what needs to be done—and you like it.*

Whatever this splintered piece of my mother's psyche had been before the Masters had gotten ahold of her, she was something else now.

You will kill me. I didn't make the conscious choice to pick up the knife from my weapons cache, but one second it was on the ground, and the next, it was in my hand. I thought of my mother's dressing room, splattered in blood. I thought of dancing on the side of the road in the snow, of my mom's face aimed heavenward, her tongue catching snowflakes.

You will kill me. The knife was heavy in my hand as she approached. *If I don't kill you first.*

My heartbeat slowed. My hand tightened around the blade. And then, without warning, I knew, the way I so often knew things about other people, that I couldn't use the blade.

I couldn't kill this monster without killing my mother, too.

Perhaps, Nightshade had told me, *someday, that choice will be yours.*

I let my hands fall to my sides. "I can't hurt you. I won't."

I expected to see victory in my opponent's eyes. Instead, I saw fear.

Why? I wondered. And then I realized. *You fight. You survive. You protect Lorelai—but what if there's nothing to protect her from?*

"I'm not a threat." I stopped moving, stopped fighting. "Home isn't a place," I said, my voice as hoarse as hers had been earlier. "It's not having a bed to come home to, or a yard, or a Christmas tree at the holidays. Home is the people who love you."

She held the knife out in front of her body as she closed the space between us, watching for any hint of movement in my hand.

I let my knife fall to the ground.

"Home is the people who love you," I said again. "I had a home growing up, and I have one now. I have people who love me, people I love. I have a family, and they would die for me." I lowered my voice to a whisper. "Just like I would die for you."

Not for *Cassandra*. Not for the Pythia. Not even for Lorelai, whoever she was and had become.

For my mom. For the woman who'd taught me to dance it off. For the one who'd kissed every skinned knee and taught me to read people and told me, every single day, that I was loved.

"I will kill you," Cassandra hissed. "I'll like it."

You want me to pick up the knife. You want me to fight.

"Forever and ever." I closed my eyes. I waited.

Forever and ever.
Forever and ever.
"No matter what."

I wasn't the one who'd spoken those words. I opened my eyes.

The woman holding the knife was shaking. "Forever and ever, Cassie. *No matter what.*"

CHAPTER 61

My mother's shaking hands explored my face. "Oh, baby," she whispered. "You got so big."

Something broke inside of me at the sound of my mother's voice, the expressiveness of her features, the familiarity of her touch.

"And so beautiful." Her voice broke. "Oh, baby. No." She jerked back. "*No, no, no* . . . You're not supposed to be here."

"As touching as this reunion is . . ." Director Sterling stood. "The task remains unchanged."

My mother tried to take a step back from me, but I wouldn't let her. I lowered my voice—too low for the watching Masters to hear. "They can't make us do this."

Her gaze went hollow. "They can make you do anything."

My eyes went to the scars on her arms, her chest—every inch of exposed skin, except for her face. Some were smooth. Some were puckered. Some were healing still.

In the stands, Malcolm Lowell stood. One by one, the Masters followed suit.

I bent to pick my knife up off the ground. We could fight—not all of them, and maybe not for long, but it was better than the alternative.

"I don't want this," my mom said. "For you."

The scars. The pain. The role of the Pythia.

"My team will find us." I channeled Lia and willed those words to sound true. "Wherever this place is, they won't stop looking. They'll figure out that the director is working against them. We just have to buy them time."

My mom stared at me, and I realized that even though she *was* the person who'd raised me and loved me and made me what I was, I still couldn't read her, not the way I could anyone else. I didn't know what she was thinking. I didn't know what she had been through—not really.

I didn't know what it meant when she nodded.

What are you saying yes to?

The sound of a door opening and shutting alerted me to the return of Malcolm Lowell. *I didn't even know he left.* When I saw what he'd gone to fetch, I stopped breathing.

Laurel.

She was born to take Malcolm's place, to be the next Nine. And now, he had his hands on her shoulders. He shoved her toward Director Sterling, who grasped Laurel by the arm.

I saw now what my mother had meant.

They can make you do anything.

The director slid a knife out of his own pocket. "You fight," he said, holding the blade to Laurel's throat, "or she dies."

The director didn't wait for a response before he began to cut. Just a little. Just a warning. Laurel didn't scream. She didn't move. But the high-pitched mewling that came out of her throat hit me like a physical blow.

"How sure are you that your team will find you?" My mother bent down to pick up her own blade. "We're halfway to the desert, in the middle of nowhere, underground. If they dig into Malcolm's past, if they go back far enough, they might see a pattern, but most people wouldn't."

Dean. Michael. Lia. Sloane.

"I'm sure," I said. "Wherever we are, they'll find us."

My mother nodded. "Okay."

"Okay?" I repeated. *What are you saying?*

She advanced on me. "We have to fight. Laurel's just a baby, Cassie. She's you, and she's me, and she's *ours*. Do you understand?"

They can make you do anything.

"You have to kill me." My mother's words sliced into me, ice-cold and uncompromising.

"No," I said.

"*Yes.*" My mother circled me, the way her alter ego had earlier. "You have to fight, Cassie. One of us has to die."

"No." I was shaking my head and backing away from her, but I couldn't make myself take my eyes off the knife.

You don't have to play the game anymore. The promise I'd

made my sister came back to me. *Not ever again. You don't have to be Nine.*

"Take the knife, Cassie," my mother said. *"Use it."*

You do it, I thought. *You kill me.* I understood now why she'd asked me how sure I was that help was coming. *If you thought you were dooming me to life as the Pythia, you'd give me mercy. You'd plunge your knife into my chest to save me from your fate.*

But I'd told her that I was sure.

A piercing scream cut through the air. Laurel wasn't silent now. She wasn't stoic. She wasn't Nine.

She's just a baby. He's hurting her. He'll kill her if I don't—
No.

"Yes," my mother said, closing the space between us. She'd always known exactly what I was thinking. She'd known me the way only someone with our particular skill set could.

Someone who loves me, forever and ever.

"Do it," my mother insisted, pressing her knife into my hand. "You have to, baby. You are the best thing I ever did—the only good thing I ever did. I can't be that for Laurel, not now." She wasn't crying. She wasn't panicked.

She was sure.

"But you can," she continued. "You can love her. You can be there for her. You can get out of here, and you can live. And to do that . . ." She placed her left hand over my right hand, guiding the knife to her chest. "You have to kill me."

Dancing in the snow. Curled up in her lap. Behavior. Personality. Environment.

I love you. I love you. I—

Her grip on my hand tightened. Her body blocking the motion from the Masters, she jerked me forward. *My hand on the knife. Her hand on mine.* I felt the blade slide into her chest. She gasped, blood blooming around the wound. I wanted to pull the knife out.

But for Laurel, I didn't.

"Forever and ever," I whispered, holding the knife in place. I held *her*. She slumped forward, bleeding, the light beginning to drain from her eyes.

I love you. I love you. I love you. I didn't look away. I didn't so much as blink, not even when I heard a door slam open.

Not even when I heard Agent Briggs's familiar voice. "Freeze!"

My mom isn't moving. Her heart isn't beating. Her eyes— they don't see me. I pulled the knife out of her chest, and her body fell to the ground as FBI agents poured into the room.

I love you. I love you. I love you.

Gone.

CHAPTER 62

On some level, I was aware of the fact that shots were being fired. On some level, I was aware of the fact that arrests were being made. But as I stood there, the bloody knife in my hand, I couldn't bring myself to look up. I couldn't watch.

I couldn't look at anything but the body.

My mother's red hair was splayed out around her, a halo of fire against the bright white of the sand. Her lips were dry and cracked, her eyes unseeing.

"Put down the knife!" Agent Sterling's voice sounded like it was coming from very far away. "Step away from the girl."

It took me a moment to realize that she wasn't talking to me. She wasn't talking about my knife. I turned, forcing my eyes to the stands.

To the director.

To Laurel.

He was crouched behind her, his knife at her throat. "We walk out of here," he said, "or the child doesn't."

"You don't kill children." It took me a moment to realize that I was the one who'd said the words. Of the hundreds of victims we'd identified as being the work of the Masters, not one of them had been a child. When Beau Donovan had failed their test, they hadn't taken a knife to his throat.

They'd left him in the desert to die.

"There are rituals," I said. "There are rules."

"And yet, you're not quite eighteen yet, are you, Cassie?" The director never took his eyes off of his daughter. "I've always believed the rules are what we make of them. Isn't that right, Veronica?"

Agent Sterling stared at her father, and for an instant, I could see the little girl she'd been. *You adored him once. You respected him. You joined the FBI for him.*

She pulled the trigger.

I heard the shot, but didn't register what I'd heard until I saw the tiny red hole in her father's forehead. Director Sterling fell to the ground. As the FBI rushed Laurel, my little sister knelt, touching the wound on her captor's forehead.

She looked up and met my eyes. "The blood belongs to the Pythia," she told me, her voice haunting, almost melodic. "The blood belongs to *Nine*."

CHAPTER 63

The EMTs who treated Laurel insisted on treating me as well. I tried to tell them that the blood wasn't mine, but the words wouldn't come.

Agent Sterling sat down beside me. "You're strong. You're a survivor. None of this was your fault."

The profiler in me knew that those words weren't just for me. I'd killed my mother. She'd killed her father.

How did a person survive that?

"As touching as this moment truly is"—a voice broke into my thoughts—"some of us had to mislead, blackmail, and/or explicitly threaten at least a half-dozen federal agents to get past the police line, and we're not the kind of people who excel at *waiting*."

I looked up to see Lia standing three feet away. Sloane was pressed to her side, a fierce look on her face. Behind them, Michael had a physical grip on Dean. Every muscle in my boyfriend's body was tensed.

Michael blackmailed the feds, I thought. *You threatened them, Dean. Explicitly.*

Dean had spent his entire life keeping his emotions carefully in check, never losing control, fighting against even a hint of violence. I knew, just by the way he was standing, the way his eyes drank me in, like a man dying of thirst in a desert, unsure whether he was beholding a mirage—*you didn't care what you had to do, who you had to hurt, what you had to threaten.*

All you care about is me.

I stood, my legs shaking as I did, and Michael let Dean go. My boyfriend caught me before I fell, and something inside me shattered. The numbness that had settled over my body receded, and suddenly I could feel everything—the ache in my throat, the ghost of the pain from the poison, Dean's body folding around mine.

I could feel the knife in my hand.

I could feel myself holding my mother and watching her die.

"I killed her." My face lay on Dean's chest, the words ripped from my mouth like a tooth pulled out by force. "Dean, I—"

"You're not a killer." Dean's right hand cupped my chin, his left gently tracing the line of my jaw. "You're the person who empathizes with every victim. You carry the weight of the world on your shoulders, and if you'd been given a choice—if it had been up to you whether it was your life on the line or anyone else's—you would have *told* the

Masters to take you." Dean's voice was rough in his throat. His dark eyes searched my own. "That's what the Masters never understood. You would have walked in there willingly, knowing you wouldn't have walked out, and not just for me or Michael or Lia or Sloane—for anyone. Because that's the person you are, Cassie. Ever since you walked into your mother's dressing room, ever since you were twelve years old, part of you believed that it was your fault, that it should have been you."

I tried to pull back from him, but he held me close.

"You've been looking—and looking and looking—for some way to make it right. You're not a killer, Cassie. You just finally accepted that sometimes, the biggest sacrifice isn't made by the person who gives up her life." He lowered his forehead to touch mine. "Sometimes, the hardest thing to be is the one who lives."

My body was shaking. My hands trembled as they found their way to his chest, his neck, his face, as if touching him, feeling him beneath the pads of my fingers, might make what he was saying true.

I love you. I love you. I love you.

I heard the sobs before I realized I was sobbing. I dug my fingers into the back of his neck, his T-shirt, his shoulders, holding on for dear life.

"I love you." Dean lifted the words from my mind. "Today, tomorrow, covered in blood, haunted and waking up in the middle of the night screaming—I love you, Cassie, and I'm here, and I'm not going anywhere."

"None of us are." Sloane's voice was quiet. I knew her well enough to know that she wasn't sure whether this was a private moment, wasn't sure if she would be wanted.

But you can't stay away.

"You aren't alone," Sloane said. "And I'm not going to ask if now would be an appropriate time to hug you, because I have calculated within a reasonable margin of error that it is."

Michael didn't say anything as he piled on behind Sloane.

Lia arched an eyebrow at me. "I didn't cry when you were gone," she informed me. "I didn't break things. I didn't feel like someone had put me in a hole."

For the first time since I'd known her, Lia's voice caught on a lie.

"How did you find me?" I did Lia the favor of changing the subject.

"We didn't," Sloane said. "Celine did."

Celine? I looked for her and saw her standing behind the police line, watching from a distance, her dark hair caught in a faint wind.

"It was the picture," Agent Sterling put in. "Of your mother and Laurel." Behind her, my little sister lay curled in the back of the ambulance, asleep.

"What about it?" I asked.

"Celine saw the resemblance between you and your mother, between your mother and Laurel, and between Laurel"—Agent Sterling's expression flickered, just for a moment—"and me."

I thought of Director Sterling telling me that some privileges—such as torturing the Pythia—were reserved for active members of the cult, while others were open to Masters who'd already handed their seat off to a replacement.

You held a knife to my throat. You let one hand gently glide down the side of my face.

I'd tried, over the past few months, not to think about the way that Laurel had been conceived.

"She's not just my sister." I met Agent Sterling's eyes. "She's your sister, too."

"We tracked the director." Agent Briggs came and stood behind Agent Sterling, as close to her as Dean was to me. "And he led us to you."

For a long moment, our FBI mentors stood there, Sterling's gaze aimed forward. I expected her to go into Agent Veronica Sterling mode, to step away from him, to point out that her father had been manipulating them—both of them—for years.

Instead, Sterling let her veneer of calm waver. She leaned back into Briggs. And his arm wrapped around her.

We're the same, I thought, watching Sterling let go. *Now more than ever.* Laurel was Agent Sterling's, and she was mine—just like what had happened in the Masters' tomb. What we'd done. What we had to live with now.

"Come on," Dean said, brushing his lips over my temple. "Let's go home."

THREE WEEKS LATER....

I buried my mother—for the second time—in Colorado. This time, the funeral wasn't a sham. This time, her body was the one in the casket. And this time, I wasn't just surrounded by the family I'd found in the Naturals program.

My father's family was there as well. Aunts and uncles and cousins. My father. Nonna.

I'd told them a version of the truth—that I'd been working with the FBI, that my mother had died at the hands of the same people responsible for my cousin Kate's death, that Laurel was my sister.

She's you, and she's me, and she's ours. My mother's words had never been far from my mind in the days since we'd wrapped up the Masters' case.

The FBI had identified and neutralized nine killers that night—seven Masters, one apprentice, and the man born to rule them all. Six killers in custody, three—Malcolm Lowell, Director Sterling, and TA Geoff—dead. The FBI was keeping the case quiet for now, but it wouldn't stay quiet for long.

In the meantime, Laurel needed something that I couldn't give her alone.

"You will come back to the house with me," Nonna declared, hoisting my little sister up like she was nothing. "We will make cookies. And you!" She pointed a finger at Michael. "You will help us."

Michael grinned. "Sir, yes, sir."

Nonna narrowed her eyes at him. "I hear you have a problem with the kissing," she said, having jumped to that conclusion when I'd been reluctant to talk about my romantic status months earlier. "If you behave yourself, I will give you some pointers."

Dean almost choked trying to keep a straight face. That was Nonna to a T—half general, half mother hen. She was the one I'd come home to—not my father, who couldn't quite look me in the eye.

Watching Nonna putting Michael handily in his place, Judd smiled slightly. "Your grandmother," he said. "She's single?"

One by one, the others cleared away, leaving me alone at my mother's gravesite. The therapist the FBI had sent me to had told me that there would be good days and bad days. Sometimes it was hard to tell the difference.

370

I wasn't sure how long I stood there by myself before I heard footsteps behind me. I turned to see Agent Briggs. He looked exactly as he had the day I'd first met him, the day he'd thrown down the gauntlet and used my mother's case to tempt me into meeting with him.

"Director." I greeted him with his new title.

"You're sure," FBI Director Briggs said, "that this is what you want?"

I *wanted* to go back to our house in Quantico, like nothing had changed. I *wanted* to save people. I *wanted* to work behind the scenes, the way we always had.

But people didn't always get what they wanted.

"This is where I need to be," I said. "If anyone can give Laurel a normal childhood, it's my grandmother. And I can't abandon her—not after everything that's happened."

Briggs studied me for a moment. "What if you didn't have to?"

I waited, knowing he wasn't the type of person to bear silence for long.

"There's a field office in Denver," Briggs said. "And I hear Michael has acquired a large house not far from your grandmother's. Dean and Sloane are in. Celine Delacroix has thrown her hat in the ring. Lia's holding out for a raise."

"We don't get paid," I commented.

Director Briggs shrugged. "You do now. We've got a task force running down the remaining Masters emeriti. The director of national security would prefer to keep any teenagers in our employ away from it, given the attention the case is likely to attract. But you're no longer minors, and there are other cases. . . ."

Other victims, other killers.

"What about Agent Sterling?" I asked.

Briggs smiled ruefully. "I proposed. She keeps turning me down—something about the two of us having been down that road before." The look on his face reminded me that Briggs had a competitive streak. He wouldn't let his ex go without a fight. "She's put in a request for a transfer to the Denver field office," Briggs added. "I believe Judd said something about making a move as well."

When I'd decided not to return to Quantico, I'd thought that I was giving up everything. But I should have realized—home wasn't a place.

"We could go to college," I said, thinking about the others. "Graduate and enroll at the FBI Academy in Quantico. Do things by the book."

"But . . ." Briggs prompted.

But we've never been normal. We've never done things by the book.

"I was thinking," I said after a moment. "Celine more than proved herself on this last case. There have to be others."

Other young people with incredible gifts. Others with no home and no direction, with ghosts in their pasts and the potential to do so much more.

"Other Naturals," Briggs filled in. "To continue the program."

Hearing him say the words gave life to something inside of me—a spark, a sense of purpose, a *flame*. Feeling that, letting myself feel it, I held his gaze and nodded.

Slowly, the newly minted director of the FBI smiled.

Game on.

ACKNOWLEDGMENTS

The Naturals series has been a labor of love for the last five years, and I owe so much to the wonderful people who helped shape and share this story. Huge thanks to my agent, Elizabeth Harding, who has been the Naturals' number one advocate from day one, and to Ginger Clark, Holly Frederick, Sarah Perillo, Jonathon Lyons, and everyone else at Curtis Brown for working tirelessly on my behalf. Over the course of the series, I have been lucky enough to work with three outstanding editors. Thank you to Cat Onder, Lisa Yoskowitz, and Kieran Viola for helping to shape every aspect of this story and pushing me to take Cassie's story to the next level. For *Bad Blood* in particular, I owe a huge debt to Kieran, who brings so much enthusiasm, wisdom, and understanding to the editorial process. I am so very proud of where we ended up!

Many thanks also go out to the wonderful team at Hyperion, especially Emily Meehan, Julie Moody, Jamie

Baker, Heather Crowley, and Dina Sherman. I'm also extremely grateful to Marci Senders, who designed the covers for this series. They fit the books so well!

While writing these books, I have gone from being a PhD student to being a professor, and I am so grateful to both Yale University and the University of Oklahoma for supporting me in my pursuit of both writing and psychology. There is so much in this series that I couldn't have written without the education I received from wonderful mentors like Laurie Santos, Paul Bloom, and Simon Baron-Cohen. An additional thank-you goes out to all of the readers who've contacted me to say that this series has stoked their interest in psychology. Stories are one way we come to understand the minds and experiences of others; for me, science is another, and it means so much to me to have met readers who share that passion!

Thank you to all of the librarians, teachers, and educators who have put this series into someone's hands, to the wonderful conferences and festivals that have let me meet so many readers, and to the fans of this series, whose passion for the teens in the Naturals program have kept me going day after day. And thank you also to the author friends who have supported me through the writing of this series, especially Rachel Vincent, Ally Carter, Sarah Rees Brennan, Carrie Ryan, Elizabeth Eulberg, Rachel Caine, and BOB. And also a huge shout-out to Rose Brock, a force of nature who I am so lucky to have as a friend!

Finally, thank you to my friends and family. To my mom and dad, thank you for coming to put food in my fridge when I was too busy to eat and for having spent the past decade supporting my writing in so many ways. To my siblings and siblings-in-law, I am so lucky to have you in my family! Thank you to Connor for keeping copies of Jen-Jen's books on hand, to Dominic and Daniel for reading Aunt Jen's books, and to Gianna, Julian, Matthew, Joey, and Colin for being yourselves. And an enormous thank you to my husband. It's hard to believe that when I started this series, we hadn't yet met. I am so very blessed to have you in my life.

To William: Thank you, little one, for changing my life and for being the world's best baby when Mommy was on deadline.

TURN THE PAGE TO SEE WHAT'S NEXT FOR THE NATURALS IN THE THRILLING NOVELLA *TWELVE*, IN PRINT FOR THE FIRST TIME!

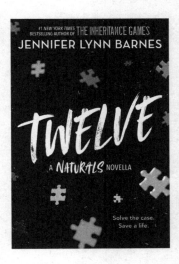

Cassie Hobbes has been working with the FBI since she was a teenager. Now twenty-three years old, she and her fellow Naturals have taken over running the program that taught them everything they know. As a unit, they're responsible for identifying new Naturals—and solving particularly impossible cases. When their latest case brings back a ghost from their past, Cassie and the other Naturals find themselves racing against the clock...and reliving their own childhood traumas.

In a small coastal town in Maine, there has been a rash of teen suicides—or at least, that's what the police believe. Mackenzie McBride, age twelve, thinks differently. Desperate to make herself heard, she stands at the top of a lighthouse, threatening to jump...unless the FBI agents who rescued her from a kidnapper at age six come to hear her out. Enter the Naturals. It doesn't take Cassie long to realize that Mackenzie isn't bluffing: she is truly convinced that the suicides are murders, and she really will jump if she can't get the FBI to believe her. To the outside world, Mackenzie is nothing more than a traumatized child. But so was Cassie, once upon a time. So were Michael, Dean, Sloane, Lia, and Celine. With a storm rolling in off the ocean and Mackenzie's position becoming more precarious by the moment, the Naturals have very little time to get to the truth about the deaths—and about twelve-year-old Mackenzie McBride.

YOU

There are names for what you do.

They cycle through your head as you stare at her body. The angle of her broken neck. The blood staining the ground beneath. There's something about the moment after impact that sticks with you.

Has always stuck with you.

It shouldn't be beautiful, but it is. You shouldn't linger, but you do. You press your index and middle fingers to your lips.

There are names for what you do. But only one matters.

Release.

CHAPTER 1

"Best, Worst, Most Improbable." Sloane paused half of a half of a beat. "Go!"

Based on her energy level—and the fact that she'd spent the first thirty-two seconds of this phone call verbally calculating the incidence of poodle-related deaths in the southwestern United States—I inferred that Michael and Dean had failed to intercept Sloane's coffee delivery that morning.

At the ripe old age of twenty-three, my former roommate still couldn't hold her caffeine.

"Somebody start," she said cheerfully, "or I will be forced to tell you the twelve most exciting wallaby statistics I know."

This was Week 10 for my fellow Naturals at the FBI Academy. *Not that I'm counting.* Sometime around Week 7, a competition had developed between the NATs—New Agent Trainees—and the NIATs—New Intelligence Analyst Trainees—to see who could sneak "Sloane the Statistical Genius" the most coffee.

I was under the impression the NIATs were winning.

"You first, Colorado." Michael Townsend sounded exactly the same on speakerphone as he did in person.

Dean sounded different. "Start with the best part of your week." My boyfriend's Southern accent had mellowed over the years, but in the past two months, I'd heard his drawl creeping back.

Quantico was home once. I fell back on an old habit, profiling Dean when I couldn't read the expression on his face. *It's also too close to your father's old hunting grounds for comfort.*

"Best part of my week." I focused on the task at hand. Phone calls didn't last long these days, and I needed this as much or more than Dean did. "I found a pair of brothers in Texas."

"Cover your ears, Redding," Michael quipped. "Cassie is going to tell us more about these brothers." I could practically *hear* him winking on the other end of the line. "Are they more handsome than Dean? Less broody? More favorable to incorporating colors into their wardrobe?"

I rolled my eyes. Dean and I had been together since we were teenagers, and Michael had taken great joy in singing the same song nearly the whole time.

"One of the brothers fits our criteria," I continued, pointedly ignoring him. "There's definitely evidence of Natural-level ability there."

In the past five years, we'd succeeded at identifying a handful of Naturals, but most had been adults. I'd sent a dozen or more to the FBI Academy, but only three had come to Colorado to be trained the way that Michael, Dean, Sloane, Lia, and I had been.

Off the books.

"The worst thing about my week," I went on, leaning my back against the wall, "is that we're still not sure *which* of the brothers is the Natural."

Every ability exists along a spectrum. That was how I'd start the conversation if we identified which brother had raised the flags in our system—and if my final analysis suggested that I could bring the kid in without doing him more harm than good. *Every spectrum has two extremes: one with very low levels of that ability and one with very high. Naturals are one in a billion. I should know.*

I was a Natural profiler.

"Are we playing Best, Worst, Most Improbable?" Lia Zhang, civilian FBI consultant, long-term thorn in my side, Natural, and—against all odds—one of my closest confidantes, appeared in the kitchen of our Colorado house.

Or, more specifically, our base of operations.

Lia plucked my cell phone from my hand, and set it to speaker. "I'm guessing Cassie told you guys about the boys in Texas."

"Best part of her week," Sloane confirmed. "And the worst."

Lia arched an eyebrow at me. She was our resident deception detector, a Natural at picking out lies *and* telling them.

"Care to try again?" she asked me.

The best part of my week really had been the development in Texas. *But the worst...*

"I'm having the dreams again." I should have hated Lia for making me admit that, but what was the point? Like me, Dean was a profiler. Michael was a Natural at reading emotions. Even if I hadn't said anything, they would have clued into the fact that something was up.

Eventually.

"You can call me, you know," Dean said on the other end of the phone line. "Any time."

I *did* know that, but I wasn't a teenager anymore. It had been five years since I'd been captured by the Masters. Five years since my mother's death. As much as I knew about the ins and outs of the human mind, I couldn't help wanting my own to work differently.

I could deal with being wounded. I didn't like feeling scarred.

"Most Improbable is next!" Sloane interjected brightly. People were harder for her to understand than numbers, but I was fairly certain she knew that I needed the distraction.

"The most improbable part of my week..." I allowed myself to be distracted and felt a grin nudging the edges of my lips upward. "Laurel made a friend."

My sister was nine years old. She'd spent the first four years of her life being raised by a cult of serial killers. To say that she was *different* would have been an understatement. Friendship didn't come easily to her. Neither did "not creeping people out."

"Her new friend," I added, "has a pony."

The idea of my morbid, introspective, too-quiet little sister with a perky, pony-riding best friend was almost unfathomable—and such a relief that I could physically feel the muscles in my stomach relaxing when I pictured the way Laurel had *almost* smiled after delivering the news in an utter deadpan.

"Did you know there's an ongoing debate about what constitutes a pony?" Sloane couldn't help herself, in part because of the caffeine and in part because she was Sloane. "Depending on who you believe, the maximum qualifying height varies between one-hundred-and-forty-two centimeters and one-hundred-and-fifty centimeters, which is also the height of one-point-four-four very tall wallabies."

There was a single beat of silence.

"The guys fall down on coffee-interception duty again?" Lia asked me.

I nodded.

"As much as I love the criticism strongly implied in that question," Michael cut in, "I'll completely ignore it and go next. Best part of my week: I annoyed six out of seven of our instructors. Worst part of my week: the seventh is proving a deceptively hard nut to crack. Most improbable...." He paused. "Lia doesn't hate me this week."

The term *on-again, off-again* had been invented for a reason. Michael and Lia were that reason.

"Best part of my week: hating Michael." Lia shot a sly smile at the phone. "Given that all of our communications are currently of the long-distance variety, expressing my distaste for his person was far more emotionally gratifying than I'd expected."

I stifled a snort.

"Worst," Lia proceeded, "the Naturals program has been assigned a new FBI liaison. If there's one thing I hate, it's breaking in a new special agent."

That was part of the reason that Michael, Dean, and Sloane had gone to Quantico. Once we'd hit eighteen, the five of us had been classified as "civilian consultants." But to work Bureau cases, we needed a Bureau team.

This was the first year any of us were old enough to attend the Academy.

"Most improbably, however," Lia continued, rounding out her trio, "our new liaison is Celine."

Celine Delacroix was Michael's half sister, just enough older that she'd already made it through new agent training. That made her Special Agent Delacroix now.

"Speaking of Celine..." Lia trailed off meaningfully. "Sloane, perhaps you'd like to go next?"

Sloane had never been one for teenage crushes, but she and Celine shared *something*. And whatever it was—lately, it had gotten more intense.

Celine had just gotten back from Quantico.

"I can't share the best part of my week or the most improbable part," Sloane said. "Due to the fact that they are both classified."

"Classified by the Bureau, or classified by Celine?" I asked.

There was a long, suspicious pause.

"The worst part of my week," Sloane replied brightly, "was blowing up Hogan's Alley. But in my defense, a person cannot, by definition, defuse a bomb unless it's operational to begin with."

And that, I thought, *is why the FBI Academy might not survive the Naturals.*

"Hogan's Alley," Lia repeated. "As in the fake town the FBI uses for training purposes?"

Sloane was quiet for a second or two. "I only blew up seventeen percent of it."

That seemed like as good a time for a subject change as any. "Your turn, Dean."

I imagined the way he would look in an FBI Academy dorm room. He'd be sitting on the end of the bed—hospital corners, if he was the one who'd made it. Getting inside his head was a matter of instinct as much as training.

You're looking at the phone and thinking about me.

"This." Dean had always been a person of few words. It took the others a moment to catch on, so I translated.

"The best part of your week," I said. "It's this."

Being separated was tough on us—all of us. Their training schedules didn't allow for much downtime, let alone regular visitation. Knowing it was temporary—measured in weeks, like an elongated summer camp—made it easier, but only just.

I closed my eyes briefly and pictured Dean again. *You're looking away from the phone now, down at your own hands, thinking of mine.*

"I'm not going to tell the two of you to get a room," Michael announced, "because that is geographically impossible. So instead, I will suggest, quite delicately, that the two of you get a *metaphorical* room."

Dean remained unruffled. After years of exposure, he was pretty much Michael-immune. "I don't think Townsend would like it if I said the worst part of my week is not being there to wake you up from the dreams, Cassie."

There had been a time when I'd been the one who'd woken Dean up from memory-ridden nightmares, instead of the reverse.

"Come now, Redding," Michael enunciated, "the worst part of your week was *clearly* losing a bet and being forced to carry a man-purse to training activities for forty-eight hours." He paused dramatically. "Some of our classmates call him Agent Man-Purse now."

"You're the only one who calls me Agent Man-Purse."

"*So far.*"

"Most Improbable?" I asked Dean. Sloane was the one who'd invented this game, and that was her favorite question.

Dean took his time with a reply. "Townsend, hand me the phone."

The sound of scuffling was audible in the background, but Dean must have come out on top, because a few seconds later, his voice came through with no background noise. "You're not on speaker anymore, Cass."

I glanced at Lia. She gave an elaborate roll of her dark

brown eyes, but handed over my phone. I took it off speaker and held it to my ear.

"What was the most improbable part of your week?" I asked again. My voice was low, but not low enough to keep Lia from hearing the question.

There was a long pause on Dean's end of the line. *You're leaving the room. You're closing the door. You lean your back against the wall. Are your eyes closed or open?*

"The most improbable part of my week"—Dean echoed my words, as if somehow, that could close the distance between Colorado and Virginia—"is the fact that my appointment with the Bureau psychologist wasn't the worst."

The FBI director had pulled strings to get my friends into the Academy. Their participation in the Naturals program was Need To Know, but their general backgrounds were not. Given the information that was out there on Dean—on Dean's serial killer *father*—even with the director's personal recommendation, the FBI Academy's admissions panel had required Dean *Redding* to jump through a handful of extra hoops—the kind of hoops designed to make sure he was psychologically intact.

"I'm glad to hear your session wasn't torture," I said. Dean wasn't much of a sharer—not with anyone but me.

Then again, these days, I wasn't much of a sharer, either.

"Cassie..." Dean let the undertone in his voice say what he wouldn't put into words.

You want to tell me that I should have come with you to the

Academy. You want to ask if my past—and the hoops they'd make me jump through—is why I did not.

"I stayed here for Laurel." That was my story, and I was sticking to it. "She's fine with me leaving on short trips, but four months? I have no idea what that would do to her." This was a conversation we'd had before. He probably knew my next words as well or better than I did. "Besides, we don't all need to be agents—or analysts. I'm happy to stay a civilian consultant if the agents I'm consulting for are the three of you."

"I know," Dean murmured.

"The program is here," I continued. "Somebody needs to run it."

Or, at least, someone would need to if the brothers in Texas panned out. If my analysis said the Naturals program would be for them—or *one* of them, anyway—what it had been for the five of us.

A sanctuary.

An opportunity.

A home.

That was the real reason I'd recruited so few young Naturals since we'd taken over. The Naturals program was designed to provide training and experience to gifted individuals whose brains were still developing—adolescents. But after everything I'd been through as a result of working with the FBI, I couldn't and wouldn't bring any kid here unless I thought they would be better off with us than in the life they were leaving behind.

Given that this was an FBI think tank devoted to using gifted teenagers to profile and catch killers?

Better was a very relative term.

Before I could say any of that out loud, a new call came in. When I saw the caller ID, I glanced back at Lia.

"Don't mind me," she said lightly. "I'm just taking note of your half of this private conversation so that I can mock and/or cross-examine you later."

I gave her a look. "Briggs is calling."

Dean heard me. "Call me later?"

"Will do." I hit a button on the phone, and as the new call picked up, I felt Dean's absence on the other end of the line like a physical thing.

Ten weeks down, ten weeks to go.

"Cassie?" FBI Director Tanner Briggs was closer to family than friend. He was the one who'd founded this program. He'd recruited me when I was seventeen years old.

He was also my boss.

"I have a case in Maine."

I waited for the details to come.

What I got was: "It has to be you."

CHAPTER 2

"Mackenzie McBride." I said the name out loud. It had been years since I'd so much as thought it, but in the time it had taken to get the assignment from Briggs, grab my go-bag, and get to the plane, it had been playing in my mind on repeat.

Little Mackenzie.

Celine stuck her head into the cockpit to let the pilot know we were ready to go, then took a seat opposite Lia and me. "Who wants to read me in?"

Special Agent Delacroix did more than live up to the title. She embodied it. It was hard to connect her to the poor little rich girl she'd been when we'd first made her acquaintance, but even in a suit, her tone businesslike, I could still see shades of the girl that Celine had been. She was an artist, evident in the calluses on her fingers and the bright print she wore beneath her steel-gray jacket. I gave it fifty-fifty odds that she'd designed the pattern on the silk shirt herself. Her expression was alert—controlled, but with a hint of adrenaline.

She still moved like a dancer or a fighter—or both.

"Mackenzie was a kidnapping victim." I tried to stick to the facts and not delve down into the emotions I associated with this particular case. "She was six years old when she was taken. By the time we were read in, the case had been cold for months."

Back in those days, the Naturals program had only allowed us access to cold cases. Mackenzie's was one of the first we'd solved as a team.

"She wanted to be a veterinarian pop star." I hadn't meant to say that, was surprised I even remembered the details after nearly six years and who-knows-how-many cases, active and cold. "Her favorite color was purple."

"Family lawyer was a lying liar who lied." Lia picked up where I left off. Back when we'd solved this case, she'd done a good job of pretending that it hadn't touched her, but nowadays she wasn't quite so intent on seeming heartless. "He was the one who took Mackenzie, then got off on the press attention surrounding it. He had her for months, hidden away in some back room or godforsaken hole."

A makeshift shack, I thought, remembering Sloane's analysis of the property. *Four feet by four feet, no windows.*

Celine flipped through the file sitting on the table between us. "Mackenzie is how old now?" The plane took off, but I barely felt it. "Twelve?"

When I was twelve years old, my mother had been

deemed missing, presumed dead. When Dean was twelve, he'd betrayed his serial killer father, resulting in Daniel Redding's arrest and the creation of the Naturals program.

When Lia was twelve...

I stopped my thoughts right there. "Mackenzie McBride is twelve years old," I confirmed. "She lives in Cape Roane, Maine." If Sloane were here, she would have rattled off every factoid and statistic imaginable about the small coastal town. I cut straight to the chase. "Cape Roane is the home of one of the tallest lighthouses in the United States, and right now..."

You climbed the stairs. You opened the window. You crawled out....

"Right now," I managed to continue, "Mackenzie is standing on the edge of that lighthouse, threatening to jump."

"Unless..." Celine said softly.

Lia finished her sentence for her. "She said she'd jump unless someone called in the FBI—specifically, the agent who found her in that shack."

Agent Briggs. He was the FBI director now. He couldn't just run off at a twelve-year-old's call. Agent Sterling, his wife, hadn't been part of the team during the Mackenzie McBride case—*and* she was thirty-six weeks pregnant.

With twins.

That left those of us who'd worked the case behind the scenes. It left me, because I was the one who'd crawled inside Mackenzie's brain, way back when.

"If her parents and the local authorities hadn't found her

threat credible," I forced myself to admit, "they wouldn't have called us."

"So we've got a potential jumper." Celine was quiet for a moment, and I wondered if she was thinking about the times in her life when she'd taken drastic measures for attention. Because she needed to matter—to be seen and heard.

Is that what this is? I directed my thoughts toward Mackenzie. *Are you just trying to make yourself heard?*

I'd been taught to profile in first person or second—never in third. But right now, I wasn't profiling. I didn't know enough about *this* Mackenzie to say with any degree of certainty what she did or did not want.

I only knew the child she'd been—and what she'd survived.

You demanded they call us in for a reason. If you really wanted to die—if you were sure—you wouldn't be up there issuing demands. That was closer to a reasonable conclusion, but I'd been taught early on how easily what you wanted to see could interfere with a profile's conclusions.

I needed to keep my head clear. I needed to hold off on conclusions. I needed to get to know Mackenzie *now*.

"We'll go straight to the lighthouse when we touch down." Celine wasn't giving orders so much as thinking out loud.

"Briggs said that the local PD already have a crisis negotiator and a child psychologist out there," I said.

Child psychologists. Half of my brain was still trying to get acquainted with Mackenzie's. *How many of those have you seen since the kidnapping? How well do you know what to say—or not to say—to convince the shrink du jour that you're normal?*

How long have you known, deep in the recesses of your mind, that normal *is a lie?*

"Cassie." Lia had to say my name twice before I tuned back in. "Aren't you forgetting to read Celine in on one little thing?" She paused, then prompted. "The *reason* Briggs said that Mackenzie wants to talk to the FBI."

Oh, right. That.

I answered in one word. "Murder."

MACKENZIE, AGE TWELVE

Mackenzie McBride has never been bothered by heights. Better to be up high, where you can see everything, than down low, boxed in, on the ground. Jumping would be easy.

The lighthouse ledge sticks out a little less than two feet. It should feel like nothing. Her legs should shake beneath her, but Mackenzie trusts her body. She knows that two feet is half of four, and for a time, four feet by four feet was her world.

Her balance is perfect. Even now, with the wind whipping at her hair and the window barricaded off behind her, she can see herself in three hundred and sixty degrees. She knows exactly what she would look like if she leapt off the edge, if she dove off it, if she fell. She can see the way her body would land in each scenario. One of her teachers tried to tell her once that what she could do, the things she knew—it was just math.

It isn't.

She rises up on her toes. A *relevé*—and a warning for the adults gathered below as well as those in the room immediately behind her. *I can step off this ledge before you can stop me.*

It would be so easy, but she doesn't want to do that. Does she? *The FBI will be here soon. They have to be. They have to listen.* If they listened, maybe she could come in. Maybe she could end this.

They have to believe me.

Because the others? The dead ones? They didn't leap or dive. They didn't dance off the edge. They didn't jump.

They were pushed.

CHAPTER 3

There was a crowd gathered outside the lighthouse. I estimated a dozen or more, ranging in age from late teens to eighties. From this distance, they couldn't make out the details of what was going on above, but they could see what I could, plain as day.

A figure. A small one. She wasn't looking down. *Your face is angled toward the sky. Your feet are close to the edge.*

My heart began beating more rapidly in my chest. In our line of work, the margin for error was never large. But this time?

It was inches.

"Excuse me." Celine had a way of parting crowds—even those intent on watching a train wreck in real time. "FBI."

That got the attention of about half of the onlookers. Pulling my gaze from the girl on the ledge, I took note of which half and followed in Celine's wake. Lia hesitated for a brief moment behind me. I knew, without glancing back at her, that she was still staring up at Mackenzie.

Lia wasn't, generally speaking, a person built for hesitation, but it was different—for all of us—when a case involved a kid.

"FBI." Celine repeated herself to the two local LEOs—law enforcement officers—posted at the door to the lighthouse.

"Aren't you a little young to be FBI?" The officer who managed to look Celine in the eye and say those words would probably soon regret it.

"I age well." Celine had an impressive deadpan. "What can I say? I moisturize." She gave him a second to process that, then issued an order. "Move."

The officers moved before they'd even realized they'd done it.

"I don't moisturize," Lia told one of them as we passed. "I made a deal with the devil to maintain my youth. You don't want to know what the devil asked for in return."

Coming from anyone else, that would have sounded flippant, but Lia could sell *any* lie. Luckily, her statement saved me from having to say anything, which was fortunate, because I looked significantly younger than either Lia or Celine.

When people called the FBI, most of them didn't expect women in their early twenties. Today, we didn't have time to prove ourselves or win hearts and minds. We didn't have time for anyone questioning us or our abilities.

Mackenzie didn't have time.

Before the door to the lighthouse had even closed behind me, I'd already sunk back into observation mode. *Behavior.*

Personality. Environment. Those were the cornerstones my mom had taught me when I was younger than Mackenzie was now. If you knew any two sides of the triangle, you could predict the third.

By the time I was a teenager, I did so effortlessly, without thinking, all the time. Being a Natural wasn't something you could turn off. With each step I took, my brain catalogued the details of the environment around me. The ground floor of the lighthouse seemed to be some kind of museum. There was a woman—early sixties—behind the counter, and two more officers—one of them, based on his clothing and posture, the ranking detective—posted at the door to the stairs.

As Celine began a round of introductions, I zeroed in on the only other person in the room—a man. *Forties. Thick hair. Rumpled clothing.* If Michael had been with us, he could have read shades of meaning in the man's expression and posture, but all I saw was the dominant emotion. *Devastation.*

"Mr. McBride." I greeted him, holding out a hand. He took mine and held on for an instant too long. "I'm Cassie Hobbes." He wouldn't remember my name later. I wasn't even sure he'd registered it. "We're here to help your daughter." That, he would process.

You already lost your little girl once. You can't lose her again. You can't just stand here.

"They won't let me upstairs," Mackenzie's father said dully. "My wife is up there. She's talking to her...."

There was only room for one, and it wasn't you. You're not the talker. That much was clear from the gaps in his words, the sporadic eye contact. I wanted to press him, to question him about his daughter. *Are you an observer, a listener, or caught up in your own world?* Those were the options—and two out of three would be useful to me.

But not now. There was such a thing as professionalism, and the FBI equivalent of bedside manner required a little finesse when it came to grilling a victim's family. I didn't have time to finesse anything at the moment.

The first and most important thing was getting to Mackenzie.

As Celine finished shaking the detective's hand and introduced Lia and me as specialist consultants, we got the thirty-second rundown of the situation. No one knew how Mackenzie had gotten all the way up to the top of the lighthouse. The staircase was typically secure, the lightroom at the top locked and used primarily for storage.

"It's not big." The detective paused, and I got the sense that he felt a need to justify his presence on the ground floor to us. "They don't want to crowd her."

He didn't specify who *they* were. It was just as well—I did best when I was left to form impressions for myself.

As we began our ascent of the lighthouse stairs, I let myself imagine Mackenzie doing the same. When Celine, Lia, and I made it to the top, I wondered if Mackenzie had been tired when she'd reached the ninth-story landing—or if she'd been buzzing.

With energy and adrenaline, dread and hope and fear.

Celine nodded to a ladder overhead. "I'll go in first."

I waited, then followed, hoisting myself up into the light-room overhead. Immediately, as I pulled myself to a standing position, I took stock of the space and the people occupying it. There were four of them: two men, two women. Mackenzie's mother was the easiest to pick out—*nurse's scrubs, dark circles under her eyes, hyperfocused on the window.* The other woman—*late thirties, early forties, professional dress, hair down*—was speaking softly to Mrs. McBride. I pegged her as the psychologist. *Even-keeled. Exactly the right degree of empathetic.*

I disliked her on instinct.

That left the two men. One of them strode toward us. The other hung back. Based on his apparel, the one who hung back appeared to be a fireman.

An axe dangled from his hand.

My gaze went to the window. It was open, but wooden boards had been nailed across the frame. From where I was standing, I could barely make out the form of Mackenzie's body through the gaps in the boards.

You climbed out the window, hammer in hand. You barricaded yourself out there. That showed a presence of mind—and forethought—that I wouldn't have expected.

"If we try to take down the boards, she'll jump." The man who'd approached us followed my gaze. He was in his late fifties, the oldest person in the room—and the one in charge.

The crisis negotiator, I thought.

"Quentin Nichols." He was good enough at reading situations to introduce himself to Celine first and good enough at reading people that his attention then settled almost immediately on me.

"Special Agent Celine Delacroix," Celine replied before nodding toward Lia and me. "Lia Zhang and Cassie Hobbes will be consulting."

"Specialists?" Nichols asked. The question embedded underneath was: *What kind?*

Before we could answer, Mrs. McBride's thin, reedy voice broke through the air. "We asked for Briggs." She shook her head, back and forth, whip-fast. "Agent Briggs. *Special Agent Tanner Briggs.*"

She was panicking out loud. *You're the talker in the family.* The scrubs she was wearing suggested that she'd come here straight from work. I recalled from the original case file that she'd gone back to school for nursing when Mackenzie had started kindergarten.

"It has to be Agent Briggs. Oh, God, please. Mackenzie said..."

"Mackenzie said that she wanted to talk to the agent who found her." I was the one who calmly responded, not Celine, not Lia. "Agent Briggs is now the director of the FBI."

I wasn't talking to Mrs. McBride—or to the crisis negotiator. I was talking to the girl outside the window, the one who'd gone still the moment we'd walked into the room.

"Mackenzie, sweetheart, we'll try again." Mrs. McBride choked on the words—or possibly on a sob.

She thought Mackenzie was going to jump.

I thought Mackenzie was listening.

"Agent Briggs isn't the one who found you." I addressed my words to her directly, trying not to think about what could happen if I misstepped, or if I'd read the situation wrong. "He's the one who came for you—but he's not the one who found you."

That got a response. Mackenzie turned.

The sharp intake of breath in the room told me that she hadn't moved this much in a while. Beside me, the crisis negotiator eased forward. The fireman did the same.

I stepped through them, right up to the window's edge. I would have had to hoist myself up to climb out through it, but the barricade rendered that possibility null and void. Instead, I angled my head up to look at Mackenzie's legs.

The way she'd angled her head toward the sky earlier.

"We found you," I said. "Lia and I did."

"Six years ago?" Mrs. McBride couldn't stop the question—or the skepticism that marked it. She'd hate herself for that later.

"You're lying," Mackenzie said, her voice shaking. I saw her feet move backward, a fraction of an inch, toward the edge. "I wanted to talk to Agent Briggs."

I had seconds to establish a rapport. I didn't know Mackenzie. I only knew where she was, what she was doing, and what I'd wanted when I was her age, and police officers had been tiptoeing around me.

Truth.

"I was seventeen years old when we found you. It was one of my first cases." The Naturals program wasn't public. I wasn't supposed to be saying any of this, but right now, security clearances were the least of my concerns. "I guess you could say that I wasn't a normal seventeen."

There was more motion outside the window, another collective flinch from those inside.

I didn't move, didn't breathe, didn't blink until Mackenzie's face appeared on the other side of the boarded frame. She was crouched on the ledge now, her knees pulled tight to her chest.

Safe. Steady—but ready to stand if you need to. Ready to jump. She'd do it, if I backed her into a corner. I knew that the way I always knew things—instinctively.

"What's your name?" Mackenzie asked me.

The muscles in my chest relaxed, but only slightly. I'd piqued her curiosity. She was engaging. We weren't out of the woods, but it was something.

"My name is Cassie," I told her. "Cassandra Hobbes."

There was a pause, maybe two seconds in length. "I'm Mackenzie." It was important to her, somehow, to maintain ownership over who and what she was. It was important to her to stay on even footing with me.

You can't let yourself feel powerless. You're out there—you're up here—*because there's a part of you that desperately needs to be in control.* If something threatened that, she'd do what she had to do.

What part of her wanted to do, because *that* was control.

"Tell me about the murders." I did the only thing that I could do. I treated her like an adult. Like a *person*. Like a witness.

Mackenzie was quiet for several seconds, and then she spoke again. "I'm not a normal twelve."

CASSIE, AGE TWELVE
Eleven years earlier

They don't want her to think of this as an interrogation room. Cassie knows that, just like she knows, objectively, that the blood has been scrubbed from her hands. They took pictures first—so many pictures of her hands, her clothes...

The blood on the walls.

Cassie wasn't there for the crime scene photos. Of course she wasn't, but she can read between the lines. *Behavior. Personality. Environment.* The BPEs are reliable when nothing and no one else is. They are constant.

Behavior. The detective pulls a chair over to her side of the table. He got her chips and a Coke, and he hands them to her now.

Environment. This is a police station, and not a well-funded one. For the detective, it's his place of business.

She's the new element here, the thing that has the potential to throw him off-kilter.

She's a kid.

She's quiet.

She's not crying.

"Is my mom dead?" Cassie's voice is low, but she beats the detective to the first question.

"We don't know, sweetheart." That answer comes quickly. The truth takes a little longer. "At this point, it seems likely."

Personality. Cassie forces herself to ignore the ringing in her ears and think. "You have kids." This time, the words that come out of her mouth aren't a question. The detective, she thinks, is probably divorced, and he probably has daughters, and it's probably hard for him not to bring his work home.

He sees his kids when he looks at her.

"I have two little girls—Ally and Maura."

The names don't fit together. He picked one, the ex-wife picked the other—or maybe one is a family name.

"I'm not your daughters," Cassie states clearly. She knows she's probably staring at him too hard. "You can ask me whatever you need to ask me. I saw people at the theater. I can describe them to you." She doesn't pause, because she knows that if she does, he'll tell her to slow down. "My mom doesn't date, but she does meet with clients one-on-one. She's a mentalist. Do you know what a mentalist is? People think she's psychic, but she's not." That seems important, when Cassie thinks back on the blood on the walls, the floor...

Too much blood.

"Maybe she fooled the wrong person," Cassie thinks out loud. "Whoever did this—they meant to. They planned it." Cassie sees it every time she closes her eyes. She sees it even when her eyes are open. "I need to go back there."

For the first time, her voice trembles. She hears it, and the detective does, too, and Cassie senses immediately that he's *relieved*. Relieved that she's showing emotion. Relieved that he can comfort her. Relieved that he can treat her like a kid.

"I need to see the evidence," Cassie insists. "The pictures you took. Are you interviewing anyone?"

She sees his answer coming, as he places a gentle hand on her shoulder.

"Breathe, sweetheart," he murmurs. "Just breathe."

CHAPTER 4

Mackenzie was backlit. There was something haunting about the image: her face visible through the wooden boards, the sun reflecting in a halo off her hair, her eyes in shadow.

"Three kids from the high school are dead." Mackenzie's voice wasn't emotionless, but it wasn't expressive, either. She said *dead* like it was any other word. "Two girls, one boy. People say it was suicide. They say the kids jumped." She paused, and I got the sense that she was watching me every bit as closely as I was observing her. "There are cliffs, where the older kids go to party. My brother goes there sometimes. He knew one of the girls."

I forced myself to concentrate on what she was saying and not just the way she was saying it. I couldn't just go through the motions here. I had to listen to her. I had to *believe* her.

I had to let her take control.

"Three victims," I repeated back to her. "Two girls, one boy." If this were a normal case, I'd be thinking victimology—what did the three have in common, what need did they fulfill for the person who'd killed them? "People say they jumped." I continued echoing Mackenzie's statement back to her, all the better to burrow into her subconscious and water the seed I'd planted when I'd told her that I wasn't normal.

We are the same.

"But you don't think they did," I continued.

"I *know* they didn't jump." Mackenzie's voice turned harsh—vicious, even.

You're angry.

I should have seen that coming. I should have been ready for it. This wasn't the kind of anger that popped up overnight. This was old and deep and more powerful than anything else she was capable of feeling.

"Tell me how you know," I said.

My understanding of emotions wasn't like Michael's. He read what someone was feeling in the moment. He looked at a person and read, based on physical cues, what they felt—and how they felt about what they felt and precisely which emotions they were trying not to show.

But what I did wasn't just about the moment. It was about who someone *was*. Emotions were a part of that, but I couldn't separate them from everything else.

Like the fact that Mackenzie had been victimized as a child.

Like the fact that the man who'd taken her had killed himself before the case could ever go to trial.

He took control. He took that from you. She wouldn't let anyone else do that, not ever again. Adults didn't get to look through her. They didn't get to make decisions for her.

They didn't get to *ignore* her.

"I saw the body." Mackenzie raised her head to the sky again, when most people in her position would have looked down. "The third one. After the first two, the adults blocked off the cliffs. There's a police officer there all the time now. They brought counselors into the schools—not just the high school. The middle school, too."

Unlike most of her classmates, Mackenzie would have been familiar with counselors, with grief, with things that no kid should have to experience.

"They talked about warning signs," Mackenzie continued bitterly. "And prevention and suicide contagion, like that's a thing."

It was a thing, but I didn't say that. I knew better.

"It didn't help." Mackenzie's voice was soft now.

How many other things haven't helped? I wondered. *How many times has someone told you what you're feeling, what you experienced, how to heal?*

I'd both been there and done that.

Stop projecting. That warning came to me in Agent Sterling's voice. My old mentor hadn't just taught me how to profile. She'd taught me to separate my instincts from the rest of my subconscious.

She'd taught me to recognize when I identified with a victim.

"What the adults said, the teachers and the parents and the *experts*—it didn't help. When the police blocked off the cliffs..." Mackenzie brought her eyes back to stare directly into mine. "The next body was found next to the church. They say she jumped off the steeple."

"She?"

"Kelley." Mackenzie's response confirmed for me what I'd suspected—she knew the third victim. *From church? Through her brother?*

That was information I could get from a source other than Mackenzie. She'd brought us here to tell us something specific. This wasn't an interrogation, and if I tried to turn it into one, I'd be treading dangerous ground.

I had to let her say what she needed to say. I had to listen. I had to believe her.

"Kelley didn't jump?" I was very careful not to tack the phrase *you think* on the front of the sentence this time. I was—almost certainly—not the first person Mackenzie had told this to.

If anyone believed you, you wouldn't be up here. You wouldn't need me.

"I saw the body." Mackenzie repeated what she'd said earlier. "I saw the way Kelley landed. The way her bones broke. She didn't jump."

Lia stepped into my peripheral vision. With the boards across the windows, the chances that Mackenzie would see her standing there were slim. I allowed myself one second to glance sideways.

Lia gave a brief nod. Mackenzie was telling the truth as she knew it—no doubt, no embellishments.

"You don't believe me, either." Mackenzie stood suddenly.

A second looking away was a second too much. She'd taken a risk telling me her truth, knowing that I might just be another in a long line of adults to dismiss it. She'd asked for the FBI. Here we were.

There was nothing left for her to ask for.

You expect me to humor you. To lie to you. To try to manipulate or control you.

From somewhere in my memory, I could hear a male voice saying, *Breathe, sweetheart. Just breathe.*

The muscles in my jaw tightened. I wasn't going to humor Mackenzie—or lie to her.

I was going to listen. And ask: "How would Kelley have landed if she'd jumped?"

Mackenzie hadn't expected the question, and that was a mark in my favor. She rose up on her toes—just slightly, her hands held out to either side. "It depends. On how close she was to the edge, how she moved. There wouldn't have been room for a running start, but she could have taken a step. Did she hold one foot out over the edge and jump from the one that remained? Did she just step off? Did she leap? Did she hold her arms out to the side and fall? How did her knees bend, how did she leap? Were her toes pointed?"

As she spoke, Mackenzie's body echoed her words in tiny,

almost imperceptible ways. There was something graceful about even the subtlest of her movements, something remarkably unperturbed, considering what she was saying—and the fact that a strong wind could take her off that edge.

"She could have landed *so* many ways." Mackenzie went suddenly still. For the first time since we'd started speaking, my stomach clenched. "She didn't."

Didn't land the way she should have.

"I know I sound crazy." Mackenzie knelt again—too fast this time, too suddenly. Behind me, her mother whimpered. The girl should have fallen. She should have at least stumbled or wavered, but she didn't. "I know that you think I'm just a kid. But I'm not. I know bodies. I know how they move. When I spar, I can see other people's moves coming. When I dance, I always know exactly how I look without ever glancing in the mirror."

Celine came to stand beside me. She caught my gaze, and I knew exactly what she was thinking.

"I'm that way," Celine told Mackenzie. "With faces."

Sloane was that way with numbers, Michael with emotions, Lia with lies.

I was that way with people—with what they wanted and needed and what they were willing to do to get it.

"You don't want to jump," I said, my voice echoing through the tight quarters. "But you will. You already know exactly how—how you'd hold your arms, the way you'd look up, not down. You'd point your toes."

The crisis negotiator grabbed me by the arm, his fingers

digging into the tendons just above the elbow. I could hear the child psychologist hiss something behind me. They thought I was being reckless, that I was saying the wrong thing, putting ideas in Mackenzie's mind.

The ideas are already there.

I ignored the negotiator's punishing grip. "You know exactly how you would land," I told Mackenzie, "because you know bodies. You know movement."

"I know," the girl on the ledge said desperately, "that Kelley didn't jump."

CELINE, AGE TWELVE
Twelve years earlier

There's not a single person at this too-formal dinner table that Celine would like to draw. To be fair, she's already drawn Michael a dozen or more times.

She knows his face almost as well as her own.

"The boys will be lining up for this one soon." Mr. Pritchett—the guest of honor—nods at Celine and smiles knowingly at her parents. "If they aren't already."

Why do grown men say such stupid things? Celine manages not to say that out loud. Her parents should truly appreciate her discretion. They're the ones who insisted that this grown-ass man—the one acting like *pretty* is the ultimate honorific an adolescent girl could receive—is important.

A valuable business connection. It is all Celine can do to keep from rolling her eyes. In a show of great restraint, she instead pictures the muscles and bones buried beneath Mr. Pritchett's healthy jowls.

"Celine isn't interested in boys yet." Her mother, college professor that she is, has just enough feminist bones in her body to add, "She's really more invested in her studies."

Studies come easily to Celine. It's the seventh grade, not rocket science.

"And her art," Michael interjects. The comment, in addition to being true, yields an immediate result: his father's attention. The shift in Thatcher Townsend's position is noticeable, even to Celine. She's done a good job of not looking at Michael's father this evening.

At the elder Townsend's face.

It's amazing, really, that no one else sees it. Not Michael, not Thatcher, not Celine's hapless father, who has no idea that she doesn't carry his DNA at all. It's all there in the bone structure that she and her father's long-time business partner share.

It's all in the face.

"You might not be interested in boys now, Celine," Michael's father says, playing to Mr. Pritchett's ego by shooting him a conspiratorial look, "but you will be someday."

You want to bet? Celine, again, restrains herself.

Michael doesn't. "Leave her alone."

Celine's stomach flips. Those words will cost Michael. Thatcher Townsend is charming. Thatcher Townsend is generous, a renowned philanthropist, an excellent businessman.

Thatcher Townsend is a monster.

Most of the time, Michael tries to hide the bruises, but he can't hide the way his nose isn't quite straight anymore.

Not from Celine. Faces don't lie. And if Michael's father has broken one bone, who says he won't break another?

No. Celine won't let that happen. *Not tonight.* She speaks up before Thatcher can turn his gaze intently toward his son. "Why?"

If she can distract Thatcher, then maybe he'll forget what Michael said. Maybe Michael won't have to stay home "sick" tomorrow. Maybe Celine won't see the echoes of it in his cheek or nasal or jaw bones, long after the bruises have healed.

"Why, what, sweetheart?" Thatcher asks indulgently. His gaze is on Celine's, but he hasn't forgotten the way Michael spoke to him.

I'll just have to make *you forget.* This isn't how Celine planned on making this particular announcement. But this is *her* truth, and *her* decision. *Screw her parents—and screw Thatcher Townsend.*

Celine smiles sweetly. "Why would I be interested in boys," she asks the table innocently, "when there are girls?"

CHAPTER 5

"You think Mackenzie's a Natural?" Lia cut straight to the chase the moment we stepped out of the room. Celine had hung back to talk down the crisis negotiator, the psychologist, and Mrs. McBride. For someone who had a fondness for throwing gasoline on fires, Celine was also surprisingly adept at putting them out. It hadn't been my intention to be inflammatory or reckless. I'd said what I needed to say to show Mackenzie that I was listening.

I wasn't just repeating her own words back to her. I *understood*. Convincing Mackenzie of that had been worth the risk of addressing her threat to jump head-on. The fact that I'd succeeded was the only reason that I'd been able to extract a promise that she would sit tight while I made some phone calls.

I'd given her something to hold on to.

I'd left her in control.

"There's only one way to find out if she's like us," I told

Lia. Feeling different didn't make a person a Natural. Believing that you knew things, that you could intuit things that other people couldn't—that didn't make you a prodigy.

The only way to tell if Mackenzie was a Natural was to find out if she was *right*.

For that, I needed Sloane. Unfortunately, the FBI Academy was not known for allowing its trainees to keep their cell phones on at all times. I circumvented the system and made a different phone call.

"Briggs." Even now that he was the FBI director, the founder of the Naturals program had a habit of answering the phone with his last name. *Efficient—and just a little egocentric.*

"I need you to get Sloane on the phone for me," I said, not bothering with *hello* any more than he had. "I also need you to get us access to everything the local PD has on three recent teenage deaths—apparent suicides. The sooner Sloane gets her eyes on those files, the better."

Maybe the detective in charge of Mackenzie's case would have handed over the files *without* receiving a phone call from the director of the FBI, and maybe he wouldn't have. Either way, I wasn't about to devote a single ounce of my attention or brain power to figuring out how to finesse the situation. My cognitive resources were already split, half focused on Mackenzie—*power* and *control* and *desperation*—and the other half working through the few facts that I knew about the trio of deaths.

If Mackenzie was right, if I proved it—she'd have a reason to come in.

Three victims. Two female, one male. All teenaged. All local. If these "suicides" really were murders, then I needed the information in the files as much as Sloane did. How far apart were the deaths, timewise? Were numbers two and three closer together or further apart than number one? I knew the third victim was female. If the first had been male, that might suggest a shift in the pattern.

The first could have been practice. The next two—the girls—they might be what you want.

"Check your phone." Lia had ducked back into the lightroom to check on Celine. Based on the first words out of her mouth when she reappeared on the landing, I concluded that Celine had probably asked her to pass that message along.

I pulled out my phone and checked my secure email. The files were there. If I had them, that meant that Sloane had them. Based on the speed with which she worked, I'd be hearing from her soon.

Not soon enough. I'd made the decision not to go back into the room until I could convince Mackenzie that I'd *done* something, that I was *doing* something. I couldn't go back just to tell her that she had to wait. In the meantime, I had to trust that Celine could handle the adults in the room—and that some part of Mackenzie would have latched on to the way Celine had responded when Mackenzie had described her awareness of her own body—of muscles and movement.

I'm that way with faces. I'd gone into this identifying with

Mackenzie and laying the groundwork for her to identify with me, but with a little space, I could see that I wasn't the only option on that front. Celine's ability was the closest to Mackenzie's. Celine was the one who moved like a fighter and a dancer, and Mackenzie had mentioned sparring and dancing both. I knew what it was like to survive trauma, but Celine was the one who'd gone to great lengths as a teenager to be seen and heard. She was comfortable with anger.

Nobody controlled her.

"Excuse me."

I looked up to see Mr. McBride making his way up the steps. Nine flights of stairs had taken a physical toll on him, but clearly he considered that the least of his problems. "Can you tell me anything?" he asked, breathing heavily. "My wife? My daughter?"

I took note of the order in which he'd asked. "They're both fine," I said. "Or as fine as they can be, under the circumstances."

Mackenzie's father ascended another step, but stopped there, below me. My phone was heavy in my hand. I had the files. I could be looking at them while waiting for Sloane's call. But I knew what it was like to be on the other end of an investigation and to feel like no one was telling you anything—or listening.

For better or worse, I could give him a minute.

"What can you tell me about Mackenzie?" I asked.

In my line of work, details were currency, and given that Sloane could feasibly call me back and say that the physical evidence *was* consistent with suicide, I needed a backup plan—one that could bring Mackenzie down off that ledge, even if she was wrong.

"Mackenzie's a good girl." Mr. McBride said that stubbornly, like he expected me to argue. When I didn't, he got nervous and pushed his hands through his hair, an alternative to wringing them. "She doesn't like attention. Not like this."

She's more like you than your wife, I translated. I wondered when that shift had happened. Mackenzie McBride had wanted to be a pop star once.

She'd *loved* attention.

"Does Mackenzie ever talk about what happened to her?" I asked.

That question shut Mr. McBride down, as immediately as if he'd had an actual off-switch and I'd pressed it.

"I have a little sister," I said, trying another tack. "I didn't know about her for years. Until she was three, almost four. What she's been through..." I thought of Laurel, of the way that she used to look at swing sets and see shackles and chains. "I won't ever fully understand it." I shook my head. "I don't make her talk about it. Sometimes, though, she says things." I paused, letting the silence work its way through his brain. "Does Mackenzie ever say things to you?"

"She said that it was small." Mr. McBride swallowed, visibly, audibly, practically with his entire body. "The place that bastard kept her, she said that it was dark, and it was small, and he'd leave her there for hours—sometimes days."

I thought of Mackenzie, standing on a ledge and looking

up at the sky. Up, not down. At least on the ledge, there was air.

At least you're in control. At least you're free.

"She said she danced."

That snapped my attention back to Mackenzie's father.

"She what?"

"She danced," he repeated. "Every day, all the time, whenever she could. Whenever it was dark. Whenever she couldn't see anything. Whenever she wanted to cry. She danced."

I thought about what it would be like to live in a four-by-four room. *You were just a kid. A kid who liked being the center of attention. A kid who wanted to be a pop star.*

He took everything away from you. He locked you up. He hurt you.

You danced.

"The older she gets, the harder it is." Mackenzie's father looked down. "I thought it would get easier, but she understands more now than she used to. The things she lived through..."

He couldn't finish that sentence.

"She dances five days a week." Mr. McBride managed a very small smile, fond and hopeful in a way that hit me like a knife to the gut. "Ballet, tap, jazz. A few years ago, she started martial arts—the kid's practically a prodigy. There's nothing physical that she can't do."

When it comes to her body—she's in control.

"Thank you," I told Mr. McBride. He asked me what I

was thanking him for, but I couldn't explain what he'd just told me—what he'd *really* told me.

If we'd had normal childhoods, Sloane had commented once, a long time ago, *we wouldn't be Naturals.* Michael had learned to read emotions because he'd *needed* to be able to read his abusive father's. Lia had grown up in a world where deception was a matter of survival. Dean's father was a serial killer.

I'd had a mother who was a mentalist, and she'd moved us around so frequently that the only relationships I was able to form with other people were in my mind.

Mackenzie McBride had been kidnapped at the age of six. I'd known that she'd been held captive. I'd known the size of the shack. I hadn't known, until this moment, what she'd done to survive.

You danced. In the dark, you danced. For hours and hours. When you had no control over anything else, you had control over the motion. Over your own muscles. Over the decision to repeat the same moves—familiar moves—again and again and again.

I suspected, but didn't know, that when Mackenzie had danced, she'd gone to a place in her mind where other things—*the bad things,* as Laurel would say—couldn't touch her. What I did know was that on the ledge, Mackenzie had said that she knew bodies, knew how they moved, knew what she looked like when she was dancing without ever looking in the mirror.

With her childhood? Her very *not normal* childhood?

That made sense. Even now, losing herself in motion, exerting physical control—it was a coping mechanism.

I'd been trying to approach this objectively. I'd been reserving judgment on whether or not Mackenzie *knew* things, the way I sometimes did.

The way we all did.

But now?

I said good-bye to Mr. McBride and started up the ladder to the lightroom. *You know bodies. You know motion.*

I'd thought that I couldn't go back in until I had proof that she was right. But right now? I didn't need proof.

I knew.

When I made it into the room, the first thing I noticed was that Celine was standing opposite the window, closer to Mackenzie than any of the others.

"You're back." Mackenzie didn't turn to look at me. I wondered if she'd seen me come into the room or if she'd heard me.

How in tune with her environment—with the bodies all around her—was she?

My phone rang, the sound almost obscene in the silence that had followed Mackenzie's statement. No matter what damage control Special Agent Delacroix had done with the adults in this room, it was a good bet that none of them quite trusted me or the way I'd chosen to approach things.

In their eyes, this was a delicate situation. *Mackenzie* was delicate and in need of kid gloves.

I looked down at my phone, then out at the girl on the ledge. "It's my colleague," I said. "The expert."

"The one who'll tell you I'm right," Mackenzie said forcefully.

My head wanted to nod, but I forced myself to answer the phone instead. "Tell me what you've got, Sloane."

SLOANE, AGE TWELVE
Eleven years earlier

"She's got to stop pulling stunts like this, Margot."

Sloane knows that the security guard's usage of the word *stunt* is a fairly recent linguistic innovation—late nineteenth century, origin unknown. Personally, she prefers the terms *exploit* and *feat*.

"What was it this time?" Sloane's mother is wearing a tight white T-shirt and jeans. Not her work clothes.

Interesting. Only 15 percent of Margot Tavish's personal wardrobe is white.

"Blackjack tables." Security keeps the reply brief. Sloane should really learn his name—just like she's already learned the placement of the three dozen security cameras in the Majesty, the blind spots, and how to work her way through the casino while minimizing the chances that she'll show up on film. It's harder to hide from the guards.

Harder, but not impossible.

"She was counting cards." Security does not sound happy about that. "For other players, Margot. Took three hands before we managed to escort her out."

"I was not *counting* anything." Sloane feels like that has to be clarified, even if clarifying it earns her a glare from an annoyed Margot. "I was tracking the number and distribution of cards that had already been played in an effort to calculate the individual probabilities of the next card being favorable to either the player or the dealer."

Security lets out what Sloane deeply suspects is an exasperated sigh. Sloane has a great deal of experience with other people's exasperation.

"No more, Margot. Kid's twelve, and she's already persona non grata on the strip. I don't need to tell you how uncomfortable this could be if word works its way up the chain of command at the Majesty."

Sloane knows the chain of command at the Majesty precisely as well as she knows the locations of the security cameras. That is, after all, the point. To get the owner's attention. To make him *see* her.

Margot puts a hand on Sloane's shoulder and pulls Sloane's smaller body back against her own. Sloane calculates that there is a 12 percent chance this is a sign of affection. More likely, it is protectiveness.

Or possibly a warning.

"If Shaw says anything, you can tell him that it's not *my* fault she's a genius."

It is not Sloane's mother's fault that Sloane is Sloane. That hurts, and it is not precisely true.

"Due to genetic polymorphism..." That is as far as Sloane gets before the security guard takes a step forward toward her mother.

The gesture appears quite threatening.

"I'm trying to help you out here, Margot. If Shaw wanted your kid around, he'd tell you."

"I'm his kid, too," Sloane says.

There is a long pause. A 12.35-second pause, by Sloane's estimation.

"Your boss has always been very clear," Margot Tavish whispers finally, "about what he does and does not want."

CHAPTER 6

"There are three cases." Sloane had gotten better, over the years, at easing me into her calculations, but I knew from experience that soon, the numbers would be flying fast.

Fast was good. Mackenzie wasn't backlit anymore. I hadn't realized it out on the landing, but in a room with a window, it was clear that the sky outside had begun to darken.

It looked like it might storm.

"The first case I analyzed," Sloane said brightly, "was a female, seventeen years old, sixty-four inches tall, approximately one hundred and forty-two pounds fully clothed. She was found in a supine position on uneven ground with a negative twelve-degree incline."

No one else could hear Sloane, but I could feel the eyes of every person in the room on me, gauging my reaction. Mrs. McBride. The psychologist. The fireman. The crisis negotiator.

Mackenzie.

"Photographs of the scene have allowed me to pinpoint the likely launch point. Working backward from the point of impact, taking into account wind resistance, vertical and horizontal distance traveled, and a range estimate for the victim's muscle density—"

"Sloane." I kept my interruption gentle.

Obligingly, my favorite human calculator cut to the chase. "She jumped."

I couldn't let my breath hitch in my throat or allow even a flicker of surprise to show on my face. Mackenzie was watching.

I'd expected Sloane to tell me that the victims had been pushed.

"Second case," Sloane continued in a tone that anyone who didn't know her well might have mistaken for cheerful. "Male, eighteen, seventy-point-two inches tall, one hundred and thirty-one pounds. Different landing pattern, different launch point on the cliff, different point of impact—same conclusion."

I wouldn't let my insides lurch. I wouldn't let myself look at Mackenzie, out on the ledge.

The boy jumped. I'd been so sure that Mackenzie was a Natural, that she was right, that I could use that to bring her down off the ledge. Now, when I got off this phone, I'd either have to lie to her or tell her that she was wrong.

That I didn't believe her.

That I was just like everyone else.

You dance five days a week. You do martial arts. You exert control over your own body when you feel like you have control of nothing else.

Right now, your body is on the ledge.
Your body could jump.

"Cassie?" Sloane's voice broke through my thoughts. "You didn't ask me about the third victim."

In the distance, I heard thunder. I'd come into this assuming we were working with a ticking clock, but if a storm was rolling in off the ocean—we had to get Mackenzie down. Even someone who had incredible control of her own body could fall if the surface she was standing on got slick.

If there was a strong enough wind.

"What about the third victim?" I said. "Kelley."

I asked that question, because I wanted the still-listening Mackenzie to know that I'd tried. I wanted her to know, regardless of the outcome, that I'd gone into this in good faith. Kelley was the only one of the three victims Mackenzie had referenced by name.

Kelley was the one who mattered to her.

"Greater vertical distance traveled, less horizontal," Sloane rattled off. "Post-mortem X-rays suggest moderate forward rotation, despite a feet-first landing. I modeled a scenario where she stepped off the ledge with one foot and shifted weight, leading to a free fall, as well as trajectories with a greater lead-up and initial vertical push—"

"Translation?" I cut in.

"The first two victims jumped." Sloane paused. "The third didn't."

I stopped breathing, and then, without warning, the air

came whooshing out of my lungs. *She was right. Mackenzie was right.*

"I'd need better photographs of the area surrounding the launch point, as well as a more detailed analysis of weather conditions, to rule out a fall, but the most likely conclusion is…"

I finished Sloane's statement for her. "The third victim was pushed."

I shouldn't have felt relieved. No part of me should have been grateful that a teenage girl had been murdered. But the third victim was the only one Mackenzie had actually seen, the one she'd based her conclusion on.

She was right. And that meant that I didn't have to tell her that she was wrong. It meant that I'd been right, too—about Mackenzie's ability, about the circumstances that had honed it.

Mackenzie McBride was a Natural.

"Kelley didn't jump." I stated the truth, plainly and loud enough for everyone in this room—and just outside of it—to hear. Mackenzie deserved to know that she was right. She deserved for everyone in this room to know it.

She deserved to be told something other than to calm down and breathe.

If someone pushed Kelley… My brain snaked its way to the obvious conclusion. *We're not just looking at suicide contagion.*

We were looking at an UNSUB who'd used a duo of tragic deaths in an attempt to disguise a third.

YOU

You are the witness. The power, the painkiller, the peace.

Strangers have no right to take that—not from you and not from those you bless.

How dare they talk about your work? Outsiders. The thought crawls beneath your skin. What do they know about this town? About its history?

About you.

CHAPTER 7

"What are you going to do?" Mackenzie demanded. She was squatting outside the window now. Her neck was bent, her forehead nearly touching the barricade.

"We'll open an investigation." Celine kept her answer to Mackenzie short and to the point. "A murder investigation. Technically, the case won't be federal, but I have a feeling that the local police department will welcome our involvement."

Briggs would make sure of it.

As I approached the window—and Mackenzie—I wished Michael was here to tell me exactly what to read into the way Mackenzie finally allowed her forehead to rest against the barricade. Was she tired? Relieved? Now that someone believed her, was the magnitude of what she'd done to get our attention sinking in?

I stopped inches away from her. The room was silent

enough that I could hear her breathing. Outside, the sky was still painted in shades of gray, but there was no thunder, no sound at all except for Mackenzie's breathing and the barest whistling of the wind.

"You'll find out who pushed her," Mackenzie said quietly. That wasn't a question—or a request. I'd expected something like hope in her tone, but I couldn't hear much emotion in it at all.

"We will." Lia stepped forward. Of the three of us, she'd interacted with Mackenzie the least, but she was also capable of speaking with a level of conviction with which an unsuspecting listener simply could not argue. "Cassie will start crawling into people's heads. I'll interrogate—witnesses, suspects, anyone who gets on my bad side."

That got a very small smile out of Mackenzie.

"Agent Delacroix will flash her badge around and put the fear of God and the FBI in this whole town," Lia promised. "It will be a sight to behold."

If Mackenzie's only reason for crawling out on that ledge had been to make someone listen, the fact that I'd confirmed her belief, and Lia's assurances of action, would have been enough to bring her in. But thinking back on my conversation with her father, I had to wonder if that was all there was to this.

You survived. You danced. And you've been dancing ever since.

"Mackenzie, baby..." Mrs. McBride had been remarkably silent the past few minutes. "Please." Mackenzie's mother was the talker in the family. "I'm sorry I didn't believe you about Kelley. We should have listened. I'm so sorry, but can't you—"

"Don't apologize," Mackenzie interrupted tersely. "It's okay."

Beside me, Lia's gaze darted almost imperceptibly toward mine. Mackenzie was lying. It wasn't okay.

A lot of things in Mackenzie's life weren't.

"Before we can leave," I said carefully, "before we can find the person who killed Kelley..."

I waited for her to fill in the blank. She had to say it herself.

"You need me to come in." Mackenzie didn't sound angry or sad, but there was something in her tone that I recognized. Something deep and cavernous, something I'd *felt*.

"You're going to be okay," I told our newest Natural, my voice catching in my throat. "Lots of things in your life—things that have happened, things that are going to happen—won't be, but you will." I let that register. No kid gloves, no sugarcoating. "You won't ever be normal, Mackenzie, but you'll be okay."

"Personally," Lia commented, "I find normal overrated."

I willed Mackenzie to hear us. *We see you. You can come down now. You can come in.*

"What if you don't catch him?" Mackenzie turned the full force of her attention back to Celine. She looked younger all of a sudden. Vulnerable. "The person who pushed Kelley. What if he gets away with it?"

He—or she, my profiler brain filled in. *Or they.* The possibilities were myriad, and I could start sorting through them just as soon as Mackenzie was in.

"Sometimes you win," Celine replied evenly, taking Mackenzie's question at face value. "Sometimes you lose. But I can promise you that we will fight like hell for Kelley. And our track record?" Celine pressed her palm flat against one of the boards. Not the one Mackenzie was leaning against. Not too close. "It's not exactly *normal*."

You're different, Mackenzie, but so are we. We see you. You aren't alone.

"You're good at what you do?" Mackenzie's voice was hoarse.

"We found you, didn't we?" Lia's tone bordered on flippant, but somehow, that made her words sound less like a rhetorical question and more like an inviolable, uncontested, naked truth.

You won't ever be normal, but you'll be okay.

"You can trust them, Mackenzie." That statement came from behind me. *The psychologist.* I'd almost forgotten she was there, that there was anyone in this room besides Mackenzie and the three of us. "We've talked about trust, haven't we?"

That was the exact wrong thing to say. I caught Mackenzie's gaze with my own, willing her to look at me—and at Lia and at Celine.

We're not humoring you. We're like you.

Before I could say that, Quentin Nichols stepped forward. "You tell us when you're ready for us to remove the barricade," the crisis negotiator said. "You're the one in control here, Mackenzie. It's your decision."

Emphasizing her control of the situation was a good move. It was the right move, one I might have made if he'd given me the chance. But he hadn't, and my gut said that the words would sound different to Mackenzie coming from him.

He's male.

"Stay back." Mackenzie jerked her head off the board, so suddenly that I was afraid it might send her flying backward. It didn't. "You don't get to *give* me control. You don't get to stand there and say..."

"Breathe, Mackenzie," the psychologist murmured behind me.

I snapped so Mackenzie didn't have to. "She's already breathing. She's *fine*."

But I knew: *You're not fine, Mackenzie. You haven't been fine in a very long time.* Something had triggered her, taken her back to a place she didn't want to go. She was fighting that—would fight it—tooth and nail.

As long as Mackenzie stayed where she was, she was in control. On the ledge, it was *her* body, *her* choice, *her* life.

Her eyes stared past me, past Lia, past Celine, past her own mother.

Straight to the psychologist—and then to Quentin Nichols.

You're small. And he's not. He has power. And you don't. Mackenzie took a step backward. It was a small one, but...

"Mackenzie," Celine said calmly, "I need you to stand very still."

I slid sideways, blocking Mackenzie's view of the men in the room as best I could. The fireman, at least, had the presence of mind to keep his mouth shut. I didn't trust Quentin Nichols to do the same.

Mackenzie probably wasn't his first jumper. This wasn't his first rodeo. But whether he saw it or not—she *was* different.

A clap of thunder boomed in the distance. Mackenzie raised her head to the sky. Her body didn't shake. She didn't waver.

"You need me to stand still," she repeated back to Celine. "And I need you to find the person who murdered Kelley."

This is control. This is setting your own terms.

"How are we supposed to find the killer if we have to stay here and babysit you?" Lia didn't pull her punches. She wasn't a profiler, but she did have a history of trauma and a deep-seated loathing for being treated like she was traumatized.

"You don't have to stay," Mackenzie said fiercely. "I can take care of myself."

We'd been so close to her coming in. If it had been just us in the room, we could have done it. I sure as hell wasn't leaving her alone with the people who'd botched this enough to keep her out there.

This is control. I wanted to believe that we could undo the damage, talk her down, but everything inside me said that now that she'd set her terms, she'd stick to them. *Your body. Your life.*

Your choice.

"I'll stay."

I'd been on the verge of saying those words, but Celine beat me to them.

"I'll stay with you," she repeated, her focus solely on Mackenzie. "And Lia and Cassie will work the case."

"Fine." Mackenzie's voice was like steel, as a gust of wind whipped her tawny brown hair against her face. She stared at Celine for a moment longer, then turned to Lia and me. "You do your jobs," she promised, "you find Kelley's killer—and I'll come down."

YOU

There are names for what you do. Mercy is one. But another? Another is art.

CHAPTER 8

"I thought that went well."

From the passenger seat of our government-issued SUV, I glared at Lia. I knew she was just pushing my buttons—because the more she pushed them, the less mental space I could devote to how I could have played things differently with Mackenzie.

Why we'd failed.

Walking away, leaving her out on that ledge, was hard, bordering on impossible. I could still see the way Mackenzie had looked from the base of the lighthouse. *Small. Still.* She was little more than a silhouette against the darkening sky. Down below, the ocean churned, angry and haphazard as it bored into the jagged shore.

The storm was getting closer. We didn't have long.

"Are you ignoring your phone on purpose, or is it just a side effect of the brooding?" Lia managed to sound genuinely curious about the answer to that question.

I looked down at my phone. Three new text messages—all from Celine.

"Agent Delacroix keeping busy?" Lia asked archly.

"Apparently, she's been making some calls." It didn't surprise me that Celine was still coordinating the investigation, even though she was the one who'd volunteered to stay behind. Objectively, Lia and I had skill sets that were more useful when it came to talking to witnesses, but Agent Delacroix was the one with the badge.

She was the one that Mackenzie was currently watching and listening to. Showing the little Natural that the case was moving would be more effective than anything anyone in that room could say to keep Mackenzie calm.

"Celine was able to get in touch with Kelley's parents," I told Lia. "They're anxious to speak with us." I rattled off the address Celine had sent, then turned my attention back to my phone—not to the texts, to my in-box—and the files. I had the length of this drive to read through Kelley's. Before we talked to our victim's parents, I needed to get acquainted with her.

Her last name was Peterson. That was one of the many things I learned en route, as I skimmed the file once and read it again. *You were a senior at Cape Roane High School. Straight-A student, doctor parents, no siblings.* A quick perusal of her social media accounts told me that she had a propensity for standing in the middle of every picture. Based on the photographs her many public mourners were posting, she also had a tendency to come to school wearing workout clothes, like she simply couldn't have been bothered to change after she hit the gym.

Her face was fully made up in every single picture.

But the thing at the forefront of my mind as Lia and I climbed the steps to the Petersons' front porch wasn't the way Kelley had looked in those pictures.

It was the way she'd looked in the autopsy photos.

"Thank you for meeting with us." I sat opposite Kelley's parents in their formal living room. The walls were tastefully decorated with a mix of abstract art and high-quality portraits—some of the whole family, some just of Kelley. Now that their daughter was dead, the moments captured in time were haunting, but the impression that I couldn't shake was the association between the portraits and the paintings.

Kelley as decoration.

Kelley as art.

"Of course." Kelley's father was the one who replied, but the way his hand was woven through his wife's made it seem like the words were a joint effort. The doctors Peterson were Type A, good-looking, driven—but whatever else they were or were not, I was certain that they'd loved their daughter.

"The agent on the phone said that there was a development in Kelley's..." Isaac Peterson didn't seem the type to stumble over words, but he hesitated just long enough for his wife to fill in.

"...case."

Not Kelley's *death*. Not *suicide*—or even *murder*. Her

case. It felt like a euphemism, as pristine as the formal white couches on which the four of us sat.

Lia leaned forward slightly. "We have reason to believe that your daughter didn't jump." Lia knew Celine had told the parents that much. It was why they'd agreed to meet with us—but it was also our strongest entry to what would doubtlessly be a difficult conversation.

"I knew it," Kelley's mom bit out. "I knew that our little girl..." She drew in a ragged breath.

Now it was her husband's turn to finish her sentence. "We knew that Kelley couldn't and wouldn't have killed herself. We told the police as much, but they're used to parents being biased when it comes to their children."

The subtext there told me that Dr. Isaac Peterson considered himself, above all, an objective and rational person. I filed that away for future reference, but paid more attention to the way that Lia tapped two fingers—middle and index—lightly against the side of my leg. The signal was subtle, but unmistakable.

She'd caught a lie.

We knew that Kelley couldn't and wouldn't have killed herself. Dr. Alice Peterson might have believed that, but her husband was the one who'd spoken those words, and he did not.

No matter what he'd told the police, no matter how objective and rational his tone, he'd doubted his daughter. He'd believed she'd jumped.

My mind went to the autopsy—not the photographs documenting the damage wreaked by impact, but the close-up shots of Kelley's lower abdomen. Scars—small, deliberate half-moons—had stretched from one of Kelley's hip bones to the next, too low to show unless she was naked.

"Were you aware that Kelley was a cutter?" I asked Kelley's father. I knew the question wouldn't be a welcome one, but I needed to get to know Kelley well enough to crawl into her head, and I needed any information, no matter how seemingly insignificant, that might give me insight into her killer's.

"Kelley put a lot of pressure on herself." Alice Peterson seemed to consider that a full and sufficient response to my question. "She was very driven."

"A perfectionist," her husband added, sitting ramrod straight.

"She was perfect." Alice's voice cracked. I glanced at Lia, but she gave no indication that Kelley's mother was lying. Whether or not Alice Peterson had believed her daughter was flawless when she was alive, now that she was gone, she was *perfect*.

Grief had a way of warping perceptions.

"Tell me about Kelley," I suggested gently. That was all it took to open the floodgates, for *both* Dr. Petersons. How beautiful Kelley was. How smart. The fact that she'd applied early to an Ivy League university. The number of times she'd made homecoming court. How mercilessly she'd been able to dismantle her opponents in debate.

As the Petersons described their perfect daughter, I thought back again to Kelley's scars. *You didn't cut your wrists, your legs, or even your stomach. You sliced below your panty line.*

She'd literally hidden her pain, preserving the image.

If you had killed yourself? I thought, slipping into her mind. *You wouldn't have wanted a closed-casket funeral.* She wouldn't have wanted to mangle the body she left behind.

You wouldn't have jumped.

"Did Kelley have any rivals?" I asked. "Was there anyone she'd had conflict with? Any issues socially?"

"Kelley was very social," her father said immediately. "Everyone loved her."

Another tap on my leg, another lie. Even in grief, Isaac Peterson knew quite well that his daughter had *not* been universally beloved.

"You can't think of anyone who might have wanted to hurt her?" Lia pressed.

"Kelley didn't always get along with other girls." Alice pursed her lips. "They could be so jealous."

That was a loaded statement if I'd ever heard one.

"And boys?" I asked.

"They all wanted to date her," Isaac said immediately. He shook his head—in memory? In denial?

"I'm guessing she had to turn a lot of would-be Romeos down." Lia gave no indication of how carefully she was studying their responses to that statement. "Was that hard for her?"

The answers came in tandem. "I think so."

"Of course."

Two taps from Lia. Neither one of them thought Kelley disliked turning people down.

"It wasn't her fault," Alice said suddenly, leaning toward us. "What happened with the Summers boy. He was obviously very ill."

I took a moment to connect the dots. Before Kelley's death, two of her classmates had killed themselves. One was a boy.

The Summers boy?

"Kelley knew the boy who jumped?" I asked.

"This is Cape Roane," her father said dismissively. "Everyone knows everyone."

And everyone loves Kelley, I echoed his earlier lie silently back at him.

"What about the other victim?" I asked. "The girl? Did she and Kelley know each other?"

There was a long pause.

"Have you been talking to the school?" Alice Peterson couldn't have bristled more if she were actually feline. I took that to mean that someone at the school might have had something less than flattering to say about her perfect daughter.

"Was Kelley ever bullied?" I asked. That was an easier question for a parent to be asked than *Was your daughter ever accused of bullying someone else?*

"There were tiffs, of course." Kelley's mother relaxed slightly. "But nothing major. Kelley knew who she was. She wasn't the type who needed anyone's approval."

Kelley's father squeezed his wife's hand. "I will say," he told me carefully, "that the last few weeks were very hard on our daughter."

The last few weeks. Since the Summers boy jumped off a cliff? Since another of Kelley's classmates did the same?

My gut said that if I pushed either of them on that point, they would end this interview, so I sidestepped. "The police file on Kelley's death indicated that she had no defensive wounds." That, along with the other suicides and Kelley's history of self-inflicted injuries, was what had biased the police in favor of the suicide interpretation. "That suggests," I explained, "that whoever pushed Kelley didn't physically engage her beforehand. She wasn't dragged up to the steeple." I kept my tone gentle, to counteract the words. "Unless her attacker had a gun, the most likely explanation is that she went willingly."

Maybe someone coerced you into going up there. Blackmailed you. Guilted you. I sorted through the possibilities, one by one. *Or maybe the person who pushed you was someone you trusted. Maybe you went willingly, because you wanted to be alone with that person.*

Or maybe you went on your own, and your killer followed.

"Would Kelley have gone up there on a dare?" I asked. "Or for privacy—or to meet someone?"

"I..." Alice bowed her head slightly, the motion more graceful than it should have been. "I don't know."

"Is there anyone she might have trusted enough to go—"

"We don't know." Isaac Peterson repeated his wife's

sentiment, and I had the distinct sense that of everything that had passed their lips during this interview, these words hurt the most.

You thought you knew your daughter, but you've realized since she died how much you don't—and didn't—know.

"Is there anyone else we should talk to?" I asked. "Anyone Kelley might have confided in? Anyone she was close to?"

That line of inquiry seemed to center Kelley's parents. Alice folded her free hand neatly in her lap, the other still woven through her husband's.

"Kelley had a lot of friends," she declared. *Kelley was popular. Kelley was perfect. Kelley was loved.* "In fact," Alice Peterson continued, her voice shaking slightly, "the pastor called to let us know that a group of students from the high school are planning a vigil for her tonight. At the church."

YOU

There's something about heights. Something pure and true. There's clarity in those final moments.
 You'll feel it again soon.

CHAPTER 9

As I stepped out of the Petersons' house, the humidity was a visceral reminder that this wasn't an ordinary case. *It's going to rain.* We weren't on an ordinary timeline, and the insight I'd been able to glean about our victim from her parents—it wasn't enough.

I couldn't let myself spare more than a passing thought for Mackenzie or the lighthouse or the angry wind whipping my hair against my face as Lia and I made our way back to the car.

I had to focus.

I pulled myself into the passenger seat, shut the door, and let my mind linger on a single word. *You.* Not Mackenzie this time. And not the killer—not yet. *Kelley.* Knowing her— how she would have reacted, the limited circumstances in which she would have climbed to the top of the steeple of her own free will, who she might have done that with—that was a piece of the puzzle I needed. *Behavior. Personality. Environment.* Victim's and killer's BPEs were intertwined.

A cell phone rang then, pulling me from my thoughts. As Lia started the car, and I reflexively buckled my seat belt, I slipped my phone from my pocket with my free hand, then realized: it wasn't ringing.

Lia's was.

She answered it and flipped the audio to speaker. "Hey, Boy Wonder."

On the other end of the line, Michael responded with all the dignity he could muster. "I appreciate a good *Batman* reference as much as the next person, but clearly, if I were a character in that particular fictional universe, I would be Batman, not Robin." He didn't give Lia the chance to gainsay him before continuing. "Hypothetically, on a scale from thrilled to ecstatic, how delighted would you be if 'Batman' commandeered a private plane, left a pleasantly worded note for the fine folks at Quantico, and made his Bat-way to the lovely town of Cape Roane to battle evildoers at your side?"

"Michael." I beat Lia to a response, but didn't get more than his name out before she cut in.

"Hypothetically speaking, have you *already* done and/or are you in the process of doing all of the above?"

"Absolutely not."

Lia rolled her eyes. "Liar." She turned toward me. "I'm going to need directions to the church."

"Spiritual awakening?" Michael asked her.

"Impending vigil for our murder victim," I corrected. It took all of three minutes for me to get Lia the directions and catch Michael up to speed on the case—all of it. *Mackenzie, what she'd seen when she looked at Kelley's body, the stakes for our newest Natural now.*

Kelley.

Her parents.

"Let's face it," Lia cut in. "Grief turns everyone into liars. It doesn't, however, make you a *good* liar—and our victim's parents, her father in particular, were very, very good." She paused. "If I were anyone else, I would have fully believed that he'd never so much as entertained the idea that his daughter had killed herself. And the wife?" Lia pressed her foot on the gas, reminding me for the umpteenth time why I really needed to stop letting her drive. "She totally didn't buy that any *tiffs* Kelley had had with her classmates were because other girls were just so jealous."

"Translation?" Michael asked.

"Far be it from me to act like a profiler," Lia replied, "but—and I say this as someone who has deeply embraced the title of lovable bitch—I deeply suspect that Kelley Peterson played to win and played for keeps."

"She was competitive," I confirmed. "With herself and with other people. I don't know that I would go so far as to call her a lovable bitch."

"You say tomato," Lia commented. "I say to-mah-to."

You were in pain, Kelley. You hid it. Did you cut down others—deliberately, precisely—the way you cut yourself? Most people tended to turn aggression either inward or outward. There was bleed-over, but it was somewhat rare to find a person with equal proclivities for both. *Power. Pain. Perfection.*

I knew Kelley now better than I had before, but it still wasn't enough.

"I sense a disturbance in the force," Michael observed on the other end of the phone line. "Heavy silence of the emotionally laden variety."

"Cassie's composing a mental poem," Lia told him. " 'Ode to a Profiler's Angst.' "

"I'm trying to figure out if Kelley was the type of person who would have climbed the steeple on her own," I corrected, "or if someone else led her up there."

Power. Pain. Perfection. It wasn't hard for me to imagine Kelley making the climb. Because she could. Because, on some level, it might hurt. *Did the killer take you by surprise? Or,* I thought, picturing the aftermath of Kelley's impact with the ground in my mind, *was it his—or her—idea?*

I could feel the shift coming. This wasn't just about Kelley anymore. I was hovering around the edges of someone else's subconscious. The UNSUB's.

The *Unknown Subject's.*

The killer's.

"We're about a minute out from the church," Lia informed me—and Michael. "When do you land, Batboy?"

"Bat*man*," Michael loftily corrected. "And fifteen minutes, give or take. Might I suggest that until then, we handle this old-school?"

"Old-school as in sneaking out of the FBI Academy like an unruly teenager and opting to ask for forgiveness instead of permission?" Lia asked innocently. All things considered, that was probably a pretty accurate depiction of what Michael had done when he'd realized that the case we were working now had ties to one of our old ones.

Michael cleared his throat. "I was thinking more along the lines of 'old-school' as in 'making liberal use of video surveillance.'"

When we'd first started out, the only way we'd been given access to witnesses was through a video feed, courtesy of our FBI handlers.

"Call me sentimental," Michael continued, "but it would hit me right in the feelings if my favorite deception detector could deal me in for old times' sake while I'm in transit. Just think about it, Zhang. You, poking around the vigil, asking questions and listening for lies, me on the lookout for anyone who's not grieving nearly as much as they'd like us to believe...."

"Be still, my heart." No one could deadpan like Lia. "I will surely be unable to control the animal attraction this nostalgia will provoke."

I snorted, but all things considered, Michael's suggestion wasn't a bad one. It wasn't unusual for killers to return to the scene of the crime, or to attend funerals, wakes, vigils, or other occasions marking the passing. *And if you are there...*

Triumph. Anger. Adrenaline. Guilt. The range of emotions Michael would be on the lookout for was wide—but I had every confidence he could spot it.

"And what is Cassie going to be doing while we take this trip down memory lane?" Lia threw the question out there, as much for my benefit as for Michael's.

If we'd had the time, I might have joined them. But the clock was ticking. We needed every advantage we could get.

"I'm going to get a feel for the crime scene and start a profile on the killer," I said.

And that was my cue to call Dean.

DEAN, AGE TWELVE

Eleven years earlier

"How are you doing, son?"

Dean stares at the FBI agent. What are the chances that Agent Briggs isn't thinking about how Dean is *doing*? What are the chances that he's thinking about what Dean has *done*?

"Fine." Fewer words are better. Dean learned that pretty quickly after his father's arrest. *Yes, ma'am* and *no, ma'am*, *yes, sir* and *no, sir*, and not causing trouble.

Not that it helps.

"You're fine," Agent Briggs repeats, eyeing the bruise on Dean's cheekbone.

"It doesn't hurt." Dean isn't lying. The pain is there, but it can't touch him. That's part of being what he is, isn't it? A lack of sensitivity to pain? To fear? To feeling?

Dean wonders, sometimes, if that's how it started for his

father. Every day, he remembers the feel of the knife in his hand. The smell of burning flesh.

"You did what you had to do, Dean. If you hadn't played your father's game, if you hadn't convinced him you *wanted* to play, he would have killed Veronica." Special Agent Tanner Briggs is awfully forgiving for someone whose wife's flesh is now branded with Dean's initials. "You hurt her so that he'd leave you alone with her."

Don't tell me I helped her escape. Don't tell me I'm the reason she's alive. Don't tell me I'm the reason my father is behind bars. He's a monster.

So am I.

"Is someone giving you a hard time?" Briggs tries again. "Because of your father?"

"I should go." Dean is twelve. He's not stupid. He knows that people want to say that they've done what they can for him.

He knows, even at twelve, that there's nothing anyone can do.

"Wait." Agent Briggs doesn't touch him, but Dean has to push down the instinct to react like he has.

No one touches me. No one should *touch me.* If Dean doesn't let people touch him, if he doesn't touch back—he can't hurt them.

He can't become his father.

"There's something else I wanted to talk to you about," Agent Briggs says suddenly. "A case."

Suddenly, Dean can hear himself think again. "Like my father's?"

"Not exactly." Briggs pauses. "The UNSUB—unknown subject—that we're currently tracking has killed at least three prostitutes in the last eight weeks."

How? The question echoes in Dean's mind, again and again until he has to ask it out loud.

"The women were beaten to death."

"Beaten bare-fisted?" For Dean, the question is automatic. He's already imagining the way the women would have fought back, the way that might have made the person beating them feel. "Or with a blunt object?"

"Neither." Briggs pauses for just a moment. "Our killer beats women to death wearing gloves."

Dean pictures it. Something gives inside of him, something visceral and hopeful and dark. Maybe he can make a difference. Maybe he can atone.

Maybe *thinking* like a killer is enough.

CHAPTER 10

Dean didn't answer when I called. I tailed Lia to the church's front office, but once she'd been directed to the youth area, where Kelley's friends—or possibly, her "friends"—were setting up for the vigil, I peeled off and stepped back outside.

In all likelihood, most of Kelley's social group still believed that she had killed herself. I knew better. Standing with my feet on solid ground, I stared up at the steeple.

The sky was dark enough to send a shiver down my spine.

With or without Dean, there was no time to spare in stepping into the UNSUB's mind. *You know your way around this church—well enough to know how to get up to the steeple. Did you know Kelley, too?*

Did she trust you?

As a profiler, my most important task was to separate the parts of a murder that were incidental from the parts that signified something specific about the killer. To the extent that a murder had been planned, the question morphed: Which parts of the plan were necessary?

Which parts were required only to fulfill your needs?

With what little I knew, I couldn't begin to guess motive yet. Maybe the killer had hated Kelley—or been fixated on her—for some time. Maybe her recent actions had drawn attention. Based on the way Kelley's parents had staunchly insisted that what happened to the Summers boy was *not* Kelley's fault, it was also possible that some people had blamed her for her classmate's suicide.

Maybe the suicides did nothing more than provide you convenient cover for Kelley's death—or maybe, in your mind, they're connected. As I addressed the killer, I couldn't even rule out the possibility that Kelley's death had been unplanned—that she'd climbed the steeple of her own volition, for her own reasons, and the killer had followed and acted on impulse.

There were too many variables. To sort through them— and I had to sort through them now, not later—I needed to concentrate on what I knew to be true. There were three elements to any murder: the victim, the location, and the method of killing.

I knew all three, and that was a start.

Victim: You chose Kelley. Why? That question could cycle too easily right back to motive, so I tried again. *Why this girl? What was it about her that got your attention? Did you see the Kelley the world saw—homecoming court and Ivy League and standing dead-center in every picture? Or did you know the real Kelley? She was vulnerable. Most people didn't see that.*

Did you? I rolled that question over in my mind. *Did she remind you of someone—or was this about her? Did she do something? Did you hate her?*

Did she trust you?

That was too many questions and not enough answers, so I turned to the next element of the crime. *Location: You killed her at a church.* I found myself pacing around the base of the building, my face tilting toward the sky the way Mackenzie's had, back at the lighthouse. *Churches are holy. Sacred. You killed this girl on holy ground.*

What did that say about our killer? For some, it might have been about sending a message, but not for an UNSUB who'd never intended for anyone to know that the victim had been murdered.

If you chose the church, you didn't choose it to send a message. You chose it for you—either for your convenience or your satisfaction. Are you religious? Or would any structure this tall do?

There was something about heights. Even standing with my feet on the ground, looking up at the way the steeple stretched into the sky, I felt it.

The higher you go, the farther away the rest of the world feels. It was just you and Kelley up there. Just Kelley and you.

On the brink of something but unable to push through, I tried Dean a second time, and this time, he answered.

"Cassie." Hearing him say my name sent a wave of something like relief—with a side of anticipation—through my body.

"Strangling someone is intimate," I said, well aware that

was *not* the way that normal girls started conversations with their boyfriends. "Shooting someone is not. But pushing them off a building…"

Pushing involves physical contact. You touched her. Did you want to? Either way, given the lack of defensive wounds, it had been quick.

"Cassie." Dean said my name again, and this time, I heard something different in his tone. The two of us were used to profiling in tandem. I profiled in second person. He profiled killers in first.

He wasn't profiling anyone or anything now.

"Briggs sent Sloane some files," I said, taking a step back. I'd assumed that Sloane had shared them, that Dean would have started sorting through them as surely as Michael, whose emotion-reading ability was of the most use in person, had taken off.

"I've seen the files," Dean told me. "All three of them."

That gave me pause. "All three?"

Sloane's conclusion had been clear: the first two victims had jumped. That was why we were focusing on Kelley—and the church.

"I'm sorry I missed your call," Dean continued. "I was getting ready to return it. I just wanted to be sure first."

"Sure?" I asked, wishing he were here, that I could see him, touch him, get a preview of some kind as to what he was thinking.

"Look at the first file," Dean said. "The photos of the victim taken at the scene."

I set my phone to speaker and went back to the original email from Briggs, pulling up the file.

The pictures.

The body.

At first, all I saw was blood and bone, a body mangled on the rocks. I knew from Mackenzie that the first two teens had jumped from a cliff, but that wasn't visible in the picture.

"Do you see it?" The moment the question exited Dean's mouth, I did. Beside the body, a foot or two removed and even with the victim's neck, was a plant of some kind, caught between two rocks. At first glance, it looked like it was growing there, but something about the positioning made me question that conclusion.

"I see it. Have you asked Sloane—"

"To ID the plant?" Dean finished. "She says it's from the genus *hedera*. Ivy. She's in the process of identifying the exact species, but she gave it a ninety-eight point seven percent chance that it doesn't grow naturally nearby."

The fingers on my right hand tightened around the phone. If the plant didn't grow nearby, that meant that it had been left there, tucked between two rocks.

"Tell me what you're thinking," Dean murmured. Something in his tone made me think that the first time I'd called, he'd been buried too deep in the UNSUB's mind to hear the phone ring. He wanted to know if he'd gone too deep, if I saw it, too.

"The first two victims weren't murdered," I said. "Sloane said they jumped."

And yet...

Without being prompted to, I downloaded a photograph of the second suicide victim. Scanning the surroundings didn't reveal any plants—flowered or otherwise—among the rocks, but there was a small collection of stones.

Four of them, clustered a foot or two to the right of the victim's neck.

"Mourning," I said, parsing through it out loud. "Or marking." I paused, then went ahead and took that logic one step further. "Someone found the bodies before the police did and marked the sites."

Were you the one who found them? Did you know them? Mourn for them?

"What are the chances of the same person finding both suicide victims?" I asked. The markers might have been different, but the positioning was the same.

Dean's response was a long time in coming. "The chances are good," he said finally, his voice reverberating in my bones, "if I watched."

YOU

There have been so many over the years. Kelley was different. Kelley was not your best work. You failed her.

You won't fail again.

CHAPTER 11

"How could our UNSUB have known in advance that there would be something *to* watch?" I asked.

Once was a coincidence. Twice was a pattern. In our line of work, patterns had meaning. Sometimes, they told us about a suspect's routine. Where they lived. How they spent their time. The radius in which they traveled.

But sometimes?

A pattern told us about the killer's need.

"I need to watch," Dean said, his words echoing my thoughts almost exactly. "The last moments...the decisions..."

"How do you know?" I asked again, the question catching my throat. "How did you know those teens were going to jump? Why were you there?"

To watch. The answer to the second question drowned out all possible responses to the first. *To mourn*.

Typically, any indicators of mourning—flowers, dressing

the victim, covering the face—were signs that an UNSUB felt some degree of remorse. The posthumous honoring of a victim was an expression of complex emotion, one that allowed a killer to simultaneously make amends and retell the story of the death in their own head.

"You didn't kill the first two," I said, feeling Dean's presence on the other end of the phone line, as surely as if he'd been there in person. "They killed themselves. They jumped."

"Kelley didn't," Dean said, his voice throaty and low. "She didn't jump."

"You didn't mark her body." Those two facts were enough of a divergence from the voyeur's MO that I should have wondered if we were talking about two different people.

But the alternative was that we were dealing with escalation.

You're the watcher. You serve as witness. But Kelley didn't go over the edge of her own volition.

"What if she was supposed to?" I asked suddenly. "What if Kelley was supposed to jump?"

I'd wondered earlier what the killer had seen in Kelley.

"She was vulnerable," I told Dean. I closed my eyes for a moment, then shifted to Kelley's perspective. "*I* was vulnerable. I climbed the steeple willingly. I just... I *hurt*."

Despite Kelley's father's objections to the contrary, he'd believed she'd killed herself.

"You were in pain," Dean said simply, "and now you're not."

Maybe I'd been looking at the markers—ivy, stone—all wrong. Maybe they weren't signs of mourning—or remorse.

Maybe they were symbols of honor. *Release.*

"I trusted you," I said, still trying to view this from Kelley's perspective. "I either told you what I was planning..."

"Or," Dean replied softly, "it was my idea."

How could an UNSUB have known in advance that two teens were going to kill themselves? *Either they told you—or it was your idea.*

Standing outside the church, looking up, it was too easy to picture Kelley up there, staring down.

"I didn't jump," I said, speaking on her behalf. "Maybe I wanted to. Maybe I thought about it. But it didn't feel right." I'd recognized earlier that Kelley wouldn't have wanted a death that would mangle her body beyond recognition. Was that what she'd realized, up on the steeple? "I didn't jump," I said fiercely. "I didn't want to."

"You were in pain," Dean repeated what he'd said earlier. "And now you're not."

"Is that what you think this is?" I asked. "Not murder, but mercy?"

"There's something holy about what I do," Dean replied steadily.

I couldn't stay in Kelley's perspective any longer. "Something holy," I echoed Dean, "about the height and the fall."

If jumping to her death *hadn't* been Kelley's idea, if someone had pushed her toward it, that suggested the manner of death held significance to the UNSUB instead. *You planted the idea in her head. You encouraged it. And when she couldn't do it...*

"It's a sacrament," Dean said. "A rite."

I thought of Kelley, looking down at the world from high up on a church. She hadn't wanted to do it. She'd *chosen* not to.

"Kelley didn't want your mercy," I said lowly, addressing the nameless, faceless killer with that much more vehemence than before.

"But," Dean countered, "she needed it." For the longest time, he was silent on the other end of the line, and I stood outside the church, my face chapped from wind, my limbs like deadweight on my body as I sorted through all I knew.

"What have you read," Dean asked me finally, fully himself and not speaking for the killer anymore, "about assisted suicide?"

The question took me by surprise, but it shouldn't have. If our UNSUB had witnessed the first two suicides, if he or she had known they were going to happen, had in any way encouraged them...

That could be seen as assistance.

And Kelley? She'd been "assisted" right over the edge.

"What do you know about mercy killings?" Dean said, amending the term he'd used before. "So-called 'angels of death' typically begin with a loved one, often one who has asked for assistance. But after that..." He trailed off for a moment. "They don't stop, and their victims aren't always willing."

"Mercy," I said, latching on to part of what Dean had said. "Even for the unwilling."

Like Kelley.

"What's the typical profile for a mercy killer?" I asked,

trying to view this objectively, trying not to think what Kelley's final moment, rushing toward the ground, realizing she'd been pushed, would have been like.

"Most often," Dean said, "you'd be looking at someone whose occupation grants them access to victims whose health has degraded to the point that they cannot fight back."

Kelley had been young and healthy—physically. Mentally, however, she'd struggled. I hadn't spent enough time on the other two files to know anything about the first two victims, but given that they *had* jumped, I had to assume that they'd had that much in common with Kelley.

Young. Vulnerable. In pain.

We were looking for someone with access to vulnerable teenagers—most likely, an adult. A teacher. A volunteer. A parent. A coach. Someone these kids trusted. Someone who could lead them right up to the brink and watch them fall.

"A mercy killer needs more than access," I said. "They need a skill set that will allow them to go undetected."

"Right," came Dean's reply. "In most cases, you'd expect some form of medical training."

Medical training. Access. "Have you ever heard of an angel of death who preys on people with mental health issues?" I asked Dean.

"No." He hesitated, just for a moment. "But I'd give it ten to one odds that the person who fits that particular profile has some kind of background in the mental health field."

We were looking for someone with access to vulnerable

teens. Someone with experience in mental health. *Someone, I thought, with psychological training, who knows exactly what to say to push someone over the edge.*

I barely felt the first drop of rain—or the second. I could see the lighthouse in the distance, and suddenly, I flashed back to the moment when I'd been close—*so close*—to talking Mackenzie down from the ledge.

"Dean," I said suddenly. "Our killer likes to watch."

My boyfriend replied, but I couldn't hear him. I couldn't form another coherent sentence, because all I could think, as the sky opened up and rain came down in sheets, was that Mackenzie was still out there on that ledge.

Right where you want her.

YOU

Poor little Mackenzie. What she's been through. What she's suffered. She needs help. Your help.

Release.

CHAPTER 12

I took off running. Cape Roane was a small town. The church and the lighthouse were separated by a matter of blocks.

"Call Lia," I told Dean, "or Michael. Tell them we have to get back to Mackenzie."

I didn't wait for a response. I just hung up and kept running. *I never should have left.* It was part and parcel of being a profiler that I tended to get absorbed in cases. I'd been so focused on Kelley and her killer, but I never should have taken my eyes off Mackenzie. From the moment I'd realized that this killer liked to watch...

I should have known you'd be there. Watching.

The lighthouse was closer now, but not close enough. My sides were already starting to burn, my lungs beginning to tighten like a vise in my chest, but I managed to keep enough presence of mind to give my cell phone a verbal command.

"Call Celine."

She answered, and I stopped running, just long enough to catch my breath—long enough to ask: "Mackenzie?"

"Everything is fine here." Celine's response was measured—unnaturally so. "The rain is a problem, but Mackenzie knows that, and we're discussing next steps."

I was soaked. Mackenzie must have been, too. *And the ledge...*

"You need to get her in," I told Celine. "And if you can't, you need to get her psychologist out of the room. Now."

As I reached the lighthouse, I could hear a voice ringing in my mind. *You can trust them, Mackenzie. We've talked about trust, haven't we?*

I'd thought the woman treating Mackenzie was incompetent. She'd said exactly the wrong thing at precisely the right moment to throw a kink in the works. If she'd kept her mouth shut, I could have talked Mackenzie down.

Maybe that was the point.

Thunder crashed, loud enough to jar my bones, but all I could think about was getting to Mackenzie.

Celine and our suspect met me halfway up the lighthouse stairs.

"Agent Delacroix said you needed a consult?" The psychologist didn't sound annoyed, but her tone was brisk. "Something about adolescent depression?"

I glanced over at Celine. Apparently, she'd had to think on her feet to get the woman out of the room without causing a scene.

Point, Agent Delacroix.

"You should get back to Mackenzie," I told Celine. "Let her know that Lia and I held up our end of the deal. She can come in."

Tell her, I didn't say, *that I know who killed Kelley.*

The psychologist stiffened. "If you're going to be talking to Mackenzie," she told Celine, "I should really be there."

I stepped up, coming even with the woman. "Please," I said. "This won't take long, and it's urgent."

I could feel Celine looking at me. I was asking her to leave me alone with a woman I believed to be a killer. Under normal circumstances, she would have refused. Based on protocol, she should have.

But with the storm—with Mackenzie still out there—protocol was the least of our worries.

"Don't worry," Celine told me, even as her eyes said *Be careful.* "We'll bring Mackenzie in."

Celine returned the way she'd come, leaving me alone with the suspect. Now I just had to keep the suspect occupied long enough for Celine and the others to talk Mackenzie down.

Without interference this time.

Also, I thought, hyperaware of the space between my body and the killer's next to me, *I have to keep you talking long enough for my backup to arrive.*

"We're trying to get a handle on the motive behind the first two suicides," I said, wishing Lia were here to sell the lie for me. "Is your practice focused on children Mackenzie's age and younger, or do you treat older adolescents as well?"

"I primarily work with teenagers," came the impatient response. "Mackenzie was referred to me by a colleague several months back. I'm afraid that without an in-depth look at your files I cannot comment on the specific cases you're interested in. I *can* say, however, that children and adolescents have emotional lives every bit as complex as that of adults. Teenagers are individuals, not statistics. I could no more talk to you about a unified motive behind adolescent suicide than I could were we discussing adults."

"I understand," I said, also comprehending that unless I wanted to turn this into a confrontation, sans backup, I needed to give her something to stay for.

You're drawn to pain. People with scars that run deep. The vulnerable ones, in need of your mercy.

"It wasn't that long ago," I said, laying the trap, "that I was a teenager myself."

There was a moment's pause, during which I registered exactly how narrow the stairs we were standing on were.

How easy it would be for her to push me.

"I have to confess, when you said you'd been working with the FBI since you were seventeen, I looked for the signs."

Keep her talking, I thought. *Give her what she wants.*

"The signs of what?" I asked.

"Psychological trauma." Her expression was neutral, but I could feel her stare crawling over my skin. "Working cases like Mackenzie's when you were still a child yourself—that's a lot to take on."

Her tone was open, almost kind, and I remembered

everything that Dean and I had concluded about our UNSUB from the files.

You see yourself as an angel of mercy. The first time you saw someone—or helped someone—commit suicide, they were probably in incredible pain, you probably loved them, and they might well have asked for your help.

You know trauma. You recognize it. Some part of you craves it.

Down below, I heard the door open and prayed that it was Lia—just like I prayed that up above, Celine and the crisis negotiator and Mackenzie's mother had talked Mackenzie down.

"I really should be getting back to my patient." The psychologist took a step up, positioning herself above me.

I said the only thing I could think of to stop her in her tracks. "I killed my mother." *You know trauma. You recognize it. You liberate the sufferer from it.* "She made me do it, but it was my hand holding the knife."

I only needed another minute, maybe two. I needed to distract her from the sound of footsteps running up the stairs toward us.

"I dream about it," I said. "All of it, all the time."

"I'm going back to Mackenzie." Her voice was sharp, her movement up the stairs sudden.

I followed and grabbed for her arm. I'd offered her a taste of my pain. It wasn't enough to keep her here—but I had to keep her away from Mackenzie.

"Let me go."

"Did you treat the Summers boy?" I asked her, hoping to

catch her off guard. "What about the girl who killed herself? Were you *treating* her, too?"

The response was chilling. "What are you trying to imply?"

In for a penny, in for a pound. "I'm implying that you wanted them to kill themselves," I said, buying precious seconds. "But you overplayed your hand with Kelley."

She jerked her arm out of my grasp, sending me flying backward into the wall. I steadied myself and prepared for another blow.

It didn't come.

"It's a mercy, isn't it?" I pressed. "What you offer them? What you do? What you *did* to Kelley."

The footsteps were right upon us now, but I couldn't afford to turn my back on the killer above me.

She leaned forward. "I had *nothing* to do with what happened to Kelley Peterson."

I saw a flash of motion out of the corner of my eye. Lia rounded the corner, Michael beside her, gun in hand. He raised it.

"You with the righteously indignant, yet distinctly guilty expression on your face! Hands in the air!"

The psychologist's gaze darted from me to Michael to Lia.

"Batman said to put your hands in the air," Lia told her. "And while you're at it, repeat what you just said about the death of Kelley Peterson."

MICHAEL, AGE TWELVE
Eleven years ago

"You're feeling annoyed." Michael Townsend offers the headmaster what passes for a twelve-year-old's most charming smile. "But also: secretly impressed with my hijinks. And is that...*anticipation* I see?" Michael gestures toward the headmaster's face. "Asymmetrical lip tilt, dilated pupils. Is someone secretly hoping for a new auditorium? Tennis courts? A donation to the development fund, perhaps?"

Michael's father has a history of buying his son's way out of trouble. Michael has a history of making that difficult.

It's a point of pride, really.

"What is it that you want, Mr. Townsend?" The headmaster has that austere, you-*will*-respect-me tone down. "What exactly are you hoping to accomplish?"

There was a time when Michael tried *not* to make his father angry, but it's easier now that he does the reverse. Now Michael sees the punches coming.

"What am I hoping to accomplish? Boarding school." Michael makes a show of examining his own knuckles as he answers the headmaster's question. "I'm hoping to get kicked out of this fine establishment, at which point my father will have no choice but to send me to boarding school. Possibly a string of boarding schools. Very far away, very in favor of generous donors with troublesome offspring."

"You *want* to be expelled?" The headmaster seems to find that preposterous—and also somewhat concerning.

"I need structure," Michael declares, propping his feet up on the edge of the headmaster's desk. "Discipline."

I need to get away from my father.

"Feet, Mr. Townsend."

Michael leaves his feet exactly where they are. He hears the secretary enter the room behind him. "Thatcher Townsend will be here shortly," she announces.

Michael can feel the muscles in his shoulders and back start to tense. He won't let them. "Wonderful man, my father," he comments.

That gets a response from the headmaster: a subtle curl of his upper lip, too slight for 99 percent of the population to see. Michael recognizes the emotion for what it is. *Distaste, not quite disgust.*

The headmaster doesn't think that Michael's father is a wonderful man. *He knows.*

"You're a school official." Michael keeps his voice light and pleasant. "That makes you a mandatory reporter, doesn't it?"

The headmaster stiffens. "You should wait outside."

"I will be thrilled to wait outside," Michael promises, "after I tell you a tale of great woe." He pauses. "You might want to pull up my attendance records as corroboration."

"Mr. Townsend—"

Michael meets his gaze. "It would be unfortunate for you to have to report one of your biggest donors for suspected child abuse." Michael doesn't enjoy thinking of himself as *abused*, so he doesn't dwell on the word.

He relishes the moment.

"Almost as unfortunate," he adds, "as if I were to report you for *not* reporting one of your biggest donors." Michael allows his feet to thump down on the floor and leans forward. "Or," he says, his voice low, "you could expel me, and I could refrain from telling you anything *unfortunate* at all."

CHAPTER 13

"I didn't push Kelley Peterson. I didn't kill her. I didn't even *know* her."

The suspect's hands were in the air. I took one step away from her, then another, easing down the staircase toward Michael and—

"True."

I whipped my head toward Lia, who shrugged. "She's telling the truth."

My heart skipped a beat, and I looked for a loophole in the psychologist's statement. *You didn't push Kelley. You didn't kill her. You didn't even know her.*

"Then why, pray tell," Michael said, his gun still pointed toward her, "do you feel guilty?"

"I don't—"

"Head tilted downward, forehead fighting furrows, gaze averted, mouth drooping—don't even get me started on the direction your eyebrows are arching." Michael lowered his weapon—most likely to put her at ease. "That combination puts you somewhere between shame and guilt, even if that lovely narrowing of your eyes and the way your muscles just tightened suggest you're pissed, too."

You didn't push Kelley. You didn't kill her. You feel guilty. I tried to make the situation compute, but it didn't, because the UNSUB we were looking for might have mourned victims, might even have felt remorse at the way things had to be, but that wasn't the dominant emotion in these kills. Neither was anger.

Exaltation. Release.

"You didn't kill Kelley," I said, trying a new tack. "You *saved* her. You didn't push her; you set her free. And you feel guilty because you weren't able to honor her passing, the way you did with the others...."

"No," the psychologist snapped. "I feel guilty because when *Mackenzie* told me that Kelley was pushed, I didn't believe her. I feel guilty that I left my most vulnerable patient—on a ledge that's getting slicker by the second—for this."

You feel guilty, I thought reflexively, *because if you'd kept your mouth shut when I was on the verge of talking Mackenzie down, she might not still be up there.*

That wasn't me profiling the killer. That was me profiling the woman standing two steps above me—and that distinction was enough to send my heart pounding in my ears.

As if from a great distance, I heard Lia confirm that every word that the psychologist had just spoken was true. Her guilt was centered on Mackenzie.

You're the reason she's still in such a precarious position. A crack of thunder drowned out every other noise in the stairwell, but not the deafening roar of my own thoughts. *But you're not the only reason.*

Mackenzie's psychologist wasn't the only one who'd spoken up and whose words had kept Mackenzie out on that ledge. *You weren't the only person in that room with a background in psychology, motivation, mental illness, and the human mind.*

I had similar training—and I was willing to lay a lot of money on it that any crisis negotiator worth his salt had the same.

You're the one in control here, Quentin Nichols had told Mackenzie. *It's your decision.*

I'd assumed that he hadn't realized how Mackenzie would take a man in a position of power *giving* her control, like it was his to dole out. But in Quentin Nichols's line of work, he *had* to know what to say, how to manipulate a target, how to defuse a dangerous situation...

Or how to blow it up.

YOU

The boards are off the windows. It's just you and Mackenzie now, separated by feet.

Soon to be inches.

Clearing the room before the FBI agent returned was the right call. You promised Mackenzie's mother that this would be over shortly.

It will be.

You wouldn't have chosen Mackenzie. She's younger than Cara was—younger than you were when Cara died—but she's hurting. You can see that. You feel it. This child is hurting. She will always hurt.

She needs you.

You didn't arrange for Mackenzie to be standing on that ledge. You didn't befriend her, didn't mentor her, didn't lead her to this place. She's not like the others, but she needs you all the same.

Needs this.

And after Kelley? Your heart ticks up a beat. You need this, too.

CHAPTER 14

I pushed past the psychologist and bolted up the stairs, aware that Michael and Lia were following on my heels, but focused only on Mackenzie. *The ledge. It's slick now. You're shivering. What's he saying to you?*

What is he nudging you to do?

I reached the ninth-story landing to find Mrs. McBride and the fireman standing to one side. Celine was on the other side of them, fighting with the door to the lightroom. It was jammed.

The ladder was up.

"Mackenzie let us take the boards off the window," Mrs. McBride told me, breathless, glowing, and fighting tears. "Quentin said she needed space—but she's coming down."

They'd left her alone with him—and based on the trouble Celine was having with the door, he'd locked them out.

"Nichols isn't talking her *down*," I told Celine, keeping my voice low. "We have to get in there. *Now.*"

It took time for the fireman to cut through the door, time for Celine to pull down what was left of the ladder.

Time we didn't have.

Per protocol, Agent Delacroix pulled herself up first. I followed a heartbeat later—screw protocol. On the far side of the room, Mackenzie stood ramrod still on the ledge, the window open, the remains of the barricade scattered on the floor.

Quentin Nichols stood between her and us—close enough that he could have pulled Mackenzie in.

If he'd wanted to.

"It's not your fault you're different," the crisis specialist was murmuring. "I'm betting that no one asked you, back then, if you wanted to be saved. If there was anything left worth saving."

Lightning flashed behind Mackenzie, sending an almost tactile shock through the room. But Mackenzie didn't jolt. Her muscles held steady. As rain and wind beat at her, her eyes stayed focused.

On the man in front of her.

"You told yourself that you came up here for Kelley, but, Mackenzie? If this were just about Kelley, you wouldn't still be out there." Quentin Nichols sounded tender.

He sounded sure.

"There's no shame," he said, "in taking control and deciding for yourself what you need."

Control. Decide. His word choices were deliberate—and given the way Mackenzie's mind worked, terrifying. He shifted his weight forward, so slightly that it might not have been visible to his target on the ledge.

She would have felt it all the same.

You know what she needs. I silently addressed Quentin. *You know that left to her own devices, she might not do it.*

"He pushed Kelley." I said the one thing guaranteed to draw the UNSUB's attention my way—the one thing sure to break through to Mackenzie. "She wouldn't jump, so he pushed her."

"I let her go," Nichols corrected, his attention still focused on Mackenzie, his tone still gentle. "Kelley was hurting. Some pain gets better—but some doesn't. What you've lived through, Mackenzie? The fight you fight every day? It's not going away."

It felt like he was telling me that—not just her.

"Part of you will always be in that shack," he continued softly, the sudden cruelty of that statement jarring. "And as long as you're there—the man responsible wins."

"No," I said, my voice like a gunshot that ricocheted through the lightroom. "You win, Mackenzie, because you're alive. Because you survived. Because that son of a bitch is in the ground, and Mackenzie McBride is still dancing."

"Step back from the window." Celine had her weapon raised and aimed at Nichols. The crisis negotiator didn't even seem to register it.

Mercy is what matters. What you and only you can give Mackenzie—no one can take that away.

"Your FBI friends think you'll come in," he told the girl

on the ledge. "They think I'm the one keeping you out there. They think you're that easily manipulated—that you're helpless and weak, and if they tell you fairy tales, you'll believe them. But I'll tell you the truth." He paused, his expression tender. "I had a sister like you. Bad things happened to her. Like you. I didn't understand then, but I do now. Some wounds can't heal. Some *people* can't heal." He took a step toward her this time—a full step. "But you don't have to do this—you don't have to *end* this—alone."

"He killed Kelley," I repeated, close to shouting now to be heard over the storm, to make her hear me. "He *wants* you to jump." No matter how much I wanted to, I couldn't tell Mackenzie that everything he'd said was a lie, because it wasn't. Even when wounds healed, the scars remained. She'd always feel them.

But this was her body. Her choice. Her life.

"Dance," I told her. She was on a ledge. It was pouring rain. That was the last thing I should have advised, but in that four-by-four shack, when she was just a little girl, Mackenzie had danced—hours upon hours, again and again, because it was *her* body.

Because no one was going to take that away.

"Don't listen to him, Mackenzie. *Dance*."

Slowly, she raised her arms, rounding them in front of her, then allowing them to part. She shifted her weight to one foot, the other toe pointing.

For the first time since we'd entered the room, Quentin Nichols turned to face Celine and me head-on.

"Hands in the air!" Celine barked. "On the ground!"

On some level, I was aware that Michael and Lia had joined us, that Celine had backup. But my attention was focused solely on the man in front of me.

The man who was close enough to Mackenzie to reach out and touch her.

"I didn't plan this," he told me.

You didn't search Mackenzie out. You didn't groom her. You didn't lead her slowly toward this, day by day.

"You planned the others," I countered. "You found them. You listened to them." I swallowed. "You made them trust you."

"I volunteer," Quentin said, closing his eyes for just a moment, the expression on his face eerily wistful. "I coach. I work with the youth group at the church."

He didn't just have one point of access, one set of hunting grounds. He'd cultivated several.

"There have been others," I stated, reading into that. "Over the years."

"I'm there for them. I help when I can. And when I can't..." He bowed his head, the motion bordering on ceremonial. "I offer release."

Behind him, Mackenzie stopped dancing. Her eyes meeting mine, she sank slowly to a sitting position.

She's coming in.

I tried not to show even a hint of relief.

"What I do is a duty," Nichols was saying, "not a pleasure."

"It's mercy," I said. I had to keep his attention on me. I couldn't let him turn around.

For a moment, I thought it was working, and then, without warning, he whirled. He saw Mackenzie. She froze. Her legs were dangling into the room. She was almost safe.

You will save her. He moved.

I lunged forward, knowing even as I did that I couldn't get to him before he reached her. A gunshot went off. My ears ringing, I hit the ground. The impact knocked the breath from my chest. I looked up, forcing my eyes to the ledge.

Mackenzie was sitting there.

Nichols was down.

Celine approached him, her freshly fired gun still in her hands. Taking use of the cover she provided, Michael knelt to feel for a pulse. I forced my eyes from the two of them, pulled myself up off the ground, and stumbled toward Mackenzie.

She slid off the ledge, into my arms. Beside us, Michael looked at Celine and shook his head.

Nichols was gone.

I wrapped my arms around Mackenzie, blocking the dead body from view, but she fought my hold and stepped aside. She wanted to see it.

To see *him*.

"For the record..." Lia managed to pull Mackenzie's attention away from the killer's corpse. "When he said that what he tried to do to you—what he did to the others—wasn't a pleasure?" Lia spat in the dead's man direction. "He lied."

LIA, AGE TWELVE

Eleven years earlier

The girl sits down, and her mother brushes her hair. Long, even strokes. "You're lucky, you know." The brush stills, then the woman wielding it corrects herself. "Blessed."

Blessed because the leader has chosen her.

Blessed because she's favored by God.

What a joke.

"Sadie." Her mother says the name she was given at birth, the one *he* knows. "This *is* a blessing."

It would have been easier if she couldn't hear, plain as day, that Mama believes that.

Believes in him.

The girl turns. She needs, just this once, for her mother to see the truth—to see her.

"I don't have visions." Truths get more potent the longer you keep them from your tongue. There's *years* of power in this one. "I never have. He doesn't have them, either. He's a liar. I'm a better one, and I will literally rip his eyes out of their sockets the next time he comes to my bed."

She was nine the first time. With the right lies—the right truths—she put him off. Until she was twelve.

"This isn't you." Her mother backs away, frightened, but the girl called Sadie—the girl who used to *be* Sadie—knows the truth.

After all, her mother was the one who told her, all those years ago—*Pretend it's not you. Whatever happens, pretend that it isn't happening to you.*

Sadie is good at pretending. *Lia* is better. After all, she's pretended to be Sadie all these years.

"I love you, Mama." Lia can make that sound and feel true without having to worry about whether or not it still is. "Even though you're planning on telling him everything I tell you, even though you'll stand back and let him put me in a hole in the ground, even though you'll watch me starving and dying of thirst and look straight through me until he gives me permission to exist again—*I love you.*"

Her mother is wearing a bracelet made of thorns—penance. She removes it, tries to force it around her daughter's wrist.

Lia lets her. As the thorns bite into her flesh, she lets her eyelashes flutter. Her face visibly softens. She dons the Sadie mask. "You did well, Mama." The words are gentle, and they sound true-true-true. Lia is leaving tonight. She knows now that no one will be coming with her. She can feel the last bit of Sadie flickering inside of her like a candle, ready to die.

She lets Sadie caress the side of her mother's face, one last time.

"Your faith is pure." Lia knows how to sell a lie, and nine-tenths of it is telling people exactly what they want to hear.

"This was a test?" Her mother is breathless. Questions can't be lies, but Lia hears the hesitation, the uncertainty. Some part of Mama has always known what the leader does to those, like Sadie, whom he calls blessed.

But the others? They aren't like Sadie, aren't like *Lia*. They don't know when someone is lying, when the leader is spitting falsehoods. They can't lie nearly so convincingly themselves.

This is the truth: there is blood on Sadie's hands, on *Lia*'s. One lie—the right lie—can doom a man. She wishes a lie could save her mother.

He's going to kill you someday. All of you.

Lia won't be here to die. "It was a test," she confirms gently. She leans forward, touches her forehead to her mother's. "Tell me you love me."

It's Lia who turns, not Sadie. It's Lia whose hair her mother is brushing. She'll always be Lia now.

"I love you, Sadie."

It would be easier, for Lia, if that were a lie.

CHAPTER 15

"Worst thing about this case." Dean sat at the end of my bed. It had taken three days—and Briggs calling in a favor—for my boyfriend to get twenty-four hours of leave from Quantico. Given that Briggs had also had to grease the wheels to excuse Michael's better-to-ask-for-forgiveness-than-permission trip to Maine, I was starting to suspect that someone at the FBI Academy was going to be read in on the Naturals program fairly soon.

"The worst thing about this case..." I took my time to feel the weight of the words. "The worst thing is knowing that Mackenzie could have died because I got it wrong."

I'd left a vulnerable twelve-year-old alone with a killer whose specialty was exploiting vulnerabilities. I knew better than to make assumptions. I knew how easily one wrong mental turn could lead even the strongest profiler astray.

And yet...

Dean took my hand in his and turned it over so that he

could trace his thumb along the lines of my palm. "Are you sure that the worst part wasn't *why* you got it wrong?"

Being a Natural didn't make a person infallible. I knew that, but I'd started working with the Bureau young enough that I also had a healthy amount of experience under my belt. Normally, when I made mistakes, they were smaller.

Normally, I self-corrected.

I didn't need to turn too much of my profiler's eye inward to know why it had been far too easy for me to see a psychologist as the enemy. I'd thought from the beginning that the woman didn't—and couldn't—understand what Mackenzie had been through.

Just like the Bureau psychologist I'd been assigned when I was a teenager had never understood me.

"You think I should see someone." I let my fingers curl slowly into a fist, and Dean cupped his hand around mine.

"I think it might help." His lips brushed, white-hot, over my knuckles.

As much as I'd fought to ignore my own scars, I'd never tried to make Dean forget his. I had never—and would never—pretend that the worst moments of his life didn't matter. I knew and accepted that *Behavior, Personality, Environment* wasn't a one-time calculation, that everything we did and experienced became a part of us.

I knew that the things that happened when we were young had the longest to burrow in.

Without our particular childhoods, none of us would have been Naturals. Lia wouldn't have been Lia without growing up in the cult. Sloane had always had an affinity for numbers, but isolation had turned them into a coping mechanism. Michael's sensitivity to emotions developed as a survival skill, and Dean understood killers because he'd been raised to be one. I'd long since accepted the role that my own childhood had played in making me a Natural profiler.

Why was it so much harder to accept that there were other traumas whose effects had formed me just as much?

"Quentin Nichols had a sister." I leaned back against the headboard, my fingers intertwining themselves with Dean's. It was easier—always—to talk about someone other than myself. "She killed herself when she was eighteen. Quentin was four years younger."

"He was there." Dean didn't make that a question.

"His family blamed him for not being able to stop it." That was what I'd been able to piece together, after the fact. "According to people who knew him, Nichols always said that was why he went into crisis negotiation—to save lives. But in reality..." I closed my eyes, just for a moment, knowing that Dean deserved more than me talking about the case because it was easier than addressing the elephant in the room.

"In reality," I continued, opening my eyes to his deep brown ones, "Nichols convinced himself that he *had* saved his sister. He was there for her, in the end. He told her it was okay. He let her go."

Dean's head tilted down toward mine. "He gave her what mercy he could."

Dean and I had always acknowledged that to do what

we did, a person needed a bit of monster in them. That was why he understood Nichols, why I could see the motive and understand it myself.

"I killed my mother." I'd said those words to Mackenzie's psychologist. I could say them to Dean now. "I was holding the knife. I felt it go into her chest."

"You couldn't stop it," Dean told me. "The knife was in your hands. Her fingers wrapped around yours."

I laid my hand on his chest. There was a spot, just inside the rib cage...

"You need to talk to someone," Dean told me.

I closed my eyes. "I know." For almost a minute, I sat there, listening to the sound of his heart, feeling it beat beneath my palm.

"Best part of this case." Dean always knew exactly when I'd reached my limit, exactly how to distract me. He laid his hand on my chest. I could feel the warmth of it through my thin white T-shirt. I could feel him feeling my heartbeat.

"The best part of this case was Mackenzie." I didn't even have to think about my answer. "Before she came in—she danced."

She was going to survive, just like she always had.

"You talked to her parents?" Dean asked.

I nodded. "She'll come to us when she's fifteen—if she still wants to."

Mackenzie's parents were hedging their bets on their daughter joining the Naturals program, but the profiler in me knew that their daughter wouldn't change her mind about this. She'd spend the next three years convincing them that normal wasn't an option.

Not for her.

Not anymore.

Without warning, Dean's mouth descended over mine. I rose up to meet him, my hands on either side of his face, my legs wrapping themselves around his body.

I wasn't normal.

Neither was he.

"The new girl can't have my room." The voice that issued that statement was completely matter-of-fact and utterly unbothered by what Dean and I were up to on the bed.

We split apart.

Laurel tilted her head to one side. "Do you prefer the screams," she asked Dean softly, "or the blood?"

There was a single beat of silence, and then Lia sauntered into the room behind my little sister.

"I give that a nine out of ten for delivery," Lia told Laurel. "But a ten for creepy content."

Laurel shrugged, her expression unchanging. "I try."

Most of the time, Laurel tried *not* to be creepy—and failed. But my sister was strangely at ease with Lia, who was already training her to use her unnatural solemnity to her advantage *and* to spot lies.

"The new girl can't have my room when she gets here," Laurel repeated emphatically. "I don't care if it's not for another three years."

Technically, my grandmother was the one raising my

sister. Technically, our base of operations was not Laurel's house. Technically, she didn't *have* a room here, but when we'd returned from this case, we'd found the bedroom Laurel sometimes stayed in completely decorated with ponies.

I belong here. That was what the expression on Laurel's tiny face said. Her mouth, in contrast, addressed Dean. "I was just messing with you about the blood." She paused. "And the screams."

I glanced at Lia, and she shrugged, which I took to mean that statement was *mostly* true.

"Come on, short stuff." Lia tweaked the end of Laurel's ponytail. "Let's leave Angsty and the Brood here to their special alone time, and I'll teach you how to convince your teacher that the dog really did eat your homework."

Before Lia could actually leave Dean and me to our own devices, her cell phone rang.

"Video call," she told us. "It's Sloane."

It took all of two seconds before Lia had helped herself to a slice of the bed. The moment she did, Laurel took off.

"Hey, Sloane." Lia answered and angled the phone's screen so that Dean and I could see.

"The nine millimeter Luger was designed by a German weapons manufacturer in 1902." Sloane's greeting was unconventional, if not entirely unexpected. "In 2015, the FBI shifted to using a one-hundred-and-forty-seven grain nine millimeter Gold Dot G2 for ammunition."

Lia took one for the team and responded to that statement.

"Either you're in the middle of weapons training, or you've spent the past forty-eight hours with Celine."

Special Agent Delacroix had fired a shot in the line of duty. She'd saved Mackenzie's life—and taken the life of a killer. There was a process that had to be followed in the wake of an event like that. Celine had to be cleared—legally and psychologically—before she could return to the field.

"Celine needs me." Sloane fiddled with something, though I couldn't quite make out what she held between her fingers. "No one has ever needed me before."

"We all need you," Dean told her. Sloane was our light in the darkness.

"Dean," Sloane said very seriously, "I hope this is not oversharing, but Celine needs me in a *very different way*." Knowing Sloane, I half expected her to share exactly what that very different way entailed—possibly with graphs, almost certainly with precise description of angles and body parts—but she spared us the explicit details and opted instead for another statistic. "Did you know that forty-six percent of Texans meditate at least once a week?"

"You don't say." Lia grinned.

Sloane frowned into the camera. "I just *did* say. And, Cassie? I looked into those brothers in Texas, and the thing is, they aren't."

"Aren't brothers?" I asked.

"Aren't in Texas," Sloane corrected. "At least, they're not there anymore. The whole family picked up and moved with no warning. Even weirder? I can't figure out where they went."

"And if *you* can't figure it out..." Michael plopped down beside Sloane and squeezed into the frame. "There's a very good chance they're off the grid."

"A ninety-seven point four percent chance," Sloane clarified.

"Exactly," Michael declared. "Now, on a somewhat unrelated note: adorable onesies for the Sterling-Briggs Wonder Twins, yay or nay?"

He held up what appeared to be a custom-made infant onesie emblazoned with the words SPECIAL AGENT BABY.

"I was thinking of putting something inappropriate, but humorous and endearing, on the back," he clarified.

There were nine and a half weeks left until Michael and Sloane would be home. Nine and a half weeks before I could look at Dean and know he wasn't leaving the next day.

Three years until Mackenzie would join the program.

Who knew how long to find the brothers.

But Briggs and Sterling's twins were expected to make their arrival early—and that meant any day.

"I vote yes on the onesies," I declared.

"All in favor?" Sloane asked formally.

I leaned back against Dean, and Lia leaned against me before we all chorused in unison, "Aye."

TURN THE PAGE TO START ANOTHER UNPUTDOWNABLE SERIES FROM JENNIFER LYNN BARNES!

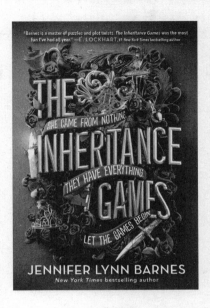

Don't miss this *New York Times* bestselling "impossible to put down" (Buzzfeed) novel with deadly stakes, thrilling twists, and juicy secrets.

Avery Grambs has a plan for a better future: survive high school, win a scholarship, and get out. But her luck changes in an instant when billionaire Tobias Hawthorne dies and leaves Avery virtually his entire fortune. The catch? Avery has no idea why—or even who Tobias Hawthorne is.

To receive her inheritance, Avery must move into the sprawling, secret-passage-filled Hawthorne House, where every room bears the old man's touch—and his love of puzzles, riddles, and codes. Unfortunately for Avery, Hawthorne House is also occupied by the family that Tobias Hawthorne just disinherited. This includes the four Hawthorne grandsons: dangerous, magnetic, brilliant boys who grew up with every expectation that, one day, they would inherit billions. Heir apparent Grayson Hawthorne is convinced that Avery must be a con woman, and he's determined to take her down. His brother Jameson views her as their grandfather's last hurrah: a twisted riddle, a puzzle to be solved. Caught in a world of wealth and privilege, with danger around every turn, Avery will have to play the game herself just to survive.

T he next day, I paid a price for sleeping in my car. My whole body ached, and I had to shower after gym, because paper towels in the bathroom at the diner could only go so far. I didn't have time to dry my hair, so I arrived at my next class sopping wet. It wasn't my best look, but I'd gone to school with the same kids my whole life. I was wallpaper.

No one was looking.

"*Romeo and Juliet* is littered with proverbs—small, pithy bits of wisdom that make a statement about the way the world and human nature work." My English teacher was young and earnest, and I deeply suspected she'd had too much coffee. "Let's take a step back from Shakespeare. Who can give me an example of an everyday proverb?"

Beggars can't be choosers, I thought, my head pounding and water droplets dripping down my back. *Necessity is the mother of invention. If wishes were horses, beggars would ride.*

The door to the classroom opened. An office aide waited for the teacher to look at her, then announced loudly enough for the whole class to hear, "Avery Grambs is wanted in the office."

I took that to mean that someone had graded my test.

———◆———

I knew better than to expect an apology, but I also wasn't expecting Mr. Altman to meet me at his secretary's desk, beaming like he'd just had a visit from the Pope. "Avery!"

An alarm went off in the back of my head, because no one was ever that glad to see me.

"Right this way." He opened the door to his office, and I caught sight of a familiar neon-blue ponytail inside.

"Libby?" I said. She was wearing skull-print scrubs and no makeup, both of which suggested she'd come straight from work. In the middle of a shift. Orderlies at assisted living facilities couldn't just walk out in the middle of shifts.

Not unless something was wrong.

"Is Dad . . ." I couldn't make myself finish the question.

"Your father is fine." The voice that issued that statement didn't belong to Libby or Principal Altman. My head whipped up, and I looked past my sister. The chair behind the principal's desk was occupied—by a guy not much older than me. *What is going on here?*

He was wearing a suit. He looked like the kind of person who should have had an entourage.

"As of yesterday," he continued, his low, rich voice measured and precise, "Ricky Grambs was alive, well, and safely passed out in a motel room in Michigan, an hour outside of Detroit."

I tried not to stare at him—and failed. *Light hair. Pale eyes. Features sharp enough to cut rocks.*

"How could you possibly know that?" I demanded. *I* didn't even know where my deadbeat father was. How could he?

The boy in the suit didn't answer my question. Instead, he

arched an eyebrow. "Principal Altman?" he said. "If you could give us a moment?"

The principal opened his mouth, presumably to object to being removed from his own office, but the boy's eyebrow lifted higher.

"I believe we had an agreement."

Altman cleared his throat. "Of course." And just like that, he turned and walked out the door. It closed behind him, and I resumed openly staring at the boy who'd banished him.

"You asked how I know where you father is." His eyes were the same color as his suit—gray, bordering on silver. "It would be best, for the moment, for you to just assume that I know everything."

His voice would have been pleasant to listen to if it weren't for the words. "A guy who thinks he knows everything," I muttered. "That's new."

"A girl with a razor-sharp tongue," he returned, silver eyes focused on mine, the ends of his lips ticking upward.

"Who are you?" I asked. "And what do you want?" *With me*, something inside me added. *What do you want with me?*

"All I want," he said, "is to deliver a message." For reasons I couldn't quite pinpoint, my heart started beating faster. "One that has proven rather difficult to send via traditional means."

"That might be my fault," Libby volunteered sheepishly beside me.

"What might be your fault?" I turned to look at her, grateful for an excuse to look away from Gray Eyes and fighting the urge to glance back.

"The first thing you need to know," Libby said, as earnestly as anyone wearing skull-print scrubs had ever said anything, "is that I had *no* idea the letters were real."

"What letters?" I asked. I was the only person in this room who didn't know what was going on here, and I couldn't shake the feeling that not knowing was a liability, like standing on train tracks but not knowing which direction the train was coming from.

"The letters," the boy in the suit said, his voice wrapping around me, "that my grandfather's attorneys have been sending, certified mail, to your residence for the better part of three weeks."

"I thought they were a scam," Libby told me.

"I assure you," the boy replied silkily, "they are not."

I knew better than to put any confidence in the assurances of good-looking guys.

"Let me start again." He folded his hands on the desk between us, the thumb of his right hand lightly circling the cuff link on his left wrist. "My name is Grayson Hawthorne. I'm here on behalf of McNamara, Ortega, and Jones, a Dallas-based law firm representing my grandfather's estate." Grayson's pale eyes met mine. "My grandfather passed away earlier this month." A weighty pause. "His name was Tobias Hawthorne." Grayson studied my reaction—or, more accurately, the lack thereof. "Does that name mean anything to you?"

The sensation of standing on train tracks was back. "No," I said. "Should it?"

"My grandfather was a very wealthy man, Ms. Grambs. And it appears that, along with our family and people who worked for him for years, you have been named in his will."

I heard the words but couldn't process them. "His *what*?"

"His will," Grayson repeated, a slight smile crossing his lips. "I don't know what he left you, exactly, but your presence is required at the will's reading. We've been postponing it for weeks."

I was an intelligent person, but Grayson Hawthorne might as well have been speaking Swedish.

"Why would your grandfather leave anything to me?" I asked.

Grayson stood. "That's the question of the hour, isn't it?" He stepped out from behind the desk, and suddenly I knew *exactly* what direction the train was coming from.

His.

"I've taken the liberty of making travel arrangements on your behalf."

This wasn't an invitation. It was a *summons*. "What makes you think—" I started to say, but Libby cut me off. "Great!" she said, giving me a healthy side-eye.

Grayson smirked. "I'll give you two a moment." His eyes lingered on mine too long for comfort, and then, without another word, he strode out the door.

Libby and I were silent for a full five seconds after he was gone. "Don't take this the wrong way," she whispered finally, "but I think he might be God."

I snorted. "He certainly thinks so." It was easier to ignore the effect he'd had on me now that he was gone. What kind of person had self-assurance that absolute? It was there in every aspect of his posture and word choice, in every interaction. Power was as much a fact of life for this guy as gravity. The world bent to the will of Grayson Hawthorne. What money couldn't buy him, those eyes probably did.

"Start from the beginning," I told Libby. "And don't leave anything out."

She fidgeted with the inky-black tips of her blue ponytail. "A couple of weeks ago, we started getting these letters—addressed to you, care of me. They said that you'd inherited money, gave us a number to call. I thought they were a scam. Like one of those emails that claims to be from a foreign prince."

"Why would this Tobias Hawthorne—a man I've never met, never even heard of—put me in his will?" I asked.

"I don't know," Libby said, "but *that*"—she gestured in the direction Grayson had gone—"is not a scam. Did you *see* the way he dealt with Principal Altman? What do you think their agreement was? A bribe...or a threat?"

Both. Pushing down that response, I pulled out my phone and connected to the school's Wi-Fi. One internet search for Tobias Hawthorne later, the two of us were reading a news headline: *Noted Philanthropist Dies at 78.*

"Do you know what *philanthropist* means?" Libby asked me seriously. "It means *rich.*"

"It means someone who gives to charity," I corrected her.

"So...*rich.*" Libby gave me a look. "What if *you* are charity? They wouldn't send this guy's grandson to get you if he'd just left you a few hundred dollars. We must be talking thousands. You could travel, Avery, or put it toward college, or buy a better car."

I could feel my heart starting to beat faster again. "Why would a total stranger leave me anything?" I reiterated, resisting the urge to daydream, even for a second, because if I started, I wasn't sure I could stop.

"Maybe he knew your mom?" Libby suggested. "I don't know, but I do know that you need to go to the reading of that will."

"I can't just take off," I told her. "Neither can you." We'd both miss work. I'd miss class. And yet...if nothing else, a trip would get Libby away from Drake, at least temporarily.

And if this is real... It was already getting harder *not* to think about the possibilities.

"My shifts are covered for the next two days," Libby informed me. "I made some calls, and so are yours." She reached for my hand. "Come on, Ave. Wouldn't it be nice to take a trip, just you and me?"

She squeezed my hand. After a moment, I squeezed back. "Where exactly is the reading of the will?"

"Texas!" Libby grinned. "And they didn't just book our tickets. They booked them *first class*."

Kim Haynes Photography

JENNIFER LYNN BARNES

is the #1 *New York Times* bestselling author of more than twenty acclaimed young-adult novels, including the Inheritance Games trilogy, *The Brothers Hawthorne*, *Little White Lies*, *Deadly Little Scandals*, *The Lovely and the Lost*, and the Naturals series: *The Naturals*, *Killer Instinct*, *All In*, *Bad Blood*, and the novella *Twelve*. Jen is also a Fulbright Scholar with advanced degrees in psychology, psychiatry, and cognitive science. She received her PhD from Yale University in 2012 and was a professor of psychology and professional writing at the University of Oklahoma for many years. She invites you to find her online at jenniferlynnbarnes.com or follow her on Twitter @jenlynnbarnes.

MORE FROM JENNIFER LYNN BARNES

THE NATURALS

DEBUTANTES   SEARCH & RESCUE

THE INHERITANCE GAMES

NOVL   LB LITTLE, BROWN AND COMPANY   theNOVL.com